GENERAL PRACTICE

ALSO BY JAMES WHITE

The Secret Visitor (1957)
Second Ending (1962)
Deadly Litter (1964)
Escape Orbit (1965)
The Watch Below (1966)
All Judgement Fled (1968)
The Aliens Among Us (1969)
Tomorrow Is Too Far (1971)
Dark Inferno (1972)
The Dream Millennium (1974)
Monsters and Medics (1977)
Underkill (1979)
Future Past (1982)
Federation World (1988)
The Silent Stars Go By (1991)
The White Papers (1996)
Gene Roddenberry's Earth: Final Conflict—The First Protector (Tor, 2000)

THE SECTOR GENERAL SERIES

Hospital Station (1962)
Star Surgeon (1963)
Major Operation (1971)
Ambulance Ship (1979)
Sector General (1983)
Star Healer (1985)
Code Blue—Emergency (1987)
The Genocidal Healer (1992)
The Galactic Gourmet (Tor, 1996)
Final Diagnosis (Tor, 1997)
Mind Changer (Tor, 1998)
Double Contact (Tor, 1999)
Beginning Operations (Orb, 2001)
Alien Emergencies (Orb, 2002)

GENERAL PRACTICE

A SECTOR GENERAL OMNIBUS

JAMES WHITE

INTRODUCTION BY
JOHN CLUTE

ORB
A TOM DOHERTY ASSOCIATES BOOK
NEW YORK

GENERAL PRACTICE: A SECTOR GENERAL OMNIBUS

Copyright © 2003 by the Estate of James White. This book is an omnibus edition composed of the novels *Code Blue—Emergency*, copyright © 1987 by James White, and *The Genocidal Healer*, copyright © 1991 by James White.

Introduction Copyright © 2003 by John Clute

Edited by Teresa Nielsen Hayden

An Orb Book
Published by Tom Doherty Associates, LLC
175 Fifth Avenue
New York, NY 10010

www.tor.com

Library of Congress Cataloging-in-Publication Data

White, James, 1928–1999
    [Code blue-emergency]
    General practice : a Sector General omnibus / James White.—
1st Orb ed.
        p. cm.
    "A Tom Doherty Associates book."
    Contents: Code blue-emergency—The genocidal healer.
    ISBN 0-765-30663-8 (acid-free paper)
    1. Science fiction, English. 2. Human-alien encounters—
Fiction. 3. Life on other planets—Fiction. 4. Space medicine—
Fiction. 5. Hospitals—Fiction. I. White, James, 1928–1999.
Genocidal healer. I. Title.

PR6073.H494C63 2003
823'.914—dc21

                                                        2003040556

First Edition: May 2003

Printed in the United States of America

P1

CONTENTS

INTRODUCTION

I n 1987, James White was about to turn sixty. For thirty years, he had been publishing stories about Sector General, a vast, self-contained multi-species hospital hanging like a great Christmas ornament in the middle of space near the galactic rim. Bolted together into loose episode chains, these stories filled six books, which Tor has recently assembled as two large omnibus volumes—*Beginning Operations* (2001) and *Alien Emergencies* (2002). The central protagonist of the six books, an inventive, intuitive, go-it-alone, extremely bright human doctor named Peter Conway, had become loved by two generations of readers. But Conway was aging—a little slower than White or his readers, out here in the real world, but fast enough—and at the very end of *Star Healer* (1985), number six of the pre-1987 volumes, he received his final promotion, to Diagnostician-in-Charge of Surgery. Readers of the series knew that had to be the end of Conway as the point-of-view protagonist of any future volumes.

Diagnosticians (as White had made clear from the get-go) were simply too *senior* in the command structure of the great hospital-hive to be heroes; in any case, they were too busy coping with the downloaded doppelgänger minds of various alien physicians—for Diagnosticians had to incorporate other-species skills in this manner, if multi-species medicine were to continue to advance—to do very much but keep order among themselves. The sight of Diagnostician Conway haring off on a mission would have been about as convincing as watching the laddish Captain Kirk bounce off the walls of that famous Hollywood backlot which stood in for every alien planet in the universe in 1967, the bounces of Kirk contributing significantly to the unique viewing experience which was *Star Trek* in its corseted pomp.

White was too clever a writer to commit that error, and he respected his creation—the Sector General hospital complex—far too deeply to treat its chain of command as risible. Conway would now have to do what commanders do: command the chain of command. There would be no orders to flout except his own. As a protagonist, then, Conway was a goner. By 1987, it was time for a change.

The two books collected here as the third Sector General omnibus show just how successfully James White responded to the challenge he had set himself. *Code Blue—Emergency* (1987) is what Brian Stableford, in his introduction to the first omnibus, called a mosaic novel: a series of stories or episodes, whether or not previously published, joined into a loose narrative. (Other terms for this very science-fictional format include A. E. van Vogt's "fixup," or "suite," which I myself would prefer to use in order to describe the essentially sequential nature of White's assembly-work.)

The Genocidal Healer (1992), on the other hand, despite one detachable flashback episode, is a genuine full-stretch novel, the first full-length tale in the entire Sector General sequence. A few others followed over White's last decade (he had been a diabetic for many years, almost completely lost his sight in the 90s, and died of a stroke in 1999, 71 years old), but *The Genocidal Healer* is perhaps the most sustained of them all, the most cumulatively energized book he would ever write about Sector General, which is, out of all the venues created over a century of science fiction, the very best place of all for good things to happen.

Let's digress for a moment, and talk about good.

In the depiction of goodness may lie the real genius of James White, the ultimate goal of all his savvy writer's tricks and sallies, for it is a terribly difficult thing for an author to make a reader want to know how a good protagonist can make good things happen in a good place in the middle of a universe filled with species who share, ultimately, the ethos which governs Sector General: that Good is normal, and that the problem of Evil, which may be defined as a lesion on the Good, *is operable.* Evil is a blockage in the flow of Good, which White tended to describe in evolutionary terms. He was an evolution Whig. On the evidence of the Sector General stories, he thought that unhampered evolutionary change generated species whose sentience was essentially benevolent. Evil was a cramp in the river of betterment. Fortunately, from the standpoint of Conway and his compeers, cramps could be operated on, excised. Sector General did not only make unhealthy organisms healthy; it rectified the immorality of blocked evolution, evolution gone awry, as Conway does with the Protectors of the Unborn in *Star Healer.*

I believe this is why some of us have been reading Sector General stories for most of our lives.

My only personal encounters with White himself were late in his life, after years of diabetes had paled him. He wore thick glasses against the fall of night. He was as thin as a wraith, a wraith smiling. I saw him at a convention, in the northeast of England I believe, in a hotel corridor. We stopped and spoke for a moment. He radiated an almost visible halo of goodness of spirit. Nothing much was said—I think I may have mumbled something about *The Watch Below* (1966), my favorite of his singleton novels—but as he continued on his way, downward saintly to some clamorous event, another thought came to me, a thought about Sector General. *Well* (I thought, more or less) *now I understand Sector General. For it is he.*

The challenge was simple, then, in 1987: to back Conway off from the forefront of the action, because he was now too *responsible* to stay there, but to retain all the while the happy kinetic flow toward greater good of the earlier volumes, which Conway had embodied so visibly, with his pertinacious problem-solving mind, and his immensely clever hands. This was vital. White must have known from the first—he was far too clever a

writer not to know pretty exactly what taproots he was sounding—that
the strength of the Sector General sequence was rooted in what might be
called the Visible Engines of First Sf, the kind of sf written by E E Smith,
whose Lensmen series haunts the corridors of White's magnificent artifact
on the galactic rim. In the sf of the 1930s, it was still possible to imagine
futures shaped by ornate technologies whose workings could be observed.
(Donato's cover to Donald Kingsbury's *Psychohistorical Crisis*, Tor 2001,
brilliantly evokes, just as Kingsbury himself evokes, the world of an older
sf: a world turned by engines of thought and steel, a world you could
touch the engine of, a world whose handles turned.)

So it is with Sector General, and the healings it enables. The engines
are visible. The great hospital "hangs" out there in the intergalactic dark,
all 384 levels aglow to the eye. Hatches gape open to embrace ships
from hyperspace. Hatches slam shut. The ships arrive and the ships
depart. Sentient beings—all of them described according to the four
letter classification system White took straight from Smith, though he
revised it in order to shed Smith's bias to the humanoid—enter the
hospital, jostle with other sentient beings along corridors used com-
munally by almost every species in the complex, quarrel (at times), make
gifts, interact, heal, are healed. It all happens in the clear. We see it all.
If a visitor is sick, it is diagnosed by healers—not by computers, or VR
simulacra under invisible remote control, or nanobots—who can do so
safely because invisible stuff like viruses does not pass between species
in this universe. If it needs an operation, Conway and/or one of his
colleagues (usually male) are there, nurses (usually female) at beck, intricate tools in hand or tentacle or proboscis, and get down to work. If
that patient's species and/or ailment was previously unknown, Conway
will unpack the maze of unknowing, and will expand the map of the
known. If a patient's problem is psychiatric—though for a long time
White banned psychological problems from Sector General, arguing
(through his protagonists) that such problems were too intangible for
multi-species hospital work—then that psychiatric problem will have
been caused, more often than not, as we've already noted, by some
visible somatic interference, some blockage of the good.

But (I think) White was too honest a writer, and loved Sector General and what it stood for too deeply, to wish to solve the Conway problem by introducing a new and younger Doc Conway to the series, because the ultimate Conway problem, over and above his seniority, lay in the fact that he was a single doctor, and that his main job in life was precisely to do doctor work as part of the intricate Sector General *modus operandi*. All too often, White was forced to give Conway his head as a loner, and to retrofit his rogue exploits into the overall picture. As White's (and our) sense of Sector General complexified, and as it became clearer and clearer that those who *ran* the great complex were on the same side as those who doctored within it, it became harder and harder to justify loner exploits. The hero of Sector General was Sector General.

The solution was to introduce characters who—whatever their medical qualifications—had somehow disqualified themselves from frontline doctoring, and who had to come to serve Sector General from, as it were, within. They had to become bureaucrats, which, as old-time readers of the series know, meant that they had to become part of Major O'Mara's staff. O'Mara is the truculent, impatient, sensitive Chief Psychologist of Sector General, and is the de facto boss of the whole shebang, though it won't be until the penultimate volume in the sequence, *Mind Changer* (1998), that he becomes its official administrator. It is O'Mara's central task to ensure that the vast congeries of interacting (and occasionally conflicting) species inhabiting Sector General, staff and patients alike, continue to behave with efficiency toward each other and toward the ultimate goal, which is to bring the greatest good—the good health which affirms the essential goodness of the evolving cosmos—to as much of the galaxy as can be reached. In order to accomplish this task, O'Mara must constantly monitor, interfere with, insult, cajole, console, in short *shake the story loose* wherever there's a blockage, real or potential. O'Mara is the healer of the hospital.

In *Code Blue—Emergency*, we meet Cha Thrat, a top-notch warrior-surgeon from the planet Sommaradva with lots of agile limbs, an impetuous acuity of mind, and a tendency to solve problems before her superiors have a chance to. As we discover through the neatly linked episodes of the text, her apprenticeship at Sector General is marked by several episodes in which her ultimate rightness is confirmed, as is her inability to operate within an ensemble. (During the course of the book, she is forced to incorporate a couple of downloaded minds, one of them the formidable Conway's, which females are not supposed to be able to abide, for reasons White never made particularly plausible; but the implications of her success are not developed in the course of this volume.) At the end of the book, O'Mara seconds her to his own staff, where the congenital jostle of her being may do some good.

In *The Genocidal Healer*—a pretty unfortunate title for a tale as full of loving kindness as this—the new recruit to O'Mara's staff is Surgeon-Captain Lioren of the planet Tarlan, also a being with lots of limbs. Lioren is wracked with guilt, as his cure for a planetary plague has—partly because of the imperious urgency with which he acts upon his diagnosis—almost killed off an entire sentient species. He wishes to be executed, but the medical councils which try him insist (rightly) on exonerating him. O'Mara assigns him to several patients who share one thing: a need to help someone in graver spiritual straits than they are. In the end—it is an ending as technically adept, and as deeply stirring, as the final paragraphs of T. H. White's *The Sword in the Stone* (1938)— Lioren discovers that, through his sacrificial exposing of his sins in order that others may forgive their own, he has become a priest.

Nowhere in the entire Sector General sequence does the moral wholeness of White's enterprise come so nakedly to the surface, almost chastening (though for only a moment) the exuberant gaiety of the stories of physicianly healing which make up the heart of the rest. White was a pacifist, and his greatest work was a series adamantly dedicated to a blanket refusal to kill. In his introduction (written a couple of years ago), Stableford notes regretfully that White, who was a native of Ulster, died before the 1999 accord brought peace to his savaged homeland. As I write (in October 2002), that brief peace is at the point of collapse. In the real world, it may be the lesions of Evil are faster than the surgeon. In the world of Sector General, the healing comes in time. White gave us a dream. It is good to remember this dream.

CODE BLUE—
EMERGENCY

CHAPTER 1

The ruler of the ship sat beside Cha Thrat at the recreation deck's viewscreen while the fuzzy blob of light that was the space hospital grew into a gigantic, complex structure ablaze with every color and intensity of light that her eyes could detect. She had strong feelings of awe, wonder, excitement, and great embarrassment.

Ruler Chiang, she had learned, carried the rank of major in the Monitor Corps Extraterrestrial Communications and Cultural Contact division. But the ruler seriously confused her at times by behaving like a warrior. Now it was sitting beside her because it felt some strange, Earth-human obligation to do so. It had wanted to pay her the compliment of allowing her to watch the approach to the hospital from its control deck, but as she was physiologically unable to enter that small and already crowded compartment, it had felt obliged to desert its post and sit with her here.

The compliment was a completely unnecessary piece of time-wasting nonsense, considering wide disparity in the social and professional levels of the people involved, but Chiang seemed to derive some pleasure from the foolishness and it had, after all, been a patient of hers.

The muted conversation in Control was being relayed with the image on the repeater screen and, while Cha Thrat's translator gave her the equivalent of every word, the particular technical jargon that the ship's warriors were using made the total meaning of what they were saying unclear. But suddenly there was a new, amplified voice whose words were simple and unambiguous, accompanied by a picture of the disgustingly hairy being who was speaking them.

"Sector General Reception," it said briskly. "Identify yourself, please. Patient, visitor, or staff; degree of urgency; and physiological classification, if known. If uncertain, please make full visual contact and we will classify."

"Monitor Corps courier vessel *Thromasaggar*," a voice from Control responded. "Short-stay docking facilities to unload patient and staff member. Crew and patient classification Earth-human DBDG. Patient is ambulatory, convalescent, treatment nonurgent. Staff member is classification DCNF and is also a warm-blooded oxygen-breather with no special temperature, gravity, or pressure requirements."

"Wait," the obnoxious creature said, and once again the image of the hospital filled the screen. A definite improvement, she thought.

"What is that thing?" she asked the ruler. "It looks like a . . . a *scroggila*. You know, one of our rodents."

"I've seen pictures of them," the ruler said, and made the unpleasant barking sound that denoted amusement with these people. "It is a Nidian DBDG, about half the body mass of an Earth-human with a very similar metabolism. Its species is highly advanced technologically and culturally, so it only looks like an outsize rodent. You'll learn to work with much less beautiful beings in that place—"

It broke off as the image of the Nidian returned.

"Follow the blue-yellow-blue direction beacons," the receptionist said. "Debark patient and staff member at Lock One Zero Four, then proceed to Dock Eighteen via the blue-blue-white beacons. Major Chiang and the Sommaradvan healer are expected and will be met."

By what? she wondered.

The ruler had given her a great deal of helpful advice and information about Sector Twelve General Hospital, most of which she did not believe. And when they entered the lock antechamber a short time later, she could not believe that the smooth, waist-high hemisphere of green jelly occupying the deck between the two waiting Earth-humans was a person.

Ruler Chiang said, "This is Lieutenant Braithwaite of the Chief Psychologist's Office, and Maintenance Officer Timmins, who is responsible for preparing your accommodation, and Doctor Danalta, who is attached to the ambulance ship, *Rhabwar*..."

Except for minor differences in the insignia on their uniforms, she could not tell the two Earth-humans apart. The large blob of green stuff on the floor, she guessed, was some kind of practical joke, or perhaps part of an initiation ritual for newcomers to the hospital. For the time being she decided not to react.

"... And this is Cha Thrat," it went on, "the new healer from Sommaradva, who is joining the staff."

Both Earth-humans moved their right hands up to waist level, then lowered them as the ruler shook its head. Cha Thrat had already told Chiang that grasping a strange person's appendage was considered quite vulgar where she came from, and it would have been much more considerate of them if they had given her some indication of their status. Ruler Chiang had spoken to them as equals, but then it had often done that while addressing subordinates on the ship. It was very careless of the ruler and most confusing for her.

"Timmins will see that your personal effects are moved to your quarters," the ruler went on. "I don't know what Danalta and Braithwaite have in mind for us."

"Nothing too onerous," Braithwaite said as the other Earth-human was leaving. "On hospital time it is the middle of the day, and the healer's accommodation will not be ready until early evening. In mid-afternoon you are due for a physical, Major. Cha Thrat is expected to be present, no doubt to receive the compliments of our medics for what was obviously a very tidy piece of, for a Sommaradvan, other-species surgery."

It looked in her direction and for some reason inclined its head forward from the neck, then went on. "Immediately following the examination both of you have appointments in Psychology: Cha Thrat for an orientation talk with O'Mara, and you for an investigation, purely a formality in your case, to ensure that there is no non-physical trauma resulting from your recent injuries. But until then . . . Have you eaten recently?"

"No," said Chiang, "and I would welcome a change from ship food."

The other Earth-human made soft barking sounds and said, "You haven't tasted a hospital meal yet. But we try hard not to poison our visitors . . ."

It broke off to apologize and explain hastily that it was making an in-hospital joke, that the food was quite palatable, and that it had been given full instructions regarding Cha Thrat's dietary requirements.

But she was only vaguely aware of what it was saying because her attention was on the hemisphere of green stuff, the surface of which had begun to ripple and pucker and grow pseudopods. It wobbled sluggishly and heaved itself upright until it was as tall as she was, its skin coloration became mottled, the wet gleam of what could only be eyes appeared, the number of short, crudely formed appendages increased until it looked like something a young child on Sommaradva might make from modeling clay. She felt sudden nausea, but her feelings of curiosity and wonder were even stronger as the body firmed out, became more finely structured, and the features appeared. Then the clothing and equipment pouch grew into place, and there was standing before her the figure of another female Sommaradvan identical in every detail to herself.

"If our Earth-human friends intend subjecting you to the environment of a multispecies dining hall within minutes of your arrival," it said in a voice that was not, thankfully, hers, "I must counteract their lack of consideration by providing you with something familiar, and friendly, to whom you can relate. It is the least I can do for a new member of the staff."

"Doctor Danalta," Braithwaite said, barking again, "is not as altruistic as it would have you think, Cha Thrat. Due to the incredibly savage environment of its planet of origin, the species evolved protective mimicry of a very high order. There are few warm-blooded oxygen-breathing life-forms in Sector General that it cannot accurately reproduce within a few minutes, as you've seen. But we suspect that any new, intelligent life-form to arrive at the hospital, be it patient, visitor, or staff, is regarded by Danalta as a challenge to its powers of physical mimicry."

"Nevertheless," she said, "I am impressed."

She stared eye to eye at her utterly alien but identical twin, thinking that the being had displayed concern for her present mental well-being by using its incredible talent to make her feel more comfortable. It was the action of a healer of rulers, and it might even be a ruler itself. Instinctively she made the gesture of respect to superiors, then belatedly realized that neither the Earth-humans nor her Danalta-copy would recognize it for what it was.

"Why, thank you, Cha Thrat," said Danalta, returning the gesture. "With protective mimicry there is an associated empathic faculty. While I don't know what the limb gesture means exactly, I could feel that I was being complimented."

Danalta, she had no doubt, was also aware of her embarrassment, but as they followed the two Earth-humans from the compartment the shape-changer did not speak of it.

The corridor outside was thronged with a menagerie of creatures, a few of whom resembled, in shape if not in size, nonintelligent species found on Sommaradva. She tried not to flinch as one of the small, red-furred bipeds of the species she had seen in charge of Reception brushed past, and she felt acutely anxious when enormous, six-limbed, multi-tentacled monsters of many times her body mass bore down on her. But not all of the creatures were frightening, or even ugly. A large crustacean with a beautifully marked carapace and hard exoskeletal limbs clicked past, its pincers opening and closing slowly as it talked to a truly lovely being who had at least thirty short, stubby legs and an overall coat of rippling, silvery fur. There were others she could not see clearly because of their protective envelopes and, in the case of the occupant of a mobile pressure vessel from which steam was escaping, she had no idea what weird or wonderful shape the vehicle was concealing.

The cacophony of hooting, chirping, gobbling, and moaning conversation could not be described, because it was totally unlike anything she had previously experienced.

"There is a much shorter route to the dining hall," Danalta said as a spiney, membraneous being who looked like some kind of dark, oily vegetable shuffled past, its physical details clouded by the thick yellow fog inside its transparent suit. "But it would mean a trip through the water-filled Chalder wards, and your protective envelopes won't be ready for another six, maybe seven days. How do you feel, and what do you think of the place so far?"

It was disconcerting and embarrassing to have Danalta, who could be nothing less than a wizard-healer of rulers, ask such questions of a mere warrior-surgeon. But the questions had been asked, and answers were expected. If the being wished to practice its art in the middle of a crowded corridor, it was certainly not her place to criticize.

Promptly she replied, "I feel confused, frightened, repelled, curious, and unsure of my ability to adapt. My confusion is such that I am unable to be more specific. I'm beginning to feel that the two Earth-humans walking in front of us, member of a species that a short time ago I would have considered totally alien, have an almost welcome normality about them. And I feel that you, because you have made yourself the most familiar and reassuring entity in the hospital, are by your very nature the most alien of all. I haven't had enough time, nor have I sufficient direct experience, to form any useful impressions or opinions about the hospital, but it may well be that the empathic faculty you possess has already made you aware of my feelings.

"Is the environment of the dining hall," she added worriedly, "much worse than this?"

Danalta did not reply at once, and the two Earth-humans had been silent for some time. The one called Braithwaite had fallen slightly behind the other, and its head was turned to one side so that the fleshy protuberance that was one of its auricular organs would be better able to pick up her words. It seemed that her feelings were of interest not only to the shape-changer. When Danalta did speak, its words resembled a lecture rather than a simple reply to her question.

"A low level of empathy is common in most intelligent life-forms," it said, "but only in one species, the natives of Cinruss, is there a perfect empathic faculty. You will meet one of them soon because it, too, is curious about newly discovered life-forms and will want to seek you out at the first opportunity. You can then compare my limited empathic faculty with Prilicla's.

"My own limited faculty," it went on, "is based on the observation of body movements, tensions, changes in skin coloration, and so on, rather than the direct reception of the subject's emotional radiation. As a healer you, too, must have a degree of empathy with your patients, and on many occasions are able to sense their condition, or changes in their condition, without direct physical investigation. But no matter how refined the faculty may be, your thoughts are still private, exclusively your own property, and it is simply your stronger feelings that I detect—"

"The dining hall," Braithwaite said suddenly. It turned into the wide, doorless entrance, narrowly avoided colliding with a Nidian and two of the silver-furred beings who were leaving, and barked softly as they made derogatory remarks about its clumsiness. It pointed. "Over there, an empty table!"

For a moment Cha Thrat could not move a single limb as she stared across the vast expanse of highly polished floor with its regimented islands of eating benches and seats, grouped by size and shape to accommodate the incredible variety of beings using them. It was much, much worse than her experience of the corridors, where she had encountered the creatures two or three at a time. Here there were hundreds of them, grouped together into species or with several different lifeforms occupying the same table.

There were beings who were terrifying in their obvious physical strength and range of natural weapons; others who were frightening, horrifying, and repugnant in the color and slime-sheen and nauseous growths covering their teguments; and many of them were the phantasms of Sommaradvan nightmare given frightful solidity. At a few of the tables were entities whose body and limb configurations were so utterly ridiculous that she had trouble believing her eyes.

"This way," said Danalta, who had been waiting for Cha Thrat's limbs to stop trembling. It led the way to the table claimed by Braithwaite, and she noticed that the furiture suited neither the physiologies of the Earth-humans nor the trio of exoskeletal crustaceans who were vacating it.

She wondered if she would ever be able to adapt to the ways of these chronically disorganized and untidy beings. At least on Sommaradva the people knew their place.

"The mechanism for food selection and delivery is similar to that on the ship," Braithwaite said as she lowered herself carefully into the dreadfully uncomfortable chair and her weight made the menu display light up. "You tap in your physiological classification and it will list the food available. Until the catering computer has been programmed with details of the combinations, consistencies, and platter displays you favor, it is likely to come in unsightly but nutritious lumps. You'll soon get used to the system, but in the meantime I'll order for you."

"Thank you," she said.

When it arrived the biggest lump looked like an uneven block of *tasam*. But it smelled like roasted *cretsi*, had the consistency of roasted *cretsi*, and, she found after trying a small corner, it tasted like roasted *cretsi*. She realized suddenly that she was hungry.

"It sometimes happens," Braithwaite continued, "that the meals of your fellow diners, or even the diners themselves, are visually distressing to the point where it is affecting your appetite. You may keep one eye on your platter and close all the others; we won't be offended."

She did as it suggested, but kept one eye slightly open so that she could see Braithwaite, who was still watching her intently while pretending, for some odd, Earth-human reason, not to do so. While she ate, her mind went back to the incident with the ship ruler on Sommaradva, the voyage, and her reception here, and she realized that she was becoming suspicious, and irritated.

"On the subject of your stronger feelings," Danalta said, seemingly intent upon resuming the lecture it had broken off at the entrance, "do you have any strong feelings against discussing personal or professional matters in the presence of strangers?"

The ship ruler, Chiang, paused with what looked like a piece of what had once been a living creature halfway to its eating orifice. It said, "On Sommaradva they prefer to hear directly what other people think of them. And conversely, the presence of interested witnesses during a discussion of their affairs is often considered beneficial."

Braithwaite, she saw, was concentrating too much attention on its disgusting meal. She turned as many eyes as would bear on the shape-changer, ignoring the many things she did not want to see in the background.

"Very well," Danalta said, turning its alien mimic's eyes on her. "You must already have realized, Cha Thrat, that your situation is unlike that of the other staff members who join the hospital for a probationary period. Appointments to Sector General are much sought after, and candidates must pass rigorous professional examinations and deep psychological investigation on their home worlds to ensure that they will have a fair chance of adapting to a multispecies hospital environment so that they will profit from our training.

"You were not screened in this manner," her alien twin went on. "There were no professional examinations, no birth-to-maturity psych profiles, no objective measure of your worth as a healer. We know only that you come with a very high recommendation, from the Cultural Contact department of the Monitor Corps and, presumably, your professional colleagues on Sommaradva, a world and society about which we know little.

"You appreciate our difficulty, Cha Thrat?" it continued. "An untrained, unprepared, single-species-oriented being could cause untold harm to itself and to the hospital staff and patients. We have to know what exactly it is that we're getting, and quickly."

The others had stopped eating and so did she, even though there was a mouth free for speaking. She said, "As a stranger arriving and expecting to take up an appointment here, I thought that my treatment showed a lack of sensitivity, but I decided that alien behavior patterns, of which I have very limited experience, were to blame. Then I began to suspect that the harsh and insensitive treatment was deliberate, and I was being tested in some fashion. You have confirmed this suspicion, but I am seriously displeased that I was not informed of the test. Secret tests, to my mind, can often show a failure in the examiner."

There was a long silence. She looked at Danalta and away again. The shape-changer's body and features and expression were the mirror of her own, and told her nothing. She turned her attention to Braithwaite, who had been taking such a continuous and covert interest in her, and waited for a reaction.

For a moment the Earth-human's two recessed eyes looked calmly into her four, and she began to feel very sure that the being was, in fact, a ruler and not a warrior as it said, "A secret test is sometimes given to avoid the unpleasantness of telling a candidate that it has failed. By pretending that no test took place, another and more acceptable reason, one that does not imply any lack of professional competence or psychological or emotional weakness, can be given for refusing the candidate an appointment. I'm sorry that you are displeased by the covert nature of the test, but in the circumstances we decided that it was better to . . . to . . ."

It broke off and began to bark quietly, as if there was something humorous in the situation, then went on. "We Earth-humans have an expression that covers your position very well. We threw you in at the deep end of the pool."

"And what," Cha Thrat said, deliberately omitting the gesture of politeness due a ruler, "did you discover from this secret test?"

"We discovered," Braithwaite said, and this time it did not bark, "that you are a very good swimmer."

CHAPTER 2

Braithwaite left before the others had finished eating, saying that O'Mara would have its intestines for hosiery supports if it was late back from lunch two days in a row. Cha Thrat knew nothing of the entity other than that it was a greatly respected and feared ruler of some kind, but the punishment for tardiness sounded a bit extreme. Danalta said that she should not worry about it, that Earth-humans frequently made such ridiculously exaggerated statements, that there was no factual basis to the remark, and that it was some kind of linguistic code they used among themselves which had a tenuous connection with the mental associative process they called humor.

"I understand," Cha Thrat said.

"I don't," Danalta said.

Ship ruler Chiang barked quietly but did not speak.

As a result, the shape-changer was their only guide on an even longer and more complicated journey to the place where Chiang was to undergo its examination—one of the casualty reception and observation wards, she was informed, reserved for the treatment of warm-blooded, oxygen-breathing patients. Danalta had returned to its original body configuration of a large, dark-green, uneven ball that guided itself, with surprising speed and accuracy, through the wheeled and walking traffic in the corridors. Was the Sommaradvan form too difficult to maintain, she wondered, or did it now feel that such psychological props were no longer necessary?

It was a surprisingly large compartment, rendered small by the number and variety of examination tables and associated equipment covering the floor and walls. There was an observation gallery for the use of visitors and trainees, and Danalta suggested that she choose the least uncomfortable chair while they were waiting. One of the silver-furred beings had already taken Chiang away to be prepared for the examination.

"We shall be able to see and hear everything that is happening," Danalta said, "but they will not hear us unless you press the transmit button, just there, on the side of your chair. You may have to use it if they ask questions."

Another silver-furred being, or perhaps it was the same one, un-dulated into the compartment, performed a seemingly purposeless act on an as-yet incomprehensible piece of equipment, then looked up at them briefly as it was leaving.

"And now we wait," Danalta went on. "But you must have questions, Cha Thrat. There is enough time to answer a few of them."

The shape-changer had retained the form of a lumpy green hemisphere, featureless except for one bulbous eye and a small fleshy protuberance that seemed to combine the functions of hearing and speech. In time, she thought, one could become used to anything—except the lack of discipline among these people, and their unwillingness to define properly their areas of authority and responsibility.

Choosing her words with care, she said, "As yet I am too ignorant and confused by all this to ask the right questions. But could I begin by asking for a detailed clarification of your own duties and responsibilities, and the class of patient you treat?"

The answer left her feeling more confused than ever.

"I don't treat patients," Danalta replied, "and unless there was a major surgical emergency, I would not be asked to do so. As for my duties, I am part of the medical team on *Rhabwar*. That is the hospital's special ambulance ship, which carries an operational crew of Monitor Corps officers and a medical team that assumes overall authority once the ship has reached the location of the vessel in distress or, as the case may be, the site of the disaster.

"The medical team," it went on, ignoring Cha Thrat's confusion, "which is led by the Cinrusskin empath, Prilicla, also comprises Pathologist Murchison, an Earth-human female; Charge Nurse Naydrad, a Kelgian experienced in space rescue work; and myself. My job is to use the shape-changing ability to reach and render first aid to casualties who might be trapped in areas inaccessible to beings of limited physical adaptability, and do whatever I can to help the injured until the rescue crew is able to extricate and move them to the ambulance ship for rapid transfer to the hospital here. You will understand that by extruding limbs and sensors of any required shape, useful work can be done in the very restricted conditions found inside a badly damaged space vessel, and there are times when I can make a valuable contribution. But in honesty I must say that the real work is done by the hospital.

"And that," it concluded, "is how I fit into this medical madhouse."

With every word, Cha Thrat's confusion had increased. Able and physically gifted this entity might be, but was it, in truth, merely a servant? But if Danalta had sensed her confusion, it mistook the reason for it.

"I have other uses, too, of course," it went on, and made a very Earth-human barking sound with its un-Earthly mouth. "As a comparative newcomer to the hospital, they send me to meet new arrivals like you on the assumption that—Pay attention, Cha Thrat! They're bringing in your ex-patient."

Two of the silver-furred beings, identified by Danalta as Kelgian operating room nurses, moved Chiang in on a powered litter, even though the ship ruler was quite capable of walking and was constantly reminding them of this fact. The Earth-human's torso was draped in a green sheet so that only its head was visible. Chiang's protests continued while they were transferring it to the examination table, until one of the nurses, in a manner completely lacking in the respect due a ruler, reminded it that it was a fully grown, mature entity who should stop acting like an infant.

Before the nurse had finished speaking, a six-legged, exoskeletal being with a high, richly marked carapace entered and approached the examination table. Silently it held out its pincers and waited while a nurse sprayed them with something that dried into a thin, transparent film.

"That is Senior Physician Edanelt," Danalta said. "It is a Melfan, physiological classification ELNT, whose reputation as a surgeon is—"

"Apologies for my personal ignorance," Cha Thrat broke in. "Beyond the fact that I am a DCNF, the Earth-human is a DBDG, and the Melfan is an ELNT, I know nothing of your classification system."

"You'll learn," the shape-changer said. "But for now, just watch and be ready for questions."

But there were no questions. While the examination proceeded, Edanelt did not speak and neither did the nurses or the patient. Cha Thrat learned the purpose of one of the mechanisms, a deep scanner that showed in minute detail the subdermal blood supply network, musculature, bone structure, and even the movement of the deepest underlying organs. The images were relayed to the observation gallery's screen, together with a mass of physiological data that was presented graphically but in a form that was completely unintelligible to her.

"That is something else you will learn," Danalta said.

Cha Thrat had been watching the screen closely, so captivated by Edanelt's meticulous charting of her surgical repair work that she had not realized that she had been thinking aloud. She looked up in time to see the arrival of yet another and even more incredible being.

"That," Danalta said simply, "is Prilicla."

It was an insect, an enormous, incredibly fragile, flying insect that was tiny in comparison with the other beings in the room. From its tubular, exoskeletal body there projected six pencil-thin legs, four even more delicately formed manipulators, and four sets of wide, iridescent wings that were beating slowly as it flew toward the examination table and hovered above it. Suddenly it flipped over, attached its sucker-tipped legs to the ceiling, and curved its extensible eyes down to regard the patient.

From somewhere in its body came a series of musical clicks and trills, which her translator relayed as "Friend Chiang, you look as if you've been in a war."

"We're not savages!" Cha Thrat protested angrily. "There hasn't been a war on Sommaradva for eight generations—"

She stopped abruptly as the long, incredibly thin legs and partly folded wings of the insect began to shake. It was as if there were a strong wind blowing through the room. Everyone on and around the examination table was staring at the little being, and then they were turning to look up at the observation gallery. At her.

"Prilicla is a true empath," Danalta said sharply. "It feels what you are feeling. Please control your emotions!"

It was very difficult to control her emotions: not only her anger at the implied insult to her now unwarlike race but also the feeling of utter disbelief that such control was necessary. She had often been forced to hide her feelings before superiors or patients, but trying to *control* them was a new experience. With a great effort, which in some obscure fashion seemed to be a negation of effort, she made herself calm.

"Thank you, new friend," the empath trilled at her. It was no longer trembling as it returned its attention to Chiang.

"I'm wasting your valuable time, Doctors," the Earth-human said. "Honestly, I feel fine."

Prilicla dropped from the ceiling to hover above the site of Chiang's recent injuries, and touched the scar tissue with a cluster of feather-light digits. It said, "I know how you feel, friend Chiang. And we are not wasting our time. Would you refuse us, a Melfan and a Cinrusskin who are both keen to enlarge our other-species experience, the opportunity of tinkering with an Earth-human, even a perfectly healthy one?"

"I suppose not," Chiang said. It made another soft, barking sound and added, "But you would have found it more interesting if you'd seen me after the crash."

The empath returned to the ceiling. To the Melfan it said, "What is your assessment, friend Edanelt?"

"The work is not as I would have performed it," the Melfan replied, "but it is adequate."

"Friend Edanelt," the empath said gently, with a brief glance in the direction of the gallery, "we are all aware, with the exception of the newest member of our staff, that you consider as merely adequate the kind of surgery which Conway himself would describe as exemplary. It would be interesting to discuss the pre- and postoperative history."

"That was my thought as well," the Melfan said. There was a rapid, irregular tapping of its six boney feet, and it turned to face the observation gallery. "Will you join us, please."

Quickly Cha Thrat disentangled herself from the alien chair and followed Danalta into the ward and across to the group at the table, aware that it was now her turn to undergo an even more searching examination, one that would establish her professional rather than her physical fitness to practice in Sector General.

The prospect must have worried her more than she realized because the empath was beginning to tremble again. And it was disconcerting, even frightening, to be so close to the Cinrusskin. On Sommaradva, large insects were to be avoided because they invariably possessed lethal stings. Her instincts told her to swat or run away from this one. She had hated insects and always avoided looking closely at them. Now she had no choice.

But there was a subtle visual attraction in the intricate symmetry of the extraordinarily fragile body and trembling limbs, whose dark sheen seemed to be reflecting colors that were not present in the room. The head was an alien, convoluted eggshell, so finely structured that the sensory and manipulatory organs that it supported seemed ready to fall off at the first sudden movement. But it was the complex structure and coloration of the partially folded wings, seemingly made of iridescent gossamer stretched across a framework of impossibly thin twigs, that made her realize that, alien or not, this insect was one of the most beautiful creatures she had ever seen—and she could see it very clearly because its limbs were no longer trembling.

"Thank you again, Cha Thrat," the empath said. "You learn quickly. And don't worry. We are your friends and are wishing for your success."

Edanelt's feet were making irregular clicking noises against the floor, a sound that might possibly be indicating impatience. It said, "Please present your patient, Doctor."

For a moment she looked down at the Earth-human, at the pink, oddly formed alien body that, as a result of the accident, had become so familiar to her. She remembered how it had looked when she first saw it: the bleeding, open wounds and the fractured, protruding bones; the general condition that strongly indicated the immediate use of comforting medication until casualty termination. Even now she could not find the words to explain why she had not ended this Earth-human's life. She looked up again at the Cinrusskin.

Prilicla did not speak, but she felt as if waves of reassurance and encouragement were emanating from the little empath. That was a ridiculous idea, of course, and probably the result of wishful and not very lucid thinking, but she felt comforted nonetheless.

"This patient," Cha Thrat said calmly, "was one of three occupants of an aircraft that crashed into a mountain lake. A Sommaradvan pilot and another Earth-human were taken from the wreck before it sank, but they were already dead. The patient was taken ashore and looked at by a healer who was insufficiently qualified, and, knowing that I was spending a recreation period in the area, he sent for me.

"The patient had sustained many incised and lacerated wounds to the limbs and torso caused by violent contact with the metal of the aircraft," she went on. "There was continuing blood loss. Differences in the appearance of the limbs on the right and left sides indicated the presence of multiple fractures, one of which was visible where it projected through the tegument of the left leg. There was no evidence of blood coming from the patient's breathing and speaking orifices, so it was assumed that no serious injuries had been sustained in the lung and abdominal areas. Naturally, very careful consideration had to be given before I agreed to take the case."

"Naturally," Edanelt said. "You were faced with treating a member of an off-planet species, one possessing a physiology and metabolism of which you had no previous experience. Or had you previous experience? Did you consider sending for same-species medical assistance?"

"I had not seen an Earth-human before that time," Cha Thrat replied. "I knew that one of their ships was in orbit around Sommaradva and that the process of establishing friendly contact was well advanced. I had heard that they were traveling widely among our principal cities, and that they often used our air transport, presumably to gain some experience of our level of technology. I sent a message to the nearest city hoping that they would relay it to the Earth-humans, but it was unlikely that it would arrive in time. The area is remote, mountainous, heavily forested, and thinly populated. The facilities were limited and time was short."

"I understand," Edanelt said. "Describe your procedure."

Remembering, Cha Thrat looked again at the network of scars and the dark, contused areas where the subdermal bleeding had not completely dispersed.

"At the time of treatment I was not aware of the fact that native pathogens have no effect on life-forms which evolved on a different planet, and it seemed to me that there was a grave danger of infection. It was also thought that Sommaradvan medication and anesthetics would be ineffective if not lethal. The only indicated procedure was to thoroughly irrigate the wounds, particularly those associated with the fractures, with distilled water. While reducing the fractures, some minor repairs were required to damaged blood vessels in the area. The incised wounds were sutured, covered, and the fractured limbs immobilized. The work was done very quickly because the patient was conscious and . . ."

"Not for long," Chiang said in a low voice. "I passed out."

". . . and the pulse seemed weak and irregular," she went on, "even though I didn't know the normal rate. The only means available to counteract shock and the effects of blood loss were external heating, provided by wood fires placed downwind so that smoke and ash would not contaminate the operative field, and pure water given intravenously when consciousness was lost. I was unsure whether our saline solution would be beneficial or toxic. I realize now that I was being overcautious, but I did not want to risk losing a limb."

"Naturally," Edanelt said. "Now describe your post-operative treatment."

"The patient regained consciousness late that evening," Cha Thrat went on. "It appeared to be mentally and verbally lucid, although the exact meaning of some words were unclear since they referred to the consigning of the faulty aircraft, the whole current situation, and myself to some hypothetical but extremely unpleasant afterlife. Since the native edible vegetation was likely to prove harmful, only water administered orally could be given. The patient complained of severe discomfort at the site of the wounds. Native pain-relief medication could not be given because it might prove toxic, so that the condition could only be treated, however inadequately, by verbal reassurance and encouragement—"

"For three days she never stopped talking," Chiang said. "Asking questions about my work, and what I would be doing after I returned to active duty, when I was pretty sure that I would be returning in a box. She talked so much, sometimes, that I just fell asleep."

There was a slight tremor apparent in Prilicla's limbs. Cha Thrat wondered if the Cinrusskin was sensitive even to the Earth-human's remembered pain.

She resumed. "In response to several urgent requests, five members of the patient's species, one of whom was a healer, arrived with supplies of suitable food and supportive medication. Progress toward recovery was rapid thereafter. The Earth-human healer gave advice on diet and medication dosage, and it was free to examine the patient at any time, but I would not allow further surgical intervention. I should explain that on Sommaradva, a surgeon will not share or in any other way avoid personal responsibility for a patient. There was strong criticism, both personal and professional, of my standpoint, particularly from the

Earth-human healer. I would not allow the patient to be moved to its ship until eighteen days after the operation, when I was convinced that full recuperation was assured."

"She watched over me," Chiang said, barking softly, "like an old mother hen."

There was silence for what seemed to Cha Thrat to be a very long time, during which everyone looked at the Melfan while it regarded the patient. It was tapping one hard-tipped leg against the floor, but the sound it made was a thoughtful rather than an impatient one.

Finally it said, "Without immediate surgical attention you would undoubtedly have died as a result of your injuries, and you were fortunate indeed to receive the necessary attention from an entity completely unfamiliar with your physiological classification. Fortunate, too, in that the entity concerned was not only skilled, resourceful, and deeply concerned with your aftercare, but made the proper use of the limited facilities available to it. I can find no serious fault with the surgical work performed here, and the patient is, indeed, wasting the hospital's time."

Suddenly they were all looking at her, but it was the empath who spoke first.

"From Edanelt," Prilicla said, "that is praise indeed."

CHAPTER 3

The private office of the Earth-human O'Mara was large, but the floor area was almost entirely covered by a variety of chairs, benches, recliners and frames designed for the use of the entities having business with the Chief Psychologist. Chiang took the indicated Earth-human chair and Cha Thrat chose a low, convoluted cage that looked as if it might not be too uncomfortable, and sat down.

She saw at once that O'Mara was an old Earth-human. The short, bristling fur covering the top and sides of its head, and the two thick crescents above its eyes, were the gray color of unpainted metal. But the heavy muscle structure apparent in the shoulders, upper limbs, and hands was not that of the other aged Earth-humans she had seen. The flexible, fleshy covers of its eyes, which were similar in color to its hair, did not droop as it studied her in every physical detail.

"You are a stranger among us, Cha Thrat," it said abruptly. "I am here to help you feel less strange, to answer questions you have been unable or unwilling to ask of others, and to see how your present abilities can be trained and extended so that they may be put to the best possible use by the hospital."

It turned its attention to Chiang. "My intention was to interview you separately, but for some reason you wish to be present during my initial talk with Cha Thrat. Can it be that you have heard, and believed, some of the things the staff say about me? Do you have delusions of being a gentleman and Cha Thrat a lady, albeit of a different physiological classification, who if not actually in distress is a friend in need of moral support? Is that it, Major?"

Chiang barked quietly but did not speak.

"A question," Cha Thrat said. "Why do Earth-humans make that strange barking sound?"

O'Mara turned its head to regard her for a long moment, then it exhaled loudly and said, "I had expected your first question to be more . . . profound. But very well. The sound is called laughing, not barking, and in most cases it is a psychophysical mechanism for the release of minor degrees of tension. An Earth-human laughs because of a sudden relief from worry or fear, or to express scorn or disbelief or sarcasm, or in response to words or a situation that is ridiculous, illogical, or funny, or out of politeness when the situation or words are *not* funny but the person responsible is of high rank. I shall not even try to explain sarcasm or the Earth-human sense of humor to you, because we don't fully understand them ourselves. For reasons that will become clearer the longer you stay here, I rarely laugh."

For some reason Chiang barked—laughed—again.

Ignoring it, O'Mara went on. "Senior Physician Edanelt is satisfied regarding your professional competence and suggests that I assign you to a suitable ward as soon as possible. Before that happens you must become more familiar with the layout, operation, and work of the hospital. You will find that it is a very dangerous and frightening place to the uninformed. At present, that is you."

"I understand," Cha Thrat said.

"The people who will impart this very necessary information," it went on, "are of many different physiological types and medical and technical specialities. They will range from Diagnosticians, Senior Physicians, and healers like, or totally unlike, yourself, to nursing staff, and laboratory and maintenance technicians. Some of them will be your medical or administrative superiors, others will be nominally subordinate to you, but the knowledge they impart is equally valuable. I'm told that you are averse to sharing patient responsibility. While learning you may, at the discretion of the doctor in charge, be allowed to practice, but under close supervision. Do you understand, and agree?"

"I do," Cha Thrat said unhappily. It was going to be her first year in the School for Warrior-Surgeons on Sommaradva all over again but, hopefully, without the attendant nonmedical problems.

"This interview," O'Mara went on, "will not decide whether or not you are accepted as a permanent member of the hospital staff. I cannot tell you what or what not to do in every situation that will arise; you must learn by observation and attention to the words of your tutors and decide that for yourself. But if there are really serious problems that you are unable to solve for yourself, you may come to me for guidance. Naturally, the fewer visits you make to this office the better disposed I shall feel toward you. I shall be receiving continuous reports on your progress, or lack of it, and it is these that will decide whether or not you remain here."

It paused briefly and moved the digits of one hand through the short gray head-fur. She watched carefully but saw no sign of dislodged parasites, and decided that the movement was an unthinking one.

"This interview," O'Mara continued, "is intended to explore some of the nonmedical aspects of your treatment of Chiang. In the short time available I would like to learn as much as possible about you as a person: your feelings, motivations, fears, likes, and dislikes, that sort of thing. Is there any area in which you would not want to answer questions, or would give obscure or false answers, because of moral or parental or community tribal conditioning during childhood or maturity? I must warn you that I am capable of detecting a lie, even the weird and wonderfully complicated lies that some of our extraterrestrials tell, but it takes time and I have none of that to waste."

She thought for a moment, then said, "There are matters involving sexual encounters that I would rather not discuss, but all other answers will be complete and truthful."

"Good!" O'Mara said. "I have no intention of entering that area and, hopefully, may never have to do so. At present I am interested in your thoughts and feelings between the time you first saw your patient and the decision to operate, any relevant discussion between the healer who was first on the scene and yourself, and the reason for the delay in starting the operation when you did take charge. If you had any strong feelings at that time, please describe and explain them if you can, and speak as the thoughts come to you."

For a moment Cha Thrat tried to recall her exact feelings at the time, then she said, "I was spending but not enjoying an enforced vacation in the area, because I would have preferred to continue working in my hospital instead of trying to devise ways of wasting time. When I heard of the accident I was almost pleased, thinking at first that the survivor was a Sommaradvan, and there was proper work for me to do. Then I saw the Earth-human's injuries and knew that the local healer would not dare touch it because he was a healer of serviles. Even though the survivor was not a Sommaradvan warrior, it was plainly a warrior injured in the course of its duty.

"I am uncertain about your units of time measurement," she went on. "The crash occurred just before sunrise, and I reached the shore of the lake where Chiang had been placed shortly before the time of the morning meal. Without proper medication or knowledge of the body structure, many things had to be considered. The sensible course would have been to allow the survivor to bleed to death or, out of kindness, expedite matters by immersing it in the lake . . ."

She stopped for a moment because O'Mara seemed to have a temporary blockage of the breathing passages, then she resumed. "After several examinations and evaluations of the risks, surgery was begun early in the afternoon. At the time I did not know that Chiang was the ruler of a ship."

The two Earth-humans exchanged looks, and O'Mara said, "That was five, maybe six hours later. Do you usually take as long as that to reach a professional decision? And would it have made any difference if you had known of Chiang's importance?"

"There were many risks to consider—I did not want to risk losing a limb," she replied sharply, sensing a criticism. "And yes, it should have made a difference. A warrior-surgeon is in the same position to a ruler as the servile-healer is in relation to a warrior. I am forbidden to practice beyond my qualifications. The penalties are most severe, even allowing for the increasingly lax standards so prevalent these days. But in this instance, well, it was a unique situation. I felt frightened, and excited, and I would probably have acted in the same way."

O'Mara said, "I'm glad you don't normally practice surgery beyond your level of competence . . ."

"It's a good thing she did," Chiang said softly.

". . . And your tutors will be relieved as well," O'Mara went on. "But I'm interested in this stratification of the Sommaradvan medical profession. Can you tell me about that?"

Puzzled by what seemed to be a nonsense question, she replied, "We are not forbidden to talk about anything. On Sommaradva there are three levels of persons—serviles, warriors, and rulers—and three levels of healers to care for them . . ."

At the bottom were the serviles, the people whose work was undemanding and repetitious—important in many respects, but completely without risk. They were a contented group, protected from gross physical damage, and the healers charged with their care used very simple procedures and medication such as herbs, poultices, and other traditional remedies. The second level, less numerous than the serviles, were the warriors, who occupied positions of responsibility and often great physical danger.

There had been no war on Sommaradva for many generations, but the warrior class had kept the name. They were the descendants of the people who had fought to protect their homelands, hunted for food, raised city defenses, and generally performed the dangerous, responsible jobs while the serviles saw to their physical needs. Now they were the engineers, technicians, and scientists who still performed the high-risk jobs associated with mining, power generation, large-scale construction, and the protection of rulers. For that reason the injuries sustained by warriors were and always had been traumatic in nature, requiring surgical intervention or repair, and this work was the responsibility of the warrior-surgeons.

The ruler-healers had even greater responsibilities and, at times, much less reward or satisfaction in their work.

Protected against all physical accident or injury, the ruler class were the administrators, academics, researchers, and planners on Sommaradva. They were the people charged with the smooth running of the cities and the continents and the world, and the ills that affected them were invariably the phantasms of the mind. Their healers dealt in wizardry, spells, sympathetic magic, and all the other aspects of nonphysical medicine.

"Even from the earliest times the practice of healing has been so divided," Cha Thrat concluded, "into physicians and surgeons and wizards."

When she finished speaking, O'Mara looked down for a moment at its hands, which were placed palms down on its desktop, and said quietly, "It's nice to know that I would rate the top level of the Sommaradvan medical profession, but I'm not sure that I like being called a wizard." It looked up suddenly. "What happens if one of your warriors or rulers gets a simple tummyache, instead of a traumatic injury or an emotional problem? Or if a servile should accidentally break a leg? Or what if a servile or a warrior is dissatisfied and wants to better itself?"

"The Cultural Contact people sent you a full report on all this," Chiang broke in, "as background material on the new medic." Apologetically it added, "The decision to send Cha Thrat was taken at the last moment, and possibly the report arrived with us on *Thromasaggar*."

O'Mara exhaled loudly, and she wondered if it was an expression of irritation at the interruption, then said, "And the hospital's internal mail system operates at a speed considerably less than that of light. Please go on, Cha Thrat."

"In the highly unlikely event of a servile having such an accident," she said, "a request for treatment would be made to a warrior-surgeon who, depending on assessment of the injuries, would or would not agree to do the work. Responsibility for a patient is not taken lightly on Sommaradva, as is shown by the delay in treating Chiang, and the loss of a life, an organ, or a limb has serious repercussions for the surgeon.

"Should a warrior or ruler require simple medical attention," she continued, "a servile-healer would be instructed, and would indeed be honored, to provide the necessary assistance.

"If a discontented servile or warrior is able as well as ambitious," she went on, "elevation to a higher level is possible. But the examinations are wide-ranging and difficult, and it is much easier to remain at the level traditionally occupied by the family or tribe or, if a release from problems and responsibilities is desired, to go down a level. Promotions, even minor promotions within a level, are not easy on Sommaradva."

"Nor are they easy here," O'Mara said. "But why did you come to Sector General? Ambition, curiosity, or a release from problems at home?"

This was an important question, Cha Thrat knew, and the quality and accuracy of the answer would have an important bearing on whether or not she was accepted by the hospital. She tried to frame the answer so that it would be accurate, truthful, and brief, but before she could reply the ship ruler was talking again.

"We were grateful to Cha Thrat for saving my life," Chiang said, speaking very quickly, "and we told her colleagues and superiors so in no uncertain language. The subject of treatment by other-species medics came up, and Sector General, where it was the rule rather than the exception. It was suggested to us, and we agreed, that Cha Thrat should come here. The Sommaradvan cultural contact is going very well and we didn't want to risk offending, perhaps insulting, them by refusing.

"I realize that we bypassed the normal candidate selection procedure," it continued. "But her already-proven ability to perform other-species surgery, on me, made us sure that you would be interested in—"

O'Mara was holding up one hand, and it had not taken its attention from Cha Thrat while the other Earth-human had been speaking. It said, "Is this a political appointment, then, which we must accept whether we like it or not? But the original question remains. Why did you want to come here?"

"I didn't want to come here," she replied. "I was sent."

Chiang covered its eyes suddenly with one hand, a gesture she had never seen it make before. O'Mara looked at her for a moment, then said, "Explain."

"When the warriors of the Monitor Corps told us of the many different intelligent species who make up the Galactic Federation," she replied, "and talked to me at great length about Sector General, where I could meet and work with many of these life-forms, I was curious, interested, but much too frightened by the prospect of meeting not one but nearly seventy different species to risk undergoing an experience that might give me a ruler's disease. I told everyone who would listen my feelings, and reminded them of my utter lack of competence in relation to the level of surgery practiced here. I was not pretending to modesty. I really was, and am, ignorant. Because I was warrior level, I could not be forced, but it was strongly suggested by my colleagues and local rulers that I come."

"Ignorance can be a temporary condition," O'Mara said. "And it must have been a pretty strong suggestion. Why was it made?"

"In my hospital I am respected but not liked," she went on, hoping that the anger in her voice was not reproduced by the translator. "In spite of being one of the first female warrior-surgeons, an innovation in itself, I am a traditionalist. I will not tolerate the reduced standards of professional behavior that are becoming increasingly prevalent, and I am critical of colleagues and superiors alike if they become lax. It was suggested to me that if I did not take advantage of the opportunity being offered by the Earth-humans, there would be a continuing increase of the nonmaterial pressures associated with my work as a surgeon. The situation was too complex for me to describe briefly, but my rulers made suggestions to the Monitor Corps, who were very reassuring and persuasive. The Earth-humans pulled while my superiors pushed, and I am here.

"Now that I am here," she ended, "I shall use my limited abilities, under direction, as best I can."

O'Mara was looking at the ship ruler now. Chiang had taken its hand away from its eyes, but its pink face was a deeper color than she had ever seen before.

"The Sommaradvan contact was widening nicely," Chiang said, "but it was at a delicate stage. We didn't want to risk refusing what seemed to them to be such a small favor. And anyway, we were pretty sure that they were giving Cha Thrat a hard time and we—I—thought she would be happier here."

"So," O'Mara said, still looking at the ship ruler, whose face was now an even deeper shade of pink, "we have not only a political appointee but an unwilling volunteer and possibly a misfit. And, out of a misplaced sense of gratitude, you tried to conceal the true situation from me. That's great!"

It turned to face Cha Thrat again and said, "I appreciate your truthfulness. This material will be useful in the preparation of your psych profile but it does not, in spite of what your misguided friend may think, preclude your acceptance by the hospital provided the other requirements are satisfied. Those you will learn during training, which will begin first thing in our morning."

The words were coming faster than before, as if O'Mara's time for talking were limited, as it went on. "In the outer office you will be given an information package, maps, class schedules, general rules, and advice, all printed in the most widely used language on Sommaradva. Some of our trainees will tell you that their first and most difficult test was finding their rooms.

"Good luck, Cha Thrat."

As she was picking her way between the alien furniture toward the door, O'Mara was saying "I'm primarily interested in your postoperative emotional condition, Major Chiang. Have there been any waking fears, recurrent nightmares, unexplained episodes of tension, with or without accompanying perspiration, associated with the operation? Any feelings of drowning, strangulation, increasing and unreasoning fear of the dark? . . ."

Truly, she thought, *O'Mara was a great wizard.*

In the outer office, the Earth-human Braithwaite gave verbal as well as printed advice together with a white band to wear on one of her upper arms. It signified to all that she was a trainee, it said, laughing, and likely to become confused and lost. Should that happen she could ask any member of the hospital staff for directions. It, too, ended by wishing her well.

Finding the way to her room was a nightmare worse, she was sure, than any that Chiang might be relating to O'Mara. She needed directions on two occasions, and each time she asked groups of the silver-furred Kelgians who seemed to be everywhere in the hospital, rather than any of the great, lumbering monsters or the squishy beings in chlorine envelopes who crowded past her. But on both occasions, in spite of the respectful manner of her request, the information was given in a most rude and abrupt fashion.

Her immediate feeling was one of severe personal offense. But then she saw that the Kelgians were rude and short-tempered even to other members of their own species, and she decided that it might be better not to upbraid them for their extreme lack of politeness toward a stranger.

When she at last located her room, the door was wide open and the Earth-human Timmins was lying prone on the floor and holding a small metal box that was making quiet noises and winking its lights.

"Just testing," Timmins said. "I'll be finished in a moment. Look around. The operating instructions for everything are on the table. If there is anything you don't understand, use the communicator to call Staff Training, they'll help you." It rolled onto its back and got to its feet in a way that was physically impossible for a Sommaradvan, and added, "What do you think of the place?"

"I'm—I'm surprised," Cha Thrat said, feeling almost shocked by its familiarity. "And delighted. It's just like my quarters at home."

"We aim to please," Timmins said. It raised one hand in a gesture she did not understand, and was gone.

For a long time she moved about the small room examining the furniture and equipment, not quite believing what she saw and felt. She knew that photographs and measurements had been taken of her quarters in the warrior-surgeon level at the Calgren House of Healing, but she had not expected such close attention to detail in the reproduction of her favorite pictures, wall coverings, lighting, and personal utilities. There were differences, too, some obvious and others subtle, to remind her that this place, despite appearances to the contrary, was not on her home world.

The room itself was larger and the furniture more comfortable, but there were no joints visible in the construction. It was as if every item had been fabricated in one piece. All the doors and drawers and fastenings in the replicas worked perfectly, which the originals had never done, and the air smelled different—in fact, it did not smell at all.

Gradually her initial feelings of pleasure and relief were being diluted by the realization that this was nothing more than a tiny, familiar bubble of normality inside a vast, alien, and terrifyingly complex structure. The fear and anxiety she was beginning to feel were greater than she had ever experienced on her incredibly distant home planet, and with them was a growing degree of loneliness so acute that it felt like an intense, physical hunger.

But she was not liked or wanted on far Sommaradva, and here, at least, they had taken positive measures to welcome her, so much so that she had to remain in this terrible place if only to discharge the obligation. And she would try to learn as much as she could before the hospital rulers decided that she was unsuitable and sent her home.

She should start learning now.

Was the hunger real, she wondered, rather than imaginary? She had not been able to eat to repletion during the earlier visit to the dining hall because her mind had been on matters other than food. She began to plan the route there, and to the location of her first lecture in the morning, from her present position. But she did not feel like another trip along the hospital's weirdly populated corridors just yet. She was very tired, and the room had a limited-menu food dispenser for trainees who did not wish to interrupt their studies by going to the dining hall.

She referred to the list of foods suited to her metabolism and tapped for medium-to-large portions. When she was feeling comfortably distended, she tried to sleep.

The room and the corridor outside were full of quiet, unidentifiable sounds, and she did not know enough to be able to ignore them. Sleep would not come and she was beginning to feel afraid again, and to wonder if her thoughts and feelings were of the kind to interest the wizard O'Mara, and that made her even more fearful for her future at Sector General. While still lying at rest, physically if not mentally, she used the ceiling projection facility of the communicator to see what was happening on the entertainment and training channels.

According to the relevant information sheet, ten of the channels continuously screened some of the Galactic Federation's most popular entertainment, current interest, and drama programs with a translator output, if required. But she discovered that while she could understand the words that the different physiological types were saying to and about each other, the accompanying actions were in turn horrifying, mystifying, ridiculous, or downright obscene to Sommaradvan eyes. She switched to the training channels.

There she had a choice of watching displays of currently meaningless figures and tabulations on the temperatures, blood pressures, and pulse rates of about fifty different life-forms, or surgical operations in progress that were visually disquieting and not calculated to lull anyone to sleep.

In desperation, Cha Thrat tried the sound-only channels. But the music she found, even when the volume was reduced to bare audibility, sounded as if it were coming from a piece of malfunctioning heavy machinery. So it was a great surprise when the room alarm began reminding her, monotonously and with steadily increasing volume, that it was time to awaken if she required breakfast before her first lecture.

CHAPTER 4

The lecturer was a Nidian who had been introduced as Senior Physician Cresk-Sar. While it was speaking, it prowled up and down the line of trainees like some small, hairy, carnivorous beast, which meant that every few minutes it passed Cha Thrat so closely that she wanted to either fold her limbs in defensive mode or run away.

"To minimize verbal confusion during meetings with other-species entities," it was saying, "and to avoid inadvertently giving offense, it is assumed that all members of the medical and support staff who do not belong to your own particular species are sexless. Whether you are addressing them directly or discussing them in their absence, you will always think of them as an 'it'. The only exception to this rule is when an other-species patient is being treated for a condition directly related to its sex, in which case the doctor must know whether it is male or female, or one of the multisexed species, if the proper treatment is to be carried out.

"I am a male Nidian DBDG," Cresk-Sar went on, "but do not think of me as 'he' or 'him'. Think of me as 'it'."

As the disgusting, hairy shape moved to within a few paces of her before turning away again, Cha Thrat thought that she would have no difficulty in thinking of this Senior Physician as "it."

With the intention of finding someone less repulsive to look at, she turned her eyes toward the trainee closest to her—one of the three silver-furred Kelgians attending the lecture. It was strange, she thought, how the Nidian's fur made her cringe inwardly while the equally alien covering of the Kelgian relaxed and calmed her like a work of great art. The fur was in constant motion, with long, slow ripples moving from the creature's conical head right down to its tail, with occasional cross-eddies and wavelets appearing, as if the incredibly fine pelt was a liquid stirred by an unfelt wind. At first she thought the movements were random, but a pattern of ripples and eddies seemed to be developing the more closely she watched.

"What are you staring at?" the Kelgian said suddenly, its translated words overlaid by the moaning and hissing sounds of its native speech. "Do I have a bald patch, or something?"

"I'm sorry, I had not meant to give offense," Cha Thrat said. "Your fur is beautiful and I couldn't help admiring it the way it moves—"

"Pay attention, you two!" the Senior Physician said sharply. It moved closer, looked up at each of them in turn, then went prowling down the line again.

"Cresk-Sar's fur," the Kelgian said softly, "is a sight. It makes me think that invisible and no doubt imaginary parasites are about to change their abode. It gives me a terrible psychosomatic itch."

This time Cresk-Sar gave them another long look, made an irritated, snuffling sound that did not translate, and continued with what it was saying.

". . . There is a great deal of illogical behavior associated with sexual differences," it went on, "and I must emphasize once again, unless the sex of a particular entity has a direct bearing on its course of treatment, the subject must be ignored if not deliberately avoided. Some of you may consider that such knowledge of another species would be helpful, conversationally useful during off-duty meetings or, as often happens in this place, when a particularly interesting piece of gossip is circulating. But believe me, in this area, ignorance is a virtue."

"Surely," said a Melfan trainee halfway down the line, "there are interspecies social occasions, shared meals or lectures, when it would be a gross act of bad manners to ignore another intelligent and socially aware person's gender. I think that—"

"And *I* think," Cresk-Sar said with a bark, or laugh, "that you are what our Earth-human friends call a gentleman. You haven't been listening. Ignore the difference. Consider everyone who is not of your own species as neuter. In any case, you would have to observe some of our other-species people very closely to tell the difference, and that in itself could cause serious embarrassment. In the case of Hudlar life-mates, who alternate between male and female mode, the behavior patterns are quite complex."

"What would happen," the Kelgian beside her said, "if they should go, completely or partly, out of synchronization?"

From the line of trainees there were a number of different sounds, none of which registered on her translator. The Senior Physician was looking at the Kelgian, whose fur, for some reason, had begun to move in rapid, irregular ripples.

"I shall treat that as a serious question," Cresk-Sar said, "although I doubt that it was intended as such. Rather than answer it myself, I shall ask one of you to do so. Would the Hudlar trainee please step forward."

So *that*, Cha Thrat thought, is a Hudlar.

It was a squat, heavy life-form with a hard, almost featureless dark-gray skin, discolored by patches of the dried paint she had seen it spraying on itself before they had entered the lecture theater, and she had decided then that it was extremely careless in its application of cosmetics. The body was supported on six heavy tentacles, each of which terminated in a cluster of flexible digits, curled inward so that the weight was borne on heavy knuckles and the fingers remained clear of the floor.

There were no body openings that she could see, not even in the head, which contained eyes protected by hard, transparent shells and a semicircular membrane that vibrated to produce the creature's words as it turned toward them.

"It is very simple, respected colleagues," the Hudlar said. "While I am presently male, Hudlars are all sexually neutral until puberty, after which the direction taken is dependent on social-environmental influences, sometimes quite subtle influences that do not involve body contact. A picture of an attractive male-mode Hudlar might impel one from neuter toward female mode, or the other way around. A conscious choice can be made if the career one intends to follow favors a particular sex. Unless one is mated, the postpuberty sex choice is fixed for the remainder of one's life.

"When two adults become life-mates," the Hudlar went on, "that is, when they join for the purpose of becoming parents and not simply for temporary pleasure, the sex changes are initiated shortly after conception. By the time the child is born the male has become much less aggressive, more attentive and emotionally oriented toward its mate, while its mate is beginning to lose the female characteristics. Following parturition, the process continues, with the father-that-was taking responsibility for the child while progressing to full female mode, and the mother develops all the male characteristics that will enable it to be a father-to-be.

"There is, of course, a time during which both life-mates are emotional neuters," the Hudlar added, "but this is a period of the pregnancy when physical coupling is contraindicated."

"Thank you," the Senior Physician said, but held up a small, hairy hand to indicate that the Hudlar should remain where it was. "Any further comments, questions?"

It was looking at the Kelgian beside her, the one who had asked the original question, but Cha Thrat spoke on impulse.

"It seems to me that the Hudlars are fortunate," she said, "in that they are not troubled by the situation of the members of one sex considering themselves innately superior to the other, as is the case on Sommaradva..."

"And on too many other worlds of the Federation," the Kelgian interjected, the fur rising into tufts behind its head.

"...I thank the Hudlar for its explanation," Cha Thrat went on, "but I was surprised to find that it is presently a male. My first thought, based on observation of what I mistakenly assumed to be cosmetic paint on its body, was that it was female."

The Hudlar's speaking membrane began to vibrate, but Cresk-Sar held its hand up for silence and said, "What are your second thoughts?"

Confused, she stared at the hairy little creature, wondering what she was expected to say.

"Come, come," Cresk-Sar barked. "Tell us what other thoughts, observations, assumptions, mistaken or otherwise, have been going through your Sommaradvan mind regarding this life-form. Think and speak clearly."

Cha Thrat turned all her eyes on it in a way that, had it been a Sommaradvan, would have elicited an immediate verbal and physical response. She said, "My first thoughts were as described. My second was that it might be Hudlar males rather than females, or perhaps both, who wear decorative paint. Then I observed that the being's movements were careful, as if it was afraid of injuring nearby people and equipment, the movements of a gentle being of immense physical strength. That taken in conjunction with the low, squat form of the body, with six rather than two or four limbs, suggested that it was a native of a dense, heavy-gravity world with comparable atmospheric pressure, where an accidental fall would be damaging. The very hard but flexible skin, which is unbroken by any permanent body orifices for the intake or elimination of food, suggested that the paint which I had observed the Hudlar spraying onto itself might be a nutrient solution."

The eyes of Cresk-Sar, and the variegated visual sensors of the other trainees, were watching her steadily. Nobody spoke.

Hesitantly she added, "Another thought, wonderful and exciting but, I expect, pure supposition, is that if this heavy-gravity, high-pressure creature can live unprotected in the hospital surroundings, its body must be capable of containing its own very high internal pressures, and an even lower pressure environment should not inconvenience it.

"It might be possible," she went on, expecting a storm of ridicule from the Nidian Senior, "for it to work unprotected in space. This would mean that—"

"At any moment," Cresk-Sar said, holding its hand up, "you will give me its physiological classification coding, even though we haven't covered that yet. Is this the first time you've seen a Hudlar?"

"I saw two of them in the dining hall," she replied, "but at the time I was too confused to know what I was seeing."

"May your confusion continue to diminish, Cha Thrat," Cresk-Sar said. Turning its head toward the others, it went on, "This trainee has displayed the qualities of observation and deduction that, when trained and refined, will enable you to live among, understand, and treat your other-species colleagues and patients. However, I would advise you not to think of a particular life-form as a Nidian, a Hudlar, a Kelgian, a Melfan, or a Sommaradvan, that is, by their planets of origin, but by their physiological classifications, DBDG, FROB, DBLF, ELNT, or DCNF. That way you will always be reminded of their pressure, gravity, and atmosphere requirements, basic metabolism and other physiological needs, and know immediately when there is a potential environmental threat to them or to yourselves."

It continued, "Should a PVSJ, a chlorine-breathing native of Illensa, accidentally rupture its pressure envelope, the risk to the being concerned and to any oxygen-breathing D, E, and F prefixes in the vicinity would be extreme. And, if you are ever called to a space rescue situation, there may be times when an urgent and accurate identification of the casualty's physiological classification, and therefore its life-support requirements, may depend on a single limb or small area of body surface glimpsed under shifting wreckage.

"You must train yourselves to be aware, instinctively, of all the differences of the people around you," Cresk-Sar went on, giving a low laugh-bark, "if only to know whom it is safe to jostle in the corridors. And now I will take you to the wards for your initial patient experience before my next class in—"

"What about the classification system?" said the silver-furred Kelgian—the DBLF, Cha Thrat corrected herself—beside her. "If it is as important as you say it is, surely you are lacking in the qualities of a teacher not to have explained it to us."

Cresk-Sar walked slowly toward the speaker, and she wondered if she could possibly reduce the verbal violence to come by asking the Senior Physician another and more politely worded question. But for some reason the Nidian completely ignored the DBLF and spoke instead to Cha Thrat.

"You will already have observed," it said, "that these Kelgian DBLF life-forms are outspoken, ill-mannered, rude, and completely lacking in tact . . ."

You should talk, Cha Thrat thought.

". . . But there are good psychophysiological reasons for this," it went on. "Because of inadequacies in the Kelgian speech organs, their spoken language lacks modulation, inflection, and all emotional expression. But they are compensated by their highly mobile fur that acts, so far as another Kelgian is concerned, as a perfect but uncontrollable mirror to the speaker's emotional state. As a result the concept of lying, of being diplomatic, tactful, or even polite is completely alien to them. A DBLF says exactly what it means or feels, because the fur reveals its feelings from moment to moment and to do otherwise would be sheer stupidity. The opposite also holds true, because politeness and the verbal circumlocution used by many species confuses and irritates them.

"You will find some of the personalities here as alien as the persons," it continued. "Considering the fact that you have met only one other-species being before your arrival here, your behavior today makes me sure that you will have not trouble in adapting to—"

"Teacher's pet," the DBLF said, its fur tufting into spikes. "I was the one who asked the question, remember?"

"That you did," Cresk-Sar replied, looking at the wall chronometer. "Tapes covering the life-form physiological classification system will be sent to your quarters sometime today. You must study the visual material they contain, carefully and repeatedly, and use your translators on the spoken commentary. But now I have time only to outline the basics of the system."

It turned suddenly and resumed its place facing them. Plainly the answer to the question was being directed toward everyone.

"Unless you have already been attached to one of the smaller, multienvironment hospitals," Cresk-Sar said, "you will normally have encountered off-world patients one species at a time, probably on a short-term basis as a result of a ship accident, and you would refer to them by their planets of origin. But I must stress once again, the rapid and accurate identification of incoming patients is vital, because all too often they are in no condition to furnish the necessary physiological data themselves. Here we have evolved a basic, four-letter physiological classification system that enables us to provide the required life-support and initial treatment pending a more detailed investigation, if that should be necessary, by Pathology. It works like this.

"The first letter denotes the level of physical evolution reached by the species when it acquired intelligence," it continued. "The second indicates the type and distribution of limbs, sense organs, and body orifices, and the remaining two letters refer to the combination of metabolism and food and air requirements associated with the home planet's gravity and atmospheric pressure, which in turn gives an indication of the physical mass and protective tegument possessed by the being."

Cresk-Sar barked softly before saying "Usually I have to remind our other-species trainees at this point that the initial letter of their classification should not be allowed to give them feelings of inferiority, because the degree of physical evolution is controlled by environmental factors and bears little relation to the degree of intelligence . . ."

Species with the prefix A, B, or C, it went on to explain, were water-breathers. On most worlds, life had originated in the sea, and these beings had developed intelligence without having to leave it. D through F were warm-blooded oxygen-breathers, into which group most of the intelligent races of the Federation fell, and the G and K types were also oxygen breathing, but insectile. The Ls and Ms were light-gravity, winged beings.

Chlorine-breathing life-forms were contained in the O and P groups, and after these came the more exotic, the more highly evolved physically, and the downright weird types. Into these categories fell the radiation-eaters, the ultra-cold-blooded or crystalline beings, and entities capable of modifying their physical structure at will. However, those beings possessing extrasensory powers, telekinesis, or teleportation sufficiently well developed to make ambulatory or manipulatory appendages unnecessary were given the prefix V regardless of their size, shape, or environmental background.

"There are anomalies in the system," the Senior Physician continued, "and these must be blamed on the lack of imagination and foresight of the originator. The AACP life-form, for example, has a vegetable metabolism. Normally the A prefix denotes a water-breather, there being nothing lower on our evolutionary coding scale than the piscatorial life-forms. But the double-A prefix, the AACPs, are mobile, intelligent vegetables, and plant life evolved before the fish.

"And now," it said, looking at the chronometer again, "you will meet some of these weird and wonderful and perhaps horrifying creatures. It is the hospital's policy to give you the earliest possible opportunity of getting to know and work with the patients and staff members. Regardless of your position or seniority in your home-planet hospitals, your rank here will be that of Junior or Trainee Nurse—until, that is, you can convince me that your professional competence warrants a higher rating.

"I am not easy to convince," Cresk-Sar added as it began moving toward the exit. "Follow me, please."

It was not easy to follow the Senior Physician because it moved fast for such a small being, and Cha Thrat had the feeling that the other trainees were more experienced in navigating the hospital corridors than she was. But then she noticed that the Hudlar—the FROB—was falling behind as well.

"For obvious reasons," the FROB said as they drew level, "the people here give me plenty of room. If you were to stay directly behind me, together we might significantly increase our speed."

She had a sudden and shocking feeling of unreality, as if she had been plunged into a nightmare world that was both terrifying and wonderful, a world in which courtesy was being shown by a horrendous beast that was capable of tearing her apart without straining a muscle on one of its six tentacles. But even if this were a dream, the proper response had to be made.

"You are most considerate," she said. "Thank you."

The being's membrane vibrated but the sound did not translate. Then it said, "About the nutrient paint you noticed earlier, to complete your information and to show how close your deductions were to the actuality, the paint is not necessary at home. There the atmosphere is so dense and thickly packed with edible, floating organisms that it resembles a semiliquid soup, a food source that, because of our high metabolic rate, is absorbed continuously. As you can see, the last paint application has almost disappeared and is due for renewal."

Before she could reply, one of the Kelgian DBLFs fell back and said, "I was nearly walked on by a Tralthan just now. This looks like a good idea. There's room for one more."

It moved closer to Cha Thrat so that they were both protected by the Hudlar's massive body. Choosing her words carefully, she said, "I do not wish to give offense, but I cannot tell the difference between one Kelgian and another. Are you the DBLF whose fur I was admiring during the lecture?"

"Admiring, you used the right word!" the Kelgian said, its fur running in concentric waves from head to tail. "Don't worry about it. If we had more than one Sommaradvan, I couldn't tell the difference either."

Suddenly the Hudlar stopped and, looking past its speaking membrane, she saw why. The whole group of trainees had halted and Cresk-Sar was beckoning to a Melfan and the other two Kelgians.

"This is a Tralthan post-op recovery ward," it said. "You two will report here after lectures every day until instructed otherwise. You don't need protective suits, the air is breathable, and trace quantities of Tralthan body odor should be ignored. Go in, you're expected."

When the party was on its way again she noticed a few of the trainees detaching themselves without being told, and assumed that they had joined the class earlier and had already been assigned wards. One of them was her Hudlar crowd controller. Very soon the group had shrunk until there was only the DBLF and herself left, and Cresk-Sar was pointing at the Kelgian.

"This is a PVSJ medical ward," it said briskly. "You will be met inside the lock antechamber and instructed in the use of your protective envelope before going through. You will then—"

"But they're chlorine-breathers in there!" the Kelgian protested, its fur standing out in spikes. "Can't you give me a ward where I can at least breathe the air? Do you *try* to make it as difficult as possible for the new people? What happens if I accidentally rupture my suit?"

"To answer your questions in turn," the Senior Physician replied, "No. You've discovered that. And the nearby patients would have their existing injuries complicated by oxygen contamination."

"What about *me*, stupid?"

"You," Cresk-Sar said, "would suffer chlorine poisoning. And what the Charge Nurse would do to you if you recovered doesn't bear thinking about."

She had to concentrate so hard on keeping pace with the Senior Physician as they descended three levels, and traversed seemingly endless and overpopulated corridors, that there was no chance to ask what she would be expected to do. But then Cresk-Sar stopped at an enormous lock entrance that was visually identified in the Galactic Federation's principal written languages—but which did not, of course, include Sommaradvan—and answered the unasked question.

"This is the hospital's AUGL ward," it said. "You will find that the patients, all natives of the ocean world of Chalderescol, are among the most visually fearsome beings you are ever likely to encounter. But they are harmless so long as you—"

"The A prefix," Cha Thrat broke in urgently, "denotes water-breathers."

"Correct," the Nidian said. "What's wrong? Is there a problem O'Mara didn't tell me about? Are you uncomfortable or afraid in water?"

"No," Cha Thrat said. "I enjoy swimming, on the surface. The problem is my lack of a protective garment."

Cresk-Sar barked and said, "There is no problem. The more complex protective equipment for heavy-gravity, high-pressure, and elevated temperature work needs time to produce, but a simple, water-impermeable, contoured envelope with air and communication systems is an easy job for the fabricator. Your suit is waiting for you inside."

This time the Senior Physician went with her, explaining that, as she was a new life-form to the hospital, it had to ensure that her equipment functioned properly and comfortably. But in the event, it was the being waiting for them in the lock antechamber who immediately took charge and did all the talking.

"Cha Thrat," it said briskly, "I am Charge Nurse Hredlichli, a PVSJ. Your protective envelope is in two pieces. Climb into the lower half, pulling on one leg at a time, in whichever order you find most convenient, using the heavier arms encircling your waist. Use the same four arms to pull on the top half, inserting the head and four shoulder-mounted arms first. You will think that the limb end-sections are small, but this is to ensure a tight fit and maximum sensitivity for the digits. Don't seal the waist joint until you know that your air supply is working. When you are sealed in, I'll show you the systems checks that must be performed at every dressing. Then you will remove the envelope and put it on again, repeating the process until we are both happy with your performance. Please begin."

Hredlichli circled her, giving advice and directions during the first three dressings, and then seemed to ignore her while it talked to the Senior Physician. The spiney, membraneous body, looking like a haphazard collection of oily, unhealthy vegetation, was obscured by the yellow chlorine fog inside the being's protective envelope. It was impossible to tell where the Charge Nurse's attention was directed, because Cha Thrat had been unable to locate its eyes.

"We are seriously understaffed at present," Hredlichli was saying, "with three of my best nurses on special post-op recovery cases to the exclusion of all else. Are you hungry?"

Cha Thrat felt that the question was for her, but was unsure of the type of answer to give—the subservient, self-negating reply expected by a ruler or the accurate, truthful kind due a warrior-level colleague. Ignorant as she was of Hredlichli's exact status, she did her best to combine the two.

"I am hungry," she replied, using the opportunity to test her suit's communicator, "but the condition is not yet so advanced that it would impair me physically."

"Good!" said Hredlichli. "As a junior-in-training you will soon discover that practically everyone and everything takes precedence over you. If this causes emotional tension, which may be expressed as verbal resentment or anger, try not to release it until you are out of my ward. You will be allowed to visit your dining hall, for a strictly limited period, as soon as someone returns to relieve you. And now I think you know how your suit works..."

Cresk-Sar turned toward the entrance. Lifting one tiny, hairy hand, it said, "Good luck, Cha Thrat."

"...So we'll go inside to the Nurses' Station," it went on, seeming to ignore the departing Nidian. "Doublecheck your suit seals and follow me."

She found herself in a surprisingly small compartment that had one transparent wall giving a view into a dim green world where the difference between the inhabitants and the decorative vegetation designed to make them feel at home was unclear. The other three sides of the room were covered by storage units, monitor screens, and equipment whose purpose she could not even guess at. The entire ceiling was devoted to brightly colored signs and geometrical shapes.

"We have a very good staff and patient safety record in this ward," the Charge Nurse went on, "and I don't want you to spoil it. Should you damage your suit and be in danger of drowning, however, mouth-to-mouth resuscitation is not advisable between oxygen- and chlorine-breathers, so you must move quickly to one of the emergency air chambers marked so"—she indicated one of the ceiling designs—"and await rescue. But the accident, or should I say the serious inconvenience, that you must guard against is pollution by patient body wastes. Filtration or replacement of the water volume in a ward this size is a major maintenance operation that would hamper our work and get us talked about in derogatory fashion all over the hospital."

"I understand," Cha Thrat said.

Why had she come to this awful place, she wondered, and could she justify to herself her immediate resignation? In spite of the warnings from O'Mara and Cresk-Sar that she would be starting at the lowest level, this was not work for a Sommaradvan warrior-surgeon. If word of what she was expected to do were to get back to her erstwhile colleagues, she would be forced into the life of a recluse. But these people were not likely to tell her people about it because, to them, such activities were so commonplace as to be unworthy of mention. Perhaps she would be found unsuitable or incompetent and dismissed from the hospital with this demeaning and unpleasant episode secret and her honor intact. But she was dreading what was coming next.

But it was not nearly as bad as she had expected.

"The patients usually know in advance when they need to evacuate," Hredlichli went on, "and will call the nurse with time to spare. Should you be called for this purpose, the equipment you require is stored in the compartment with its door marked like this." A frondlike arm appeared inside its protective envelope, pointing to another distinctively marked panel on the ceiling, then to its distant, brightly lit twin that shone through the green dimness of the ward. It went on, "But don't worry, the patient will know all about the operation of the equipment and will prefer to help itself. Most of them dislike using the thing, you'll find that Chalders embarrass easily, and any who are not immobilized will prefer to use the room marked with that symbol. It is a long, narrow compartment barely large enough to contain one Chalder and is operated by the user. Extraction and filtration of the wastes is automatic, and if anything goes wrong it is a Maintenance problem."

Hredlichli's appendage rose again to point toward the confusion of shapes at the other end of the ward. "If you need help with a patient, ask Nurse Towan. Most of its time is being spent with a seriously ill patient, so don't distract it unnecessarily. Later today I shall instruct you on the Chalder optimum pulse rate, pressure, and body temperature, and how and where to obtain them. The vital signs are taken and recorded at regular intervals, the frequency depending on the condition of the patient. You will also be shown how to sterilize and dress surgical wounds, which is not a simple job on a water-breather, and in a few days you may be allowed to do it yourself. But first you must get to know your patients."

The appendage was pointing at a doorless opening into the main ward. A sudden paralysis seemed to be affecting all twelve of Cha Thrat's limbs, and she tried desperately to delay any movement by asking questions.

"Nurse Towan," she said. "What species is it?"

"An AMSL," the Charge Nurse replied. "A Creppellian octopoid, and Sector General qualified, so you have nothing to worry about. The patients know that we are being assigned a new-species trainee and are expecting you. Your body configuration is well suited to the water medium, so I suggest that you go in and begin by teaching yourself how to move about the ward."

"Please, a further question," Cha Thrat said desperately. "The AMSL is a water-breather. Why aren't all of the medical attendants here water-breathers? Wouldn't it be simpler if they were Chalders, the same species as their patients?"

"You haven't even met a patient and already you're trying to reorganize the ward!" Hredlichli said, producing another appendage from somewhere and gesticulating with them both. "There are two reasons why we don't do as you suggest. One is that very large patients can be effectively treated by small medics, and Sector General was designed with precisely that situation in mind. The second is structural. Personnel accommodation and recreation space is at a premium here, and can you imagine how much of it would be taken up by the life-support requirements of, say, a basic medical and nursing staff of one hundred water-breathing Chalders?

"But enough of this," the Charge Nurse said impatiently. "Go into the ward and act as if you know what you're doing. We'll talk later. If

I don't go for lunch this instant, they'll find me in a corridor dead from malnutrition . . ."

It seemed like a very long time before she was able to venture into the green immensity of the ward, and then she swam only as far as a structural support less than five body-lengths from the entrance. The harsh, angular contours of the metal had been visually softened by irregular areas of paint and the attachment of artificial foliage, Cha Thrat saw as she swam around it, no doubt to make it resemble the vegetation of the home world.

Hredlichli had been right; she was able to adapt quickly to movement in water. When she kicked out with her feet and simultaneously swept the four mid-arms downward, she spurted forward and coasted for three body-lengths. When one or two of the mid-arms were held steady and the hands angled, quite delicate directional and positional control was possible. Previously she had never been able to remain under water for more than a few moments, and she was beginning to really enjoy the sensation. She continued to circle the structural member, moving up and down its entire length and examining the artificial vegetation even more closely. There were clusters of what could have been underwater fruit, which glowed with multihued light at her approach, revealing themselves to be a part of the ward lighting system. But the pleasures of discovery were short-lived.

One of the long, dark-green, motionless shadows lying along the floor of the ward had detached itself and was rushing silently toward her. It slowed, took monstrous, terrifying, three-dimensional form and began to circle her slowly as she had been circling the structural support.

The creature was like an enormous, armored fish with a heavy, knife-edged tail, a seemingly haphazard arrangement of stubby fins, and a thick ring of ribbon tentacles projecting from the few gaps in its organic body-armor. The tentacles lay flat along its sides when it was moving forward, but they were long enough to reach beyond the thick, blunt wedge of the head. One tiny, lidless eye watched her as it circled closer.

Suddenly the head divided to reveal a vast pink cavern of a mouth edged with row upon row of enormous white teeth. It drifted closer, so that she could even see the periodic fogging of the water around its gills. The mouth opened even wider.

"Hello, Nurse," it said shyly.

CHAPTER 5

Cha Thrat was not sure whether the AUGL ward's duty roster had been drawn up by Charge Nurse Hredlichli or a seriously deranged computer overlooked by the Maintenance staff, and she could not ask without calling into question someone's level of mental competence. It was unbalanced, she thought, whether "it" referred to the roster, some anonymous Maintenance entity, or Hredlichli itself. After six days and two and a half nights darting about like an overworked minnow among her outsized Chalders, she had been given two whole days in which she could do whatever she liked—provided that part of the free time was spent at her studies.

The proportion suggested by their noxious Nidian tutor, Cresk-Sar, was ninety-nine percent.

Sector General's corridors held fewer terrors for her now, and she was trying to decide whether to go exploring or continue studying when her door signal sounded.

"Tarsedth?" she called. "Come in."

"I hope that question refers to my purpose in calling," the Kelgian trainee said as it undulated into the room, "and not another expression of doubt regarding my identity. You should know me by *now!*"

Cha Thrat also knew that no reply was often the best reply.

The DBLF came to a halt in front of the viewscreen and went on.

"What's *that*, an ELNT lower mandible? You're lucky, Cha Thrat. You've gotten the hang of this physiological classification business a lot faster than the rest of us, or is it just that you study every waking minute? When Cresk-Sar pulled that three-second visual on us and you identified it as a blow-up of an FGLI large metatarsal and phalange before the picture was off the screen—"

"You're right, I was lucky," Cha Thrat broke in. "We had Diagnostician Thornnastor in the ward two days earlier. There was a small misunderstanding, a piece of clumsiness on my part, while we were presenting the patient for examination. For a few moments I had a very close look at a Tralthan large toe while the foot was trying not to step on me."

"And I suppose Hredlichli jumped on you with all five of those squishy things it uses for feet?"

"It told me . . ." Cha Thrat began, but Tarsedth's mouth and fur had not stopped moving.

"I'm sorry for you," it went on. "That is one tough chlorine-breather. It was Charge Nurse on my PVSJ ward before it applied for other-species duty with the Chalders, and I've been told all about it, including something that happened between it and a PVSJ Senior Physician on Level Fifty-three. I wish I knew what did happen. They tried to explain it to me but who knows what is right, wrong, normal, or utterly scandalous behavior where chlorine-breathers are concerned? Some of the people in this hospital are *strange*."

Cha Thrat stared for a moment at the thirty-limbed, silvery body that sat like a furry question mark in front of the viewscreen. "I agree," she said.

Returning to the original question, Tarsedth said, "Are you in trouble with Hredlichli? About your clumsiness when a Diagnostician was in the ward, I mean? Will it report you to Cresk-Sar?"

"I don't know," Cha Thrat replied. "After we'd finished the evening surgical round, it said that I should take myself out of its sight for the next two days, and no doubt I would enjoy that as much as it would. Did I tell you that it allows me to change some of the surgical dressings now? Under its supervision, of course, and the wounds concerned are almost healed."

"Well," Tarsedth said, "your trouble can't be too serious if it's having you back again. What are you going to do with your two days? Study?"

"Not all the time," she replied. "I want to explore the hospital, the areas where my protective suit will take me, that is. Cresk-Sar's high-speed tour and lecture sessions don't give me enough time to stop and ask questions."

The Kelgian dropped another three or four sets of limbs to the floor, a clear indication that it was about to leave.

"You'll be living dangerously, Cha Thrat," it said. "I'm content to learn about this medical madhouse a little at a time; that way I'm less likely to end up as one of the casualties. But I've been told that the recreation level is well worth a visit. You could start your explorations from there. Coming?"

"Yes," she said. "There at least the heavies will be relaxing and at rest, and not charging along the corridors like mobile disasters waiting to happen to us."

Later, Cha Thrat was to wonder how she could have been so wrong. The signs over the entrance read:

RECREATION LEVEL, SPECIES DBDG, DBLF, DBPK, DCNF, EGCL, ELNT, FGLI, & FROB. SPECIES GKMN & GLNO AT OWN RISK.

For members of the staff whose written languages were not represented, the same information was repeated endlessly via translator.

"DCNF," Tarsedth said. "They've got your classification up there already. Probably a routine updating by Personnel."

"Probably," Cha Thrat said. But she felt very pleased and, for the first time, important.

After days spent in crowded hospital corridors, her tiny room, and the even more cramped confines of the suit she had to wear in the tepid, green depths of the AUGL ward, the sheer size of the place made her feel insecure and unsteady. But the spaciousness, the open sky, and the long distances were apparent rather than real, she soon realized, and the initial shock diminished quickly to become a feeling of pleased surprise.

Trick lighting and some inspired landscaping had given the recreation level its illusion of tremendous spaciousness. The overall effect was of a small tropical beach enclosed on two sides by cliffs and open to a sea that stretched out to a horizon rendered indistinct by heat haze. The sky was blue and cloudless, and the water of the bay was deep blue shading to turquoise where the waves ran onto the bright, golden sand of the beach.

Only the light from the artificial sun, which was too reddish for Cha Thrat's taste, and the alien greenery fringing the beach and cliffs kept it from looking like a tropical bay anywhere on Sommaradva.

But then, space was at a premium in Sector General, she had been told before her first visit to the dining hall, and the people who worked together had to eat together. Now it seemed that they were expected to play together as well.

"Realistic cloud effects are difficult to reproduce," Tarsedth volunteered, "so rather than risk them looking artificial, they don't bother trying. The Maintenance person who suggested I come here told me that. It also said that the best thing about the place was that the gravity was maintained at half Earth-normal, which is close enough to half Kelgia- and Sommaradva-normal. The people who like to rest actively can be more active, and the others find the sand softer to lie on—Watch out!"

Three Tralthans on a total of eighteen massive feet went thundering past them and plowed into the shallows, scattering sand and spray over a wide area. The half-G conditions that allowed the normally slow and ponderous FGLIs to jump about like bipeds also kept the sand they had disturbed airborne for a long time before it settled back to the beach. Some of it had not settled because Cha Thrat was still trying to blink it out of her eyes.

"Over there," Tarsedth said. "We can shelter between the FROB and the two ELNTs. They don't look as if they are very active resters."

But Chat Thrat did not feel like lying still and doing nothing but absorb artificial sunlight. She had too much on her mind, too many questions of the kind that could not be asked without the risk of giving serious offense, and she had found in the past that strenuous physical activity rested the mind—sometimes.

She watched a steep, low-gravity wave roll in and break on the beach. Not all of the turbulence in the bay was artificial—it varied in proportion to the number, size, and enthusiasm of the swimmers. The most favored sport, especially among the heaviest and least streamlined life-forms, was jumping into the bay from one of the springboards set into the cliff face. The boards, which seemed to her to be dangerously high until she remembered the reduced gravity, could be reached through tunnels concealed within the cliff. One board, the highest of them all, was solidly braced and without flexibility, probably to avoid the risk of an overenthusiastic diver fracturing its cranium on the artificial sky.

"Would you like to swim?" she asked suddenly. "That is, I mean, if DBLFs can."

"We can, but I won't," the Kelgian said, deepening the sandy trench it had already dug for itself. "It would leave my fur plastered flat and unable to move for the rest of the day. If another DBLF came by I wouldn't be able to talk to it properly. Lie down. Relax."

Cha Thrat folded her two rear legs and gently collapsed into a horizontal position, but it must have been obvious even to her other-species friend that she was not relaxed.

"Are you worried about something?" Tarsedth asked, its fur rippling and tufting in concern. "Cresk-Sar? Hredlichli? Your ward?"

Cha Thrat was silent for a moment, wondering how a Sommarad-van warrior-surgeon could explain the problem to a member of a species whose cultural background was completely different, and who might even be a servile. But until she was sure of Tarsedth's exact status, she would consider the Kelgian her professional equal, and speak.

"I do not wish to offend," she said carefully, "but it seems to me that, in spite of the wide-ranging knowledge we are expected to acquire, the strange and varied creatures we care for, and the wonderful devices we use to do it, our work is repetitious, undignified, without personal responsibility, invariably performed under direction, and well, *servile*. We should be doing something more important with our time, or such a large proportion of it, than conveying body wastes from the patients to the disposal facility."

"So that's what's bothering you," Tarsedth said, twisting its conical head in her direction. "A deep, incised wound to the pride."

Cha Thrat did not reply, and it went on. "Before I left Kelgia I was a nursing superintendent responsible for the nursing services on eight wards. Same-species patients, of course, but at least I had come up through nursing. Some of the other trainees, yourself included, were doctors, so I can imagine how they—and you—feel. But the servile condition is temporary. It will be relieved when or if we complete our training to Cresk-Sar's satisfaction. Try not to worry about it. You are learning other-species medicine, if you excuse the expression, from the bottom up.

"Try taking more interest in the other end of the patient," Tarsedth added, "instead of concerning yourself with the plumbing all the time. Talk to them and try to understand how their minds work."

Cha Thrat wondered how she could explain to the Kelgian, who was a member of what seemed to be an advanced but utterly disorganized and classless civilization, that there were things that a warrior-surgeon should and should not do. Even though the medical fraternity on Sommaradva could not have cared less what happened to her, in Sector General she had been forced by circumstances into behavior that was wrong, in both the negative and positive sense, for someone of her professional status. She was acting above and below her level of competence, and it worried her.

"I do talk to them," she said. "One especially, and it says that it likes talking to me. I try not to favor any particular patient, but this one is more distressed than the others. I shouldn't be talking to it as I'm not qualified to treat it, but nobody else can or will do anything for the patient."

Tarsedth's fur rippled with concern. "Is it terminal?"

"I don't know. I don't think so," Cha Thrat replied. "It's been a ward patient for a very long time. Seniors examine it sometimes with advanced trainees present, and Thornnastor spoke to it when the Diagnostician was in the ward with another patient, but not to ask about its condition. I haven't access to its case history, but I'm pretty sure that the medication prescribed for it is palliative rather than curative. It is not neglected or ill treated so much as politely ignored. I'm the only one who will listen to its symptoms, so it talks to me at every opportunity. I shouldn't talk to it, not until I know what's wrong with it, because I'm not qualified."

The movement of Tarsedth's fur settled down to a more even rhythm as it said, "Nonsense! Everybody is qualified to talk, and a bit of verbal sympathy and encouragement can't harm your patient. But if its condition is incurable, your ward water would be teeming with Diagnosticians and Seniors intent on proving otherwise. That's the way things work here; nobody gives up on *anybody*. And your patient's problem will give you something to think about while you do the less attractive jobs. Or don't you want to talk to it?"

"Yes," Cha Thrat said, "I'm very sorry for the great, suffering brute, and I want to help it. But I'm beginning to wonder if it is a ruler, in which case I should not be talking to it."

"Whatever it is, or was, on Chalderescol," Tarsedth said, "has no bearing, or shouldn't have, on its treatment as a patient. What harm can a little nonmedical sympathy and encouragement do either of you? Frankly, I don't see your difficulty."

Patiently Cha Thrat said again, "I'm not qualified."

Tarsedth's fur was moving in a manner that denoted impatience. "I still don't understand you. Talk, don't talk to it. Do whatever you want to do."

"I *have* talked to it," Cha Thrat said, "and that's what worries me— Is something wrong?"

"Can't it leave me alone!" said Tarsedth, its fur tufting into angry spikes. "I'm sure that's Cresk-Sar coming this way, and it's seen our trainee badges. The first question it will ask is why we aren't studying. Can't we ever escape from its infuriating 'I have questions for you' routine?"

The Senior Physician detached itself from a group of two other Nidians and a Melfan who had been moving toward the water's edge and stopped, looking down at them.

"I have questions for both of you," it said inevitably, but unexpectedly went on. "Are you able to relax in this place? Does it enable you to forget all about your work? Your Charge Nurses? Me?"

"How can we forget about you," Tarsedth said, "when you're here, and ready to ask us why we're here?"

The Kelgian's seeming rudeness was unavoidable, Cha Thrat knew, but her reply would have to be more diplomatic.

"The answer to all four questions is, not entirely," she said. "We were relaxing but were discussing problems relating to our work."

"Good," Cresk-Sar said. "I would not want you to forget your work, or me, entirely. Have you a particular problem or question that I can answer for you before I rejoin my friends?"

Tarsedth was burrowing deeper into the artificial sand and pointedly ignoring their tutor who, now that it was off duty, seemed to Cha Thrat to be a much less obnoxious Nidian. Cresk-Sar deserved a polite response, even though the recent topic of discussion, the psychological and emotional problems associated with the removal of other-species body wastes, was not an area in which a Senior Physician would have firsthand experience. Perhaps she could ask a general question that would satisfy both the social requirements of the situation and her own curiosity.

"As trainees," Cha Thrat said, "we are assigned to the less pleasant, nonmedical ward duties, in particular those involving organic wastes. These are an unpleasant but necessary by-product common to all species whose food is ingested, digested, and eliminated. However, there must be wide differences in the chemical composition of other-species wastes. Since the hospital was designed so far as was possible to be a closed ecological system, what becomes of all this material?"

Cresk-Sar seemed to be having difficulty with its breathing for a moment, then it replied, "The system is not completely closed. We do not synthesize all our food or medication and, I am pleased to tell you, there are no intelligent life-forms known to us who can exist on their own or any other species' wastes. As for your question, I don't know the answer, Cha Thrat. Until now the question has never come up."

It turned away quickly and went back to its Melfan and Nidian friends. Shortly afterward the ELNT started to make clicking sounds with its mandibles while the furry DBDGs barked, or perhaps laughed, loudly. Cha Thrat could not find anything humorous in the question. To the contrary, she found the subject actively unpleasant. But the loud, untranslatable noises coming from the group showed no sign of stopping—until they were drowned out by the sharp, insistent, and even louder sounds coming from the public address system.

"*Emergency,*" it blared across the recreation level and from her translator. "*Code Blue, AUGL ward. All named personnel acknowledge on nearest communicator and go immediately to the AUGL ward. Chief Psychologist O'Mara, Charge Nurse Hredlichli, Trainee Cha Thrat. Code Blue. Acknowledge and go at once to—*"

She missed the rest of it because Cresk-Sar had come back and was glaring down at her. It was neither barking nor laughing.

"Move yourself!" it said harshly. "I'll acknowledge the message and go with you. As your tutor I am responsible for your medical misdeeds. Hurry."

As they were leaving the recreation level it went on, "A Code Blue is an emergency involving extreme danger to both patients and medical staff, the kind of trouble during which untrained personnel are ordered to stay clear. But they have paged you, a trainee, and, of all people, Chief Psychologist O'Mara.

"What have you *done?*"

CHAPTER 6

C ha Thrat and the Senior Physician arrived at the AUGL ward minutes before O'Mara and Charge Nurse Hredlichli, and joined the other three nurses on duty—two Kelgian DBLFs and a Melfan ELNT—who had abandoned their patients to take shelter in the Nurses' Station.

This normally reprehensible behavior was not being considered as a dereliction of medical duty, the tutor explained, because it was the first time in the hospital's wide experience in staff-patient relations that a Chalder had become violently antisocial.

In the green dimness at the other end of the ward a long, dark shadow drifted slowly from one side-wall to the other, as Cha Thrat had seen many of the mobile, bored, and restless Chalders doing while she had been on duty. Except for a few pieces of decorative greenery detached and drifting untidily between the supports, the ward looked peaceful and normal.

"What about the other patients, Charge Nurse?" Cresk-Sar asked. As the Senior Physician present it had overall medical responsibility. "Is anyone hurt?"

Hredlichli swam along the line of monitors and said, "Disturbed and frightened, but they have sustained no injuries, nor has their food and medication delivery system been damaged. They've been very lucky."

"Or the patient is being selective in its violence—" O'Mara began, then broke off.

The long shadow at the other end of the ward had foreshortened and was enlarging rapidly as it rushed toward them. Cha Thrat had a glimpse of fins blurred by rapid motion, ribbon tentacles streaming backward, and the serried ranks of gleaming teeth edging the enormous, gaping mouth before it crashed against the transparent wall of the Nurses' Station. The wall bulged inward alarmingly but did not collapse.

It was too large for the doorless entrance, she saw, but it changed position and moved three of its tentacles inside. They were not long enough or strong enough to pull anyone outside to the mouth, although one of the Kelgian nurses had a few anxious moments. Disappointed, the Chalder turned and swam away, with detached vegetation eddying its wake.

O'Mara made a sound that did not translate, then said, "Who is the patient, and why was trainee Cha Thrat called?"

"It is the long-stay patient, AUGL-One Sixteen," the Melfan nurse replied. "Just before it became violent it was calling for the new nurse, Cha Thrat. When I told the patient that the Sommaradvan would be absent for a few days, it stopped communicating and has not spoken to us since, even though its translator is still in position and working. That is why the trainee's name was included when I called in the Code Blue."

"Interesting," the Earth-human said, turning its attention to Cha Thrat. "Why did it want you especially, and why should it start taking the ward apart when you weren't available? Have you established a special relationship with AUGL-One Sixteen?"

Before she could reply, the Nidian said urgently, "Can the psychological ramifications wait, Major? My immediate concern is for the safety of the ward patients and staff. Pathology will give us a fast-acting anesthetic and a dart gun to pacify the patient, and then you can—"

"A dart gun!" one of the Kelgians said, its fur rippling in scorn. "Senior Physician, you are forgetting that your dart has to travel through water, which will slow it down, and then penetrate that organic suit of armor One Sixteen wears! The only sure way of placing the dart effectively would be to shoot it into the soft tissues of the inner mouth. To place it accurately, the person using the gun would have to be very close and might find itself following the dart into the open mouth, with immediately fatal results. I am not volunteering!"

Before Cresk-Sar could reply, Cha Thrat turned to the Senior Physician and said, "If you will explain what exactly it is that I must do, I shall volunteer for this duty."

"You lack the training and experience to—" began the Nidian, and broke off as O'Mara held up its hand for silence.

"Of course you will volunteer," O'Mara said quietly. "But why, Cha Thrat? Are you exceptionally brave? Are you naturally stupid? Do you have an urge to commit suicide? Or are you, perhaps, feeling a measure of responsibility and guilt?"

"Major O'Mara," Hredlichli said firmly, "this is not the time for apportioning responsibility or undertaking deep analysis. What is to be done about Patient One Sixteen? And my other patients?"

"You're right, Charge Nurse," O'Mara said. "I shall do it my way, by attempting to pacify and reason with One Sixteen. I've spoken to it many times, enough for it to tell me apart from other Earth-humans if I wear this lightweight suit. While I'm working with it I may also need to talk to Cha Thrat, so stay by the communicator, trainee."

"No need, I'll go with you," Cha Thrat said firmly. Silently she began the mental and moral exercises that were supposed to help reconcile her to an untimely ending of her life.

"And I," O'Mara said, making another sound that did not translate, "will be too busy with our demented friend to stop you. Come along, then."

"But it is only a *trainee*, O'Mara!" Cresk-Sar protested. "And in a lightweight suit it might recognize you, all right, as a convenient piece of plastic-wrapped meat. This life-form is omnivorous and until recently they—"

"Cresk-Sar," the Earth-human said, as it swam toward the entrance. "Are you trying to worry me?"

"Oh, very well," the Nidian said. "But I, too, shall do things my way, in case you can't talk yourselves through this problem. Charge Nurse, signal immediately for a four-unit patient transfer team with heavy-duty suits, dart guns, and physical restraints suitable for a fully conscious and uncooperative AUGL . . ."

The tutor was still talking as Cha Thrat swam into the ward behind O'Mara.

For what seemed a very long time they hung silent and motionless in the middle of the ward, watched by an equally still and silent patient from the cover of a patch of torn artificial greenery. O'Mara had told her that they should not do anything that One Sixteen might construe as a threat, that they must therefore appear defenseless before it, and that the first move was up to the patient. Cha Thrat thought that the Earth-Human was probably right, but her whole body was slippery with perspiration, and much warmer than could be explained by the temperature of the green, lukewarm water outside her protective suit. Plainly she was not yet completely reconciled to the ending of her existence.

The voice of the Senior Physician in her suit 'phones made her twitch in every limb.

"The transfer team is here," Cresk-Sar said quietly. "Nothing much is happening at your end. Can I send them in to move the other patients into OR? It will be a tight squeeze in there, but they will be able to receive treatment and be comfortable for a few hours, and you will have One Sixteen all to yourselves."

"Is the treatment urgent?" O'Mara asked softly.

"No," Cha Thrat said, answering the question before Cresk-Sar could relay it to the Charge Nurse. "Just routine observation and recording of vital signs, wound dressing changes, and administration of supportive medication. Nothing really urgent."

"Thank you, Trainee," Hredlichli said in a tone as corrosive as the atmosphere it breathed, then went on. "I have been Charge Nurse here for a short time, Major O'Mara, but I feel that I, too, have the patient's trust. I would like to join you."

"No, to both of you," the Earth-human said firmly. "I don't want our friend to be frightened or unsettled by too many comings and goings within the ward. And Hredlichli, if your protective suit were to rupture, contact with water is instantly lethal to a chlorine-breather, as you very well know. With us oxygen-breathers, we can drown in the stuff if help doesn't reach us in time, but it isn't poisonous or—Uh-oh!"

Patient AUGL-One Sixteen was silent but no longer still. It was rushing at them like a gigantic, organic torpedo, except that torpedoes did not have suddenly opening mouths.

Frantically they swam apart so as to give the attacking Chalder two targets instead of one, the theory being that while it was disposing of one the other might have enough time to make it to the safety of the Nurses' Station. But this was planning for a remote contingency, the Earth-human had insisted. O'Mara would not believe that AUGL-One Sixteen, who was normally so shy and timid and amenable, was capable of making a lethal attack on anyone.

On this occasion it was right.

The vast jaws snapped shut just before the Chalder swept through the gap that had opened between them. Then the great body curved upward and over them, dove, and began swimming around them in tight circles. Turbulence sent them spinning and twisting like leaves at the center of a whirlpool. Cha Thrat did not know whether it was circling them in the vertical or horizontal plane, only that it was so close that she could feel the compression waves every time the jaws snapped shut, which was frequently. She had never felt so helpless and disoriented and frightened in all her life.

"Stop this nonsense, Muromeshomon!" she said loudly. "We are here to help you. Why are you behaving like this?"

The Chalder slowed but continued to circle them closely. It mouth gaped open and it said, "You cannot help me, you have said that you are not qualified. Nobody here can help me. I do not wish to harm you, or anyone else, but I am frightened. I am in great pain. Sometimes I want to hurt everyone. Stay away from me or I will hurt you . . ."

There was a muffled, underwater clang as its tail flicked out and struck her air tanks a glancing blow, sending her spinning again. An Earth-human hand grasped one of her waist limbs, steadying her, and she saw that the patient had returned to its dark corner and was watching them.

"Are you hurt?" O'Mara asked, releasing its grip. "Is your suit all right?"

"Yes," Cha Thrat said, and added, "It left very quickly. I'm sure the blow was accidental."

The Earth-human did not reply for a few moments, then it said, "You called Patient One Sixteen by name. I am aware of its name because the hospital requires this information for possible notification of the next-of-kin, but I would not consider using its name unless there were very exceptional circumstances, and then only with its permission. But somehow you have learned its name and are using it as lightly and thoughtlessly as you would Cresk-Sar's or Hredlichli's, or my name. Cha Thrat, you must never—"

"It told me its name," Cha Thrat broke in. "We exchanged names while we were discussing my observations regarding the inadequacy of its treatment."

"You discussed . . ." O'Mara said incredulously. It made an untranslatable noise and went on. "Tell me what exactly you said to it."

Cha Thrat hesitated. The AUGL had left its dark corner and was moving toward them again, but slowly. It stopped halfway down the ward and hung with its fins and tail still and the ribbon tentacles spread like an undulating, circular fan around it, watching and probably listening to every word they said.

"On second thought, *don't* tell me," O'Mara said angrily. "I'll tell you what I know about the patient first, then you can try to reduce my level of ignorance. That way we will avoid repetition and save time. I don't know how much time it will give us to talk without another interruption. Not a lot, I suspect, so I'll have to speak quickly . . ."

Patient AUGL-One Sixteen was a long-stay patient whose time in Sector General exceeded that of many of the medical staff. The clinical picture had been and still remained obscure. Several of the hospital's top Diagnosticians had examined it, finding signs of strain in certain areas of the patient's body plating that partly explained its discomfort— a being who was largely exoskeletal, lazy, and something of a glutton could only put on weight from the inside. The generally agreed diagnosis was hypochondria and the condition incurable.

The Chalder had become seriously ill only when there was talk of sending it home, and so the hospital had acquired a permanent patient. It did not mind. Visiting as well as hospital medics and psychologists had given it a going over, and continued to do so, as did the interns and nurses of all the life-forms represented on the staff. It had been probed, pried into, and unmercifully pounded by trainees of varying degrees of gentleness, and it loved every minute of it. The hospital's teaching staff were happy with the arrangement and so was the Chalder.

"Nobody mentions going home to it anymore," O'Mara ended. "Did you?"

"Yes," Cha Thrat said.

O'Mara made another untranslatable noise and she went on quickly. "This explains why the nurses ignored it when other patients needed treatment, and supports my own diagnosis of an unspecified ruler's disease that—"

"Listen, don't speak!" the Earth-human said sharply. The patient seemed to be drifting closer. "My department has tried to get to the root causes of One Sixteen's hypochondria, but I was not required to solve its problem so it remained unsolved. This sounds like an excuse, and it is. But you must understand that Sector General is not and can never be a psychiatric hospital. Can you imagine a place like this where a large proportion of the multispecies patients, the mere sight of which gives sane people nightmares, are physically fit and mentally disturbed? Can you imagine the problems of other-species treatment and restraint? It is difficult enough to be responsible for the mental well-being of the staff without adding disturbed patients, even a harmlessly disturbed patient like One Sixteen, to my load. When a medically ill patient displays signs of mental instability it is kept under close observation, restrained if necessary, and returned to its own people for the appropriate treatment as soon as it is physically well enough to be discharged."

"I understand," Cha Thrat said. "The explanation excuses you."

The Earth-human grew pinker in the face, then said, "Listen carefully, Cha Thrat, this is important. The Chalders are one of the few intelligent species whose personal names are used only between mates, members of the immediate family, or very special friends. Yet you, an other-species stranger, have been told, and have spoken aloud, One Sixteen's personal name. Have you done this in ignorance? Do you realize that this exchange of names means that anything you may have said to it, or any future action you may have promised, is as binding as the most solemn promise given before the highest imaginable physical or metaphysical authority?"

"Do you realize now how serious this is?" O'Mara went on in a tone of quiet urgency. "Why did it tell you its name? What, exactly, was said between you?"

She could not speak for a moment because the patient had moved very close, so close that she could see the individual points of its six rows of teeth. A strangely detached and uncaring portion of her mind wondered what evolutionary imperative had caused the upper three rows to be longer than the lower set. Then the jaw snapped shut with a bony crash that was muffled by the surrounding water, and the caring part of her mind wondered what it would sound like if a limb or her torso were between those teeth.

"Have you fallen asleep?" O'Mara snapped.

"No," she said, wondering why an intelligent being had asked such a stupid question. "We talked because it was lonely and unhappy. The other nurses were busy with a post-op patient and I was not. I told it about Sommaradva and the circumstances that led to me coming here, and some of the things I would be able to do if I qualified for Sector General. It said that I was brave and resourceful, not sick and old and increasingly fearful like itself.

"It said that many times it dreamed of swimming free in the warm ocean of Chalderescol," she went on, "instead of this aseptic, water-filled box with its plastic, inedible vegetation. It could talk about the home world to other AUGL patients, but much of their post-op recovery time was spent under sedation. The medical staff were pleasant to it and would talk, on the rare occasions when they had time to do so. It said that it would never escape from the hospital, that it was too old and frightened and sick."

"Escape?" O'Mara said. "If our permanent patient has begun to regard the hospital as a prison, that is a very healthy sign, psychologically. But go on, what were you saying to it?"

"We spoke of general subjects," she replied. "Our worlds, our work, our past experiences, our friends and families, our opinions—"

"Yes, yes," the Earth-human said impatiently, looking at One Sixteen, who was edging closer. "I'm not interested in the small talk. What did you say that might have brought on this trouble?"

Cha Thrat tried to choose the words that would describe the situation concisely, accurately, and briefly as she replied, "It told me about the space accident and injuries that brought it here originally, and the continuing but irregular episodes of pain that keep it here, and of its deep unhappiness with its existence generally.

"I was uncertain of its exact status on Chalderescol," she went on, "but from the way it had described its work I judged it to be an upper-level warrior, at least, if not a ruler. By that time we had exchanged names, so I decided to tell it that the treatment being provided by the hospital was palliative rather than curative, and it was being treated for the wrong sickness. I said that its malady was not unknown to me and, although I was not qualified to treat the condition, there were wizards on Sommaradva capable of doing so. I suggested, on several occasions, that it was becoming institutionalized and that it might be happier if it returned home."

The patient was very close to them now. Its massive mouth was closed but not still, because there was a regular chewing motion that suggested that the teeth were grinding together. The movement was accompanied by a high-pitched, bubbling moan that was both frightening and strangely pitiful.

"Go on," O'Mara said softly, "but be very careful what you say."

"There is little more to tell," Cha Thrat said. "During our last meeting I told it that I was leaving for a two-day rest period. It would speak only of the wizards, and wanted to know if they could cure its fear as well as the pains. It asked me as a friend to treat it, or send for one of our Sommaradvan brothers who would be able to cure it. I told it that I had some knowledge of the spells of the wizards, but not enough to risk treating it, and that I lacked the status and authority to summon a wizard to the hospital."

"What was the response to that?" O'Mara asked.

"None," Cha Thrat said. "It would not speak to me thereafter."

Abruptly they were looking into the AUGL's open mouth, but it was keeping its uncomfortably short distance as it said, "You were not like the others, who did nothing and promised nothing. You held out the hope of a cure by your wizards, then withdrew it. You cause me pain that is many times worse than that which keeps me here. Go away, Cha Thrat. For your own safety, go away."

The jaws crashed shut and it swept around them and headed for the other end of the ward. They could not see clearly but, judging by the voices coming from the Nurses' Station, it seemed intent on wrecking the place.

"My patients!" Charge Nurse Hredlichli burst out. "My new treatment frames and medication cabinets . . ."

"According to the monitors," Cresk-Sar broke in, "the patients are still all right, but they've been lucky. I'm sending in the transfer team now to knock out One Sixteen. It will be a bit tricky. Both of you get back here, quickly."

"No, wait," O'Mara said. "We'll try talking to it again. This is not a violent patient and I don't believe that we are in any real danger." On Cha Thrat's frequency it added, "But there is always a first time for being wrong."

For some reason a picture from Cha Thrat's childhood rose suddenly to the surface of her adult mind. She saw again the tiny, many-colored fish that had been her favorite pet, as it circled and butted desperately and hopelessly against the glass walls of its bowl. Beyond those walls, too, lay an environment in which it would quickly asphyxiate and die. But that small fish, like this overlarge one, was not thinking of that.

"When One Sixteen gave you its name," O'Mara said with quiet urgency, "it placed a binding obligation on both of you to help the other in every way possible, as would a life-mate or a member of your family. When you mentioned the possibility of a cure by your Sommaradvan wizards, regardless of the efficacy of such other-species treatment, you were expected to provide the wizard regardless of any effort, cost, or personal danger to yourself."

There were noises of tearing metal and the complaining voices of the other AUGLs being transmitted through the green water, and Hredlichli sounded very agitated. O'Mara ignored them and went on. "You must keep faith with it, Cha Thrat, even though your wizards might not be able to help One Sixteen any more than we can. And I realize that you haven't the authority to call in one of your wizards. But if Sector General and the Monitor Corps were to put their combined weight behind you—"

"They wouldn't come to this place," Cha Thrat said. "Wizards are notoriously unstable people, but they are not stupid—It's coming back!"

This time One Sixteen was coming at them more slowly and deliberately, but still too fast for them to swim to safety, nor could the transfer team with their anesthetic darts reach them in time to do any good. There was no sound from the patients in the ward and the beings watching from the Nurses' Station. As the AUGL loomed closer she could see that its eyes had the feral, manic look of a wounded predator, and slowly it was opening its mouth.

"Use its *name*, dammit!" O'Mara said urgently.

"Mu-Muromeshomon," she stammered. "My—my friend, we are here to help you."

The anger in its eyes seemed to dim a little so that they reflected more of its pain. The mouth closed slowly and opened again, but only to speak.

"Friend, you are in great and immediate danger," the AUGL said. "You have spoken my name and told me that the hospital cannot cure me with its medicines and machines, and it no longer tries, and you will not help me even though you have said that a cure is possible. If our positions were reversed I would not act, or refuse to act, as you have done. You are an unequal friend, without honor, and I am disappointed and angry with you. Go away, quickly, and protect your life. I am beyond help."

"No!" Cha Thrat said fiercely. The mouth was opening wider, the eyes were showing a manic gleam once more, and she realized that when the AUGL attacked, she would be its first victim. Desperately she went on. "It is true that I cannot help you. Your sickness does not respond to the healer's herbs or the surgeon's knife, because it is a ruler's disease that requires the spells of a wizard. A Sommaradvan wizard might cure you but, since you are not yourself a Sommaradvan, there is no certainty. Here there is the Earth-human, O'Mara, a wizard with experience of treating rulers of many different life-forms. I would have approached it about your case at once but, being a trainee and unsure of the procedure, I was about to request a meeting for another, an unimportant, reason during which I would have spoken of you in detail..."

The AUGL had closed its mouth but was moving its jaws in a way that could be indicating anger or impatience. She went on quickly. "In the hospital I have heard many people speak of O'Mara and his great powers of wizardry—"

"I'm the Chief Psychologist, dammit," O'Mara broke in, "not a wizard. Let's try to be factual about this and not make more promises we can't possibly keep!"

"You are *not* a psychologist!" Cha Thrat said. She was so angry with this Earth-human who would not accept the obvious that for a moment she almost forgot about the threat from One Sixteen. Not for the first time she wondered what obscure and undefined ruler's disease it was that made beings who possessed high intelligence, and The Power in great measure, behave so stupidly at times. Less vehemently, she went on. "On Sommaradva a psychologist is a being, neither servile-healer nor warrior-surgeon, who tries to be a scientist by measuring brain impulses or bodily changes caused by physical and mental stress, or by making detailed observations of behavior. A psychologist tries to impose immutable laws in an area of spells and nightmares and changing realities, and tries to make a science of what has always been an art, an art practiced only by wizards."

They were both watching her, eyes unblinking, motionless. The patient's expression had not changed but the Earth-human's face had gone a much deeper shade of pink.

"A wizard will use or ignore the instruments and tabulations of the psychologist," she continued, "to cast spells that influence the complex, insubstantial structures of the mind. A wizard uses words, silences, minute observation, and intuition to compare and gradually change the sick, internal reality of the patient to the external reality of the world. That is the difference between a psychologist and a wizard."

The Earth-human's face was still unnaturally dark. In a voice that was both quiet and harsh it said, "Thank you for reminding me."

Formally Cha Thrat said, "No thanks are required for that which needs to be done. Please, may I remain here to watch? Before now I have never had the chance to see a wizard at work."

"What," the AUGL asked suddenly, "will the wizard do to me?"

It sounded curious and anxious rather than angry, and for the first time since entering the ward she began to feel safe.

"Nothing," O'Mara said surprisingly. "I shall do nothing at all . . ."

Even on Sommaradva the wizards were full of surprises, unpredictable behavior and words that began by sounding irrelevant, ill chosen, or stupid. What little of the literature that was available to one of the warrior-surgeon level, she had read and reread. So she composed herself and, with great anticipation, watched and listened while the Earth-human wizard did nothing at all.

The spell began very subtly with words, spoken in a manner that was anything but subtle, describing the arrival of AUGL-One Sixteen at the hospital as the commanding officer and sole survivor of its ship. The vessels of water-breathing species, and especially those of the outsize denizens of Chalderescol, were notoriously unwieldy and unsafe, and it had been exonerated of all blame for the accident both by the Monitor Corps investigators and the authorities on Chalderescol—but not by itself. This was realized when the patient's physical injuries had healed and it continued to complain of severe psychosomatic discomfort whenever the subject of returning home was discussed.

Many attempts were made to make the patient realize that it was punishing itself, cutting itself off from its home and friends, for a crime that was very probably imaginary, but without success—it would not consciously admit that it had committed a crime, so telling it that it was not guilty had no effect. A Chalder's most prized possession was its personal integrity, and as an authority that integrity was unassailable. AUGL-One Sixteen was a sensitive, intelligent, and highly qualified being who, outwardly, was a submissive and cooperative patient. But where its particular delusion was concerned it was as susceptible to influence as the orbit of a major planet.

And so Sector General had acquired a permanent patient, an AUGL specimen in perfect health and a continuing and strictly unofficial challenge to its Department of Psychology, because only in the hospital could it be pain-free and relatively happy.

Silently Cha Thrat apologized to the Earth-human for thinking that it had been negligent, and listened in admiration as the spell took positive form.

"And now," O'Mara went on, "due to a combination of circumstances, a significant change has occurred. The talks with transient AUGL patients have made you increasingly homesick. Your anger over your neglect by the medical staff has been growing because, subconsciously, you yourself were beginning to suspect that you were not sick and their attention was unnecessary. And then there was the unwarranted, but for you fortunate, interference by Trainee Cha Thrat, who confirmed your suspicion that you were not being treated as a patient.

"You have much in common with our outspoken trainee," it continued. "Both of you have reasons, real or imaginary, for not wanting to go home. On Sommaradva as on Chalderescol, personal integrity and public honor are held in high regard. But the trainee is woefully ignorant of the customs of other species and, when you took the unprecedented step of saying your name to a non-Chalder, it disappointed and hurt you grievously by continuing to act toward you as had the other members of the staff. You were driven to react violently but, because of the constraints imposed by your personality type, the violence was directed at inanimate objects.

"But," the Earth-human went on, "the simple act of giving your name to this sympathetic and untutored Sommaradvan, whom you had known only a few days, is the clearest possible indication of how badly you wanted help to get away from the hospital. You *do* still want to go home?"

AUGL-One Sixteen replied with another high-pitched, bubbling sound that did not translate. Its eyes watched only the Earth-human, and the muscles around its closed jaws were no longer clenched into iron rigidity.

"It was a stupid question," O'Mara said. "Of course you want to go home. The trouble is, you are afraid and also want to stay here. A dilemma, obviously. But let me try to solve it by telling you that you are once again a patient here, subject to the hospital regimen and my own special and continuing treatment, and until I pronounce you cured you will *not* go home . . ."

On the surface the situation had not changed, Cha Thrat thought admiringly. The hospital still retained its permanent AUGL patient, but now there was doubt about the permanency of the arrangement. Now it fully understood its position and had been given a choice, to stay or leave, and its departure date was unspecified so as to relieve its natural fears about leaving. But it was no longer completely satisfied with its life in the hospital, and already the Earth-human wizard was altering its internal reality by gently stressing the rehabilitative aspects of the therapy. Material would be provided by the Monitor Corps on the changes that had occurred on the home world in its absence, which would be useful if it decided to leave and informative should it stay, and there would be regular and frequent visits by O'Mara itself and other persons it would specify.

Oh, yes, she thought as it talked on, this Earth-human wizard was good.

The transfer team and their anesthetic dart guns had long since left the Nurses' Station, which meant that Cresk-Sar and Hredlichli must have decided that the danger from AUGL-One Sixteen had passed. Looking at the passive and distress-free patient who was hanging on O'Mara's every word, she was in entire agreement with them.

"... And you should now realize," the Earth-human was saying, "that if you want to go, and can convince me that you are able to adapt to home-planet life, I shall with great pleasure and reluctance kick you out. You have been a patient for a very long time and, among many members of the senior staff, our professional concern has developed into the personal variety. But the best thing that a hospital can do for a friend is to send it away, as quickly as possible, cured.

"Do you understand?" O'Mara ended.

For the first time since the Earth-human had begun talking to it, AUGL-One Sixteen turned its attention to Cha Thrat. It said plaintively, "I am feeling much better, I think, but confused and worried by all that I must do. Was that a spell? Is O'Mara a good wizard?"

Cha Thrat tried to control her enthusiasm as she said, "It is the beginning of a very fine spell, and it is said that a really good wizard makes its patient do all the hard work."

O'Mara made another one of its untranslatable noises and signaled Hredlichli that it was safe for the nurses to return to their patients. As they turned to leave AUGL-One Sixteen, who was once again its friendly and docile self, the Chalder spoke again.

"O'Mara," it said formally, "you may use my name."

When they were again in the air of the lock antechamber and all but Hredlichli had their visors open, the Charge Nurse said angrily, "I don't want that—that interfering *sitsachi* anywhere near me! I know that One Sixteen is going to get better and leave sometime, and I'm glad about that. But just look at the place! Wrecked, it is! I refuse to allow that trainee in my ward. That's final!"

O'Mara looked at the chlorine-breather for a moment, then in the quiet, unemotional tones of a ruler it said, "It is, of course, within your authority to accept or refuse any trainee. But Cha Thrat, whether or not it is accompanied by me, will be granted visiting facilities whenever and as often as the patient itself or myself consider it necessary. I do not foresee a lengthy period of treatment. We are grateful for your cooperation, Charge Nurse, and no doubt you are anxious to return to your duties."

When Hredlichli had gone, Cha Thrat said, "There was no opportunity to speak until now, and I am unsure how my words will be received. On Sommaradva good work is expected of a wizard or any high-level ruler, so that the praise of a subordinate for a superior is unnecessary and insulting. But in this case—"

O'Mara held up a hand for silence. It said, "Anything you say, whether complimentary or otherwise, will have no effect on what is to happen to you, so save your breath.

"You are in serious trouble, Cha Thrat," it went on grimly. "The news of what happened here will soon be all over the hospital. You must understand that to a Charge Nurse the ward is its kingdom, the nursing staff its subjects, and troublemakers, including trainees who exercise too much initiative too soon, are sent into exile, which can, in effect, mean home or to another hospital. I'd be surprised if there is a single Charge Nurse willing to accept you for practical ward training."

The Earth-human paused, giving her a moment to assimilate its words, then went on. "You have two options. Go home, or accept a nonmedical and servile position with Maintenance."

In a more sympathetic tone than she had ever heard it use before, Cresk-Sar said, "You are a most promising and diligent trainee, Cha Thrat. If you were to take such a position you would still be able to visit and talk to One Sixteen, and attend my lectures, and watch the teaching channels during your free time. But without practical ward experience you could not hope to qualify here.

"If you don't resign," the Senior Physician went on, "it may well be that you will discover firsthand the answer to the question you asked me this morning on the recreation level."

Cha Thrat remembered that question very well, and the amusement it had caused among the tutor's friends. She also remembered her initial feelings of shock and shame when her duties as a trainee nurse had been explained to her. Nothing could be more demeaning for a warrior-surgeon than that, she had thought at the time, but she had been wrong.

"I am still ignorant of the laws governing the hospital," she said. "But I realize that I have transgressed them in some fashion and must therefore accept the consequences. I shall not take the easy option."

O'Mara sighed and said, "It is your decision, Cha Thrat."

Before she could reply, the Nidian Senior Physician was talking again. "Putting it into Maintenance would be a criminal waste," the tutor protested. "It is the most promising trainee in its class. If we were to wait until the Hredlichli outcry died down, or until the grapevine is overloaded with another scandal, you might be able to find a ward that would take it for a trial period and—"

"Enough," O'Mara said, visibly relenting. "I don't believe in having second thoughts because the first are usually right. But I'm tired and hungry and I, too, have had enough of your trainee.

"There is such a ward," it went on. "FROB Geriatric, which is chronically understaffed and may be desperate enough to accept Cha Thrat. It is not a ward where I would normally assign a trainee who is not of the patients' own species, but I shall speak to Diagnostician Conway about it at the first opportunity.

"Now go away," it ended sourly, "before I cast a spell consigning both of you to the center of the nearest white dwarf."

As they were heading for the dining hall, Cresk-Sar said, "It's a tough ward and, if anything, the work is even harder than a job in Maintenance. But you can say whatever you like to the patients and nobody will mind. Whatever else happens, you can't get into trouble there."

The Nidian's words were positive and reassuring, but its voice carried undertones of doubt.

CHAPTER 7

She was given two extra days off duty, but whether they were a reward for her help with AUGL-One Sixteen or because it took that long for O'Mara to arrange for her transfer to FROB Geriatric, Cresk-Sar would not say. She paid three lengthy visits to One Sixteen in the AUGL ward, during which her reception was enough to turn its tepid water to ice, but she would not risk returning to the recreation level or exploring the hospital. There was less chance of getting into trouble if she stayed in her room and watched the teaching channels.

Tarsedth pronounced her certifiably insane and wondered why O'Mara had not confirmed this diagnosis.

Two days later she was told to present herself at FROB Geriatric in time for morning duty and to make herself known to the DBLF nurse in charge. Cresk-Sar said that it would not need to introduce her on this occasion because Charge Nurse Segroth, and probably every other being on the hospital staff, would have heard all about her by now. That may have been the reason why, on her meticulously punctual arrival, she was given no opportunity to speak.

"This is a surgical ward," Segroth said briskly, indicating the banks of monitors occupying three walls of the Nurses' Station. "There are seventy Hudlar patients and a nursing staff of thirty-two counting yourself. All the nurses are warm-blooded oxygen-breathers of various species, so you will not need environmental protection other than a gravity compensator and nasal filters. The FROBs are divided into pre- and post-op patients, segregated by a light- and soundproof partition. Until you learn your way around you will not concern yourself, or go anywhere near, a post-op patient."

Before Cha Thrat had time to say that she understood, the Kelgian ran on. "We have an FROB trainee and classmate here who will, I'm sure, be happy to answer any questions you are afraid to ask me."

Silvery fur puckered into irregular waves along its flanks in a way, she had learned from observing Tarsedth, that indicated anger and impatience. It continued. "From what I've heard of you, Nurse, you are the type who will already have studied the available Hudlar material and will be eager to make a contribution. Don't even try. This is a special project of Diagnostician Conway, we are breaking new surgical ground here, so your knowledge is already out of date. Except for those times when you are required by O'Mara for AUGL-One Sixteen, you will do nothing but watch, listen, and occasionally perform a few simple duties at the direction of the more experienced nurses or myself.

"I would not want to be embarrassed," she ended, "by you producing a miracle cure on your first day."

It was easy to pick out her FROB classmate from among the other nurses on duty—they were either Kelgian DBLFs or Melfan ELNTs—and even easier to tell it apart from all the FROB patients. She could scarcely believe that there was such a horrifying difference between a mature and an aged Hudlar.

Her classmate's speaking membrane vibrated quietly on her close approach. It said, "I see you've survived your first encounter with Segroth. Don't worry about the Charge Nurse; a Kelgian with authority is even less charming than one without. If you do exactly as it tells you, everything will be fine. I'm glad to see a friendly, familiar face in the ward."

It was an odd thing to say, Cha Thrat thought, because Hudlars did not possess faces as such. But this one was trying hard to reassure her and she was grateful for that. It had not, however, called her by name, and whether the omission was deliberate or due to an oversight she did not know. Perhaps the Hudlars and Chalders had something in common besides great strength. Until she was sure that their names could be used without giving offense, they could call each other "Nurse" or "Hey, you!"

"I'm spraying and sponging-off at the moment," the Hudlar trainee said. "Would you like to strap on a spare nutrient tank and follow me around? You can meet some of our patients."

Without waiting for her reply, it went on. "This one you won't be able to talk to because its speaking membrane has been muffled so that the sounds it makes will not distress the other patients and staff. It is in considerable discomfort that does not respond very well to the pain-killing medication, and, in any case, it is incapable of coherent speech."

It was immediately obvious that this was not a well Hudlar. Its six great tentacles, which normally supported the heavy trunk in an upright position for the whole of its waking and sleeping life, hung motionless over the sides of its support cradle like rotted tree trunks. The hard patches of callus—the knuckles on which it walked while its digits were curled inward to protect them against contact with the ground—were discolored, dry, and cracking. The digits themselves, usually so steady and precise in their movements, were twitching in continual spasm.

Large areas of its back and flanks were caked with partially absorbed nutrient paint, which would have to be washed off before the next meal could be sprayed on. As she watched, a milky perspiration was forming on its underside and dripping into the suction pan under its cradle.

"What's wrong with it?" Cha Thrat asked. "Can it, is it being cured?"

"Old age," the nurse said harshly. In a more controlled and clinical tone it went on. "We Hudlars are an energy-hungry species with a greatly elevated metabolic rate. With advancing age it is the food absorption and waste elimination mechanisms, both of which are normally under voluntary control, that are first to suffer progressive degeneration. Would you respray this area as soon as I've washed off the dried food, please?"

"Of course," Cha Thrat said.

"This in turn causes a severe impairment in the circulation to the limbs," the Hudlar went on, "leading to increasing deterioration in the associated nerve and muscle systems. The eventual result is general paralysis, necrosis of the limb extremities, and termination."

It used the sponge briskly and moved clear to enable Cha Thrat to apply fresh nutrient, but when it resumed speaking its voice had lost some of its former clinical calm.

"The most serious problem for the Hudlar geriatric patient," it said, "is that the brain, which requires a relatively small proportion of the available energy, remains organically unimpaired by the degenerative process until a few moments after its double heart has ceased to function. Therein lies the real tragedy. Rare indeed is the Hudlar mind that can remain stable inside a body which is disintegrating painfully all around it. You can understand why this ward, which has been recently extended for the Conway Project, is the closest that the hospital comes to providing treatment for psychologically disturbed patients.

"At least," it added, forcing a lighter tone as they moved to the next patient, "that was so until you started analyzing your AUGL-One Sixteen."

"Please don't remind me of that," Cha Thrat said.

There was another thick, cylindrical muffler encasing the next patient's speaking membrane, but either the sounds the Hudlar was making were too loud for it or the equipment was faulty. Much of what it was saying, which was clearly the product of advanced dementia and great pain, was picked up by her translator.

"I have questions," Cha Thrat said suddenly. "By implication they may be offensive to you, and perhaps critical of Hudlar philosophical values and professional ethics. On Sommaradva the situation within the medical profession may be different. I do not wish to risk insulting you."

"Ask," the other nurse said. "I shall accept your apology, if required, in advance."

"Earlier I asked if these patients could be cured," she said carefully, "and you have not yet replied. Are they incurable? And if so, why were they not advised to self-terminate before their condition reached this stage?"

For several minutes the Hudlar continued to sponge stale nutrient from the second patient's back without speaking, then it said, "You surprise but do not offend me, Nurse. I cannot myself criticize Sommaradvan medical practice because, until we joined the Federation a few generations ago, curative medicine and surgery were unknown on my world. But do I understand correctly that you urge your incurable patients to self-terminate?"

"Not exactly," Cha Thrat replied. "If a servile-healer or warrior-surgeon or a wizard will not take personal responsibility for curing a patient, the patient will not be cured. It is given all the facts of the situation, simply, accurately, and without the kindly but misguided lying and false encouragement that seem to be so prevalent among the nursing staff here. There is no attempt to exert influence in either direction; the decision is left entirely to the patient."

While she was speaking the other had stopped working. It said, "Nurse, you must never discuss a patient's case with it in this fashion, regardless of your feelings about our medical white lies. You would be in very serious trouble if you did."

"I won't," Cha Thrat said. "At least not until, or unless, the hospital once again gives me the position and responsibilities of a surgeon."

"Not even then," the Hudlar said worriedly.

"I don't understand," she said. "If I accept total responsibility for a patient's cure—"

"So you were a surgeon back home," the other nurse broke in, obviously wanting to avoid an argument. "I, too, am hoping to take home a surgical qualification."

Cha Thrat did not want an argument, either. She said, "How many years will that take?"

"Two, if I'm lucky," the Hudlar replied. "I don't intend going for the full other-species surgical qualification, just basic nursing and the FROB surgical course, taken concurrently. I joined the new Conway Project, so I'll be needed at home as soon as I can possibly make it.

"And to answer your earlier question," it added. "Believe it or not, Nurse, the condition of the majority of these patients will be alleviated if not cured. They will be able to lead long and useful lives that will be pain-free, mentally and, within limits, physically active."

"I'm impressed," Cha Thrat said, trying to keep the incredulity she felt from showing in her voice. "What is the Conway Project?"

"Rather than listen to my incomplete and inaccurate description," the Hudlar replied, "it would be better for you to learn about the project from Conway itself. It is the hospital's Diagnostician-in-Charge of Surgery, and it will be lecturing and demonstrating its new FROB major operative techniques here this afternoon.

"I shall be required to observe the operation," it went on. "But we will need surgeons so badly and in such large numbers that you would only have to express an interest in the project, not actually join it, to be invited to attend. It would be reassuring to have someone beside me who is almost as ignorant as I am."

"Other-species surgery," Cha Thrat said, "is my principal interest. But I've only just arrived in the ward. Would the Charge Nurse release me from duty so soon?"

"Of course," the FROB said as they were moving to the next patient. "Just so long as you do nothing to antagonize it."

"I won't," she said, then added, "at least, not deliberately."

There was no muffler around the third patient's speaking membrane, and a few minutes before their arrival it had been having an animated conversation about its grandchildren with a patient across the ward. Cha Thrat spoke the ritual greeting used by the healers on Sommaradva and, it seemed, by every medic in the hospital.

"How are you feeling today?"

"Well, thank you, Nurse," the patient replied, as she knew it would.

Plainly the being was anything but well. Although it was mentally alert and the degenerative process had not yet advanced to the stage where the pain-killing medication had no effect, the mere sight of the surface condition of the body and tentacles made her itch. But, like so many of the other patients she had treated, this one would not dream of suggesting that her ability was somehow lacking by saying that it was *not* well.

"When you've absorbed some more food," she said while her partner was busy with its sponge, "you will feel even better."

Fractionally better, she added silently.

"I haven't seen you before, Nurse," the patient went on. "You're new, aren't you? I think you have a most interesting and visually pleasing shape."

"The last time that was said to me," Cha Thrat said as she turned on the spray, "it was by an overardent young Sommaradvan of the opposite sex."

Untranslatable sounds came from the patient's speaking membrane and the great, disease-wasted body began twitching in its cradle. Then it said, "Your sexual integrity is quite safe with me, Nurse. Regrettably, I am too old and infirm for it to be otherwise."

A Sommaradvan memory came back to her, of seriously wounded and immobilized warrior-patients of her own species trying to flirt with her during surgical rounds, and she did not know whether to laugh or cry.

"Thank you," she said. "But I may need further reassurance in this matter when you become convalescent..."

It was the same with the other patients. The Hudlar nurse said very little while the patients and Cha Thrat did all the talking. She was new to the ward, a member of a species from a world about which they knew nothing, and a subject, therefore, of the most intense but polite curiosity. They did not want to discuss themselves or their distressing physical conditions, they wanted to talk about Cha Thrat and Sommaradva, and she was pleased to satisfy their curiosity—at least about the more pleasant aspects of her life there.

The constant talking helped her to forget her growing fatigue and the fact that, in spite of the gravity compensators reducing the weight of the heavy nutrient tank to zero, the harness straps were making a painful and possibly permanent impression on her upper thorax. Then suddenly there were only three patients left to sponge and feed, and Segroth had materialized behind them.

"If you work as well as you talk, Cha Thrat," the Charge Nurse said,

"I shall have no complaints." To the Hudlar, it added, "How is it doing, Nurse?"

"It assists me very well, Charge Nurse," the FROB trainee replied, "and without complaint. It is pleasant and at ease with the patients."

"Good, good," Segroth said, its fur rippling in approval. "But Cha Thrat belongs to another one of those species that require food at least three times a day if a pleasant disposition is to be maintained, and the midday meal is overdue. Would you like to finish the rest of the patients by yourself, Nurse?"

"Of course," the Hudlar said as Segroth was turning away.

"Charge Nurse," Cha Thrat said quickly. "I realize that I've only just arrived, but could I have permission to attend the—"

"The Conway lecture," Segroth finished for her. "Naturally, you'll find any excuse to escape the hard work of the ward. But perhaps I do you an injustice. Judging by the conversations I have overheard on the sound sensors, you have displayed good control of your feelings while talking with the patients and, considering your surgical background, the practical aspects of the lecture should not worry you. However, if any part of the demonstration distresses you, leave at once and as unobtrusively as possible.

"Permission would normally be refused a newly joined trainee like yourself," it ended, "but if you can make it to the dining hall and back inside the hour, you may attend."

"Thank you," Cha Thrat said to the Kelgian's already departing back. Quickly she began loosening the nutrient tank harness.

"Before you go, Nurse," the Hudlar trainee said, "would you mind using some of that stuff on me? I'm starving!"

Cha Thrat was among the first to arrive and stood—Hudlars did not use chairs, so the FROB lecture theater did not provide them—as close as possible to the operating cradle while she watched the place fill up. There was a scattering of Melfan ELNTs, Kelgian DBLFs, and Tralthan FGLIs among those present, but the majority were Hudlars in various stages of training. She was hemmed in by FROBs, so much so that she did not think that she would be able to leave even if she should want to, and she assumed—she still could not tell them apart—that the one standing closest to her was her partner of the morning.

From the conversations going on around her it was obvious that Diagnostician Conway was regarded as a very important being indeed, a medical near-deity in whose mind resided, by means of a powerful spell and the instrumentation of O'Mara, the knowledge, memories, and instincts of many other-species personalities. Having seen the hapless condition of the FROB ward's pre-op patients, she was looking forward with growing anticipation to seeing it perform.

In appearance Conway was not at all impressive. It was an Earth-human DBDG, slightly above average in height, with head fur that was a darker gray than the wizard O'Mara's.

It spoke with the quiet certainty of a great ruler, and began the lecture without preamble.

"For any of you who may not be completely informed regarding the Hudlar Project, and who may be concerned with the ethical position, let me assure you that the patient on which we will be operating today, its fellows in the FROB ward, and all the other geriatric and pre-geriatric cases waiting in great distress on the home world, are all candidates for elective surgery.

"The number of cases is so great—a significant proportion of the planetary population, in fact—that we cannot possibly treat them in Sector General . . ."

As the Earth-human Diagnostician talked on, Cha Thrat became increasingly disheartened by the sheer magnitude of the problem. A planet that contained, at any given time, many millions of beings in the same horrifying condition as the patients she had been recently attending was an idea that her mind did not want to face. But it became clear that Conway had faced it and was working toward an eventual solution—by training large numbers of the medically untutored Hudlars, assisted by other-species volunteers, to help themselves.

Initially, Sector General would provide basic tuition in FROB physiology, pre- and postoperative nursing care, and training in just one simple surgical procedure. The successful candidates, unless they displayed such an unusually high aptitude that they were offered positions on the staff, would return home to establish their own training organizations. Within three generations there would be enough own-species specialist surgeons to make this dreadful and hitherto unavoidable scourge of the Hudlars a thing of the past.

The sheer scale and what appeared to be the utter, criminal irresponsibility of the project shocked and sickened Cha Thrat. Conway was not training surgeons, it was turning out vast numbers of conscienceless, organic machines! She had been surprised when the Hudlar trainee had mentioned the time required for qualification, and it was possible that the hospital's tutors would be able to provide the necessary practical training during that short period. But what about the long-term indoctrination, the courses of mental and physical exercises that would prepare the candidates for the acceptance of responsibility and pain, and the long, presurgery novitiate? As the Diagnostician talked on, there was no mention of these things.

"This is incredible!" Cha Thrat said suddenly.

Softly the Hudlar beside her said, "Yes, indeed. But be quiet, Nurse, and listen."

"The degree and extent of the suffering among aging FROBs is impossible to imagine or describe," the Earth-human was saying. "If the majority of the other races in the Federation were faced with the same problem, there would be one simple, if completely unsatisfactory, answer for the individuals concerned. But the Hudlars, unfortunately or otherwise, are philosophically incapable of self-termination.

"Would you bring in Patient FROB-Eleven Thirty-two, please."

A mobile operating frame driven by a Kelgian nurse glided to a stop in front of the Diagnostician. It held the patient—one of the Hudlars she had sprayed that morning—already prepared for surgery.

"The condition of Eleven Thirty-two," the Earth-human went on, "is too far advanced for surgical intervention to reverse the degenerative processes completely. However, today's procedure will ensure that the remainder of the patient's life will be virtually pain-free, which, in turn, means that it will be mentally alert, and, it will be able to lead a useful if not very active life. With Hudlars who elect for surgery before the onset of the condition, and there are few members in the age groups concerned who do not so elect, the results are immeasurably better.

"Before we begin," it continued, unclipping the deep scanner, "I would like to discuss the physiological reasons behind the distressing clinical picture we see before us . . ."

What miracle of irresponsible and illegal surgery, Cha Thrat wondered sickly, *could make Eleven Thirty-two well again?*

But her curiosity was outweighed by a growing fear. She did not know whether or not she could bear to hear the answers that this terrible Earth-person would give, and still retain her sanity.

"In common with the majority of the life-forms known to us," the Diagnostician continued, "the primary cause of the degenerative process known as aging is caused by increasing loss of efficiency in the major organs and an associated circulatory failure.

"With the FROB life-form," it went on, "the irreversible loss of function and the abnormal degree of calcification and fissuring in the extremities is aggravated by the demand for nutrient, which is no longer available.

"From your FROB physiology lectures," it continued, "you know that a healthy adult of the species possesses an extremely high metabolic rate that requires a virtually continuous supply of nutrient, which is metabolized, via the absorption mechanism, to supply major organs such as the two hearts, the absorption organs themselves, the womb when the entity is in gravid female mode, and, of course, the limbs. These six immensely strong limbs form the most energy-hungry system of the body, and demand close to eighty percent of the total nutrient metabolized.

"If this excessive demand is removed from the energy equation," the Diagnostician said slowly and emphatically, "the nutrient supply to less-demanding systems is automatically increased to optimum."

There was no longer any doubt in Cha Thrat's mind regarding the surgical intentions of the Earth-human, but still she was trying to convince herself that the situation was not quite as bad as it seemed. With quiet urgency she asked, "Do this life-form's limbs regenerate?"

"That is a stupid question," the Hudlar beside her said. "No, if such were the case, the limb musculature and circulation would not have degenerated to their present state in the first place. Please be quiet, Nurse, and listen."

"I meant the Earth-human's limbs," Cha Thrat said insistently, "not the patient's."

"No," the Hudlar impatiently said. When she tried to ask other questions, it ignored her.

Conway was saying, "The major problem encountered while performing deep surgery on any life-form evolved for heavy gravity and high atmospheric pressure conditions is, of course, internal organ displacement and decompression damage. But with this type of operation there is no real problem. The bleeding is controlled with clamps, and the procedure is simple enough for any of you advanced trainees to perform it under supervision.

"In fact," the Diagnostician added, showing its teeth suddenly, "I shall not even lay a cutter on this patient. The responsibility for the operation will be collectively yours."

A quiet, polite uproar greeted the Earth-human's words and the trainees surged closer to the barrier, imprisoning Cha Thrat within a barricade of metal-hard Hudlar bodies and tentacles. So many conversations were going on at once that several times her translator was overloaded, but from what she did hear it seemed that they were all in favor of this utterly shameful act of professional cowardice, and stupidly eager rather than afraid to take surgical responsibility.

She had never in her wildest and most fearful imaginings expected anything like this, nor thought to prepare herself for such a vicious and demoralizing attack on her ethical code. Suddenly she wanted away from this nightmare with its group of demented and immoral Hudlars. But they were all too busy flapping their speaking membranes at each other to hear her.

"Quiet, please," Diagnostician Conway said, and there was silence. "I don't believe in springing surprises, pleasant or otherwise, but sooner or later you Hudlars will be performing multiple amputations like this on your home world hour after hour, day after day, and I feel that you should get used to the idea sooner rather than later."

It paused to look at a white card it was holding in one hand, then said, "Trainee FROB-Seventy-three, you will begin."

Cha Thrat had an almost overwhelming urge to shout and scream that she wanted out and far away from this hellish demonstration. But Conway, a Diagnostician and one of the hospital's high rulers, had commanded silence, and the discipline of a lifetime could not be broken—even though she was far from Sommaradva. She pushed silently against the wall of Hudlar bodies enclosing her on three sides, but her attempts to pass through were ignored if they were even noticed. Everyone's eyes were focused exclusively on the operating cradle and patient FROB-Eleven Thirty-two and, in spite of her attempts to look elsewhere, hers were turned in the same direction.

It was obvious from the start that Seventy-three's problem was psychological rather than surgical, and caused by the close proximity of one of the hospital's foremost Diagnosticians watching every move it made. But Conway was being both tactful and reassuring during its spoken commentary on the operation. Whenever the trainee seemed hesitant, it managed to include the necessary advice and directions without making the recipient feel stupid and even more unsettled.

There was something of the wizard in this Diagnostician, Cha Thrat thought, but that in no way excused its unprofessional behavior.

"The Number Three cutter is used for the initial incision and for removing the underlying layers of muscle," Conway was saying, "but some of us prefer the finer Number Five for the venous and arterial work, since the smoother edges of the incisions make suturing much easier as well as aiding subsequent healing.

"The nerve bundles," it went on, "are given extra length and covered with inert metal caps, and are positioned just beneath the surface of the stump. This facilitates the nerve impulse augmentors that will later control the prosthetics . . ."

"What," Cha Thrat wondered aloud, "are prosthetics?"

"Artificial limbs," the Hudlar beside her said. "Watch and listen; you can ask questions afterward."

There was plenty to see but less to hear because Trainee FROB-Seventy-three was working much faster and no longer seemed to be in need of the Diagnostician's covert directions. Not only could Cha Thrat look directly at the operative field, but the internal scanner picture was also being projected onto a large screen above and behind the patient, so that she could watch the careful, precise movements of the instruments within the limb.

Then suddenly there was no limb—it had fallen stiffly, like the diseased branch of a tree, into a container on the floor—and she had her first view of a stump. Desperately she fought the urge to be physically sick.

"The large flap of tegument is folded over the stub limb," Conway was saying, "and is attached by staples that dissolve when the healing process is complete. Because of the elevated internal pressure of this life-form and the extreme resistance of the tegument to puncturing by needle, normal suturing is useless and it is advisable, in fact, to err on the generous side where the staples are concerned."

There had been unsavory rumors of cases like this on Sommaradva, traumatic amputation of limbs during a major industrial or transportation accident, after which the casualty had survived, or insisted on surviving. The wounds had been discreetly tidied up, usually by young, nonresponsible and as yet unqualified warrior-surgeons or even, if nobody else was available, by an amenable servile-healer. But even when the warriors concerned had sustained the wounds as a result of an act of bravery, the matter was hushed up and forgotten as quickly as possible.

The casualties went into voluntary exile. They would never dream of revealing their disabilities or deformities to the public gaze, nor would they have been allowed to do so. On Sommaradva they had too much respect for their bodies. And for people to parade around with mechanical devices replacing their limbs was abhorrent and unthinkable.

"Thank you, Seventy-three, that was well done," the Earth-human said, glancing once again at its white card. "Trainee Sixty-one, would you like to show us what you can do?"

Abhorrent and repulsive though it was, Cha Thrat could not take her eyes from the operating cradle while the new FROB demonstrated its surgical prowess. The depth and positioning of every incision and instrument was burned into her memory as if she were watching some horrid but fascinating perversion. Sixty-one was followed by two other advanced trainees, and patient FROB-Eleven Thirty-two was left with only two of its six limbs remaining in place.

"There is still a fair degree of mobility in one of the forelimbs," Conway said, "and, considering the advanced age and reduced mental adaptability, I feel that it should be left intact for psychological as well as physiological reasons. It may well be that the increased blood and available nutrient supply due to the absence of the other limbs will partially improve the muscle condition and circulation in this one. As you can see, the other forelimb has degenerated virtually to the point of necrosis and must be removed.

"Trainee Cha Thrat," it added, "will perform the amputation."

Suddenly they were all looking at her, and for a moment Cha Thrat had the ridiculous feeling that she was in the center of a three-dimensional picture, frozen in this nightmare for all eternity. But the real nightmare lay a few minutes in the future, when she would be forced into a major professional decision.

Her partner from the ward vibrated its speaking membrane quietly. "This is a great professional compliment, Nurse."

Before she could reply, the Diagnostician was speaking again, to everyone.

It said, "Cha Thrat is a native of a newly discovered world, Sommaradva, where it was a qualified surgeon. It has prior experience of other-species surgery on an Earth-human DBDG, a life-form that it had encountered for the first time only a few hours earlier. In spite of this, the work was skillfully done, Senior Physician Edanelt tells me, and undoubtedly saved the entity's limb and probably its life. And now it can further increase its other-species surgical experience with a much less difficult procedure on an FROB."

Encouragingly it ended, "Come forward, Cha Thrat. Don't be afraid. If anything should go wrong, I will be here to help."

There was a great, cold fear inside her mixed with the helpless anger of having to face the ultimate challenge without adequate spiritual preparation. But the Diagnostician's concluding words, suggesting that her natural fear might somehow keep her from doing the work, filled her with righteous anger. It was a hospital ruler and, no matter how misguided and irresponsible its orders to her had seemed, they would be obeyed—that was the law. And no Sommaradvan of the warrior class would show fear before anyone, and that included a group of other-species strangers. But still she hesitated.

Impatiently the Earth-human said, "Are you capable of performing this operation?"

"Yes," she said.

Had it asked her if she *wanted* to perform the operation, Cha Thrat thought sadly as she moved toward the cradle, the answer would have been different. Then, with the incredibly sharp FROB Number Three cutter in her hand, she tried again.

"What," she asked quickly, "is my precise responsibility in this case?"

The Earth-human took a deep breath and let it out slowly, then said, "You are responsible for the surgical removal of the patient's left forelimb."

"Is it possible to save this limb?" she asked hesitantly. "Can the circulation be improved, perhaps by surgical enlargement of the blood vessels, or by—"

"No," said Conway firmly. "Please begin."

She made the initial incisions and proceeded exactly as the others had done, without further hesitation or need of prompting by the Diagnostician. Knowing what was to happen, she suppressed her fear and steadfastly refused to worry about or feel the pain until the moment it would engulf her. She was utterly determined now to show this strange, highly advanced but seemingly nonresponsible medic how a truly dedicated warrior-surgeon of Sommaradva was expected to behave.

As she was inserting the last few staples into the flap covering the stump, the Diagnostician said warmly, "That was fast, precise, and quite exemplary work, Cha Thrat. I am particularly impressed by—What are you *doing*?"

She thought that her intentions were obvious as soon as she lifted the Number Three cutter. Sommaradvan DCNFs did not possess forelimbs as such but, she thought proudly, the removal of a left-side medial limb would satisfy the professional requirements of the situation. One quick, neat slice was enough, then she looked at it lying in the container among the Hudlar limbs and gripped the stump tightly to control the bleeding.

Her last conscious memory of the episode was of Diagnostician Conway shouting above the general uproar into the communicator.

"FROB lecture theater on the double," it was saying urgently. "One DCNF, a traumatic amputation, self-inflicted. Ready the OR on Level Forty-three, dammit, and assemble a microsurgery team!"

CHAPTER 8

She could not be sure about the time required for her post-op recuperation, only that there had been lengthy periods of unconsciousness and a great many visits from Chief Psychologist O'Mara and Diagnosticians Thornnastor and Conway. The DBLF nurse assigned to her made caustic comments about the special attention she was receiving from the hospital's hierarchy, the quantity of food she was moving for a supposedly sick patient, and about a newly arrived Nidian trainee whose furry little head had been turned by Cresk-Sar of all people. But when she tried to discuss her own case it was obvious from the Kelgian nurse's agitated fur that that was a forbidden subject.

It did not matter because, by accident or design, the medication she was receiving had the effect of making her feel as if her mind was some kind of dirigible airship, moving at her direction but detached and floating free of all mundane problems. It was, she realized, a very comfortable but suggestible state.

During one of its later visits, O'Mara had suggested that, regardless of her reasons for acting as she had, she had discharged her particularly strict professional obligations, so that no further action was required on her part. The limb had been completely severed and removed from the torso. The fact that Conway and Thornnastor had together performed some very fancy microsurgery to reattach it, with no loss of function or feeling, was a piece of good fortune that she should accept gratefully and without guilt.

It had taken a long time to convince the wizard that she had already arrived at the same conclusion, and that she was grateful, not only for her good fortune, but to Diagnosticians Conway and Thornnastor for giving her back the limb. The only part of the incident that continued to puzzle her, she had told O'Mara, was the adverse reaction of everyone to the noble and praiseworthy thing she had done.

O'Mara had seemed to relax then, and it had proceeded with a long, devious spell that involved subjects which Cha Thrat had considered too personal and sensitive to be discussed with a fellow Sommaradvan, much less a stranger. Perhaps it was the medication that reduced her feelings of shock and outrage, and made the suggestions of the wizard seem worthy of consideration rather than outright rejection.

One of its suggestions had been that, when viewed nonsubjectively, the action she had taken had been neither noble nor praiseworthy, but a little bit silly. By the end of that visit she almost agreed with it, and suddenly she was allowed visitors.

Tarsedth and the Hudlar trainee were the first callers. The Kelgian came bustling forward to ask how she was feeling and to examine her scars, while the FROB remained standing in silence just inside the entrance. Cha Thrat wondered if there was anything bothering it, forgetting for the moment that her medication frequently caused her to vocalize her thoughts.

"Nothing," said Tarsedth. "Just ignore the big softie. When I arrived it was outside the door, don't know for how long, afraid that the mere sight of another Hudlar would give you some kind of emotional relapse. In spite of all that muscle, Hudlars are sensitive souls. According to what O'Mara told Cresk-Sar, you are unlikely to do anything sudden or melodramatic. You are neither mentally unbalanced nor emotionally disturbed. Its exact words were that you were normally crazy but not certifiably mad, which is the condition of quite a few people who work in this place."

It turned suddenly to regard the FROB, then went on. "Come closer!

It is in bed, with a limb and most of its body immobilized, it has been blasted into low orbit with tranquilizers, and it isn't likely to bite you!"

The Hudlar came forward and said shyly, "We all, everyone who was there, wish you well. That includes Patient Eleven Thirty-two, who is pain-free now and making good progress. And Charge Nurse Segroth whose good wishes were, ah, more perfunctory. Will you recover the full use of the limb?"

"Don't be stupid," Tarsedth broke in. "With two Diagnosticians on the case it doesn't dare not make a complete recovery." To Cha Thrat it went on. "But so much has been happening to you recently that I can't keep up. Is it true that you ticked off the Chief Psychologist in front of everybody in the Chalder ward, called it some kind of witch-doctor, and reminded it of its professional duty toward Patient AUGL-One Sixteen? According to the stories going around—"

"It wasn't quite as bad as that," Cha Thrat said.

"It never is," the DBLF said, its fur subsiding in disappointment. "But the business during the FROB demonstration, now. You can't deny or diminish what happened there."

"Perhaps," the Hudlar quietly said, "it would rather not talk about that."

"Why not?" Tarsedth asked. "Everyone else is talking about it."

Cha Thrat was silent for a moment as she looked up at the head and shoulders of the Kelgian projecting like a silver-furred cone over one side of her bed and the enormous body of the Hudlar looming over the other. She tried to make her unnaturally fuzzy mind concentrate on what she wanted to say.

"I would prefer to talk about all the lectures I've missed," she said finally. "Was there anything especially interesting or important? And would you ask Cresk-Sar if I could have a remote control for the view-screen, so I can tune in to the teaching channels? Tell it that I have nothing to do here and I would like to continue with my studies as soon as possible."

"Friend," Tarsedth said, its fur rising into angry spikes, "I think you would be wasting your time."

For the first time she wished that her Kelgian classmate was capable of something less than complete honesty. She had been expecting to hear something like this, but the bad news could have been broken more gently.

"What our forthright friend should have told you," the Hudlar said, "is that we inquired about your exact status from Senior Physician Cresk-Sar, who would not give us a firm answer. It said that you were guilty not so much of contravening hospital rules but of breaking rules that nobody had dreamed of writing. The decision on what to do with you has been referred up, it said, and you could expect a visit from O'Mara quite soon.

"When asked if we could bring you lecture material," it ended apologetically, "Cresk-Sar said no."

It did not make any difference how it was broken, she thought after they had gone, the news was equally bad. But the sudden, raucous sound of her bedside communicator kept her from dwelling for too long on her troubles.

It was Patient AUGL-One Sixteen who, with Charge Nurse Hredlichi's cooperation, was shouting into one of the Nurses' Station communicators from the entrance to the Chalder ward. It began by apologizing for the physiological and environmental problems that kept it from visiting her in person, then told her how much it was missing her visits—the Earth-human wizard O'Mara, it said, lacked her sympathetic manner and charm—and it hoped she was recovering with no physical or mental distress.

"Everything is fine," she lied. It was not a good thing to burden a patient with its medic's troubles, even when the medic was temporarily a patient. "How are you?"

"Very well, thank you," the Chalder replied, sounding enthusiastic in spite of the fact that its words were reaching her through two communicators, a translator, and a considerable quantity of water. "O'Mara says that I can leave and rejoin my family very soon, and can start contacting the space administration on Chalder about my old job. I'm still young for a Chalder, you know, and I do really feel well."

"I'm very happy for you, One Sixteen," Cha Thrat said, deliberately omitting its name because others might be listening who were not entitled to use it. She was surprised by the strength of her feelings toward the creature.

"I've heard the nurses talking," the Chalder went on, "and it seems like you are in serious trouble. I hope all goes well for you, but if not, and you have to leave the hospital . . . Well, you are so far from Sommaradva out here that if you felt like seeing another world on your way home, my people would be pleased to have you for as long as you liked to stay. We're pretty well advanced on Chalderescol and your food synthesis and life-support would be no problem.

"It's a beautiful world," it added, "much, much nicer than the Chalder ward . . ."

When the Chalder eventually broke contact, she settled back into the pillows, feeling tired but not depressed or unhappy, thinking about the ocean world of Chalderescol. Before joining the AUGL ward she had studied the library tape on that world with the idea of being able to talk about home to the patients, so she was not completely unfamiliar with the planet. The thought of living there was exciting, and she knew that, as an off-planet person entitled to call Muromeshomon by name, its family and friends would make her welcome however long or short her stay. But thoughts like that were uncomfortable because they presupposed that she would be leaving the hospital.

Instead she wondered how the normally shy and gentle Chalder had been able to prevail upon the acid-tongued Hredlichli to use the Nurses' Station communicator as it had done. Could it have forced cooperation by threatening to wreck the place again? Or, more likely, had the Chalder's call to her been supported, perhaps even suggested, by O'Mara?

That, too, was an uncomfortable thought, but it did not keep her awake. The continuing spell of the Earth-human wizard or the medication it had prescribed, or both, were still having their insidious effect.

During the days that followed she was visited singly and, where physiological considerations permitted, in small groups by her classmates. Cresk-Sar came twice but, like all the other visitors, the tutor would not talk about medical matters at all. Then one day O'Mara and Diagnostician Conway arrived together and would discuss nothing else.

"Good morning, Cha Thrat, how are you feeling?" the Diagnostician began, as she knew it would.

"Very well, thank you," she replied, as it knew she would. After that she was subjected to the most meticulously thorough physical examination she had ever experienced.

"You've probably realized by now that all of this wasn't strictly necessary," Conway said as it replaced the sheet that had been covering her body. "However, it was my first opportunity to have a really close look at the DCNF physiological classification as a whole, as opposed to one of the limbs. Thank you, it was interesting and most instructive.

"But now that you are completely recovered," it went on, with a quick glance toward O'Mara, "and will require only a course of exercises before you would be fit for duty, what are we going to do with you?"

She suspected that it was a rhetorical question, but she badly wanted to reply to it. Anxiously she said, "There have been mistakes, misunderstandings. They will not occur again. I would like to remain in the hospital and continue my training."

"*No!*" Conway said sharply. In a quieter voice it went on. "You are a fine surgeon, Cha Thrat—potentially a great one. Losing you would be a shameful waste of talent. But keeping you on the medical staff, with your peculiar ideas of what constitutes ethical behavior, is out of the question. There isn't a ward in the hospital that would accept you for practical training now. Segroth took you only because O'Mara and I requested it.

"I like to make my surgery lectures as interesting and exciting as possible for the trainees," Conway added, "but there are limits, dammit!"

Before either of them could say the words that would send her from the hospital, Cha Thrat said quickly, "What if something could be done that would guarantee my future good behavior? One of my early lectures was on the Educator tape system of teaching alien physiology and medicine that, in effect, gives the recipient an other-species viewpoint. If I could be given such a tape, one with a more acceptable, to you, code of professional behavior, then I would be sure to stay out of trouble."

She waited anxiously, but the two Earth-humans were looking at each other in silence, ignoring her.

Without the Educator or physiology tape system, she had learned, a multispecies hospital like Sector General could not have existed. No single brain, regardless of species, could hold the enormous quantity of physiological knowledge required to successfully treat the variety of patients the hospital received. But complete physiological data on any patient's species was available by means of an Educator tape, which was simply the brain record of some great medical mind belonging to the same or a similar species as the patient to be treated.

A being taking such a tape had to share its mind with a completely alien personality. Subjectively, that was exactly how it felt; all of the memories and experiences and personality traits of the being who had donated the tape were impressed on the receiving mind, not just selected pieces of medical data. An Educator tape could not be edited and the degree of confusion, emotional disorientation, and personality dislocation caused to a recipient could not be adequately described even by the Senior Physicians and Diagnosticians who experienced it.

The Diagnosticians were the hospital's highest medical rulers, beings whose minds were both adaptable and stable enough to retain permanently up to ten physiology tapes at one time. To their data-crammed minds was given the job of original research into xenological medicine and the treatment of new diseases in newly discovered life-forms.

But Cha Thrat was not interested in subjecting herself voluntarily, as had the Diagnosticians, to a multiplicity of alien ideas and influences. She had heard it said among the staff that any person sane enough to be a Diagnostician had to be mad, and she could well believe it. Her idea represented a much less drastic solution to the problem.

"If I had an Earth-human, a Kelgian, even a Nidian personality sharing my mind," she persisted, "I would understand why the things I sometimes do are considered wrong, and would be able to avoid doing

them. The other-species material would be used for interpersonal behavioral guidance only. As a trainee I would not try to use its medical
or surgical knowledge on my patients without permission."

The Diagnostician was suddenly overcome by an attack of coughing.
When it recovered it said, "Thank you, Cha Thrat. I'm sure the patients
would thank you, too. But it's impossible to . . . O'Mara, this is your
field. You answer it."

The Chief Psychologist moved close to the bedside and looked down
at her. It said, "Hospital regulations do not allow me to do as you ask,
nor would I do so if I could. Even though you are an unusually strong
and stubborn personality, you would find it very difficult to control the
other occupant of your mind. It *isn't* an alien entity fighting for control,
but because the type of leading medical specialist who donates the tapes
is frequently a very strong-minded and aggressive person used to getting
its own way, it would feel as if it is taking control. The ensuing purely
subjective conflict could give rise to episodes of pain, skin eruptions,
and more troublesome organic malfunctionings. All have a psychosomatic basis, of course, but they will hurt you just as much as the real
thing. The risk of permanent mental damage is great and, until a trainee
has learned to understand the external personalities of the beings around
it, it would not receive one of their Educator tapes.

"In your case there is an additional reason," O'Mara added. "You
are a female."

Sommaradvan prejudices, she thought furiously, *even here in Sector
General!* and made a sound that at home would have resulted in an
immediate and probably violent breakdown in communication. Fortunately, the sound did not translate.

"The conclusion you have just jumped to is wrong," O'Mara went
on. "It is simply that the females of all the two-sexed species yet
discovered have evolved with certain peculiarities, as opposed to abnormalities, of mind. One of them is a deeply rooted, sex-based fastid-
iousness and aversion toward anything or anyone entering or trying to
possess their minds. The only exception is in the situation when life-
mating has taken place, where, in many species, the processes of physical

and mental sharing and the feelings of possession complement each other. But I can't imagine you falling in love with an other-species mind impression."

"Do male entities," Cha Thrat asked, both satisfied and intrigued by the explanation, "receive mind recordings from other-species females, then? Could *I* be given a female tape?"

"There is only one recorded instance of that . . ." O'Mara began.

"Let's not go into that," Conway broke in, its face becoming a darker shade of pink. "I'm sorry, Cha Thrat, you cannot be given an Educator tape, now or ever. O'Mara has explained why, just as he has explained the political circumstances of your arrival here and the delicate state of the cultural contact on Sommaradva that would be jeopardized if we simply dismissed you from the hospital. Wouldn't it be better for all concerned if you left of your own free will?"

Cha Thrat was silent for a moment, her eyes turned toward the limb that she had thought would be lost forever, trying to find the right words. Then she said, "You don't owe me anything for my work on ship ruler Chiang. I have already explained, during my first meeting with the Chief Psychologist, that the delay in attending to its injuries was caused by my not wanting to lose a limb because if, as a result of my decision to perform the operation it lost a limb, then so would I. As a warrior-surgeon I cannot escape a responsibility willingly accepted.

"And now," she went on, "if I were to leave the hospital as you suggest, it would not be of my own free will. I cannot do, or leave undone, something that I know to be wrong."

The Diagnostician was also looking at the replaced limb. "I believe you," it said.

O'Mara exhaled slowly and half turned to leave. It said, "I'm very sorry I didn't pick up on that 'losing a limb' remark you made at our first meeting; it would have saved us all a lot of trouble. Against my better judgment I relented after the AUGL-One Sixteen business, but the bloody drama during the FROB demonstration was too much. The remainder of your stay here will not be very pleasant because, in spite of the earlier recommendations you've had from Diagnostician Conway and myself, nobody wants you anywhere near their patients.

"Let's face it, Cha Thrat," it ended as both Earth-humans moved toward the door, "you're in the doghouse."

She heard them talking with a third person in the corridor, but the words were too muffled for translation. Then the door opened and another Earth-human entered. It was wearing the dark-green uniform of the Monitor Corps and looked familiar.

Cheerfully it said, "I've been waiting outside in case they couldn't talk you into leaving, and O'Mara was pretty sure they wouldn't. I'm Timmins, in case you don't remember me. We have to have a long talk.

"And before you ask," it went on, "the doghouse, so far as you're concerned, is the Maintenance Department."

CHAPTER 9

It was obvious from the beginning that Lieutenant Timmins did not consider its job to be either servile or menial, and it was not long before the Lieutenant had her beginning to feel the same way. It wasn't just the Earth-human's quiet enthusiasm for its job, there was also the portable viewer and set of study tapes it had left at her bedside that convinced her that this was work for warriors—although not, of course, for warrior-surgeons. The wide-ranging and complex problems of providing technical and environmental support for the sixty-odd—some of them very odd indeed—life-forms comprising the hospital's patients and staff made her earlier medical and physiological studies seem easy by comparison.

Her last formal contact with the training program was when Cresk-Sar arrived, carried out a brief but thorough examination, and, subject to the findings of the eye specialist, Doctor Yeppha, who would be visiting her shortly, pronounced her physically fit to begin the new duties. She asked if there would be any objection to her continuing to view the medical teaching channels in her free time, and the Senior Physician told her that she could watch whatever she pleased in her spare time, but it was unlikely that she would ever be able to put any of the medical knowledge gained into practice.

It ended by saying that while it was relieved that she was no longer the Training Department's responsibility, it was sorry to lose her and that it joined her erstwhile colleagues in wishing her success and personal satisfaction in the new work she had chosen.

Doctor Yeppha was a new life-form to her experience, a small, tripedal, fragile being that she classified as DRVJ. From the furry dome of its head there sprouted, singly and in small clusters, at least twenty eyes. She wondered whether the overabundance of visual sensors had any bearing on its choice of specialty, but thought it better not to ask.

"Good morning, Cha Thrat," it said, taking a tape from the pouch at its waist and pushing it into the viewer. "This is a visual acuity test designed primarily to check for color blindness. We don't care if you have muscles like a Hudlar or a Cinrusskin, there are machines to do the really heavy work, but you have to be able to see. Not only that, you must be able to clearly identify colors and the subtle shades and dilution of color brought about by changes in the intensity of the ambient lighting. What do you see there?"

"A circle made up of red spots," Cha Thrat replied, "enclosing a star of green and blue spots."

"Good," Yeppha said. "I am making this sound much simpler than it really is, but you will learn the complexities in time. The service bays and interconnecting tunnels are filled with cable looms and plumbing all of which is color coded. This enables the maintenance people to tell at a glance which are power cables and which the less dangerous communication lines, or which pipes carry oxygen, chlorine, methane, or organic effluvia. The danger of contamination of wards by other-species atmospheres is always present, and such an environmental catastrophe should not be allowed to occur because some partially sighted nincompoop has connected up the wrong set of pipes. What do you see now?"

And so it went on, with Yeppha putting designs in subtly graduated colors on the screen and Cha Thrat telling it what she saw or did not see. Finally the DRVJ turned off the viewer and replaced the tape in its pouch.

"You don't have as many eyes as I do," it said, "but they all work. There is no bar, therefore, to you joining the Maintenance Department. My sincere commiserations. Good luck!"

The first three days were to be devoted exclusively to unsupervised lessons in internal navigation. Timmins explained that whenever or wherever an emergency occurred, or even if a minor fault was reported, the maintenance people were expected to be at the site of the trouble with minimum delay. Because they would normally be carrying tools or replacement parts with them on a self-powered trolley, they were forbidden the use of the main hospital corridors, except in the direst of emergencies—staff and patient traffic there was congested enough as it was without risking a vehicular thrombosis. She was therefore expected to find her way from A to B, with diversions through H, P, and W, without leaving the service bays and tunnels or asking directions of anyone she might meet.

Neither was she allowed to make an illegal check on her position by emerging into the main corridor system to go to lunch.

"Wearing the lightweight protective envelope will probably be unnecessary," Timmins said as he lifted the grating in the floor just outside her room, "but maintenance people always wear them in case they have to pass through an area where there may be a nonurgent seepage of own-species toxic gas. You have sensors to warn you of the presence of all toxic contaminants, including radiation, a lamp in case one of the tunnels has a lighting failure, a map with your route clearly shown, a distress beacon in case you become hopelessly lost or some other personal emergency occurs, and, if I may say so, more than enough food to keep you alive for a week much less a day!

"Don't worry and don't try to hurry, Cha Thrat," it went on. "Look on this as a long, leisurely walk through unexplored territory, with frequent breaks for a picnic. I'll see you outside Access Hatch Twelve in Corridor Seven on Level One Twenty in fifteen hours, or less."

It laughed suddenly and added, "Or possibly more."

The service tunnels were very well lit, but low and narrow—at least so far as the Sommaradvan life-form was concerned—with alcoves set at frequent intervals along their length. The alcoves were puzzling in that they were empty of cable runs, pipes, or any form of mechanisms, but she discovered their purpose when a Kelgian driving a powered trolley came charging along the tunnel toward her and yelled, "Move aside, stupid!"

Apart from that encounter she seemed to have the tunnel to herself, and she was able to move much more easily than she had ever been able to do in the main corridor whose floor was now above her head. Through the ventilator grilles she could clearly hear the sounds of thumping and tapping and slithering of other-species ambulatory appendages overhead, and the indescribable babble of growling, hissing, gobbling, and cheeping conversation that accompanied it.

She moved forward steadily, careful not to be surprised by another fast-moving vehicle as she consulted her map, and occasionally stopped to dictate notes describing the size, diameter, and color codings on the protective casings of the mechanisms and connecting pipes and cable runs that covered the tunnel walls and roof. The notes, Timmins had told her, would enable it to check her progress during the test, as well as give her an important check on her general location.

The power and communication lines would look the same anywhere in the hospital, but most of the plumbing here bore the color codings for water and the atmospheric mixture favored by the warm-blooded, oxygen-breathing life-forms that made up more than half of the Federation's member species. Under the levels where they breathed chlorine, methane, or super-heated steam the colors would be much different and so would be her protective clothing.

A mechanism that did not appear to be working caught her attention. Through its transparent cover she could see a group of unlit indicators and a serial number that probably meant something to the entities who had built the thing, but to nobody else who was not familiar with their written language. She located and pressed the plate of the audible label and switched on her translator.

"I am a standby pump on the drinking water supply line to the DBLF ward Eighty-three diet kitchen," it announced. "Functioning is automatic when required, currently inoperative. The hinged inspection panel is opened by inserting your general-purpose key into the slot marked with a red circle and turning right through ninety degrees. For component repair or replacement consult Maintenance Instructions Tape Three, Section One Twenty. Don't forget to close the panel again before you leave.

"I am a standby pump . . ." it was beginning again when she took her hand away, silencing it.

At first she had been worried by the thought of traveling continuously along the low, narrow service tunnels, even though O'Mara had assured Timmins that her psych profile was free of any tendency toward claustrophobia. All of the tunnels were brightly lit and, she had been told, they remained so even if they were unoccupied for long periods. On Sommaradva this would have been considered a criminal waste of power. But in Sector General the additional demand on the main reactor for continuous lighting was negligible, and was more than outweighed by the maintenance problem that would have been posed if fallible on-off switches had been installed at every tunnel intersection.

Gradually her route took her away from the corridors and the alien cacophony of the people using them, and she felt more completely and utterly alone than she had believed it possible to feel.

The absence of outside sounds made the subdued humming and clicking of the power and pumping systems around her appear to grow louder and more threatening, and she took to pressing the audible labels at random, just to hear another voice—even though it was simply a machine identifying itself and its often mystifying purpose.

Occasionally she found herself thanking the machine for the information.

The color codings had begun to change from the oxygen-nitrogen and water markings to those for chlorine and the corrosive liquid that the Illensan PVSJ metabolism used as a working fluid, and the corridors were shorter with many more twists and turns. Before her confusion could grow into panic, she decided to make herself as comfortable as possible in an alcove, substantially reduce the quantity of food she was carrying, and think.

According to her map she was passing from the PVSJ section downward through one of the synthesizer facilities that produced the food required by the chlorine-breathers and into the section devoted to the supply of the AUGL water-breathers. That explained the seemingly contradictory markings and the square-sectioned conduits that made hissing, rumbling noises as the solid, prepackaged PVSJ food was being moved pneumatically along them. However, a large corner of the AUGL section had been converted to a PVSJ operating room and post-op observation ward, and this was joined to the main chlorine section by an ascending spiral corridor containing moving ramps for the rapid transfer of staff and patients, since the PVSJs were not physiologically suited to the use of stairs. The twists and turns of the service tunnel were necessary to get around these topologically complex obstructions. But if she got safely past this complicated interpenetration of the water- and chlorine-breathing sections, the journey should be much simpler.

There was no shortage of vocal company. Warning labels, which spoke whether she pressed them or not, advised her to check constantly for cross-species contamination.

Provision had been made to take food without unsealing her protective suit, but her sensors showed the area clear of toxic material in dangerous quantities, so she opened her visor. The smell was an indescribable combination of every sharp, acrid, heavy, unpleasant, and even pleasant smell that she had ever encountered but, fortunately, only in trace quantities. She ate her food, quickly closed the visor, and moved on with increased confidence.

Three long, straight sections of corridor later she realized that her confidence had been misplaced.

According to her estimates of the distances and directions she had traveled, Cha Thrat should be somewhere between the Hudlar and Tralthan levels. The tunnel walls should have been carrying the thick, heavily insulated power cables for the FROBs' artificial gravity grids and at least one distinctively marked pipe to supply their nutrient sprayers, as well as the air, water, and return waste conduits required by the warm-blooded, oxygen-breathing FGLIs. But the cable runs bore color combinations that should not have been there, and the only atmosphere line visible was the small-diameterpipe supplying air to the tunnel itself. Irritated with herself, she pressed the nearest audible label.

"I am an automatic self-monitoring control unit for synthesizer process One Twelve B," it said importantly. "Press blue stud and access panel will move aside. Warning. Only the container and audible label are reusable. If faulty, components must be replaced and not repaired. Not to be opened by MSVK, LSVO, or other species with low radiation tolerance unless special protective measures are taken."

She had no desire to open the cabinet, even though her radiation monitor was indicating that the area was safe for her particular life-form. At the next alcove she had another look at her map and list of color codings.

Somehow she had wandered into one of the sections that were inhabited only by automatic machinery. The map indicated fifteen such areas within the main hospital complex, and none of them was anywhere near her planned route. Plainly she had taken a wrong turning, perhaps a series of wrong turnings, soon after leaving the spiral tunnel connecting the PVSJ ward with its new operating room.

She moved on again, watching the tunnel walls and roof in the hope that the next change in the color codings would give her a clue to where she might be. She also cursed her own stupidity aloud and touched every label she passed, but soon decided that both activities were nonproductive. It was a wise decision because, at the next tunnel intersection, she heard distant voices.

Timmins had told her not to speak to anyone or to enter any of the public corridors. But, she reasoned, if she was already hopelessly off-course then there was nothing to stop her taking the side tunnel and moving toward the sound. Perhaps by listening at one of the corridor ventilating grilles she might overhear a conversation that would give her a clue to her present whereabouts.

The thought made Cha Thrat feel ashamed but, compared with some of the things she had been forced to think about recently, it was a small, personal dishonor that she thought she could live with.

There were lengthy breaks in the conversation. At first the voices were too quiet and distant for her translator to catch what was being said, and when she came closer the people concerned were indulging in one of their lengthy silences. The result was that when she came to the next intersection, she saw them before there was another chance to overhear them.

They were a Kelgian DBLF and an Earth-human DBDG, dressed in Maintenance coveralls with the additional insignia of Monitor Corps rank. There were tools and dismantled sections of piping on the floor between them and, after glancing up at her briefly, they went on talking to each other.

"I wondered what was coming at us along the corridor," the Kelgian said, "and making more noise than a drunken Tralthan. It must be the new DCNF we were told about, on its first day underground. We mustn't talk to it, not that I'd want to, anyway. Strange-looking creature, isn't it?"

"I wouldn't dream of talking to it, or vice versa," the DBDG replied. "Pass me the Number Eleven gripper and hold your end steady. Do you think it knows where it's going?"

The Kelgian's conical head turned briefly in the direction Cha Thrat was headed, and it said, "Not unless it was feeling that the tunnel walls were closing in on it, and it wanted to treat threatened claustrophobia with a jolt of agoraphobia by walking on the outer hull. This is no job for a Corps senior non-com shortly, if what the Major says is true, to be promoted Lieutenant."

"This is no job for anybody, so don't worry about it," the Earth-human said. It turned to look pointedly along the corridor to the left. "On the other hand, it could be contemplating a visit to the VTXM section. Stupid in a lightweight suit, of course, but maintenance trainees have to be stupid or they'd try for some other job."

The Kelgian made an angry sound that did not translate, then said,

"Why is it that nowhere in the vast immensity of explored space have we discovered yet a single life-form whose body wastes smell nice?"

"My furry friend," the Earth-human said, "I think you may have touched upon one of the great philosophical truths. And on the subject of inexplicable phenomena, how could a Melfan Size Three dilator get into their waste-disposal system and travel through four levels before it gummed up the works down here?"

She could see the Kelgian's fur rippling under its coveralls as it said, "Do you think that DCNF is stupid? Is it going to stand there watching us all day? Is it intending to follow us home?"

"From what I've heard about Sommaradvans," the DBDG replied, still not looking directly at her, "I'd say it wasn't so much stupid as a bit slow-witted."

"Definitely slow-witted," the Kelgian agreed.

But Cha Thrat had already realized that, cloaked though they were by statements that were derogatory and personally insulting, the overheard conversation had contained three accurate points of reference which would easily enable her to establish her position and return to the planned route. She regarded the two maintenance people for a moment, sorry that she was forbidden to speak to them as they were to her. Quickly she made the formal sign of thanks between equals, then turned away to move in the only direction the two beings had *not* discussed.

"I think," the Kelgian said, "it made a rude gesture with its forward medial limb."

"In its place," the Earth-human replied, "I'd have done the same."

During the remainder of that interminable journey she double-checked every change of direction and kept watch for any unexpected alterations in color codings on the way to Level One Twenty, and paused only once to make another large dent in her food store. When she opened Access Hatch Twelve and climbed into Corridor Seven, Timmins was already there.

"Well done, Cha Thrat, you made it," the Earth-human said, showing its teeth. "Next time I'd better make the trip a little longer, and a lot more complicated. After that I'll let you help out with a few simple jobs. You may as well start earning your keep."

Feeling pleased and a little confused, she said, "I thought I arrived early. Have I kept you waiting long?"

Timmins shook its head. "Your distress beacon was for your own personal reassurance in case you felt lost or frightened. It was part of the test. But we keep permanent tracers on our people at all times, so I was aware of every move you made. Devious, aren't I? But you passed very close to a maintenance team at one stage. I hope you didn't ask them for directions. You know the rule."

Cha Thrat wondered if there was any rule in Sector General so inflexible that it could not be bent out of shape, and she hoped that the outer signs of her embarrassment could not be read by a member of another species.

"No," she replied truthfully, "we didn't speak to each other."

CHAPTER 10

I n the event, she was not given a job until Timmins had shown her the full range and complexity of the work that, one day, she might be capable of taking on. It was obvious that the Earth-human was quietly but intensely proud of its Maintenance Department and, with good reason, was showing off while trying to instill a little of its own pride in her. True, much of the work was servile, but there were aspects of it that called for the qualities of a warrior or even a minor ruler. Unlike the rigid stratification of labor practiced on Sommaradva, however, in the Maintenance Department advancement toward the higher levels was encouraged.

Timmins was doing an awful lot of encouraging, and seemed to be spending an unusually large proportion of its time showing her around.

"With respect," she said after one particularly interesting tour of the low-temperature methane levels, "your rank and obvious ability suggest that you have more important uses for your time than spending it with me, your most recent and, I suspect, most technically ignorant maintenance trainee. Why am I given this special treatment?"

Timmins laughed quietly and said, "You mustn't think that I'm neglecting more important work to be with you, Cha Thrat. If I'm needed I can be contacted without delay. But that is unlikely to happen because my subordinates try very hard to make me feel redundant.

"You should find the next section particularly interesting," it went on. "It is the VTXM ward, which, strange as it may seem, forms part of the main reactor. You know from your medical lectures that the Telfi are a gestalt life-form who live by the direct absorption of hard radiation, so that all patient examination and treatment is by remote-controlled sensors and manipulators. To be assigned to maintenance in this area you would need special training in—"

"Special training," Cha Thrat broke in, beginning to lose her patience, "means special treatment. I have already asked this question. Am I being given special treatment?"

"Yes," the Earth-human said sharply. It waited while a refrigerated vehicle containing one of the frigid-blooded SNLU methane-breathers rolled past, then went on. "Of course you are being given special treatment."

"Why?"

Timmins did not reply.

"Why do you not answer this simple question?" she persisted.

"Because," the Earth-human said, its face deepening in color, "your question does not have a simple answer, and I'm not sure if I am the right person to give it to you, since I might also give offense, cause you mental pain, insult you, or make you angry."

Cha Thrat walked in silence for a moment, then said, "I think that your consideration for my feelings makes you the right person. And a subordinate who has acted wrongly may indeed feel mental pain or anger or intense self-dislike but surely, if the superior speaks justly, no offense can be taken nor insult given."

The Earth-human shook its head in a gesture, she had learned, that could mean either negation or puzzlement. It said, "There are times, Cha Thrat, when you make me feel like the subordinate. But what the hell, I'll try to answer. You are being accorded special treatment because of the wrong we did to you and the mental discomfort we have caused, and there are several important people who feel obligated to do something about it."

"But surely," she said incredulously, "I am the one who has behaved wrongly."

"That you have," Timmins said, "but as a direct result of us wronging you first. The Monitor Corps are responsible for allowing, no, *encouraging* you to come here in the first place, and waiving the entry requirements. The wrongdoing that followed this combination of misguided gratitude for saving Chiang's life and sheer political opportunism was the inevitable result."

"But I wanted to come," Cha Thrat protested, "and I still want to stay."

"To punish yourself for recent misdeeds?" Timmins asked quietly. "I've been trying to convince you that we are originally to blame for those."

"I am not mentally or morally warped," she replied, trying to control her anger at what, on her home world, would have been a grave insult. "I accept just punishment, but I would not seek to inflict it on myself. There are some very disquieting and unpleasant aspects to life here, but in no level of Sommaradvan society could I be subject to such a variety and intensity of experience. That is why I would like to stay."

The Earth-human was silent for a moment, then it said, "Conway, O'Mara, and Cresk-Sar among others, even Hredlichli, were sure that your reasons for wanting to stay here were positive rather than negative and that there was little chance of my getting you to agree to a return home . . ."

It broke off as Cha Thrat stopped dead in the corridor.

Angrily she said, "Have you been discussing with all these people my deeds and misdeeds, my competence or incompetence, perhaps my future prospects, without inviting me to be present?"

"Move, you're causing a traffic problem," Timmins said. "And there is no reason for anger. Since that business during the Hudlar demo there isn't a single being in the hospital who has *not* talked about your deeds, misdeeds, competence, or lack thereof, and your highly questionable future prospects in the hospital. Having you present at all those discussions was not possible. But if you want to know what was said about you in great and interminable detail—the serious discussions, that is, as opposed to mere hospital gossip—I believe O'Mara has added the recordings to your psych file and might play them back to you on request. Or again, he might not.

"Alternatively," it went on when they were moving again, "you may wish me to give you a brief summary of these discussions, inaccurate in that the excess verbiage and the more impolite and colorful phraseology will be deleted."

"That," Cha Thrat said, "is what I wish."

"Very well," it replied. "Let me begin by saying that the Monitor Corps personnel and all of the senior medical staff members involved are responsible for this situation. During the initial interview with O'Mara you mentioned that the lengthy delay in your decision to treat Chiang was that you did not want to lose a limb. O'Mara assumed, wrongly, that you were referring only to Chiang's limb, and he thinks that in an other-species interview he should have been more alert to the exact meaning of the words spoken, and that he is primarily responsible for your self-amputation.

"Conway feels responsible," it went on, "because he ordered you to perform the Hudlar limb removal without knowing anything about your very strict code of professional ethics. Cresk-Sar thinks it should have questioned you more closely on the same subject. Both of them believe that you would make a fine other-species surgeon if you could be deconditioned and reeducated. And Hredlichli blames itself for ignoring the special friendship that developed between you and AUGL-One Sixteen. And, of course, the Monitor Corps, which is originally responsible for the problem, suggested a solution that would give the minimum displeasure to everyone."

"By transferring me to Maintenance," she finished for it.

"That was never a serious suggestion," the Earth-human said, "because we couldn't believe that you would accept it. No, we wanted to send you home."

A small part of her mind was moving her body forward and around the heavier or more senior staff members, while the rest of it felt angry and bitterly disappointed in the life-form beside her that she had begun to think of as a friend.

"Naturally," Timmins went on, "we tried to take your feelings into account. You were interested in meeting and working with off-planet life-forms, so we would give you a cultural liaison position, as an advisor on Sommaradvan affairs, on our base there. Or on *Descartes,* our largest specialized other-species contact vessel, which will be orbiting your world until another new intelligent species is discovered somewhere. Your position would be one of considerable responsibility, and could not be influenced in any way by the people who dislike you on Sommaradva.

"Naturally, nothing could be guaranteed at this stage," it continued. "But subject to your satisfactory performance with us you would be allowed to choose between a permanent position with the Corps' Sommaradva establishment as an interspecies cultural advisor or as a member of the contact team on *Descartes.* We tried to do what we thought was best for you, friend, and everyone else."

"You did," Cha Thrat said, feeling her anger and disappointment melting away. "Thank you."

"We thought it was a reasonable compromise," Timmins said. "But O'Mara said no. He insisted that you be given a maintenance job here in the hospital and have the Corps induction procedures attended to as quickly as possible."

"Why?"

"I don't know why," it replied. "Who knows how a Chief Psychologist's mind works?"

"Why," she repeated, "must I join your Monitor Corps?"

"Oh, that," Timmins said. "Purely for administrative convenience. The supply and maintenance of Sector General is our responsibility, and anyone who is not a patient or on the medical staff is automatically a member of the Monitor Corps. The personnel computer has to know your name, rank, and number so as to be able to pay your salary and so we can tell you what to do.

"Theoretically," it added.

"I have never disobeyed the lawful order of a superior..." Cha Thrat began, when it held up its hand again.

"A Corps joke, don't worry about it," Timmins said. "The point I'm trying to make is that our Chief Psychologist bears the administrative rank of major, but it is difficult to define the limits of his authority in this place, because he orders full Colonels and Diagnosticians around, and not always politely. Your own rank of junior technician, Environmental Maintenance, Grade Two, which became effective as soon as we received O'Mara's instructions, will not give you as much leeway."

"Please," she said urgently, "this is a serious matter. It is my understanding that the Monitor Corps is an organization of warriors. It has been many generations on Sommaradva since our warrior-level citizens fought together in battle. Peace and present-day technology offer danger enough. As a warrior-surgeon I am required to heal wounds, not inflict them."

"Seriously," the Earth-human said, "I think your information on the Corps came chiefly from the entertainment channels. Space battles and hand-to-hand combat are an extremely rare occurrence, and the library tapes will give you a much truer, and more boring, description of what we do and why we do it. Study the material. You'll find that there will be no conflict of loyalty between your duties to the Corps, your home world, or your ethical standards.

"We've arrived," it added briskly, pointing at the sign on the heavy door before them. "From here on we'll need heavy radiation armor. Oh, you've another question?"

"It's about my salary," she said hesitantly.

Timmins laughed and said, "I do so hate these altruistic types who consider money unimportant. The pay at your present rank isn't large. Personnel will be able to tell you the equivalent in Sommaradvan currency, but then there isn't much to spend it on here. You can always save it and your leave allowance and travel. Perhaps visit your AUGL friend on Chalderescol sometime, or go to—"

"There would be enough money for an interstellar trip like that?" she broke in.

The Earth-human went into a paroxym of coughing, recovered, then said, "There would *not* be enough money to pay for an interstellar trip. However, because of the isolated position of Sector General, free Corps transport is available for physiologically suitable hospital personnel to travel to their home planets or, with a bit of fiddling, to the planet of your choice. The money could be spent there, enjoying yourself. Now will you please get into that armor?"

Cha Thrat did not move and the Earth-human watched her without speaking.

Finally she said, "I am being given special treatment, shown areas where I am not qualified to work and mechanisms that I can't hope to use for a very long time. No doubt this is being done as an incentive, to show me what is possible for me to achieve in the future. I understand and appreciate the thinking behind this, but I would much prefer to stop sightseeing and do some simple, and useful, work."

"Well, good for you!" Timmins said, showing its teeth approvingly. "We can't look directly at the Telfi anyway, so we aren't missing much. Suppose you begin by learning to drive a delivery sled. A small one, at first, so that an accident will damage you more than the hospital structure. And you'll have to really master your internal geography, and be able to navigate accurately and at speed through the service tunnel network. It seems to be a law of nature that when a ward or diet kitchen has to be resupplied, the requisition is always urgent and usually arrives late.

"We'll head for the internal transport hangar now," it ended, "unless you have another question?"

She had, but thought it better to wait until they were moving again before asking it.

"What about the damage to the AUGL ward for which I was indirectly responsible?" she said. "Will the cost be deducted from my salary?"

Timmins showed its teeth again and said, "I'd say that it would take about three years to pay for the damage caused by your AUGL friend. But when the damage was done you were one of the medical trainee crazies, not a serious and responsible member of the Maintenance Department, so don't worry about it."

She did not worry about it because, for the rest of the day, there were far more important things to worry about—principally the control and guidance of the uncontrollable and misguided, multiply accursed heap of machinery called an antigravity sled.

In operation the vehicle rode a repulsion cushion so that there was no contact with the deck, and changes in direction were effected by lowering friction pads, angling the thrusters, or, for fine control, leaning sideways. If emergency braking was necessary, the power was switched off. This caused the vehicle to drop to the deck and grind noisily to a halt. But this maneuver was discouraged because it made the driver very unpopular with the service crew who had to realign the repulsor grids.

By the end of the day her vehicle had slipped and spun all over the transport hangar floor, hit every collapsible marker that she was supposed to steer around, and generally displayed a high level of noncooperation. Timmins gave her a packet of study tapes, told her to look over them before next morning, and said that her driving was pretty good for a beginner.

Three days later she began to believe it.

"I drove a sled with a trailer attached, both fully loaded, from Level Eighteen to Thirty-three," she told Tarsedth, when her one-time classmate visited her for the customary evening gossip. "I did it using only the service tunnels, and without hitting anything or anybody."

"Should I be impressed?" the Kelgian asked.

"A little," Cha Thrat said, feeling more than a little deflated. "What's been happening to you?"

"Cresk-Sar transferred to me LSVO Surgical," Tarsedth said, its fur rippling in an unreadable mixture of emotions. "It said I was ready to broaden my other-species nursing experience, and working with a light-gravity life-form would improve my delicacy of touch. And anyway, it said, Charge Nurse Lentilatsar, the rotten, chlorine-breathing slimy slob, was not entirely happy with the way I exercised my initiative. What tape is that? It looks massively uninteresting."

"To the contrary," Cha Thrat said, touching the pause stud. The screen showed a picture of a group of Monitor Corps officers meeting the great Earth-human MacEwan and the equally legendary Orligian Grawlya-Ki, the true founders, it was said, of Sector General hospital. "It's the history, organization, and present activities of the Monitor Corps. I find it very interesting, but ethically confusing. For example, why must a peace-keeping force be so heavily armed?"

"Because, stupid, it couldn't if it wasn't," Tarsedth said. It went on quickly. "But on the subject of the Monitor Corps I'm an expert. A lot of Kelgians join these days, and I was going to try for a position as Surgeon-Lieutenant, a ship's medic, that is, and might still do it if I don't qualify here.

"Of course," it went on enthusiastically, "there are other, nonmilitary, openings . . ."

As the Galactic Federation's executive and law-enforcement arm, the Monitor Corps was essentially a police force on an interstellar scale, but during the first century since it had come into existence it had become much more. Originally, when the Federation had comprised a rather unstable alliance of only four inhabited systems—Nidia, Orligia, Traltha, and Earth—its personnel had been exclusively Earth-human. But those Earth-humans were responsible for discovering other inhabited systems, and more and more intelligent life-forms, and for establishing friendly contact with them.

The result was that the Federation now numbered among its citizens close on seventy different species—the figure was constantly being revised upward—and the peace-keeping function had taken second place to that of the Survey, Exploration, and Other-species Communications activities. The people with the heavy weaponry did not mind because a police force, unlike an army, feels at its most effective when there is nothing for it to do but keep in training by carving up the odd mineral-rich asteroid for the mining people, or clearing and leveling large tracts of virgin land on a newly discovered world in preparation for the landing of colonists.

The last time a Monitor Corps police action had been indistinguishable from an act of war had been nearly two decades ago, when they had defended Sector General itself from the badly misguided Etlans, who had since become law-abiding citizens of the Federation. A few of them had even joined the Corps.

"Nowadays membership is open to any species," Tarsedth continued, "although for physiological reasons, life-support and accommodation problems on board the smaller ships, most of the space-going personnel are warm-blooded oxygen-breathers.

"Like I said," the Kelgian went on, undulating forward and restarting the tape, "there are lots of interesting openings for restless, adventurous, home-hating types like us. You could do worse than join."

"I have joined," Cha Thrat said. "But driving a gravity sled isn't exactly adventurous."

Tarsedth's fur spiked in surprise, then settled down again as it said, "Of course you have. Stupid of me, I'd forgotten that all nonmedical staff are automatically coopted into the Monitor Corps. And I've seen how you people drive. Adventurous verging on the suicidal best describes it. But you made a good decision. Congratulations."

The decision had been made for her, Cha Thrat thought wryly, but that did not mean that it was necessarily a wrong decision. They had settled back to watch the remainder of the Monitor Corps history tape when Tarsedth's fur became agitated again.

"I'm worried about you and the Corps people, Cha Thrat," the Kelgian said suddenly. "They can be a bit stuffy about some things, easygoing about others. Just study and work hard. And think carefully before you do anything that will get you kicked out."

CHAPTER 11

Time slipped past and Cha Thrat felt that she was making no progress at all, until one day she realized that she was performing as routine tasks that only a little earlier would have been impossible. Much of the work was servile but, strangely, she was becoming increasingly interested in it and felt proud when she did it well. Sometimes the morning assignments contained unpleasant surprises.

"Today you will begin moving power cells and other consumables to the ambulance ship *Rhabwar*," Timmins said, consulting its worksheet. "But there is a small job I want you to do first—new vegetable decoration for the AUGL ward. Study the attachment instructions before you go so that the medics will think you know what you're doing . . . Is there a problem, Cha Thrat?"

There were other and more senior technicians in her section—three Kelgians, an Ian, and an Orligian—waiting for the day's assignments. She doubted her ability to take over one of their jobs, and hers was probably too elementary for the Lieutenant to consider swapping assignments, but she had to try.

Perhaps the Earth-human would accord her some of the earlier special treatment that, for some reason, had been completely absent since she had been put to work.

"There is a problem," Cha Thrat said quietly. The note of pleading in her voice was probably lost in the process of translation, she thought as she went on. "As you know, I am not well liked by Charge Nurse Hredlichli, and my presence in the AUGL ward is likely to cause, at very least, verbal unpleasantness. The bad feeling for which I am largely responsible may fade in time, but right now I think that it would be better to send someone else."

Timmins regarded her silently for a moment, then it smiled and said, "Right now, Cha Thrat, I wouldn't want to send anyone else to the AUGL ward. Don't worry about it.

"Krachlan," it went on briskly. "You are for Level Eighty-three, another fault reported in the power converter at Station Fourteen B. We may have to replace the unit . . ."

All the way to the Chalder level, Cha Thrat seethed quietly as she wondered how such a stupid, insensitive, cross-species miscegenation as Timmins had risen to its high rank and responsibilities without sustaining mortal injury at the hands, claws, or tentacles of a subordinate. By the time she reached the AUGL ward and entered inconspicuously by the service tunnel lock, she had calmed sufficiently to remember a few, a very few, of Timmins's good qualities.

She was relieved when nobody came near her as she went to work. All of the patients and nursing staff seemed to be congregated at the other end of the ward and dimly, through the clouded green water, she could see the distinctive coveralls of a transfer team member. Plainly something of great interest was happening back there, which meant that with luck she would be able to complete her work undisturbed and unnoticed.

Seemingly it was not to be her lucky day.

"It's you again," said the familiar, acid-tongued voice of Hredlichli, who had approached silently from behind her. "How long will it take for you to finish hanging that vile stuff?"

"Most of the morning, Charge Nurse," Cha Thrat replied politely.

She did not want to get into an argument with the chlorine-breather, and it seemed as if one were about to start. She wondered if it was possible to forestall it by doing all the talking herself on a subject that Hredlichli could not argue about, the improved comfort of its patients.

"The reason for it taking so long to install, Charge Nurse," she said quickly, "is that this vegetation isn't the usual plastic reproduction. I've been told that it has just arrived from Chalderescol, that it is a native underwater plant-form, very hardy and requiring the minimum of attention, and that it releases a pleasant, waterborne aroma that is said to be psychologically beneficial to the recuperating patient.

"Maintenance will periodically check its growth and general health," she went on before the chlorine-breather could respond, "and supply the nutrient material. But the patients could be given the job of caring for it, as something interesting to do to relieve their boredom, and to leave the nurses free to attend—"

"Cha Thrat," Hredlichli broke in sharply, "are you telling me how I should run my ward?"

"No," she replied, wishing not for the first time that her mouth did not run so far ahead of her mind. "I apologize, Charge Nurse. I no longer have responsibility for any aspect of patient care, and I did not wish to imply that I did. While I am here I shall not even talk to a patient."

Hredlichli made an untranslatable sound, then said, "You'll talk to one patient, at least. That is why I asked Timmins to send you here today. Your friend, AUGL-One Sixteen, is going home, and I thought you might want to wish it well—everybody else in the ward seems to be doing so. Leave that disgusting mess you're working on and finish it later."

Cha Thrat could not speak for a moment. Since the transfer to Maintenance she had lost contact with her Chalder friend, and knew only that it was still on the hospital's list of patients under treatment. The most she had hoped for today, and it had been a pretty forlorn hope, was that Hredlichli would allow her a few words with the patient while she was working. But this was completely unexpected.

"Thank you, Charge Nurse," she said finally. "This is most considerate of you."

The chlorine-breather made another untranslatable noise. It said, "Since I was appointed Charge Nurse here I've been agitating to have this antiquated underwater dungeon redecorated, reequipped, and converted into something resembling a proper ward. Thanks to you that is now being done, and once I recovered from the initial trauma of having my ward wrecked, I decided that I owed you one.

"Even so," it added, "I shall not suffer terminal mental anguish if I don't see you again after today."

AUGL-One Sixteen had already been inserted into its transfer tank and only the hatch above its head remained to be sealed, after which it would be moved through the lock in the outer hull and across to the waiting Chalder ship. A group comprised of well-wishing nurses, visibly impatient transfer team members, and the Earth-human O'Mara hung around the opening like a shoal of ungainly fish, but the loud, bubbling sounds from the tank's water-purifying equipment made it difficult to hear what was being said. As she approached, the Chief Psychologist waved the others back.

"Keep it short, Cha Thrat, the team is behind schedule," O'Mara said, turning away and leaving her alone with the ex-patient.

For what seemed a long time she looked at the one enormous eye and the great teeth in the part of its head visible through the open seal, and the words she wanted to speak would not come. Finally she said, "That looks like a very small tank, are you comfortable in there?"

"Quite comfortable, Cha Thrat," the Chalder replied. "Actually, it isn't much smaller than my accommodation on the ship. But that constriction will be temporary, soon I'll have a planetary ocean to swim in.

"And before you ask," the AUGL went on, "I am feeling fine, really well, in fact, so you don't have to go poking about in this pain-free and disgustingly healthy body checking my vital signs."

"I don't ask questions like that anymore," Cha Thrat said, wishing suddenly that she could laugh like Earth-humans to hide the fact that she did not feel like laughing. "I'm in Maintenance now, so my instruments are much larger and would be very much more uncomfortable."

"O'Mara told me about that," the Chalder said. "Is the work interesting?"

Neither of them, Cha Thrat felt sure, were saying the things they wanted to say.

"Very interesting," she replied. "I'm learning a lot about the inner workings of this place, and the Monitor Corps pays me, not very much, for doing it. When I've saved enough to take some leave on Chalderescol, I'll go and see how everything is with you."

"If you visited me, Cha Thrat," the AUGL broke in, "you would not be allowed to spend any of your hard-earned Monitor currency on Chalderescol. As you are a name-user and off-world member of my family, they would be deeply insulted, and would probably have you for lunch, if you tried."

"In that case," Cha Thrat said happily, "I shall probably visit you quite soon."

"If you don't swim clear, Technician," said an Earth-human in Transfer Team coveralls who had appeared beside her, "we'll seal you in the tank now, and you can damn well travel there with your friend!"

"Muromeshomon," she said quietly as the seal was closing, "may you fare well."

When she turned to go back to the unplanted vegetation, Cha Thrat's mind was concentrated on her Chalder friend to such an extent that she did not think of the impropriety of what she, a mere second-grade technician, said to the Earth-human Monitor Corps Major as she passed it.

"My congratulations, Chief Psychologist," she said gratefully, "on a most successfull spell."

O'Mara responded by opening its mouth, but not even an untranslatable sound came out.

The three days that followed were spent on the *Rhabwar* resupply job, bringing crew consumables and time-expired equipment to the largely Earth-human maintenance people charged with bringing the ambulance ship to peak operating efficiency, and occasionally assisting with the installation of some of the simpler items. On its next trip *Rhabwar* would be carrying Diagnostician Conway, a former leader of its medical team, and the present crew did not want it to find any cause for complaint.

On the fourth day, Timmins asked Cha Thrat to wait while the other assignments were given out.

"You seem to be very interested in our special ambulance ship," the Lieutenant said when they were alone. "I'm told that you've been climbing all over and through it, and mostly when it's empty and you are supposed to be off-duty. Is this so?"

"Yes, sir," Cha Thrat said enthusiastically. "It is a complex and beautifully functional vessel, judging by what I've heard and seen, and it is almost a miniature version of the hospital itself. The casualty treatment and other-species environmental arrangements are especially..." She broke off, to add warily, "I would not try to test or use any of this equipment without permission."

"I should hope not!" the Lieutenant said. "All right, then. I have another job for you, on *Rhabwar*, if you think you can do it. Come with me."

It was a small compartment that had been converted from a post-op recovery room, and it still retained its direct access to the ELNT Operating Theater. The ceiling had been lowered, which indicated that the occupant-to-be either crawled or did not stand very tall, and the plumbing and power supply lines, revealed by the incomplete wall paneling, bore the color codings for a warm-blooded oxygen-breather with normal gravity and atmospheric pressure requirements.

The wall panels that were in place had been finished to resemble rough planking with a strangely textured grain which resembled a mineral rather than wood. There was an untidy heap of decorative vegetation on the floor waiting to be hung, and beside it a large picture of a landscape that could have been taken in any forested lakeland on Sommaradva, if it had not been for subtle differences in the tree formations.

The framework and padding of a small, low-level bed was placed against the wall facing the entrance. But the most noticeable feature of the room, after she had blundered painfully against it, was the transparent wall that divided it in two. At one end of the wall there was a large door, outlined in red for visibility, and a smaller, central opening that contained remote handling and examination equipment capable of reaching across to the bed.

"This room is being prepared for a very special patient," Timmins said. "It is a Gogleskan, physiological classification FOKT, who is a personal friend of Diagnostician Conway. The patient, indeed its whole species, has serious problems about which you can brief yourself when you have more time. It is a gravid female nearing full term. There are psychological factors that require that it receives constant reassurance, and Conway is clearing his present workload during the next few weeks so that he will be free to travel to Goglesk, pick up the patient, and return with it to Sector General in plenty of time before the event takes place."

"I understand," Cha Thrat said.

"What I want you to do," Timmins went on, "is to set up a smaller and simpler version of this accommodation on *Rhabwar*'s casualty deck. You will draw the components from Stores and be given full assembly instructions. The work is slightly above your present technical level, but there is ample time for someone else to complete the job if you can't do it. Do you want to try?"

"Oh, yes," she said.

"Good," the Earth-human said. "Look closely at this place. Pay special attention to the attachment fittings of the transparent wall. Don't worry too much about the remote-controlled manipulators because the ship has its own. The patient restraints will have to be tested, but only under the supervision of one of the medical team who will be visiting you from time to time.

"Unlike this compartment," it went on, "your casualty deck facility will be in use only during the trip from Goglesk to the hospital, so the wall covering will be a plastic film, painted to represent the wood paneling here and applied to the ship's inner plating and bulkheads. This saves on installation time and, anyway, Captain Fletcher would not approve of us boring unnecessary holes in his ship. When you think you understand what you will be doing, collect the material from Stores and take it to the ship. I'll see you there before you go off-duty . . ."

"Why the transparent wall and remote handling equipment?" Cha Thrat asked quickly, as the Lieutenant turned to go. "An FOKT classification doesn't sound like a particularly large or dangerous life-form."

". . . To answer any questions not covered by your information tape," it ended firmly. "Enjoy yourself."

The days that followed were not particularly enjoyable except in retrospect. The tri-di drawings and assembly instructions gave her a permanent headache during the first day and night but, from then on, Timmins's visits to check on progress became less and less frequent. There were three visits from Charge Nurse Naydrad, the Kelgian member of the medical team who, Tarsedth informed her, was an expert in heavy rescue techniques.

Cha Thrat was polite without being subservient and Naydrad, in the manner of all Kelgians, was consistently rude. But it did not find fault with her work, and it answered any questions that it did not consider either irrelevant or stupid.

"I do not fully understand the reason for the transparent division in this compartment," she said during one of its visits. "The Lieutenant tells me it is for psychological reasons, so that the patient will feel protected. But surely it would feel more protected by an opaque wall and a small window. Is the FOKT in need of a wizard as well as an obstetrician?"

"A *wizard?*" said the Kelgian in surprise, then it went on. "Of course, you must be the ex-medical trainee they're all talking about who thinks O'Mara is a witch-doctor. Personally, I think you're right. But it isn't just the patient, Khone, who needs a wizard, it's the whole planetary population of Goglesk. Khone is a volunteer, a test case and a very brave or stupid FOKT."

"I still don't understand," Cha Thrat said. "Could you explain, please?"

"No," Naydrad replied. "I don't have the time to explain all the ramifications of the case, especially to a maintenance technician who has a morbid curiosity but no direct concern, or who feels lonely and wants to talk instead of work. Be glad you have no responsibility, this is a very tricky one.

"Anyway," it went on, pointing toward the viewer and reference shelves at the other side of the compartment, "our copy of the case-history tape runs for over two hours, if you're that interested. Just don't take it off the ship."

She continued working, in spite of a constant temptation to break off for a quick look at the FOKT tape, until the maintenance engineer who had been checking Control poked its Earth-human head into the casualty deck.

"Time for lunch," it said. "I'm going to the dining hall. Coming?"

"No, thank you," she replied. "There's something I have to do here."

"This is the second time in three days you've missed lunch," the Earth-human said. "Do Sommaradvans have some kind of crazy work ethic? Aren't you hungry, or is it just an understandable aversion to hospital food?"

"No, yes very, and sometimes," Cha Thrat said.

"I've a pack of sandwiches," it said. "Guaranteed nutritious, non-toxic to all oxy-breathers and if you don't look too closely at what's inside, you should be able to make them stay down. Interested?"

"Very much," Cha Thrat replied gratefully, thinking that now she would be able to satisfy her complaining stomach and spend the whole lunch period watching the FOKT tape.

The muted but insistent sound of the emergency siren brought her mind back from Goglesk and its peculiar problems to the realization that she had spent much longer than the stipulated lunch period watching the tape, and that the empty ship was rapidly filling with people.

She saw three Earth-humans in Monitor Corps green go past the casualty deck entrance, heading toward Control, and a few minutes later the lumpy green ball that was Danalta rolled onto the casualty deck. It was closely followed by an Earth-human, wearing whites with Pathology

Department insignia, who had to be the DBDG female, Murchison; then Naydrad and Prilicla entered, the Kelgian undulating rapidly along the deck and the insectile Cinrusskin empath using the ceiling. The Charge Nurse went straight to the viewer, which was still running the FOKT tape, and switched it off as two more Earth-humans came in.

One of them was Timmins and the other, judging by the uniform insignia and its air of authority, was the ship's ruler, Major Fletcher. It was the Lieutenant who spoke first.

"How long will it take you to finish here?" it said.

"The rest of today," Cha Thrat replied promptly, "and most of the night."

Fletcher shook its head.

"I could bring in more people, sir," Timmins said. "They would have to be briefed on the job, which would waste some time. But I'm sure I could shorten that to four, perhaps three hours."

The ship ruler shook its head again.

"There is only one alternative," the Lieutenant said.

For the first time Fletcher looked directly at Cha Thrat. It said, "The Lieutenant tells me that you are capable of completing and testing this facility yourself. Are you?"

"Yes," Cha Thrat said.

"Have you any objections to doing so during a three-day trip to Goglesk?"

"No," she said firmly.

The Earth-human looked up at Prilicla, the leader of the ship's medical team, not needing to speak.

"I feel no strong objections from my colleagues to this being accompanying us, friend Fletcher," the empath said, "since this is an emergency."

"In that case," Fletcher said as it turned to go, "we leave in fifteen minutes."

Timmins looked as if it wanted to say something, a word of caution, perhaps, or advice, or reassurance. Instead it held up a loosely clenched fist with the opposable thumb projecting vertically from it in a gesture she had not seen it make before, and then it, too, was gone. Cha Thrat heard the sound of its feet on the metal floor of the ship's boarding tube and, in spite of the four widely different life-forms closely surrounding her, suddenly she felt all alone.

"Don't worry, Cha Thrat," Prilicla said, the musical trills and clicks of its native speech backing the translated words. "You are among friends."

"There's a problem," Naydrad said. "No acceleration furniture to suit that stupid shape of yours. Lie down on a casualty litter and I'll strap you in."

CHAPTER 12

The FOKT facility was completed and thoroughly tested, first by Naydrad and then, on the orders of Major Fletcher, by *Rhabwar*'s engineer officer, Lieutenant Chen. That, apart from brief meetings on the way to or from the combination dining area and recreation deck, was her only direct contact with any of the ship's officers.

It was not that they tried to discourage such contact between the officer-ruler level and a being of the lowest technical rank, or that they deliberately tried to make her feel inferior. They did neither. But all Monitor Corps personnel who passed the very high technical and academic requirements for service on interstellar ships were automatically considered, at least to the status-conscious mind of a Sommaradvan, to be as close to ruler status as made no difference. Without meaning to give offense they kept slipping into a highly technical and esoteric language of their own, and they made her feel very uncomfortable.

In any case she felt more at home with the civilian medics than with the beings who, apart from a few small but significant badges on their collars, wore the same uniform as she did. As well, it was impossible to be in the same company as Prilicla without feeling very comfortable indeed. So she made herself as inconspicuous as her physiology would permit, reminded herself constantly that she now belonged to the maintenance rather than the medical fraternity, and tried very hard not to join in while the others were discussing the mission.

Goglesk had been a borderline case so far as the Cultural Contact people were concerned. Full contact with a technologically backward culture could be dangerous because, when the Monitor Corps ships dropped out of their skies, they could never be sure whether they were giving the natives evidence of a future technological goal at which they could aim or a destructive inferiority complex. But the Gogleskans, in spite of their backwardness in the physical sciences and the devastating racial psychosis that forced them to remain so, were psychologically stable, at least as individuals, and their planet had not known war for many thousands of years.

The easiest course would have been for the Corps to withdraw and leave the Gogleskan culture to continue as it had been doing since the dawn of its history, and write their problem off as insoluble. Instead they had made one of their very few compromises by setting up a small base for the purposes of observation, investigation, and limited contact.

Progress for any intelligent species depended on increasing levels of cooperation among its individuals and family or tribal groups. On Goglesk, however, any attempt at close cooperation brought drastically reduced intelligence, a mindless urge to destruction, and serious physical injury in its wake, so that the Gogleskans had been forced into becoming a race of individualists who had close physical contact only during the brief reproductive period or while caring for the very young.

The problem had come about as the result of a solution forced on them in presapient times. They had been a food source for every predator infesting their oceans, but they, too, had evolved natural weapons of offense and defense—stings that paralyzed or killed the smaller lifeforms and long cranial tendrils that gave them the faculty of telepathy by contact. When threatened by large predators they had linked bodies and minds together to the size required to neutralize any attacker with their combined stings.

There was fossil evidence on Goglesk of a titanic struggle for survival between them and a gigantic and particularly ferocius species of ocean predator, a battle that had raged for many, many thousands of years.

The FOKTs had won in the end, and had evolved into intelligent land-dwellers, but they had paid a terrible price.

In order to sting to death one of those giant predators, physical and telepathic link-ups of hundreds of individual FOKTs had been required. A great many of them had perished, been torn apart or eaten during every such encounter, and the consequent and oft-repeated death agonies of the slain had been shared telepathically by every single member of the groups. In an attempt to reduce their suffering, the effects of the group telepathy had been diluted by the generation of a mindless urge to destroy indiscriminately everything within reach. But even so, the mental scars inflicted during their prehistory had not healed.

Once heard, the audible signal emitted by Gogleskans in distress that triggered the process could not be ignored at either the conscious or unconscious levels, because that call to join represented only one thing—the threat of ultimate danger. And even in present times, when such threats were imaginary or insignificant, it made no difference. A joining led inevitably to the mindless destruction of everything in their immediate vicinity—housing, vehicles, mechanisms, books, or art objects—that they had been able to build or accomplish as individuals.

That was why the present-day Gogleskans would not allow, except on very rare occasions, anyone to touch or come close to them or even address them in anything but the most impersonal terms, while they fought helplessly and, until Conway's recent visit to the planet, hopelessly against the conditioning imposed on them by evolution.

It was plain to Cha Thrat that the only subjects that the medical team wanted to discuss were the Gogleskan problems in general and Khone in particular, and they talked about them endlessly and without arriving anywhere except back to where they had started. Several times she had wanted to make suggestions or ask questions, but found that if she kept quiet and waited patiently, a form of behavior that had always been foreign to her nature, the ideas and the questions were suggested and answered by one of the others.

Usually it was Naydrad who asked such questions, although much less politely than Cha Thrat would have done.

"Conway should be here," the Kelgian said, fur ruffling in disapproval. "It made a promise to the patient. There should be no excuses."

The yellow-pink face of Pathologist Murchison deepened in color. On the ceiling Prilicla's iridescent wings were quivering in response to the emotional radiation being generated below, but neither the empath nor the female Earth-human spoke.

"It is my understanding," Danalta said suddenly, moving the eye it had extruded to regard the Kelgian, "that Conway was successful in breaching the conditioning of just one Gogleskan, by an accidental, dangerous, and unprecedented joining of minds. For this reason the Diagnostician is the only other-species being who has any chance of approaching the patient closely, much less of touching it before or during the birth. Even though the call came much earlier than expected, there must be many others in the hospital who are capable and willing to take over the Diagnostician's workload for the few days necessary for the trip.

"I, too, think that Conway should have come with us," the shape-changer ended. "Khone is its friend, and it promised to do so."

While Danalta was speaking, Murchison's face had retained the deep-pink coloration except for patches of whiteness around its lips, and it was obvious from Prilicla's trembling that the Pathologist's emotional radiation was anything but pleasant for an empath.

"I agree with you," Murchison said in a tone that suggested otherwise "that nobody, not even the Diagnostician-in-Charge of Surgery, is indispensable. And I'm not defending him simply because he happens to be my life-mate. He can call for assistance from quite a few of the Senior Physicians who are capable of performing the work. But not quickly, not while surgery is actually in progress. And the briefings for his operating schedule would have taken time, two hours at least. The Goglesk call had the Most Urgent prefix. We had to leave at once, without him."

Danalta did not reply, but Naydrad's fur made discontented waves as the Kelgian said, "Is this the only excuse Conway gave you for breaking its promise to the patient? If so, it is unsatisfactory. We have all had experience with emergencies arising that necessitated people doing other people's work, without notice or detailed briefings. There is a lack of consideration being shown for its patient—"

"Which one?" Murchison asked angrily. "Khone or the being presently under his knife? And an emergency, in case you've forgotten, occurs spontaneously or because a situation is out of control. It should not be caused deliberately simply because someone feels honorbound to be somewhere else.

"In any case," it went on, "he was in surgery and did not have time to say more than a few words, which were that we should leave at once without him, and not worry about it."

"Then it is you who is making excuses for your life-mate's misbehavior . . ." Naydrad began when Prilicla, speaking for the first time, interrupted it.

"Please," it said gently, "I feel our friend Cha Thrat wanting to say something."

As a Senior Physician and leader of *Rhabwar's* medical team it would have been quite in order for Prilicla to tell them that their continued bickering was causing it discomfort, and that they should shut their speaking orifices forthwith. But she also knew that the little empath would never dream of doing any such thing, because the resultant feelings of embarrassment and guilt over the pain they had caused their inoffensive, well-loved, and emotion-sensitive team leader would have rendered it even more uncomfortable.

It was therefore in Prilicla's own selfish interests to give orders indirectly so as to minimize the generation of unpleasant feelings around it. If it felt her wanting to speak, it was probable that it could also feel that she, too, was wanting to reduce the current unpleasantness.

They were all staring at her, and Prilicla had ceased trembling. Plainly the emotion of curiosity was much less distressing than that which had gone before.

"I, too," Cha Thrat said, "have studied the Goglesk tape, and in particular the material on Khone—"

"Surely this is no concern of yours," Danalta broke in. "You are a maintenance person."

"A most inquisitive maintenance person," Naydrad said. "Let it speak."

"A maintenance person," she replied angrily, "should be inquisitive about the being for whose accommodation she is responsible!" Then she saw Prilicla begin to tremble again, and controlled her feelings as she went on. "It seems to me that you may be concerning yourselves needlessly. Diagnostician Conway did not speak to Pathologist Murchison as if it felt unduly concerned. What exactly did the message from Goglesk say about the condition of the patient?"

"Nothing," Murchison said. "We know nothing of the clinical picture. It isn't possible to send a lengthy message from a small, low-powered base like Goglesk. A lot of energy is needed to punch a signal through hyperspace so that—"

"Thank you," Cha Thrat said politely. "The technical problems were covered in one of my maintenance lectures. What did the message say?"

Murchison's face had deepened in color again as it said, "The exact wording was 'Attention, Conway, Sector General. Most Urgent. Khone requires ambulance ship soonest possible. Wainright, Goglesk Base.' "

For a moment Cha Thrat was silent, ordering her thoughts, then she said, "I am assuming that Healer Khone and its other-species friend have been keeping themselves informed regarding each other's progress. Probably they have been exchanging lengthier, more detailed and perhaps personal messages carried aboard the Monitor Corps courier vessels operating in this sector, which would avoid the obvious disadvantages of information transmitted through hyperspace."

Naydrad's fur was indicating that it was about to interrupt. She went on quickly. "From my study of the Gogleskan material, I am also assuming that Khone is, within the limits imposed by its conditioning, an unusually thoughtful and considerate being who would be unwilling to inconvenience its friends unnecessarily. Even if Conway had not mentioned the subject directly, Khone would already have learned from its sharing of the Earth-human's mind the full extent of the duties, responsibilities, and workload carried by a Diagnostician. And Conway, naturally, would be equally well informed about Khone's mind and its probable reaction to that knowledge.

"As the being who wished to be responsible for this patient," she continued, "the hyperspace signal was for Conway's attention. But it urgently requested an ambulance ship, not the presence of the Diagnostician.

"Conway knew why this was so," Cha Thrat went on, "because it also knew as much about Gogleskan pregnancies as Khone itself did, so it might be that the literal wording of the signal released Conway from the promise. Knowing that its patient required nothing more than fast transport to the hospital, the Diagnostician was not overly concerned, and it told you not to be concerned, either, by its absence.

"It may well be," she ended, "that the recent criticism of Diagnostician Conway's seemingly unethical behavior was without basis."

Naydrad turned toward Murchison and made the closest thing to an apology that a Kelgian could make as it said, "Cha Thrat is probably right, and I am stupid."

"Undoubtedly right," Danalta joined in. "I'm sorry, Pathologist. If I was in Earth-human form right now, my face would be red."

Murchison did not reply but continued to stare at Cha Thrat. The Pathologist's face had returned to its normal coloration, but otherwise displayed no expression that she could read. Prilicla drifted toward her until she could feel the slight, regular down-draft from its wings.

"Cha Thrat," the Cinrusskin said quietly, "I have a strong feeling that you have made a new friend . . ."

It broke off as the casualty deck's speaker came to life with the overamplified voice of Fletcher.

"Senior Physician, Control here." it said. "Hyperspace Jump complete and we are estimating the Goglesk orbiting maneuver in three hours, two minutes. The lander is powered up and ready to go, so you can transfer your medical gear as soon as convenient.

"We are in normal-space radio contact with Lieutenant Wainright," it went on, "who wants to talk to you about your patient, Khone."

"Thank you, Captain," Prilicla replied. "We want to talk about Khone as well. Please relay friend Wainright's message to the casualty deck here and to the lander bay when we move out. We can work as we talk."

"Will do," Fletcher said. "Relay complete. You are through to Senior Physician Prilicla, Lieutenant. Go ahead."

In spite of the distortion caused by the translation into Sommaradvan, Cha Thrat could detect the deep anxiety in Wainright's voice. She listened carefully with only part of her mind on the job of helping Naydrad load medical equipment onto the litter.

"I'm sorry, Doctor," it said, "the original arrangements for the pickup on our landing area will have to be scrapped. Khone isn't able to travel, and sending transport manned by off-planet people to collect it from its town will be tricky. At a time like this the natives are particularly, well, twitchy, and the arrival of visually horrifying alien monsters to carry it and its unborn child away could cause a joining and—"

"Friend Wainright," Prilicla interrupted gently, "what is the condition of the patient?"

"I don't know, Doctor," the Lieutenant replied. "When we met three days ago it told me that Junior would arrive very soon and would I please send for the ambulance ship. It also said that it had to make arrangements to have its patients cared for, and that it would come to the base shortly before the lander was due. Then a few hours ago a message was relayed verbally to the base saying that it could not move from its house, but the bearer of the message could not tell me whether the cause was illness or injury. Also, it asked if you had another power pack for the scanner Conway left with it. Khone has been impressing its patients with that particular marvel of Federation medical science and the energy cell is flat, which would explain why Khone was unable to give us any clinical information on its own present condition."

"I'm sure you are right, friend Wainright," Prilicla said. "However, the patient's sudden loss of mobility indicates a possibly serious condition that may be deteriorating. Can you suggest a method of getting it into the lander, quickly and with minimum risk to itself and its friends?"

"Frankly, no, Doctor," Wainright said. "This is going to be a maximum-risk job from the word go. If it was a member of any other species we know of, I could load it onto my flyer and bring it to you within a few minutes. But no Gogleskan, not even Healer Khone, could sit that close to an off-planet creature without emitting a distress call, and you know what would happen then."

"We do," Prilicla said, trembling at the thought of the widespread, self-inflicted property damage to the town and the mental anguish of the inhabitants that would ensue.

The Lieutenant went on. "Your best bet would be to ignore the base and land as close as possible to Khone's house, in a small clearing between it and the shore of an inland lake. I'll circle the area in a flyer and guide you down. Maybe we can devise something on the spot. You'll need some special remote handling devices to move it out, but I can help you with the external dimensions of Khone's house and doorways . . ."

While Cha Thrat helped the rest of the medical team move equipment into the lander, Wainright and the empath continued to wrestle with the problem. But it was obvious that they had no clear answers and were, instead, trying to provide for all eventualities.

"Cha Thrat," Prilicla said, breaking off its conversation with the base commander. "As a nonmember of the crew I cannot give you orders, but we'll need as many extra hands down there as we can assemble. You are particularly well equipped with manipulatory appendages, as well as an understanding of the devices used to move and temporarily accommodate the patient, and I feel in you a willingness to accompany us."

"Your feeling is correct," Cha Thrat said, knowing that the intensity of excitement and gratitude the other's words had generated made verbal thanks unnecessary.

"If we load any more gadgetry into the lander," Naydrad said, "there won't be enough space for the patient, much less a hulking great Sommaradvan."

But there was enough space inside the lander to take all of them, especially when those not wearing gravity compensators, which was everyone but Prilicla, were further compressed by the lander's savage deceleration. Lieutenant Dodds, *Rhabwar*'s astrogation officer and the lander's pilot, had been told that speed had priority over a comfortable ride, and it obeyed that particular order with enthusiasm. So fast and uncomfortable was the descent that Cha Thrat saw nothing of Goglesk until she stepped onto its surface.

For a few moments she thought that she was back on Sommaradva, standing in a grassy clearing beside the shore of a great inland lake and with the tree-shrouded outlines of a small, servile township in the middle distance. But the ground beneath her feet was not that of her home planet, and the grass, wildflowers, and all the vegetation around her were subtly different in color, odor, and leaf structure from their counterparts on Sommaradva. Even the distant trees, although looking incredibly similar to some of the lowland varieties at home, were the products of a completely different evolutionary background.

Sector General had seemed strange and shocking to her at first, but it had been a fabrication of metal, a gigantic artificial house. *This* was a different world!

"Is your species afflicted with sudden and inexplicable bouts of paralysis?" Naydrad asked. "Stop wasting time and bring out the litter."

She was guiding the powered litter down the unloading ramp when Wainright's flyer landed and rolled to a stop close beside them. The five Earth-humans who manned the Goglesk base jumped out. Four of them scattered quickly and began running toward the town, testing their translation and public address equipment as they went, while the Lieutenant came toward the lander.

"If you have anything to do that involves two or more of you working closely together," it said quickly, "do it now while the flyer is hiding you from view of the town. And when you move out, remain at least five meters apart. If these people see you moving closer together than that, or making actual bodily contact by touching limbs, it won't precipitate a joining, but it will cause them to feel deeply shocked and intensely uncomfortable. You must also—"

"Thank you, friend Wainright," Prilicla said gently. "We cannot be reminded too often to be careful."

The Lieutenant's features deepened in color, and it did not speak again until, walking i a well-separated line abreast, they were approaching the outskirts of the town.

"It doesn't look like much to us," Wainright said softly, the feelings behind its words making Prilicla tremble, "but they had to fight very hard every day of their lives to achieve it, and I think they're losing."

The town occupied a wide crescent of grass and stony outcroppings enclosing a small, natural harbor. There were several jetties projecting into deep water, and most of the craft tied up alongside had thin, high funnels and paddle wheels as well as sails. One of the boats, clearly the legacy of a past joining, was smoke-blackened and sunk at its moorings. Hugging the water's edge was a widely separated line of three- and four-story buildings, made of wood, stone, and dried clay. Ascending ramps running around all four walls gave access to the upper levels, so that from certain angles the buildings resembled thin pyramids.

These, according to the Goglesk tape, were the town's manufacturing and food-processing facilities, and she thought that the smell of Gogleskan raw fish was just as unpleasant as that of their Sommaradvan counterparts. Perhaps that was the reason why the private dwellings, whose roofs and main structural supports were provided by the trees around the edge of the clearing, were so far away from the harbor.

As they moved over the top of a small hill, Wainright pointed out a low, partially roofed structure with a stream running under it. From their elevated position they could see into the maze of corridors and tiny rooms that was the town's hospital and Khone's adjoining dwelling.

The Lieutenant began speaking quietly into its suit mike, and she could hear the words of warning and reassurance being relayed at full volume from the speakers carried by the four Earth-humans who had preceded them.

"Please do not be afraid," it was saying. "Despite the strange and frightening appearance of the beings you are seeing, they will not harm you. We are here to collect Healer Khone, at its own request, for treatment in our hospital. While we are transferring Khone to our vehicle we may have to come very close to the healer, and this may accidentally cause a call for joining to go out. A joining must not be allowed to happen, and so we urge everyone to move away from your homes, deep into the forest or far from the shore, so that a distress signal will not reach you. As an additional safeguard, we will place around the healer's home devices that will make a loud and continuous sound. This sound will be as unpleasant to you as it is to us, but it will merge with and change the sound of any nearby distress signal so that it will no longer be a call for joining."

Wainright looked toward Prilicla and when the empath signaled its approval, it changed to the personal suit frequency and went on. "Record and rerun that, please, until I either amend the message or tell you to stop."

"Will they believe all that?" Naydrad called suddenly from its position along the line. "Do they really trust us off-planet monsters?"

The Lieutenant moved several paces down the hill before replying. "They trust the Monitor Corps because we have been able to help them in various ways. Khone trusts Conway for obvious reasons and as their trusted healer, it has been able to convince the townspeople that Conway's horrifying friends are also worthy of trust. The trouble is, Gogleskans are a race of loners who don't always do as they're told.

"Some of them," it went on, "could have good reasons for not wanting to leave their homes. Illness or infirmity, young children to be cared for, or for reasons that seem good only to a Gogleskan. That's why we have to use the sound distorters."

Naydrad seemed satisfied but Cha Thrat was not. Out of consideration for Prilicla, who would suffer everyone else's feelings of anxiety as well as her own, she remained silent.

Like everyone else in Maintenance, she knew about those distorters. Suggested and designed by Ees-Tawn, the department's head of Unique

Technology, in response to one of Conway's long-term Gogleskan requirements, the devices were still in the prototype stage. If successful they would go into mass production until they were in every Gogleskan home, factory, and seagoing vessel. It was not expected that the devices would eliminate joinings entirely, but with sensitive audio detectors coupled to automatic actuators, it was hoped that the link-ups that did occur would be limited to a few persons. That would mean that a joining's destructive potential would be negligible, shorter in duration, and psychologically less damaging to the beings concerned.

Under laboratory conditions the distorters were effective against several FOKT distress call recordings provided by Conway, but the device had yet to be tested on Goglesk itself.

The stink of fish worsened, and the sound of the monitors broadcasting the Lieutenant's message grew louder as they neared the hospital. Apart from a few glimpses she had of the Earth-humans moving between the houses at the edge of the clearing, there were no signs of life in the town.

"Stop sending now," Wainright briskly said. "Anyone who hasn't acted on the message by now doesn't intend to. Harmon, take up the flyer and give me an aerial view of this area. The rest of you place the distorters around the hospital, then stand by. Cha Thrat, Naydrad, ready with the litter?"

Quickly, Cha Thrat positioned the vehicle close to the entrance of Khone's dwelling, ran out the rear ramp, and opened the canopy in readiness to receive the patient. They could not risk touching Khone within sight of other Gogleskans and were hoping that the little healer would come out and board the vehicle itself. In case it did not, Naydrad would send in its remote-controlled probe to find out why.

Because they would make conversation difficult—and so far nothing had happened that could cause any Gogleskan to emit a distress call—the distorters remained silent.

"Friend Khone," Prilicla said, and the waves of sympathy, reassurance, and friendship emanating from it were almost palpable. "We have come to help you. Please come out."

They waited for what seemed like a very long time, but there was neither sight nor sound of Khone.

"Naydrad . . ." Wainright began.

"I'm doing it," the Kelgian snapped.

The tiny vehicle, bristling with sound, vision, and biosensors as well as a comprehensive array of handling devices, rolled across the uneven surface and into Khone's front entrance, pushing aside the curtain of woven vegetable fibers that hung there. The view all around it was projected onto the litter's repeater screen.

Cha Thrat thought that the probe itself, to someone who did not know its purpose, was a frightening object. Then she reminded herself that Diagnostician Conway, and through it Khone, knew all about such mechanisms.

The probe revealed nothing but a deserted house.

"Perhaps friend Khone required special medication from the hospital and went to get it," Prilicla said worriedly. "But I cannot feel its emotional radiation, which means that it is either far from here or unconscious. If the latter, then it may require urgent attention, so we cannot afford to waste time by searching every room and passageway in the hospital with the probe. It will be quicker if I search for it myself."

Its iridescent wings were beating slowly, already moving it forward when it went on. "Move well back, please, so that your conscious feelings will not obscure the fainter, unconscious radiation of the patient."

"Wait!" the Lieutenant said urgently. "If you find it, and it awakens suddenly to see you hovering above it . . ."

"You are correct, friend Wainright," Prilicla said. "It might be frightened into sending out a distress call. Use your distorters."

Cha Thrat quickly moved back with the medical team beyond the range of maximum sensitivity for the Cinrusskin's empathic faculty, and they adjusted their headsets to deaden external sounds while enabling them to communicate with each other. As a screaming, moaning, whistling cacophony erupted from the distorter positions around the hospital, Cha Thrat wondered about the depth of unconsciousness of their patient. The noise was enough to wake the dead.

It was more than enough to rouse Khone.

CHAPTER 13

feel it!" Prilicla called, excitement causing its hovering flight to become wildly unstable. "Friend Naydrad, send in the probe. The patient is directly beneath me, but I don't want to risk frightening it by a sudden, close approach. Quickly, it is very weak and in pain."

Now that it had an accurate fix on Khone's position, Naydrad quickly guided the probe to the room occupied by the Gogleskan. Prilicla rejoined the others around the litter's repeater screen where the sensor data was already being displayed.

The pictures showed the interior of one of the hospital's tiny examination rooms with the figure of Khone lying against the low wall that separated the healer and patient during treatment. A small table contained a variety of very long-handled, highly polished wooden implements that appeared to be probes, dilators, and spatulas for the nonsurgical investigation of body orifices, some jars of local medication, and, incongruously, the lifeless x-ray scanner left by Conway. A few of the instruments had fallen to the floor, and it seemed likely that Khone had been examining a patient on the other side of the wall when the healer had collapsed. It was also probable that the patient concerned had originated the last message received by Wainright.

"I am Prilicla, friend Khone," the empath said via the probe's communicator. "Do not be afraid . . ."

Wainright made an untranslatable sound to remind Prilicla that, apart from the initial words of identification, Gogleskans did not address each other as persons and became mentally distressed if anyone tried to do so.

"This device will not cause pain or harm," Prilicla continued more impersonally. "Its purpose is to lift the patient, very gently, and convey it to a position where expert attention is available. It is beginning to do so now."

On the repeater screen Cha Thrat saw the probe extend two wide, flat plates and slide them between the floor and Khone's recumbent body.

"*Stop!*"

The two voices, Khone's through the communicator and Prilicla's in response to the Gogleskan's blast of emotional radiation, sounded as one. The empath's fragile body was shaking as if caught in a high wind.

"I'm sorry, friend Khone . . ." it began, then remembering, went on. "Sincere apologies are tendered for the severe discomfort caused to the patient. Even greater gentleness will be striven for in future. But is the patient-healer able to furnish information on the exact position of, and possible reasons for, the pain?"

"Yes and no," Khone said weakly. Its pain had diminished because Prilicla was no longer trembling. It went on. "The pain is located in the area of the birth canal. There is loss of function and diminished sensation in the lower limbs, and the upper limbs and the medial area are similarly but less markedly affected. The cardiac action is accelerated and respiration is difficult. It is thought that the birth process had begun and was interrupted, but the reason is unknown because the scanner has not worked for some time and it is doubted if the patient's digits retain sufficient dexterity to change the power cell."

"The probe mounts its own scanner," Prilicla said reassuringly, "and its visual and clinical findings will be transmitted to the healers out here. It will also change the power cell in the other scanner so that the patient will be able to aid the healers outside with its own Gogleskan observations and experience."

The empath began trembling again, but Cha Thrat had the feeling that the shaking was due to its personal concern for Khone rather than a return of the other's pain.

"The scanner is being deployed now," Prilicla went on. "It will approach closely but will not touch the patient."

"Thanks are expressed," Khone said.

As she watched the increasingly detailed scan of Khone's pelvic area, Cha Thrat grew more and more angry over her ignorance of Gogleskan physiology. And it made little difference that the degree of ignorance of Prilicla, Murchison, and Naydrad was only slightly less than her own. The one person with the ability to help Khone now was many light-years away in Sector General, and there was a strong probability that even the presence of the Diagnostician Conway would not have resolved this problem.

"The healer-patient can see for itself," Prilicla said gently, "that the fetus is large and is improperly presented to the birth canal. It is also pressing against the major nerve bundles and impeding the blood supply to the muscles in the area, making it impossible for the fetus to be expelled in its present position.

"Would the healer-patient agree," the empath went on, "that the birth cannot proceed without immediate surgical intervention?"

"No!" Khone said vehemently, forgetting to be impersonal. "You must not touch me!"

"But we're your ..." Prilicla began. It hesitated for an instant, then went on. "Only friends wishing to help the patient are here. The psychological difficulties are understood. If necessary the probe can be instructed to administer sedative medication so that the patient will be unconscious and unaware of being touched while the operation is in progress."

"No," Khone said again. "The patient must be conscious during and for a short period following the birth. There are things that the parent must do for the new-born. Can your mechanism be instructed to perform the operation? The patient would be less frightened by the touch of a machine than that of an off-world monster."

Prilicla trembled again with the emotional effort needed to make a negative reply. It said, "Regrettably not. The remote-controlled manipulators are not sufficiently accurate or responsive for such a delicate procedure. If an observation might be made, the patient is in a severely weakened state and may shortly become unconscious without the assistance of medication."

Khone was silent for a moment, then with a note of desperation in its voice the Gogleskan said, "It is consciously realized that the off-world healers feel friendship and deep concern for the patient. But subconsciously, on the darker, unthinking levels of the mind, the close approach of one of these visually horrifying creatures would represent an immediate and deadly threat to the life of the patient, which would inevitably lead to a call for joining."

"The call would not be heard," Prilicla said, and explained the purpose of the sound distorters. But Khone's reply set the empath trembling again.

"A call for joining," it said, "presupposes a condition of extreme mental distress that is followed by a massive and uncontrolled expenditure of physical energy. The effect on the patient and fetus could lead to termination."

Quickly Prilicla said, "Time is short and the clinical condition is deteriorating rapidly. Risks must be taken. The probe mechanism can be made to provide two-way vision, and pictures of the off-world friends will be sent. Will the patient choose from among them the least frightening being, who will then try to assist it?"

While the litter's vision pickup swung to cover each of them in turn, Khone was saying "The Earth-humans are familiar and trusted, as are the Cinrusskin and Kelgian seen during the earlier visit to Goglesk, but all of them would arouse blind, instinctive terror if they approached closely. The other two beings are unfamiliar, both to the recollection of the patient or in the memories of the Earth-human Conway. Are they healers?"

There was a note of relief in the empath's voice as it replied, "Both are recent arrivals at the hospital and were unknown to Conway at the time of its first visit. The small, globular being is Danalta, an entity capable of taking any required physical form including, if desirable, that of a Gogleskan, or of extruding any limbs or sensory organs necessary for the repair or alleviation of an organic malfunction. It will work under the Senior Physician's direction and is an ideal choice for—"

"*A shape-changer!*" Khone broke it. "Apologies are tendered to this entity, whose nonphysical qualities are doubtless admirable, but the thought of such a being is terrifying, and its close approach in the guise of one of my people would be unbearably repugnant. No!

"The tall creature," it added, "would be much less disturbing."

"The tall being," said Prilicla apologetically, "is a hospital maintenance technician."

"And previously," Cha Thrat added quietly, "a warrior-surgeon of Sommaradva, with other-species experience."

The empath was trembling again, and this time because of the storm of mixed feelings being generated by the other members of the medical team.

"Apologies are tendered," Prilicla said hastily. "A short delay is necessary. This matter requires discussion."

"For clinical reasons," Khone replied, "the patient-healer hopes that the delay will be very short."

It was Pathologist Murchison who spoke first. It said, "Your other-species experience is limited to an Earth-human DBDG and a Hudlar FROB, both involving simple, external surgery to a limb. Neither of them or, for that matter, your own DCNF classification, bears any resemblance to a Gogleskan FOKT. After that Hudlar limb-for-a-limb business, I'm surprised you want to take the responsibility."

"If this goes wrong," Naydrad joined in, its fur twitching with concern, "if the patient or newborn terminate, I don't know what piece of medical melodrama you will pull in atonement. Better keep out of this."

"I don't know why," Danalta said, in a tone that suggested that its feelings were hurt, "it prefers an ungainly, stiff-boned life-form like Cha Thrat to me."

"The reason," Khone said, making them realize that they had forgotten to switch off the probe's communicator, "is degrading and probably insulting to the being concerned, but it should be mentioned in case the Sommaradvan finds it necessary to withdraw its offer."

Khone went on. "There are physical, psychological, and perhaps ridiculous reasons why this being might closely approach, but not touch except with long-handled instruments, the patient."

There were few visual similarities between the FOKT and DCNF classifications, Khone explained, except in the eyes of very young Gogleskans who tried to make models of their parents. But the mass of hair covering the ovoid body, the four short, splayed-out legs, the digital clusters, and the four long, cranial stings, were beyond their sculptoring skill. Instead they produced lumpy, conical shapes made from mud and grass, into which they stuck twigs that were not always straight or of uniform thickness. The results, on a much smaller scale, had a distinct resemblance to the body configuration of a Sommaradvan.

These crudely fashioned models were fabricated during the years preceding the change from childhood to maturity, when the young adult's stings became a threat to its parent's life, and they were kept and treasured by both parent and offspring as reminders of the only times in their lives when they could feel in safety the warmth and closeness of extended contact with another of their kind.

It was a memory that, in their later and incredibly lonely adult lives, helped keep them sane.

Murchison was the first to react after Khone finished speaking. The Pathologist looked at Cha Thrat and said incredulously, "I think it is telling us that you look like an oversized Gogleskan equivalent of an Earth teddy bear!"

Wainright gave a nervous laugh, and the others did not react. Probably they were as ignorant about teddy bears as Cha Thrat was. However, if the creature resembled her in many ways, it could not be entirely unbeautiful.

"The Sommaradvan is willing to assist," Cha Thrat said, "and offense has not been taken."

"And neither," Prilicla said, turning its eyes toward her, "will responsibility be taken."

The musical trills and clickings that were the Cinrusskin's native speech changed in pitch, and for the first time in Cha Thrat's experience the little empath's translated words carried the firmness and authority of a ruler as it went on. "Unless the Sommaradvan can give an unqualified assurance that there is no possibility of a recurrence of the Hudlar amputation, the Sommaradvan will not be allowed to assist.

"The healer-maintenance technician is being used for one reason only," it continued, "because the close proximity of the more experienced healers is contraindicated for this patient. It will consider itself simply as an organic probe whose mind, sensors, and digits are under the direction of the Senior Physician, who accepts sole responsibility for treatment and subsequent fate of the patient. Is this clearly understood?"

The idea of sharing or, in this instance, completely relegating responsibility for her actions to another person was repugnant to a warrior-surgeon, even though she could understand the reasons for it. But stronger than her feeling of shame was the sudden, warm upsurge of gratitude and pride at once again being called to work as a healer.

"It is understood," she said.

Silently the empath indicated that it was changing from the probe frequency, so as not to be verbally hampered by having to use the listening Gogleskan's impersonal mode of speech.

"Thank you, Cha Thrat," it said quickly. "Use my Cinrusskin instruments, they are best suited to your upper digits and I would feel more comfortable directing you in their use. Fit the protective devices before trying to do anything else; you could not help the patient if you were to be paralyzed by its stings. When you are with Khone, make no sudden movements that might frighten it without first explaining the reason for them. I shall be monitoring friend Khone's emotional radiation from here, and will warn you if any action causes a sudden increase of fear. But you are well aware of the situation, Cha Thrat. Please hurry."

Naydrad had her carrier pack already filled and waiting. She added the replacement power cell for Khone's scanner and began climbing from the top of the litter on to the hospital roof.

"Good luck," Murchison said. Naydrad ruffled its fur and the others made untranslatable noises.

The roof sagged alarmingly under Cha Thrat's weight, and one of her forefeet went right through the flimsy structure, but it was a much quicker route than crawling through a maze of low-ceilinged corridors. She dropped into the uncovered passageway leading to Khone's room, crouched awkwardly onto two knees and three of her medial limbs, and, with Prilicla warning the patient of her arrival, moved only her head and shoulders through the entrance. For the first time she was able to study a Gogleskan FOKT at close quarters.

"The intention," Cha Thrat said carefully, "is not to touch the patient directly."

"Gratitude is expressed," Khone replied in a voice that was barely audible above the sound of the distorters.

The mass of unruly hair and spikes that covered the erect, ovoid body were less irregular in color and position than the probe pictures had suggested. The body hair had mobility, although not to the extent as that possessed by the Kelgians, and lying motionless amid the multicolored cranial fur were a number of long, pale tendrils that were used only during a joining to link the member minds of the group. Four small, vertical orifices, two for breathing and speaking and two for food ingestion, encircled its waist.

The spikes covering the body were highly flexible, grouped together into digital clusters, and were capable of fine manipulation, and the lower body was encircled by a thick apron of muscle, under which the four short legs could be withdrawn when the being wished to rest.

Now it lay on its side, a position from which even a fully fit and active Gogleskan would have difficulty in recovering.

Quietly Cha Thrat said, "Instruct the probe to bring the scanner here. When the power cell has been replaced, return it to within easy reach of the patient, then move the machine aside."

To Khone she went on. "Unlike the visiting healers, the patient has been unaware of its own condition and an immediate self-examination is requested. Since the patient is also a healer with extensive knowledge of its own life processes, any comments or suggestions it cares to make would be helped to the off-planet colleagues."

Prilicla's voice came from her earpiece but not the probe's speaker, which meant that the empath wanted to talk to her alone. It said, "That was well spoken, Cha Thrat. No patient, no matter how ill or injured, wants to feel completely useless and dependent. Otherwise well-intentioned healers sometimes forget that."

That was one of the first lessons she had learned at the medical school on Sommaradva. Another, which had obviously been learned by Prilicla, was that junior medics facing a new and difficult job benefited from encouragement."

"The patient," Khone said suddenly, "is unable to guide the scanner."

There was nothing in the Cinrusskin's instrument pack long enough to reach Khone from Cha Thrat's present position. Impersonally she asked, "Is it permitted to use the Gogleskan instruments?"

"Of course," Khone said.

On the side table there was a set of long, expanding tongs, made from highly polished wood and with hinges of a soft, reddish metal, used for bringing instruments or dressings to bear on the otherwise untouchable Gogleskan patients. Lying beside them was a thin, conical object that had been fashioned crudely from dried clay, with short twigs and straw stuck all over it. She had mistaken it at first for a piece of decorative or aromatic vegetation. Now that she knew what it was, Cha Thrat thought that its resemblance to the aesthetically pleasing Sommaradvan body shape was close only in the eyes of a very sick Gogleskan.

Awkwardly at first, she used the tongs to lift the scanner from the limp grasp of Khone's digits and moved it over the abdominal area. While the patient was concentrating on the screen, she edged further into the room and closer to the patient. The unnatural position of her bent forelegs and spine, and the fact that virtually her entire body weight was being supported on medial limbs normally used only for manipulation, was threatening to send the associated muscles into spasm. To ease them she rocked very slowly from side to side, moving a little closer each time.

"The Sommaradvan healer is larger than was expected," Khone said suddenly, looking up from the scanner. It did not take Prilicla to tell her that the Gogleskan was very frightened.

Cha Thrat held herself motionless for a moment, then said, "The Sommaradvan healer, despite its size, will no more harm the patient than the sculptured likeness lying on the floor. The patient must surely know this."

"The patient knows this," Khone agreed, with a distinct trace of anger in its voice. "But has the Sommaradvan healer ever suffered nightmares, in which it is haunted, and hunted, by dark and fearful creatures of the undermind intent on its destruction? And instead of fleeing in unreasoning fear, has it ever tried to stop in the midst of such a nightmare, and think through or around its terror, and turned to face these dreadful phantasms, and tried to look upon them as friends?"

Ashamed, Cha Thrat said, "Apologies are tendered, and admiration for the patient-healer who is trying to do, who is doing, that which the stupid and insensitive Sommaradvan healer would find impossible."

Prilicla's voice sounded in her earpiece. "You have irritated friend Khone, Cha Thrat, but its fear has receded a little."

She took the opportunity of moving closer and said, "It is realized that the patient-healer's intentions toward the Sommaradvan are friendly, and any harm that might befall it would be the result of a purely instinctive reaction or accident. Both eventualities can be avoided by rendering the stings harmless . . ."

Khone's emotional reaction to that suggestion had both Prilicla and Cha Thrat badly worried, but time was running out for this patient and, if anything was going to be done for it, there was no real alternative to capping those stings. The little Gogleskan knew that as well as they did. It was being asked to surrender its only remaining weapon.

Cha Thrat dared not move a muscle other than her larynx, and that one was being seriously overworked as she tried to convince Khone's unconscious as well as its already half-conscious conscious mind that, in a truly civilized society, weapons were unnecessary. She told it that she, too, was a female, although she had yet to produce an offspring. She spoke of her most personal feelings, many of them petty rather than praiseworthy, about her past life and career on Sommaradva and in Sector General, and of the things she had done wrong in both places.

The team members waiting impatiently by the litter must be wondering if she had contracted a ruler's disease and had lost contact with the reality of the situation, but there was no time to stop and explain. Somehow she had to get through to the Gogleskan's dark undermind and convince it that psychologically she was leaving herself as open and defenseless by what she was telling it as Khone was by relinquishing its only natural weapons.

She could hear Naydrad's voice, which was being picked up by the Cinrusskin's headset, demanding to know whether Khone was a psychiatrist as well as a healer, and if so, the stupid Sommaradvan had picked the wrong time to lie on its couch! Prilicla did not speak and she went on talking unhurriedly to the patient whose voice, like the rest of it, seemed to be paralyzed by fear.

Suddenly there was a response.

"The Sommaradvan has problems," Khone said. "But if intelligent beings did not occasionally do stupid things, there would be no progress at all."

Cha Thrat was unsure whether the Gogleskan's words represented some deep, philosophical truth or were merely the product of a mind clouded by pain and confusion. She said, "The problems of the healer-patient are much more urgent."

"There is agreement," Khone said. "Very well, the stings may be covered. But the patient must be touched only by the machine."

Cha Thrat sighed. It had been too much to hope that a few highly personal revelations would demolish the conditioning of millennia. Without moving any closer, she held the scanner in position with the long tongs and used the rear medial limb to open her pack so that the probe's manipulators, which were being guided with great precision by Naydrad, could extract the sting covers.

Those covers had been designed to contain the needle-pointed stings and absorb their venom. Once in position, they released an adhesive that would ensure that they remained so until Khone reached Sector General. This property of the covers had not been mentioned to the patient. But with the distorters making it impossible for any call for joining to be heard by the other townspeople and its stings rendered impotent, the Gogleskan would be unable to avoid direct physical contact with one of the frightful off-worlders.

Considering the rapidly worsening clinical picture, the sooner that happened the better.

But Khone was not stupid and probably it had already realized what was to happen, which would explain its growing agitation as two, then three of the four sting covers were placed in position. Now it was moving its head weakly from side to side, deliberately avoiding the last cover. Quickly Cha Thrat tried to give it something else to think about.

"As can be clearly observed in the scanner and bio-sensor displays," she said impersonally, "the fetus is being presented laterally to the birth canal and is immobilized in this position. It has exerted pressure on important blood vessels and nerve connections to the parent's mid- and lower body, which has resulted in loss of muscle function and sensation and, unless relieved, will lead to necrosis in the areas concerned. The umbilical is also being increasingly compressed as the involuntary muscles continue trying to expel the fetus. The fetal heartbeat is weak, rapid, and irregular, and the vital signs of the parent are not good, either. Has the patient-healer any suggestion or comments on this case?"

Khone did not reply.

Only Prilicla would know how much Cha Thrat's coldly impersonal tone belied her true feelings toward the incredibly brave little creature who lay like a tumbled haystack so close to her, but still too far away in the non material distances of the mind for her to be able to help it. Yet they were alike in so many ways, she thought. Both had taken risks that no other members of their species were willing to take—she had treated an off-world life-form she had never seen before, and Khone had volunteered itself for treatment by off-worlders. But of the two, Khone was the braver and its risks the greater.

"Is this condition rare or common among gravid females," she asked quietly, "and what is the normal procedure in such cases?"

The other's voice was so weak that the reply was barely audible as it said, "The condition is not rare. Normal procedure in such cases is to administer massive doses of medication that enables the patient and fetus to terminate with minimum discomfort."

Cha Thrat could think of nothing to say or do.

In the stillness of Khone's room she became increasingly aware of the external noises: the constant whistling and hissing of the distorters; and coming to her through the empath's communicator, the voice of Naydrad complaining about the difficulty of capping the stings of a patient who would not cooperate; and more quietly, Murchison, Danalta, and Prilicla itself as they suggested and quickly discarded a number of wildly differing procedures.

"The medical team's voices are unclear," Cha Thrat said anxiously. "Has anything been decided? What are the immediate instructions?"

Suddenly the voices became loud and very clear indeed, because they were coming from the probe's speaker as well as her own earpiece. Naydrad, its attention concentrated on the probe's remote-controlled manipulators as it tried to fit the last sting cover, must have decided that she wanted more volume and reacted to her statement without thinking.

The conversation was completely unguarded.

Prilicla was speaking, quietly and reassuringly, and clearly unaware that its words were reaching Khone as well as herself, Cha Thrat realized. The intense and conflicting emotional radiation emanating from the other team members grouped so closely around it was keeping the empath from detecting her own sudden burst of surprise and fear.

"Cha Thrat," it said, "there has been some argument, which has since been resolved in your favor, regarding who should perform the operation. Friend Khone's need is urgent, its condition has deteriorated to the stage where the risk of moving it out for surgery is unacceptable, and your only option is to—"

"No!" she said urgently. "Please stop *talking!*"

"Do not be distressed, Cha Thrat," the empath continued, mistaking the reason for the objection. "Your professional competence is not in doubt, and Pathologist Murchison and myself have studied Conway's notes on the FOKT life-form, as have you, and we will guide you at every stage of the procedure and take complete responsibility throughout.

"Immediate surgical intervention is required to relieve this condition," it went on. "As soon as the last sting is capped, you will use a Number Eight scalpel to enlarge the birth opening with an incision from the pelvis up to the—What is happening?"

There was no need to tell it what was happening because in the time taken to ask the question it already knew the answer. Khone, faced with the imminent prospect of a major surgical attack, had reacted instinctively by emitting the call for joining and was trying to sting to death the only strange, and therefore threatening, being within reach. With its legs virtually paralyzed, Khone was twisting violently from side to side and using its digital clusters to pull itself toward Cha Thrat.

The remaining uncapped sting, long, yellow, and with tiny drops of venom already oozing from its point, was swaying and jerking closer. Frantically Cha Thrat pushed backward with the forefeet and medial limbs, launching herself toward the Gogleskan and grasping the base of the sting with three of her upper hands.

"Stop it!" she shouted above the noise of the call. Forgetting to be impersonal, she went on. "Stop moving or you'll injure yourself and the young one. I'm a friend, I want to help you. Naydrad, cap it! Cap it quickly!"

"Hold it still, then," the Kelgian snapped back, swinging the probe's manipulator arm above Khone's jerking head. "Hold it very still."

But that was not easy to do. Her upper, neck-level arms and digits had been evolved for more precise and delicate operations and lacked the heavy musculature of the medial limbs, and using them meant that Khone's head and her own were almost touching. She strained desperately to tighten her ridiculously weak grip on the sting, sending waves of pain into her neck and upper thorax. She knew that if those fingers slipped the sting would immediately be plunged into the top of her head.

The medical team would probably get to her quickly enough to save her life, but not those of Khone and the fetus, which was their only reason for being here. She was wondering how Murchison, the Diagnostician's life-mate; and Prilicla, its long-term friend; and Cha Thrat herself would face Conway with the news of Khone's death when Naydrad shouted, "Got it!"

The last sting was covered. She could relax for a moment. But not Khone, who was still jerking and writhing on the floor and stabbing ineffectually at her with all four of its capped stings. Close up, the sound of its distress call was like a gale whistling and howling through a ruined building.

"At least the distorters are working," Wainright said, and added warningly, "but hurry it up, they won't last much longer."

She ignored the Earth-human and grasped tufts of the Gogleskan's hair in her upper and medial hands, trying vainly to hold it motionless. Pleadingly she said, "Stop moving. You're wasting what little strength you've got. You'll die and the baby will die. Please stop moving. I'm not an enemy, I'm your *friend*!"

The call for joining was still howling out with undiminished volume, making her wonder how such a small creature could make so great a noise, but its physical movements were becoming noticeably less violent. Was it a symptom of sheer physical weakness, or was she getting through to the Gogleskan? Then she saw that the long, pale tendrils on its head were uncurling from the concealing hair and were standing out straight. Two of them fell slowly to lie along the top of her own head, and suddenly Cha Thrat wanted to scream.

Being Khone's friend was much, much worse than being its enemy.

CHAPTER 14

There was fear as she had never known it before—the sudden, overriding, and senseless fear of everything and everyone that was not joined tightly to her for the group defense; and a terrible, blind fury that diminished the fear; and the memories and expectation of pains past, present, and to come. And with those fearful memories there came a dreadful and confused nightmare of all the frightful and painful things that had ever happened to her—on Sommaradva and Goglesk and in Sector General. Many elements of the nightmare were utterly strange to her; the feeling of terror at the sight of Prilicla, which was ridiculous, and the sense of loss at the departure of the male Gogleskan who had fathered the child within her. But now there was no fear of the outsized, off-world animated doll who was trying to help her.

Even with the confusion of fear, pain, and alien experiences dulling her capacity to think, the conclusion was inescapable. Khone had invaded her mind.

Now she *knew* what it was like to be a Gogleskan; at a time like this the choice was simple. Friends joined and enemies—everyone and everything that was not part of the group—were attacked and destroyed. She wanted to break everything in the room, the furniture, instruments, decorations, and then tear down the flimsy walls, and she wanted to drag Khone around with her to help her do it. Desperately she tried to control the blind and utterly alien fury that was building up in her.

Amid the storm of Gogleskan impressions a tiny part of her own mind surfaced for a moment, observing that the tight grip she retained on Khone's fur must have fooled its subconscious into believing that she had joined with it, and was therefore a friend worthy of mind-sharing.

I am Cha Thrat, she told herself fiercely, *once a Sommaradvan warrior-surgeon and now a trainee maintenance technician of Sector General. I am not Khone of Goglesk and I am not here to join and destroy . . .*

But this was a joining, and memories of a larger, more destructive joining came crowding into her mind.

She seemed to be standing on top of a land vehicle stopped on high ground overlooking the town, watching the joining as it happened. The Earth-human Wainright was beside her, warning her that the Gogleskans were dangerously close, that they should leave, that there was nothing she could do and, for some strange reason, while it was saying these things it sometimes called "Doctor" but more often "sir." She felt very bad because she knew that the joining had been her fault, that it had happened because she had tried to help, and had touched, an industrial accident casualty. Below her she could clearly see Khone attaching itself to the other Gogleskans without being able to understand the reason, and at the same time she *was* Khone and knew the reason.

With individual Gogleskans hurrying to join it from nearby buildings, moored ships, and surrounding tree dwellings, the group-entity became a great, mobile, stinging carpet that crawled around large buildings and engulfed small ones as if it did not know or care what it was doing. In its wake it left a trail of smashed equipment, vehicles, dead animals, and a capsized ship. The group-entity moved inland to continue its self-destructive defense against an enemy out of prehistory.

In spite of the terrible fear of that nonexistent enemy in Khone's mind, which was now her mind, Cha Thrat tried to make herself think logically about what had happened to her. She thought of the wizard O'Mara and how it had said that Educator tapes would never be for her, and remembered the reasons it had given. Now she knew what it was like to have a completely alien entity occupying her mind, and she wondered if her sanity would be affected. Perhaps the fact that Khone, like herself, was a female might make a difference.

But there was a growing realization that it was not only Khone's mind and memories that she had to contend with. The memory and viewpoint from the top of the land vehicle was not from the Gogleskan's mind, nor her own. There were memories of the ambulance ship and the exploits of its medical team that were definitely not her own, and some vivid and—to her—fearful and wonderful recollections of events in Sector General that were totally outside her experience. Had O'Mara been right? Were factual recollections and insane fantasies intermingling, and she was no longer sane?

But she did not think she was insane. Madness was supposed to be an escape from a too-painful reality to a condition that was more bearable. There was too much pain here and the memories or fantasies were too painfully sharp. And one of them was of Lieutenant Wainright standing beside her, its head on a level with hers, and calling her "sir."

With a sudden shiver of fear and wonder she realized what was happening. She was sharing Khone's mind, and Khone had earlier shared it with someone else.

Conway!

For some time Cha Thrat had been aware of Prilicla's voice in her earpiece, but the words were just sounds without meaning to her already overloaded mind. Then she felt its warmth and sympathy and reassurance all around her, and the pain and confusion receded a little so that the meaning came through.

"Cha Thrat, my friend," the empath was saying, "please respond. You have been holding onto the patient's fur for the past few minutes, not doing anything and not answering us. I am on the roof directly above you, and your emotional radiation distresses me. Please, what is wrong? Have you been stung?"

"N-no," she replied shakily, "there is no physical damage. I feel badly confused and frightened, and the patient is—"

"I can read your feelings, Cha Thrat," Prilicla said gently, "but not the reason for them. There is nothing to be ashamed of, you've already done more than could be reasonably expected of you, and it was unfair of us to let you volunteer for this operation in the first place. We are in danger of losing the patient. Please withdraw and let me perform the surgery—"

"No," Cha Thrat said, feeling Khone's body twitch in her hands. The long, silvery tendrils that were the organic conductors for the uniquely Gogleskan form of telepathy-by-wire were still lying across her head, and anything Cha Thrat felt or heard or thought was immediately available to Khone, who did not like the idea of an alien monster operating on it, for reasons that were both personal and medical. Cha Thrat added, "Please give me a moment. I'm beginning to regain control of my mind."

"You are," Prilicla said, "but hurry."

Incredibly, it was her mind-partner who was doing most to aid the process. In common with the rest of its long-suffering and nightmare-ridden species, it had learned how to control and compartmentalize its thinking, feelings, and natural urges so that the enforced loneliness necessary to avoid a joining was not only bearable but, at times, happy. And now the Conway-memories of Sector General and some of its monstrous patients were surging into the forefront of her mind.

Be selective, Khone was telling her. *Use only what is useful.*

All the memories and experience of a Sommaradvan warrior-surgeon, a Gogleskan healer, and half an Earth-human lifetime spent in Sector General were hers, and with that vast quantity of other-species medical and physiological expertise available she could not believe that, even at this late stage, the Khone case was hopeless. Then from somewhere in that vast and incredibly varied store of knowledge, the glimmerings of an idea began to take shape.

"I no longer feel that surgical intervention is the answer," she said firmly, "even as a last resort. It is unlikely that the patient would survive."

"Who the blazes does it think it is?" Murchison said angrily. "Who's in charge of this op, anyway? Prilicla, pin its ears back!"

Cha Thrat could have answered both questions, but did not. She knew that her words and tone had been wrong for someone in her lowly position—she sounded much too self-assured and authoritative. But there was no time for either long explanations or pretensions of humility, and it would be better if the true explanation was never given. With any luck Pathologist Murchison would believe, and go on believing, that Cha Thrat was a self-opinionated maintenance technician and one-time trainee nurse with delusions of grandeur and, for the time being at least, the team leader was leaving her ears unpinned.

"Explain," Prilicla said.

Quickly Cha Thrat reviewed the current clinical picture, gravely worsened now by the extreme debilitation that, even in a healthy Gogleskan, followed a joining. When she said that Khone lacked the strength and physical resources to withstand major surgery—it would have to be a cesarean procedure rather than a simple enlargement of the birth opening—she spoke with absolute certainty because she had the patient-healer's viewpoint of the case as well as her own. But she did not mention that, saying instead that Khone's emotional radiation would confirm her observations.

"It does," the empath said.

She went on quickly. "The FOKT classification is one of the few life-forms capable of resting in the upright position, although they can also lie down. Since their ancestors emerged from the oceans, their bodies and internal organs have been acted on by vertical G forces, as are those of the Hudlars and Tralthans and Rhenithi. I am reminded of a case in Tralthan Maternity a few years ago that was broadly similar to this one and required—"

"You didn't learn *that* from Cresk-Sar," Murchison broke in suddenly. "Trainee nurses aren't told about the near-failures, at least not in first year."

"I liked to study odd cases outside the syllabus," Cha Thrat lied smoothly, "and I still do, when I'm not engrossed in a maintenance manual."

Her emotional radiation would tell the Cinrusskin that she was lying, but it could only guess at what she was lying about. All it said was "Describe your procedure."

"Before I do," she went on quickly, "please remove the canopy from the litter and reposition the gravity grids to act laterally in opposite directions. Set the body restraints to the size and weight of the patient under anything up to an alternating plus and minus three Gs. Move the probe into the passageway, so I can step from it onto the roof. Hurry, please. I'm bringing out the patient now and will explain on the way . . ."

Cradling the barely conscious Khone in two medial arms and with all of her free hands gripping its fur tightly to make it feel that it was still joined to a friend, she climbed awkwardly onto the roof and sidled back the way she had come. Prilicla hovered anxiously above her all the way, Naydrad complained bitterly that its litter would never be the same again, and Murchison reminded it that they had a maintenance technician, or something, with them.

She continued to grip the Gogleskan's fur while Naydrad expertly fitted the restraints and Murchison attached an oxygen supply to all breathing orifices. With her head touching Khone's and the long, silvery tendrils still making contact, she checked that the other had a clear view of the scanner display, which she in her present awkward position did not, then braced herself and gave the signal to begin.

Cha Thrat felt her head and upper limbs being pulled sideways as Naydrad fed power to the gravity grid positioned above the patient's head. It was difficult to keep her balance because her lower body and legs were out side the influence of the artificial gravity field. But so far as Khone was concerned, it was tied upside-down to the litter under double, increasing to treble and Gogleskan standard gravity pull.

"Heart rate irregular," Prilicla reported quietly. "Blood pressure increasing in the upper body and head, respiration labored, minor displacement of thoracic organs, but the fetus hasn't moved."

"Shall I increase the pull to four Gs?" Naydrad asked, looking at Prilicla. But it was Cha Thrat who replied.

"No," she said. "Give it two Gs alternating as rapidly as possible between normal and reverse pull. You've got to try to shake Junior loose."

Now she was being knocked from side to side, as if by the soft, invisible paws of some great beast, while the patient was suffering the same maltreatment in the vertical plane. She managed to keep her head and the hands gripping Khone's fur steady, but she was feeling a growing nausea that reminded her of childhood bouts of travel sickness.

"Friend Cha Thrat, are you all right?" Prilicla asked. "Do you wish to stop?"

"Can we spare the time?"

"No," the empath replied, then: "The fetus is moving! It is—"

"Reverse, two Gs steady," Cha Thrat said quickly, effectively standing Khone on its head again.

"—now pressing against the upper womb," Prilicla continued. "The umbilical is no longer being compressed, and pressure on the blood vessels and nerve linkages in the area has been relieved. The muscles are beginning rapid, involuntary contractions..."

"Enough to expel the fetus?" she broke in.

"No," it replied. "They are too weak to complete the birth process. In any case the fetus is still not in the optimum position."

Cha Thrat used a swear word that was definitely not Sommaradvan, and said, "Can we reposition and refocus the gravity grids so as to pull the fetus into the proper position for—"

"I would need time to—" Naydrad began.

"There isn't any time," said Prilicla. "I'm surprised friend Khone is still with us."

This was not going nearly as well as the remembered case in the Tralthan maternity ward had gone, and there was no consolation in telling herself that, in this instance, the life-form was strange and the operating facilities virtually non-existent. Khone's mind was no longer sending or receiving impressions, so that she could not even make the Last Apology to it for her failure.

"Please do not distress yourself, friend Cha," the Cinrusskin went on, beginning to tremble violently. "No blame can be attached to you for attempting a task that, because of the peculiar circumstances, none of us were able to do. Your present emotional radiation is worrying me. Remember, you aren't even a member of the medical team, you have no authority, and the responsibility for allowing you to try this procedure is not yours . . . You have just thought of something?"

"We both know," Cha Thrat said, so quietly that her voice reached only Prilicla, "that I have made it my responsibility. And yes, I've thought of something."

In a louder voice she went on quickly. "Naydrad, we need a rapid one-G push-pull this time, just enough to keep the fetus moving. Danalta, the muscle wall around the womb is thin, and relaxed due to the patient's unconsciousness. Will you produce some suitable limbs and hands? Prilicla will tell you the size and shape needed, and use the scanner to direct your movements of the fetus into the proper position. Murchison, will you stand by to help withdraw it, if or when it is born?"

Apologetically she added, "I cannot assist you. For the time being it would be better if I retained the closest possible physical contact with the patient. My feeling is that, unconscious or not, it will derive a greater measure of emotional comfort from my doing so."

"Your feeling is correct," Prilicla said. "But time is short, friends. Let's do it."

While Naydrad kept the fetus twitching slowly within the womb, and Danalta, using appendages whose shape and movements would give Cha Thrat bad dreams for many nights to come, tried to press and turn it into optimum position, she tried desperately to get through to her deeply unconscious mind-partner.

You will be all right. Your child will be all right. Hang on, please don't die on me!

It was like thinking into a black and bottomless pit. For an instant she thought there was a flicker of awareness, but it was probably that the feeling had come because she wanted it to be so. She turned her head slightly, so as not to break contact with the long, silvery tendrils, and wished that she was in a position to see the scanner display.

"It's in optimum position now," Prilicla said suddenly. "Danalta, move your hands lower. Be ready to press when I tell you if the fetus starts turning again. Naydrad, two Gs steady, down!"

For a moment there was silence except for the whistling of the distorters, which now seemed to be wavering in intensity as they labored like the patient, on reduced power, to perform their function. Time was running out for both of them. Everyone's attention was on Khone, and even Prilicla was watching the scanner display too intently to describe what it was seeing.

"I see the head!" Murchison said suddenly. "The top of the head only. But the contractions are too weak, they aren't helping very much. The legs are at maximum spread, but the fetal head is moving down, then back again, by a fraction of an inch with each contraction. Shall I try surgical enlargement of the—"

"No surgery," Cha Thrat said firmly. Even if the patient survived it, she had shared Khone's mind and knew that serious psychological damage would result from the inflicting of a surgical wound—not to mention the aftermath when close physical contact would be necessary to provide treatment and change dressings—on one whose species was virtually untouchable. The brief physical and mental contact with Conway and Cha Thrat had knocked a large hole in Khone's Gogleskan conditioning, but psychologically it was still a strong and very rigid structure.

But there was no time to explain her feeling or argue her point of view. Murchison had straightened up and was looking questioningly at Prilicla, who shook in the emotional winds blowing from all sides but said nothing.

"It would be better if we tried to assist the natural process," Cha Thrat went on. "Naydrad, I want alternating positive and reverse gravity again, this time between zero and three Gs down, initially for the next five contractions. And watch out for major displacement of other organs. This species has never been subjected to increased G forces—"

"I see the whole head now!" Murchison broke in excitedly. "And shoulders. Dammit, I've *got* the wee bugger!"

"Naydrad," Cha Thrat said quickly, "maintain three Gs down for a moment until the afterbirth is out, then return to normal gravity conditions. Murchison, place the newborn between the digital clusters just to the left of my head. My feeling is that Khone will derive greater reassurance from holding on to its little one than from me holding on to its parent."

She watched as Khone's digits curled instinctively around the tiny form, which looked to the Sommaradvan part of her mind like a slimy, twitching little horror and which the Gogleskan portion insisted was a thing of indescribable beauty. Reluctantly she lifted her head from Khone's and released her grip on its fur.

"Your feeling is accurate, Cha Thrat," Prilicla said, "The patient, although still unconscious, is already emoting more strongly."

"But wait," Murchison said worriedly. "We were told that it must be conscious if it was to take care of the newborn properly. We've no idea what . . ."

She broke off because Cha Thrat, who now knew everything that the Gogleskan healer had known, was busily doing all that was necessary. It was contrary to her Sommaradvan upbringing to tell a deliberate lie, but the situation was fraught with all sorts of interpersonal difficulties and was too complicated for her to take the time needed to tell the truth.

Instead, Cha Thrat waited until the umbilical had been neatly severed and sealed off and the patient's lower limbs disposed more comfortably, then said smoothly, "There are a number of physiological similarities between the FOKT life-form and my own and, in any case, we females have certain instincts in these matters."

The Earth-human shook its head doubtfully and said, "Your female instincts are a lot stronger, and more precisely directed, than mine."

"Friend Murchison," Prilicla said, its voice sounding loud because all but two of the distorters had ceased their whistling, "let us discuss female instincts at a more convenient time. Friend Naydrad, replace the litter canopy, turn up the internal heating three points, and maintain a pure oxygen atmosphere and watch out for signs of delayed shock. The emotional radiation indicates a condition of grave debility, but it is stable, there is no immediate danger, and circulation and mobility are returning to the lower limbs. We will all feel better, and especially the patient, when it has the ship's intensive-care equipment looking after it. Please move quickly.

"All except Cha Thrat," it added gently. "With you, my Sommaradvan friend, I would like private words."

Driven by Naydrad and with Danalta and Wainright flanking it, the litter was already moving off. But Pathologist Murchison was hanging back, its face deep pink and wearing an expression that Cha Thrat could now read and understand.

"Don't be *too* hard on it, Prilicla," Murchison said. "I think it did a very good job, even if it is inclined to forget who's in charge at times. I mean, well, let's just say that with Cha Thrat, Maintenance Department's gain was the medical staff's loss."

As Murchison turned abruptly to hurry after the litter, Cha Thrat watched it from three different and confusing viewpoints and with three sets of very mixed feelings. To her Sommaradvan mind it was a small, flabby, and unlovely DBDG female. To the Gogleskan mind it was just another off-planet monster, friendly but frightening. But from her Earth-human viewpoint it was an altogether different entity, one that for many years she had known to be highly intelligent, second only to Thornnastor in its professional standing, friendly, sympathetic, fair-minded, beautiful, and sexually desirable. Some of these aspects of its personality had just been demonstrated, but the sudden physical attraction Cha Thrat felt toward it, and the associated mind-pictures of horrible alien grapplings and intimacies, frightened her so badly that the Gogleskan part of her mind wanted to call for a joining.

Murchison was a female Earth-human and Cha Thrat was a female Sommaradvan. She *had* to stop feeling this stupid attraction toward a member of another species who was not even male, because in that direction lay certain madness. She remembered the discussion about Educator tapes with the wizard, O'Mara, and her own experience of sharing her mind with those of Kelgians, Tralthans, Melfans among others.

But that was not *her* experience, she reminded herself firmly. She was and would remain Cha Thrat. The Gogleskan and Earth-human who seemed to be occupying her mind were guests, one of them a particularly troublesome guest where thoughts of the entity Murchison were concerned, but they should not be allowed to influence her personal feelings. It was ridiculous to think, or feel, otherwise.

When the disturbing figure of Murchison had disappeared into the middle distance and Cha Thrat was feeling more like herself than two other people, she said, "And now, I suppose, comes the pinning back of the ears of a big-headed and grossly insubordinate technician with delusions of medical grandeur?"

Prilicla had alighted on the roof above Khone's doorway so that its eyes would be on a level with Cha Thrat's. It said gently, "Your emotional control is excellent, friend Cha. I compliment you. But your supposition is wrong. However, your obvious understanding of the Earth-human terms you have just used, and your earlier behavior during a very tricky clinical situation, leads me to speculate about what might possibly have happened to you.

"I am merely thinking aloud, you understand," it went on. "You are not required, in fact you are expressly forbidden to say whether my speculations are accurate or not. In this matter I would prefer to remain officially ignorant."

It was evident from the first few words that the empath knew exactly what had happened to Cha Thrat, even though its certainties were mentioned as suspicions. It suspected that Cha Thrat had shared minds with Khone, that the Gogleskan's mind had previously been shared with that of Conway, and it was the Diagnostician's medical expertise and initiative that had surfaced before and during the birth of Khone's child. For this reason the Cinrusskin was not offended by the incident—a Senior Physician was far outranked by a Diagnostician, even one who was temporarily in residence within the mind of a subordinate. And neither would the other team members feel offended if they were to suspect the truth.

But they must not suspect, at least until Cha Thrat was safely lost in the maintenance tunnels of Sector General.

"From your recent emotional radiation," Prilicla went on, "I suspect that you had strong if confused feelings of a sexual nature toward friend Murchison that were not pleasant for your Sommaradvan self. But consider the intensity of Murchison's embarrassment if it suspected that you, an entity of a completely different physiological classification forced by circumstances to work in close proximity with it, were regarding it with the eyes and the same strength of feeling as that of its life-mate. And if the others were to suspect as well, the emotional radiation from the team would be extremely painful and distressing to me."

"I understand," Cha Thrat said.

"Pathologist Murchison is highly intelligent," the Cinrusskin continued, "and in time she will realize what has happened, if she doesn't learn it from Khone first. That is why I would like you to explain this delicate situation to friend Khone at the first opportunity, and ask for its silence in this matter.

"Friend Khone," Prilicla added gently, "has the memories and feelings of Cha Thrat as well as Conway."

For a moment Cha Thrat could not speak as the Gogleskan healer's mind threatened to engulf her own with its peculiar mixture of fear, curiosity, and parental concern. Finally she said, "Will Khone be able to speak?"

"I have the feeling, not a suspicion, that both our Gogleskans are doing well," Prilicla replied, shaking out its wings in readiness for flight. "But now, if we don't end this conversation soon, the others will wonder what I am doing to you, and will be expecting you to arrive back bruised and bleeding."

The idea of Prilicla inflicting any kind of injury on anyone was so ridiculous that even a Gogleskan as well as a Sommaradvan and Earth-human considered it funny. Cha Thrat laughed out loud as, with the down-draft from the empath's wings stirring her hair, they followed the others back to the lander.

"You realize, friend Cha," the empath said, its trembling limbs a visible apology for the words that would diminish her pleasure, "that O'Mara will have to be told."

CHAPTER 15

B y the time they had been transfered from the lander to the special FOKT accommodation of *Rhabwar*'s casualty deck, both patients were fully conscious and making loud hissing noises. The sounds that the younger one was making did not translate, but Khone's were divided into repeated expressions of gratitude for its survival and weak but very insistent reassurances about its clinical condition. The healer's self-diagnosis was supported by the biosensors and confirmed by the less tangible but even more accurate findings of the emotion-sensitive Prilicla. And now that it was separated from its friendly off-world monsters, and its subconscious fears thereby allayed, by a thick transparent partition, Khone was quite happy to speak to anyone at any time.

That included the nonmedical crew members who, with Captain Fletcher's permission, left their positions in Control and the Power Room briefly to congratulate the patient and tell complimentary lies about the obvious intelligence, parental resemblance, and great beauty of the new arrival, a male child of greater than average weight. In spite of Prilicla's urgings that it should rest and refrain from overexcitement, the atmosphere around Khone's accommodation more closely resembled a birthday party than the casualty deck of an ambulance ship.

When Captain Fletcher arrived, they did not need an emphatic faculty to feel the atmosphere change. To Khone the Earth-human made a perfunctory inquiry about its health, then turned quickly to Prilicla.

"I need a decision, Senior Physician," it went on, "one that only you people can make. The hospital signaled us a few minutes ago, saying that an emergency beacon had been detected in this sector. The distressed ship is about five hours subspace flight away; the distress beacon was not one of the types used by the Federation, so the casualties might be a species new to us. That makes it difficult to estimate the time needed for the rescue. It could take a couple of days rather than hours.

"The question is," it ended, "do your patients require hospitalization before or after we respond to this distress call?"

It was not an easy decision to make because their patients, although stable and not in need of urgent treatment, belonged to a life-form about which little was known clinically, so that unexpected complications might arise at any time. Surprisingly the discussion, which was animated but necessarily brief, was ended by Khone itself.

"Please, friends," it said during one of the rare lulls, "Gogleskan females recover quickly once the birth trauma is over. I can assure you, both as a healer and a parent, that such a delay will not endanger either of us. Besides, here we are receiving much better attention than would be possible anywhere on Goglesk."

"You're forgetting something," Murchison said quietly. "We may be going into a disaster situation possibly involving a life-form completely new to us. It is conceivable that they might horrify or scare even us, much less a Gogleskan leaving its planet for the first time."

"They might," Khone replied, "but they would almost certainly be in a worse condition than I am."

"Very well," Prilicla said, turning back to the Captain. "It seems that friend Khone has reminded us of the priorities and of our duty as healers. Tell the hospital that *Rhabwar* will respond."

Fletcher disappeared in the direction of Control, and the Cinrusskin went on. "We should now eat and sleep, since there might not be an opportunity to do either for some time. The patients' biosensors will be monitored automatically and any change in condition signaled to me at once. They need rest, too, and they wouldn't get it if I left a team member on duty. Come along, everyone. Sleep well, friend Khone."

It flew gracefully into the gravity-free central well and up toward the dining and recreation deck, followed in more orthodox fashion by Naydrad, Danalta, Murchison, and Cha Thrat. But just before they began their weightless climb, Murchison gripped the ladder with one hand and placed the other on one of her medial limbs.

"Wait, please," it said. "I would like to speak to you."

Cha Thrat stopped but did not speak. The sensation of alien digits gently enclosing her arm and the sight of the flabby, pink Earth-human face looking up at her were giving rise to feelings that no Sommaradvan, much less a female one, had any business harboring. Slowly, so as not to give offense, she disengaged the limb from the other's grip and sought for emotional control.

"I'm worried about this ship rescue, Cha Thrat," it said, "and the effect on you of the casualties we may have to treat. Disaster injuries can be pretty bad, collision fractures and explosive decompressions for the most part, and as a rule there are very few survivors. You don't seem to be able to keep your Sommaradvan nose out of the medical area, but this time you must try, try really hard, not to get involved with our casualties."

Before Cha Thrat could reply, it went on. "You did some very nice work with Khone, even though I'm still not sure what exactly was going on, but you were very lucky. If Khone or the infant or both of them had died, how would you have felt? More important, what would you have done to yourself?"

"Nothing," Cha Thrat said, trying hard to tell herself that the expression on the pink face below her was one of friendly concern for an other-species subordinate and not something more personal. Quickly she went on. "I would have felt very bad, but I would not have injured myself again. The code of ethics of a warrior-surgeon is strict, and even on Sommaradva there were colleagues who did not observe it as I have done, and who envied and disliked me for my own strict observance. To me the code remains valid, but in Sector General and on Goglesk there are other and equally valid codes. My viewpoints have changed ..."

She stopped herself, afraid that she had said too much, but the other had not noticed that she had used the plural.

"We call that broadening the mind," Murchison said, "and I'm relieved and pleased for you, Cha Thrat. It's a pity that ... Well, I meant what I said about you being the Maintenance Department's gain and our loss. Your superiors find you a bit hard to take at times, and after the Chalder and Hudlar incidents I can't imagine you being accepted for ward training by anyone. But maybe if you waited until the fuss died down, and didn't do anything else to get yourself noticed, I could speak to a few people about having you transfered back to the medical staff. How do you feel about that?"

"I feel grateful," she replied, trying desperately to find a way of ending this conversation with a being who was not only sympathetic and understanding as a person, but whose physical aspect was arousing in her other feelings of the kind usually associated with the urge to procreate. Most definitely, she thought, this was a problem that could only be resolved by one of O'Mara's spells. Quickly she added, "I also feel very hungry."

"Hungry!" Murchison said. As the Earth-human turned to resume climbing to the dining area, it laughed suddenly and said, "You know, Cha Thrat, sometimes you remind me of my life-mate."

She was able to rest after the meal but not sleep and, after three hours of trying, she made the excuse to herself that Khone's life-support and synthetic food delivery systems needed checking. She found the Gogleskan awake, as well, and they talked quietly while it fed the infant. Soon afterward they were both asleep and she was left to stare silently at the complex shapes of the casualty deck equipment, which looked like weird, mechanical phantasms in the night-level lighting, until the arrival of Prilicla.

"Have you been able to speak with friend Khone?" the Cinrusskin asked, hovering over the two Gogleskans.

"Yes," Cha Thrat replied. "It will do as you suggested, to avoid embarrassing us."

"Thank you, friend Cha," Prilicla said. "I feel the others awake and about to join us. We should be arriving at any—"

It was interrupted by a double chime that announced their emergence into normal space, followed a few minutes later by the voice of Lieutenant Haslam speaking from Control.

"We have long-range sensor contact with a large ship," the communications officer said. "There are no indications of abnormal radiation levels, no expanding cloud of debris, no sign of any catastrophic malfunction. The vessel is rotating around its longitudinal axis as well as spinning slowly end over end. We are locking the telescope into the sensor bearing and putting the image on your repeater screen."

A narrow, fuzzy triangle appeared in the center of the screen, becoming more distinct as Haslam brought it into focus.

It went on. "Prepare for maximum thrust in ten minutes. Gravity compensators set for three Gs. We should close with it in less than two hours."

Cha Thrat and Khone watched the screen with the rest of the medical team, who were making Prilicla tremble with the intensity of their impatience. They were as ready as it was possible to be, and the more detailed preparations would have to wait until they had some idea of the physiological classification of the people they were about to rescue. But it was possible for the ship ruler to draw conclusions, even at long range.

"According to our astrogation computor," Fletcher said, "the nearest star is eleven light-years distant and without planets, so the ship did not come from there. Although large, it is still much too small to be a generation ship, so it is highly probable that it uses a form of hyperdrive similar to our own. It does not resemble any vessel, past, current, or under development, on the Federation's fleet list.

"In spite of its large size," the Captain went on, "it has the aerodynamically clean triangular configuration typical of a vessel required to maneuver in a planetary atmosphere. Most of the star-traveling species that we know prefer, for technical and economic reasons, to keep their combined atmosphere-and-space vessels small and build the larger nonlanders in orbit where streamlining is unnecessary. The two exceptions that I know of build their space-atmosphere ships large because the crews needed to operate them are themselves physically massive."

"Oh, great," Naydrad said. "We'll be rescuing a bunch of giants."

"This is only speculative at the moment," the Captain said. "Your screen won't show it, but we're beginning to resolve some of the structural details. That ship was not put together by watchmakers. The overall design philosophy seems to have been one of simplicity and strength rather than sophistication. We are beginning to see small access and inspection panels, and two very large features that must be entry locks. While it is possible that these are cargo locks that double as entry ports for personnel who are physically small, the probability is that these people are a very large and massive life-form—"

"Don't be afraid, friend Khone," Prilicla broke in quickly. "Even a demented Hudlar couldn't break through the partition Cha Thrat put around you, and our casualties will be unconscious anyway. Both of you will be quite safe."

"Reassurance and gratitude are felt," the Gogleskan said. With a visible effort it added, more personally, "Thank you."

"Friend Fletcher," the empath said, returning its attention to the Captain, "can you speculate further about this life-form, other than that it is large and probably lacks digital dexterity?"

"I was about to," the Captain said. "Analysis of internal atmosphere leakage shows that—"

"Then the hull has been punctured!" Cha Thrat said excitedly. "From within or without?"

"Technician," said the ship ruler, reminding her of her position and her insubordination with the single word. "For your information, it is extremely difficult, expensive, and unnecessary to make a large, space-going structure completely airtight. It is more practical to maintain the vessel at nominal internal pressure and replace the negligible quantity of air that escapes. In this case, had escaping air not been observed, it would almost certainly have meant that the ship was open to space and airless.

"But there are no signs of collision or puncture damage," Fletcher went on, "and our sensor data and analysis of the atmosphere leakage suggests that the crew are warm-blooded oxygen-breathers with environmental temperature and pressure requirements similar to our own."

"Thank you, friend Fletcher," Prilicla said, then joined the others who were silently watching the repeater screen.

The image of the slowly rolling and spinning ship had grown until it was brushing against the edges of the screen, when Murchison said, "The ship is undamaged, uncontrolled, and, the sensors tell us, there is no abnormal escape of radiation from its main reactor. That means their problem is likely to be disease rather than traumatic injuries, a disabling or perhaps lethal illness affecting the entire crew. Under illness I would include the inhalation of toxic gas accidentally released from—"

"No, ma'am," said Fletcher, who had maintained the communicator link with Control. "Toxic contamination of the air supply system on that scale would have shown up in our leak analyses. There's nothing wrong with their air."

"Or," Murchison went on firmly, "the toxic material may have contaminated their liquid or food supply, and been ingested. Either way, there may be no survivors and nothing for us to do here except posthumously investigate, record the physiology of a new life-form, and leave the rest to the Monitor Corps."

The rest, Cha Thrat knew, would mean carrying out a detailed examination of the vessel's power, life-support, and navigation systems with the intention of assessing the species' level of technology. That might provide the information that would enable them to reconstruct the elements of the ship's course before the disaster occurred and trace it back to its planet of origin. Simultaneously, an even more careful evaluation of the nontechnical environment—crew accommodation and furnishings, art or decorative objects, personal effects, books, tapes, and self-entertainment systems—would be carried out so that they would know what kind of people lived on the home planet when they succeeded in finding it, as they ultimately would.

And eventually that world would be visited by the Cultural Contact specialists of the Monitor Corps and, like her own Sommaradva, it would never be the same again.

"If there are no survivors, ma'am," Fletcher said regretfully, "then it isn't a job for *Rhabwar*. But we'll only know when we go inside and check. Senior Physician, do you wish to send any of your people with me? At this stage, though, getting inside will be a mechanical rather than a medical problem. Lieutenant Chen and Technician Cha Thrat, you will assist me with the entry—Wait, something's happening to the ship!"

Cha Thrat was very surprised that Fletcher wanted her to help with such important work, badly worried in case she might not be able to perform to his expectations, and more than a little frightened at the thought of what might happen to them when they got inside the distressed ship. But the feelings were temporarily submerged at the sight of what was happening on the screen.

The ship's rate of spin and roll were increasing as they watched, and irregular spurts of vapor were fogging the forward and aft hull and the tips of the broad, triangular wings. She suffered a moment's sympathetic nausea for anyone who might be inside the vessel and conscious, then Fletcher's voice returned.

"Attitude jets!" it said excitedly. "Somebody must be trying to check the spin, but is making it worse. Maybe the survivor isn't feeling well, or is injured, or isn't familiar with the controls. But now we know someone is alive in there. Dodds, as soon as we're in range, kill that spin and lock on with all tractors. Doctor Prilicla, you're in business again."

"Sometimes it's nice," Murchison said, speaking to nobody in particular, "to be proved wrong."

While Cha Thrat was donning her suit, she listened to the discussion between the medical team members and Fletcher that, had it not been for the presence of the gentle little empath, would have quickly developed into a bitter argument.

It was plain from the conversation that the Captain was *Rhabwar's* sole ruler so far as all ship operations were concerned, but at the site of a disaster its authority had to be relinquished to the senior medical person on board, who was empowered to use the resources of the ship and its officers as it saw fit. The main area of contention seemed to be the exact point where Fletcher's responsibility ended and Prilicla's began.

The Captain argued that the medics were not, considering the fact that the distressed ship was structurally undamaged, on the disaster site until it got them into the ship, and until then they should continue to obey its orders or, at very least, act on its advice. Its advice was that they should remain on *Rhabwar* until it had effected an entry, because to do otherwise was to risk becoming casualties themselves if the injured or ill survivor—who had already made a mess of checking its ship's spin with the attitude jets—decided to do something equally unsuccessful and much more devastating with the main thrusters.

If the medical team was waiting outside the distressed ship's entry lock when thrust was applied, they would either be smashed against the hull plating or incinerated by its tail flare, and the rescue would be aborted because of a sudden lack of rescuers.

Fletcher's reasons for wanting the medics to remain behind until the other ship had been opened were sound, Cha Thrat thought, even though they had given her a new danger to worry about. But the medical team had been trained for the fastest possible rescue and treatment of survivors, and they were particularly anxious not to waste time in this case when there might only be one. By the time she was leaving for the airlock, a compromise had been worked out.

Prilicla would accompany Fletcher, Chen, and herself to the ship. While they were trying to get inside, the empath would move up and down the outer hull and try to pinpoint the locations of survivors by their emotional radiation. The rest of the medical team would hold themselves ready for a fast recovery of casualties as soon as the way was open.

She had been waiting only a few minutes in the lock antechamber when Lieutenant Chen arrived.

"Good, you're here already," the Earth-human said, smiling. "Help me move our equipment into the lock, please. The Captain doesn't like to be kept waiting."

Without giving the impression that it was lecturing her, Chen discussed the purpose of the equipment they were moving from the nearby stowage compartment to the lock, so that Cha Thrat felt her level of ignorance was being reduced without the feelings of stupidity and inferiority that so often accompanied that process. She decided that the Earth-human was a considerate and helpful person, in spite of its rank, and one with whom she might risk a small insubordination.

"This is in no sense a criticism of the ship ruler," she said carefully, "but I am concerned lest Captain Fletcher is giving me credit for more technical experience than I in fact possess. Frankly, I'm surprised it wanted me along."

Chen made an untranslatable sound and said, "Don't be surprised, Technician, or worried."

"Regrettably," Cha Thrat said, "I am both."

For a few minutes the Lieutenant went on talking about the sections of portable airlock they were carrying that, when deployed and attached with fast-setting sealant around the entry port of the other ship, would enable *Rhabwar*'s boarding tube to join the two vessels and allow the medics to do their work unhampered by spacesuits.

"But rest your mind, Cha Thrat," Chen went on. "Your maintenance chief, Timmins, spoke to the Captain about you. It said that you are pretty bright, learn quickly, and we should give you as much work to do as possible. We should do this because, once the FOKT's accommodation was finished, you would have nothing to do and might fret. It said that, with your past performance in the hospital, the medical team wouldn't allow you anywhere near one of their patients."

It laughed suddenly and went on. "Now we know how wrong Timmins was. But we still intend to keep you busy. You have four times as many hands as I have, and I can't think of a better tool-carrier. Do I offend you, Technician?"

The question had been asked of the trainee technician and not the proud warrior-surgeon she had been, so the answer had to be "No."

"That's good," Chen said. "Now, close and seal your helmet, and double-check your safety-line attachments. The Captain's on his way."

And then she was outside, festooned with equipment and drifting with the two Earth-humans across the short distance to the distressed vessel, which was now held by the rigid, nonmaterial beams of *Rhabwar*'s tractors. While immobilizing the other ship, their own had acquired a proportion of its spin. But the countless stars that wheeled endlessly around the apparently motionless vessels aroused a feeling not of nausea but wonder.

Prilicla was already there when they arrived, having exited by the casualty deck's airlock, and was patrolling along the hull in its careful search for the emotional radiation that would indicate the presence of survivors.

CHAPTER 16

A s soon as they were standing upright and held to the gray, un-painted hull plating by their boot magnets, and with the bulk of *Rhabwar* hanging above them like a shining and convoluted white ceiling, the Captain began to speak.

It said, "There are only so many ways for a door to open. It can hinge in or outward, slide vertically or laterally, unscrew clockwise or anticlockwise or, if the builders are sufficiently advanced in the field of molecular engineering, an opening could be dilated in an area of solid metal. We have yet to encounter a species capable of the latter and, if we ever do, we'll have to be very careful indeed, and remember to call them 'sir.' "

Before it had joined the Monitor Corps, she had learned, Fletcher had been a ruler-academic and one of Earth's foremost, and certainly most youthful, authorities on Extraterrestrial Comparative Technology, and the old habits died hard. Even on the hull of an alien ship that might apply thrust at any moment, it was lecturing—and remembering to include the occasional dry little joke. It was also speaking for the benefit of the recorders, in case something sudden and melodramatic happened.

"We are standing on a large door or hatch that is rectangular in shape with rounded corners," it went on, "so the probability is that it will open in or out. Below us, according to the sensors, is a large, empty compartment, which means that it has to be a cargo or personnel lock rather than an equipment access or inspection panel. The hatch is featureless, so the external actuator mechanism should be behind one of the small panels in the door surround. Technician, the scanner, please."

Because this particular scanner was designed to see into the vital organs of metal-encased machines rather than the softer structures of flesh and blood, it was much larger and heavier than its medical counterpart. In her eagerness to appear fast and efficient, Cha Thrat miscalculated the inertia and sent it crashing into the hatch cover, where it left a long, shallow dent before the Captain brought it to a halt.

"Thank you," Fletcher said drily, and added, "We are, of course, making no secret of our presence. A covert entry and our sudden appearance inside their ship might frighten the survivors, if there are any."

Chen made an untranslatable noise and said, "Whacking the hull with a sledgehammer would have been even better."

"Sorry," Cha Thrat said.

Two of the small panels concealed retractable lighting fixtures and the remaining one turned out to be a large rocker switch set flush with the hull plating. Fletcher warned them to stand clear, then pressed with its palm on both ends of the switch in turn. It had to press very hard, so hard that it had pushed its leg and arm magnets away from the hull, before anything happened.

A sudden rush of air from the edge of the slowly opening hatch sent Fletcher spinning away. Cha Thrat, who had the advantage of four foot-magnets holding her down, grabbed it by one leg and brought the Captain into contact with the hull again.

"Thank you," Fletcher said, as the fog of escaping air cleared, then went on. "Everyone inside. Doctor Prilicla, come quickly. The opening of the lock is sure to register on their control deck. If there are any survivors up there, now is the most likely time for them to get nervous and apply thrust . . ."

"There *are* survivors, friend Fletcher," the empath broke in. "One of them is forward, probably on the control deck, and several groups of them farther aft, but none in your immediate area. Out here I am too far from the sources to be able to detect individual emotional radiation, but the predominant feelings are of fear, pain, and anger. It is the intensity of the anger that worries me, friend Fletcher, so go carefully. I am returning to *Rhabwar* for the rest of the medical team."

With the scanner they were able to identify and trace the actuator wiring to a set of two rocker switches. The first one was locked in position, and when they pressed the second, the lock's outer seal closed behind them, after which the first one moved freely and opened the inner seal, simultaneously turning on the lighting.

Fletcher said a few words for the recorders about the intense greenish-yellow lighting that would, on later analysis, give useful information about the crew's visual organs and an indication of the type and proximity of their sun to the home planet. Then it led the way from the lock chamber into the corridor.

"The corridor is about four meters high, square in cross-section, well lit, unpainted, and gravity-free," the Captain went on. "We assume an artificial gravity system, currently malfunctioning or possibly switched off, because the inner surfaces are bare of ladders, climbing nets, or handholds that the crew would need to get about in the weightless condition. At this level the section of corridor visible to us follows the lateral curvature of the inner hull, and opposite the lock entrance there is a wide opening through which we can see two ramps, one ascending and the other descending, which lead, presumably, to other decks. We are taking the ascending one."

Consulting the analyzer strapped to its arm, the Captain went on. "Nothing toxic in the air, pressure low but still breathable, temperature normal. Open your visors so we can talk together without tying up the suit frequencies."

Fletcher and Chen launched themselves into the air above the ascending ramp. Less expertly, Cha Thrat did likewise and was halfway to the top when the others arrived—and dropped suddenly onto the deck with a muffled crash of equipment and a much less quiet burst of strong language. She had enough warning to be able to land on her feet.

"The artificial gravity system," the Captain said, when it had picked itself up again, "is still operating in this area. Move quickly, please, we're looking for survivors."

Large inward-opening doors with simple latch fastenings lined the corridor, and under Fletcher's direction, the search became a routine process. First unlatch the door, push it wide open while standing well back in case something nasty came through it, then search the compartment quickly for crew members. But the compartments held only racks of equipment or containers of various shapes and sizes whose labels they could not read, and nothing that in any way resembled furniture, wall decorations, or clothing.

So far, Fletcher reported, the ship's interior seemed incredibly spartan and utilitarian, and it was beginning to worry about the kind of people who would build and crew such a vessel.

At the top of the next ramp, in another section of corridor that was gravity-free, they saw one of them. It was hanging weightless, spinning slowly and occasionally bumping against the ceiling.

"Careful!" Fletcher warned as Cha Thrat moved forward for a closer look. But there was no danger because she could recognize a cadaver when she saw one, regardless of its species. A hand placed on its thick, heavily veined neck confirmed the absence of a pulse and a body temperature that was much too low for a warm-blooded oxygen-breather who was alive.

The Captain joined her and said, "This is a big one, almost twice the mass of a Tralthan, physiological classification FGHI . . ."

"FGHJ," Cha Thrat corrected.

Fletcher broke off and took a deep breath, which it expelled slowly through its nose. When it spoke she could not be sure whether the Captain was being what Earth-humans called sarcastic, or simply asking a question of a subordinate who appeared to have more knowledge in a particular area than it had.

"Technician," it said, laying heavy emphasis on the first word, "would you like to take over?"

"Yes," she said eagerly, and went on. "It has six limbs, four legs and two arms, all very heavily muscled, and is hairless except for a narrow band of stiff bristles running from the top of the head along the spine to the tail, which seems to have been surgically shortened at an early age. The body configuration is a thick cylinder of uniform girth between the fore and rear legs but the forward torso narrows toward the shoulders and is carried erect. The neck is very thick and the head small. There are two eyes, recessed and looking forward, a mouth with very large teeth, and other openings that are probably aural or olfactory sense organs. The legs . . ."

"Friend Fletcher," Prilicla broke in gently. "Would you please switch on your vision pickup and spotlight, and hold them very steady? We want to see what Cha Thrat is describing."

Suddenly every surface detail of the dead FGHJ was illuminated by a light even more intense than that of the corridor.

"You won't see a good picture," the Captain said. "The shielding effects of the ship's hull will cause fogging and distortion."

"That is understood," the empath said. "Friend Naydrad is preparing the large pressure litter. We will be with you very soon. Please continue, Cha Thrat."

"The legs terminate in large, reddish-brown hooves," she went on, "three of which are covered by thick, heavily padded bags fastened tightly at the tops, possibly to deaden the sound their feet make on the metal deck. Cylinders of metal, padded on the inner surfaces, encircle all four legs just below knee-level, with short lengths of chain attached to them. The links at the end of the chains have been broken or forced apart.

"The creature's hands are large, with four digits," she continued, "and do not appear particularly dexterous. There is a complicated harness suspended from and belted around the upper torso and flanks. Pouches of different sizes are attached to the harness. One of them is open and there are small tools scattered around the body."

"Technician," the Captain said, "remain here until the medic team arrives, then follow us. We're supposed to find and help the live ones and—"

"No!" Cha Thrat said without thinking. Then apologetically she added, "I'm sorry, Captain. I mean, be very careful."

Chen was already moving down the corridor, but the Captain checked itself as it was about to follow.

"I am always careful, Technician," it said quietly, "but why do you think I should be very careful?"

"I do not have a reason," she said, with three of her eyes on the cadaver and one on the Earth-human, "only a suspicion. On Sommar-adva there are certain people, warriors as well as serviles, who behave badly and without honor toward their fellow citizens and, on rare occasions, grievously injure or kill them. These lawbreakers are confined on an island from which there is no escape. On the vessel that transports them to this island the non-crew accommodation lacks comfort, and the prisoners themselves are immobilized by leg restraints. With respect, the similarities to our present situation are obvious."

Fletcher was silent for a moment, then it said, "Let's take your suspicion a stage further. You think this might be a prison ship, in distress not because of a technical malfunction but because its prisoners have broken free and may have killed or injured all or part of the crew before they realized that they were unable to work the ship themselves. Perhaps some crew members are holed up somewhere, in need of medical attention, after inflicting serious casualties among the escapees."

Fletcher looked briefly at the cadaver, then returned its attention to Cha Thrat.

"It's a neat theory," it went on. "If true, we are faced with the job of convincing the ship's crew and a bunch of unruly prisoners, who are on less than friendly terms with each other, that we would like to help all of them without becoming casualties ourselves. But is it true? The leg restraints support your theory, but the harness and tool pouches suggest a crew member rather than a prisoner.

"Thank you, Cha Thrat," it added, turning to follow Chen, "I shall bear your suspicions in mind, and be very careful."

As soon as the Captain had finished speaking, Prilicla said quickly, "Friend Cha, we can see wounds all over the body surface, but the details are indistinct. Describe them please. And do they support your theory? Are they the type of injuries that might be sustained by an entity being moved violently about inside a spinning ship, or could they have been inflicted deliberately by another member of the same species?"

"On your answer," Murchison joined in, "depends whether or not I go back for a heavy-duty spacesuit."

"And I," Naydrad said. Danalta, who belonged to a species impervious to physical injury, remained silent.

She looked closely at the brightly lit surfaces of the corridor for a moment, then gently rotated the cadaver so that its entire body was presented to the vision pickup. She was trying to think like a warrior-surgeon while at the same time remembering one of the basic physics tapes she had viewed as a trainee technician.

"There are a large number of superficial contusions and abrasions," she said, "concentrated on the flanks, knees, and elbows. They appear to have been made by grazing contact with the metal of the corridor, but the wound that caused its death is a large, depressed fracture located on and covering the top of the skull. It does not look as if it was caused by any type of metal tool or implement but by violent contact with the corridor wall. There is a patch of congealed blood, comparable to the area of the injury, on the wall where I am directing the vision pickup.

"Remembering that the cadaver's position in the vessel is approximately amidships," she went on, wondering if the Captain's lecturing manner was a psychological contagion, "it is unlikely that the spinning could have been responsible for such a grievous head injury. My conclusion is that the being, whose legs are very strong, misjudged a jump in weightless conditions and hit its head against the wall. The lesser wounds could have been caused while it was tumbling, unconscious and dying, inside the spinning ship."

Murchison's voice sounded relieved as it said, "So you're telling us that it had an accident, that no other antisocial type bashed in its skull?"

"Yes," Cha Thrat said.

"I'll be with you in a few minutes," it said.

"Friend Murchison," Prilicla began anxiously.

"Don't worry, Doctor," said the Pathologist. "If anyone or anything nasty threatens, Danalta will protect us."

"Of course," the shape-changer said.

While she was waiting for them to arrive, Cha Thrat continued to study the cadaver while listening to the voices of Prilicla, Fletcher, and *Rhabwar's* communications officer. The Cinrusskin's empathic faculty had given it approximate locations for the survivors who, apart from the single crew member in Control, seemed to be gathered together in three small groups of four or five persons on one deck. But the Captain had decided that it would be better to make contact with a single crew member before approaching a group, and was heading directly for the survivor on the Control deck.

Cha Thrat steadied the cadaver and took one of its large, strong hands in two of her upper manipulators. The fingers were short and stubby and tipped with claws that had been trimmed short, and none of the digits were opposable. In this species' prehistory she could imagine those clawed hands conveying freshly killed food to the mouth that even now was filled with long and very nasty-looking teeth. It did not, she thought, look like a member of a species capable of building ships that traveled between the stars.

It did not look, well, *civilized.*

"You can't always judge by external appearance," Murchison said, making Cha Thrat realize that she had been thinking aloud. "Your Chalder friend from the AUGL ward makes this one look like a pussycat."

The rest of the medical team were following closely behind the Pathologist: Naydrad guiding the litter; Prilicla walking the ceiling on its six, sucker-tipped legs; and, as she watched, Danalta extruded a thicker, sucker-tipped limb of its own and attached itself to the wall like some watchful, alien vegetable.

Quickly Murchison attached its instrument pack to the wall with magnetic pads and used larger magnets and webbing to immobilize the cadaver. It said, "Our friend here was unlucky, but at least it is helping the others. I can do things to it which I would not think of doing to a living survivor, and without wasting time on—"

"Dammit, this is *ridiculous!*" a voice said in their suit phones, so distorted by surprise and incredulity that she did not recognize it at first as belonging to the Captain. Fletcher went on. "We're on the control deck and we've found another crew member, alive, apparently uninjured, occupying one of five control positions. The other four positions are empty. But the survivor is wearing restraints on all four legs and is chained to its control couch!"

Cha Thrat turned away and left without speaking. The Captain had told her that she should follow Chen and itself as soon as the medical team arrived, and she wanted to do just that before Fletcher had a chance to countermand the earlier order. Her curiosity about this strange, chained-up ship's officer was so intense that it was almost painful.

It was not until she had ascended two decks that she noticed Prilicla silently following her.

Fletcher was saying "I've tried communicating with it, with the translator and my making the usual friendly signs. *Rhabwar's* translation computer is capable of converting simple messages into any conceivable language that is based on a system of word-sounds. It growls and barks at me but the sounds don't translate. When I approach closely it acts as if it wants to tear my head off. At other times its body and limb movements are erratic and uncoordinated, although it seems anxious to be free of its leg restraints."

Prilicla and Cha Thrat arrived at that moment, and the Captain added, "See for yourselves."

The Cinrusskin had taken up a position on the ceiling just inside the entrance, well away from the crew member's wildly flailing arms. It said, "Friend Fletcher, the emotional radiation disturbs me. There are feelings of anger, fear, hunger, and blind, unthinking antagonism. There is a coarseness and intensity in these emotions not usually found in beings possessing high intelligence."

"I agree, Doctor," the Captain said, moving back instinctively as one of the clawless hands stabbed out at its face. "But these couches were designed for this particular life-form, and the controls, switches, and doorhandles that we've seen so far in the ship are suited to those particular hands. At the moment it is completely ignoring the controls, and the sudden increase in spin we noticed during our approach was probably caused by it accidentally striking the keys concerned.

"Its couch, like the other four, is mounted on runners," Fletcher went on. "It has been moved back to the limit of its travel, which makes it very difficult for the being's hands to reach the control consoles. Have you any ideas, Senior Physician, because I haven't."

"No, friend Fletcher," Prilicla said, "but let us move to a lower deck where it cannot see or hear us."

A few minutes later it continued. "The levels of fear, anger, and antagonism have diminished, and its hunger remains at the same intensity. For reasons that aren't clear to me at the moment, the crew member's behavior is irrational and emotionally unstable. But it is in no immediate danger where it is, and it is not in any pain. Friend Murchison."

"Yes?" the Pathologist responded.

"When you are examining that cadaver," it went on, "pay special attention to the head. It has occurred to me that the cranial injury may not have been an accident, but was deliberately self-inflicted in response to acute and continuing cranial discomfort. You should look for evidence of an area of infection or cell degeneration affecting the brain tissues, which may have adversely affected or destroyed its higher centers of mentation and emotional control.

"Friend Fletcher," it went on without waiting for a reply, "we must quickly locate and check the condition of the other survivors. But carefully, in case they are behaving like our friend in Control."

With Prilicla's empathic faculty to guide them, they quickly found the three large dormitory compartments containing the remaining conscious survivors, five in one room and four in each of the others. The doors were not locked but the occupants had not used the simple latch system that would have opened them from the inside. The artificial gravity system was in operation, and the brief look they were able to catch before the occupants spotted and began to attack them showed plain, undecorated metal walls and flooring that was covered by disordered bedding and wrecked waste-disposal equipment. The smell, Cha Thrat thought, could have been cut with a knife.

"Friend Fletcher," Prilicla said as they were leaving the last dormitory, "all of the crew members are physically active and without pain, and if it wasn't for the fact that they are clearly no longer capable of working their ship, I would say that they are quite healthy. Unless friend Murchison discovers a clinical reason for their abnormal behavior, there is nothing we can do for them.

"I realize that I am being both cowardly and selfish," it went on, "but I do not want to endanger our casualty deck equipment and terrify friend Khone by moving in close on twenty oversized, overactive, and, at present, underintelligent life-forms who—"

"I agree," Fletcher said firmly. "If that lot got loose, they could wreck my ship and not just the casualty deck. The alternative is to keep them here, extend *Rhabwar*'s hyperspace envelope, and Jump both ships to Sector General."

"That was my thought as well, friend Fletcher," Prilicla replied. "Also, that you rig the boarding tube so that we can have rapid access to the survivors, that we gather samples of all packets and containers likely to hold this life-form's food or nutritious fluids. The only symptom these people display is intense hunger and, considering the size of their teeth, I would like to relieve it as soon as possible in case they start eating each other."

"And," the Pathologist's voice joined in, "you want me to analyze the samples so as to tell you which containers hold paint and which soup?"

"Thank you, friend Murchison," the empath said, and went on. "As well as your cranial investigation would you look at the cadaver's general metabolism with a view to suggesting a safe anesthetic for use on these people, something fast-acting that we can shoot into them at a distance.

They must all be anesthetized very quickly because—"

"For fast work like that," Murchison broke in, "I'll need *Rhabwar*'s lab, not a portable analyzer like this one. And I'll need the whole team to help me."

"Because," Prilicla resumed quietly, "I have a feeling that there is another survivor who is not healthy and active and hungry. Its emotional radiation is extremely weak and characteristic of an entity who is deeply unconscious and perhaps dying. But I am unable to locate it because of the stronger, overriding emanations from the conscious survivors. That is why, as soon as the samples are gathered for friend Murchison, I would like every hole, corner, or compartment large enough to hold an FGHJ searched.

"It must be done quickly," the Cinrusskin ended, "because the feeling is very weak indeed."

Awkwardly Fletcher said, "I understand, Senior Physician, but there is a problem. Pathologist Murchison needs all of the medical team and extending *Rhabwar*'s hyperenvelope and realigning our tractors for the Jump and deploying the boarding tube will require all of the ship's officers..."

"Which leaves me," Cha Thrat said quietly, "with nothing to do."

"... So which should be given priority?" the Captain went on, seeming not to have heard her. "The search for your unconscious FGHJ, or getting it and the rest of them to Sector General as quickly as possible?"

"I will search the ship," she said, more loudly.

"Thank you, Cha Thrat," Prilicla said, "I felt you wanting to volunteer. But think carefully before you decide. The survivor, should you find it, will be too weak to harm you. But there are other dangers. This ship is large, and as strange to us as it is to you."

"Yes, Technician," the Captain said. "These aren't the maintenance tunnels at Sector General. The color codings, if present, will mean something entirely different. You can't make assumptions about anything you see, and if you accidentally foul a control link... Very well, you may search, but stay out of trouble.

Fletcher turned to look at Prilicla and added plaintively, "Or do you feel me feeling that I'm wasting my breath?"

CHAPTER 17

With the printouts from *Rhabwar's* sensors providing information on the ship's layout, and in particular on the size and
location of its empty spaces, Cha Thrat began a rapid and methodical
search of the alien vessel. She ignored only the control deck, the occupied dormitories, and areas close to the ship's reactor that the sensor
maps showed to be uninhabitable by the FGHJ life-form or, for that
matter, any other species who were not radiation-eaters. She was very
careful to check all interiors with sound sensors and the heavy-duty
scanner before opening every door or panel. She was not afraid, but
there were times when shivers marched like tiny, icy feet along the length
of her spine.

It usually happened when the realization came that she was searching an alien starship for survivors of a species whose existence she could
not have imagined a short time ago, at the direction of other unimaginable beings from a place of healing whose size, complexity, and occupants were like the solid manifestations of a disordered mind. But the
unthinkable and unimaginable had become not only thinkable but acceptable to her, and all because a discontented and unloved warrior-
surgeon of Sommaradva had risked a limb and her professional
reputation to treat an injured off-world ship ruler.

At the thought of what her future would have been had she not taken that risk she shivered again, in dread.

Even though the first search was to be a fast, perfunctory one, it took much longer than Cha Thrat had expected. By the time it was completed, *Rhabwar*'s boarding tube was in position, and she could feel and hear the empty grumbling of both her stomachs.

Prilicla told her to relieve these symptoms before making her report.

When she arrived on the casualty deck, Prilicla, Murchison, and Danalta were working on the cadaver while Naydrad and Khone, its hairy body pressed against the transparent dividing wall, watched with an interest so intense that only the Cinrusskin sensed her arrival.

"What's wrong, friend Cha?" the empath asked. "Something disturbed you on the ship. I felt it even here."

"This," she replied, holding up one of the leg restraints that Murchison had removed from the cadaver and discarded before the dead FGHJ had been moved to *Rhabwar*. "The chain is not locked to the leg cuff, it is attached with a simple spring-loaded bolt that can be released easily when pressure is applied just here."

She demonstrated, then went on. "When I was searching the control deck area I looked at the crew member chained to its couch, without being seen, and noticed that similar fastenings hold the chains to all four of its leg cuffs. It and the cadaver here could have freed themselves simply by releasing the fastenings, which are within easy reach of its hands. It did not have to break free, and neither does the crew member chained to the control couch, who nevertheless continues to struggle violently against restraints that it could so easily remove. It is all very puzzling, but I think we must now discard the theory that any of these people were prisoners under restraint."

They were all watching her closely as she went on. "But what is affecting them? What is it that leaves a crew member normally a responsible, highly trained individual capable of guiding a starship, in such a state that it cannot unfasten its couch restraints? What has rendered the other crew members incapable of opening their own dormitory doors or finding food for themselves? Why has their behavior degenerated to that of unthinking animals? Could contaminated food, or the absence of specific foods, have caused this? And before you left me, the Senior Physician suggested that an organism might have invaded the brain tissues. Is it possible that—"

"If you will stop asking questions, Technician," Murchison broke in crossly, "I'll have a chance to answer some of them. No, the food supply is plentiful and contains nothing toxic to this life-form. I have analyzed and identified several varieties carried on the ship, so you will be able to feed them when you go back. As for the brain tissues, there are no indications of damage, circulatory impairment, infection, or any pathological abnormality.

"I found trace quantities of a complex chemical structure that, in the metabolism of this life-form, would act as a powerful tranquilizer. The residual material suggests that a massive dose was absorbed perhaps three or four days ago, and the effect has since worn off. A large supply of this tranquilizer was found in one of the cadaver's harness pouches. So it seems that the crew members tranquilized themselves before confining themselves to the control couch and their dormitories."

There was a long silence that was broken by Khone, who was holding up its offspring where the scrawny little entity could see all the strange creatures on the other side of its transparent panel. Cha Thrat wondered if the Gogleskan was already trying to weaken the young one's conditioning, even at the tender age of two days.

Impersonally it said, "It is hoped that the time of more intelligent and experienced healers will not be wasted by this interruption, but on Goglesk it is accepted that in certain circumstances, and against their will, otherwise intelligent and civilized beings will behave like vicious and destructive animals. Perhaps the entities on the other vessel have a similar problem, and must take strong and repeated doses of medication to keep their animal natures under control so that they can live civilized lives, and make progress, and build starships.

"Perhaps they are starved," Khone ended, "not of food but of their civilizing drug."

"A neat idea," Murchison said warmly, then matching the Gogleskan's impersonal tone it went on. "Admiration is felt for the originality of the healer's thinking but, regrettably, the medication concerned would not increase awareness and the ability to mentate, it would decrease it to the point where continuous use would cause these people to spend their entire lives in a state of semi-consciousness."

"Perhaps," Cha Thrat joined in, "the state of semi-consciousness is pleasant and desirable. It shames me to admit it, but on Sommaradva there are people who deliberately affect and often damage their minds with substances for the purely temporary pleasure they give the user . . ."

"Sommaradva's shame," Naydrad said angrily, "is shared by many worlds in the Federation."

". . . And when these harmful substances are withdrawn suddenly from habitual users," she went on, "their behavior becomes irrational and violent and similar, in many respects, to that of the FGHJs on the other ship."

Murchison was shaking its head. "Sorry, no again. I cannot be absolutely certain because we are dealing with the metabolism of a completely new life-form here, but I would say that the traces found in the cadaver's brain was a simple tranquilizer that deadens rather than heightens awareness, and is almost certainly nonaddictive. Had this not been so I would have suggested using it as an anesthetic.

"And before you ask," the Pathologist went on, "progress with the anesthetic is slow. I have gone as far as I can go with the physiological data provided by the cadaver, but to produce one that will be safe to use in large doses I require blood and gland secretion samples from a living FGHJ."

Cha Thrat was silent for a moment, then she turned to include Prilicla as she said, "I could not find any trace of injured or unconscious survivors during my preliminary search, but I shall search again more diligently when the required samples have been obtained. Is the being still alive? Can you give me even an approximate guide to its location?"

"I can still feel it, friend Cha," Prilicla replied. "But the cruder, conscious emoting of the other survivors is obscuring it."

"Then the sooner Pathologist Murchison has its samples the sooner we'll have the anesthetic to knock out the emotional interference," Cha Thrat said briskly. "My medial digits are strong enough to restrain the arms of the FGHJ on the control couch while my upper manipulators take the samples. From which veins and organs, and in what quantities, must they be removed?"

Murchison laughed suddenly and said, "Please, Cha Thrat, let the medical team do something to justify its existence. You will hold the crew member tightly to its couch, Doctor Danalta will position the scanner, and I will obtain the samples while—"

"Control here." Fletcher's voice broke in from the wall speaker. "Jump in five seconds from ... now. The extra mass of the distressed ship will delay our return somewhat. We are estimating Sector General parking orbit in just under four days."

"Thank you, friend Fletcher," Prilicla said.

Suddenly there was the familiar but indescribable sensation, unseen, unheard, and unfelt but indisputably present, that signaled their removal from the universe of matter to the tiny, unreal, and purely mathematical structure that the ship's hyperdrive generators had built around them. She forced herself to look through the casualty deck's direct vision panel. The tractor and pressor beams that laced the ships rigidly together were invisible, so that she saw only the ridiculously flimsy boarding tube joining them and, at the bottom of the metal chasm formed by the two hulls, the heaving, flickering grayness that seemed to reach up through her eyes and pull her very brain out of focus.

She returned her attention to the solid, familiar if temporarily unreal world of the casualty deck before hyperspace could give her an eyestrain headache.

Cha Thrat had time for only a few words with Khone before following Murchison, Danalta, and Naydrad to the boarding tube. The Charge Nurse was helping her carry packages of the material that Murchison had identified as food, and she had only to compare them with the hundreds of others in the other ship's stores to be able to feed all of the surviving crew members until they bulged at the seams.

Her last sight of the casualty deck for a long time, although she did not know it just then, was of Senior Physician Prilicla hovering above the widely scattered remains of the cadaver and interspersing its quiet words to Khone with untranslatable cluckings and trillings to the younger Gogleskan.

"If we can spare the time," Cha Thrat said to the Pathologist when they were standing around the control couch and its agitated and weakly struggling occupant, "we could feed it before taking your samples. That might make the patient more contented, and amenable."

"We can spare the time for that," Murchison replied, then added, "There are times, Cha Thrat, when you remind me of somebody else."

"Who do we know," Naydrad asked in its forthright Kelgian manner, "who's that weird?"

The Pathologist laughed but did not reply, and neither did Cha Thrat. Without realizing it, Murchison had moved into a sensitive and potentially highly embarrassing area, and, if it ever did learn exactly what had happened to the Sommaradvan's mind on Goglesk, it should be from its life-mate, Conway, and not Cha Thrat—Prilicla had been quite insistent about that.

There was surprisingly little variety in the FGHJs' food containers— two differently shaped plastic bottles, one holding water and the other a faintly odorous nutrient liquid, and there were uniform blocks of a dry, spongy material wrapped in a thin plastic film with a large ring for tearing it open. The liquid and solid foods were synthetic, according to Murchison, but nutritionally tailored to the requirements of the FGHJs' metabolism, and the small quantities of nonnutrient material present were probably there to excite the taste buds.

But when Cha Thrat tossed one of the packages into the crew member's hands, it began tearing at it with its teeth without removing the plastic wrapping. The simple, spring-loaded caps sealing the bottles were also ignored. It tore open the neck of the container with its teeth and sucked out the liquid that it had not already spilled down its chest.

A few minutes later the Pathologist made an untranslatable sound and said, "Its table manners certainly leave a lot to be desired, but it doesn't appear to be hungry anymore. Let's get started."

Feeding the crew member made no perceptible difference to its behavior except, perhaps, to give it more strength to resist them. By the time Murchison had withdrawn its samples, Naydrad, Cha Thrat, and the Pathologist itself were displaying several areas of surface bruising and Danalta, whose body could not be injured or deformed except by the application of ultrahigh temperatures, had been forced into some incredible shape-changes in order to help them immobilize the brute. When the task was done, Murchison sent Naydrad and Danalta ahead with its test samples while it remained, breathing rapidly, and with its eyes fixed on the crew member.

"I don't like this," it said.

"It worries me, too," Cha Thrat said. "However, if a problem is restated often enough, in different words, a solution sometimes emerges."

"I suppose some wise old Sommaradvan philosopher said that," Murchison said drily. "I'm sorry, Technician. What were you going to say?"

"An Earth-human Lieutenant called Timmins said it," she replied. "And I was about to restate the problem, which is that we are faced with a ship's crew who are apparently suffering from a disease that leaves them completely healthy, but mindless. Not only can they not operate their own undamaged and fully functioning ship, they do not remember how to unfasten their leg restraints, unlatch doors, or open food containers. They have become like healthy animals."

Murchison said quietly, "The problem is being restated, but in the same words."

"The living quarters are bare and comfortless," Cha Thrat went on, "which made us think at first that this was a prison ship. But is it possible that the crew members, for reasons that may be psychological and associated with space-travel, or a disease that affects them during space travel, know that bodily comforts, pleasant surroundings, and valued personal possessions would be wasted on them during a voyage because they *expect* to become animals. Perhaps the condition is brief, episodic, and temporary, but on this occasion something went wrong and it became permanent."

"Now," Murchison said, twitching her shoulders in the movement that Earth-humans called a shiver, "the words are different. But if it is of any help to you, among the samples Naydrad brought me for analysis there was medication as well as food. The medication was of one kind only, the tranquilizer capsules of the type found on the cadaver, in a form intended for oral self-administration. So you may be right about them expecting the condition and taking steps to reduce accidental damage to themselves during the mindless phase. But it's strange that Naydrad, who looks very carefully for such things, found only this one type of medication, and no sign of any instruments for the purposes of examination, diagnosis, or surgery. Even if they knew in advance that they were going to take sick, it looks as if the ship's crew did not include a medic."

"If anything," Cha Thrat said, "this new information increases the problem."

Murchison laughed, but the pallor of its normally pink face showed that it found nothing humorous in the situation. It said grimly, "I could not find anything wrong with the being I examined, apart from the accidental head injury that killed it, nor can I see anything clinically wrong with the other crew members. But *something* has tracelessly destroyed their higher centers of intelligence and wiped their minds clean of all memory, training, and experience so that they are left with nothing but the instincts and behavior patterns of animals.

"What kind of organism or agency," it ended with another shiver, "could cause such a selectively destructive effect as that?"

Cha Thrat had a sudden urge to wrap her medial arms around the Pathologist and comfort it, and an upsurge of the kind of emotion that no Sommaradvan, male or female, should feel for an Earth-human. With difficulty she controlled the feelings that were not her own and said gently, "The anesthetic might give you the answer. We are seeing patients in whom the disease, or whatever, has run its course. If they are knocked out and we found the other one, isn't it possible that the disease might not have run its course with this survivor, or the survivor has natural resistance to it? By studying the disease and the resistant patient you might discover the cure for all of them."

"The anesthetic, yes," Murchison said, and smiled. "Your tactful way of reminding a stupid Pathologist of the elements of her job would do credit to Prilicla itself. I'm wasting time here."

It turned to leave, then hesitated. Its face was still very pale.

"Whatever it is that is affecting these people," it said grimly, "is outside my clinical experience, and possibly that of the hospital. But there should be no danger to us. You already know from your medical lectures that other-species pathogens can effect only life-forms that share a common planetary and evolutionary background, and have no effect on off-planet organisms. But there are times when, in spite of everything we know to the contrary, we wonder if we will someday run into the exception that proves the rule, a disease or a clinical condition that is capable of crossing the species barrier.

"The mere possibility that this might be that exception," it went on very seriously, "is scaring the hell out of me. If this should be our bacteriological bogeyman, we must remember that the disease does not appear to have any physical effects. The onset and symptomology of the condition are more likely to be psychological rather than physical. I shall discuss this with Prilicla, and we shall be watching you for any marked behavioral changes, just as you must keep a watch on your own mental processes for uncharacteristic thoughts or feelings."

The Pathologist shook its head in obvious self-irritation. "Nothing can harm you here, I'm as sure of that as I can possibly be. But please, Cha Thrat, be very careful anyway."

CHAPTER 18

She did not know how long she spent watching the mindless struggling of the FGHJ on its couch, and its strong, blunt-fingered hands that had guided this great vessel between the stars before she left the control deck, feeling depressed and angry at her inability to produce a single constructive idea, to begin collecting food for the other, still-hungry crew members. But when she entered the nearest food storage compartment a few minutes later, she was startled to find Prilicla already there.

"Friend Cha," the empath said, "there has been a change of plan..."

The anesthetic that Murchison was producing would have to be tested, in minute but gradually increasing doses, initially on the FGHJ in Control. That process could take anything up to three days before the Pathologist could pronounce it safe for use. Prilicla felt sure that the survivor did not have three days and another method of pacifying the crew members, not as effective as anesthesia, must be tried. Adequate supplies of the crew's own tranquilizers were available, and large doses of these would be added to the crew's food and drink in the hope that, heavily tranquilized and with their hunger satisfied, the intensity of their emotional radiation would be reduced to a level where the empath could isolate and locate the remaining and seriously ill or injured survivor.

"I would like all of the crew members to be fed and tranquilized as quickly as possible," Prilicla went on. "Our friend's emotional radiation is characteristic of a mind of high intelligence presently degraded by pain, rather than one in the condition of its crew-mates, but it grows steadily weaker. I fear for its life."

At Prilicla's direction she heavily dosed the liquid food and water, then distributed it quickly to the dormitories while the Cinrusskin moved from deck to deck, with its empathic faculty extended to its maximum range and sensitivity. With full stomachs and dulled minds—some of them even went to sleep—the crew members' emotional radiation became less obtrusive, but otherwise the results were negative.

"I still can't get a fix," Prilicla said, its body trembling to its own as well as Cha Thrat's disappointment. "There is still too much interference from the conscious survivors. All we can do now is return to *Rhabwar* and try to assist friend Murchison. Your charges will not grow hungry again for some time. Coming?"

"No," she said, "I would prefer to continue the normal, physical search for your dying survivor."

"Friend Cha," Prilicla said, "must I remind you again that I am not a telepath, and that your secret, inner thoughts remain your own property. But your feelings are very clear to me, and they are of low-intensity excitement, pleasure, and caution, with the excitement predominating and the caution barely detectable. This worries me. My guess is that you have had an idea or come to a conclusion of some kind, which will involve personal risk before it can be proved or disproved. Would you like to tell me about it?"

The simple answer would have been "No," but she could not bring herself to hurt the empath's hypersensitive feelings with such a verbal discourtesy. Instead she said carefully, "It may be that the idea came as a result of my ignorance regarding your empathic faculty, hence my reticence in mentioning it until I was sure that it had some value and I would avoid embarrassment."

Prilicla continued to hover silently in the center of the compartment, and Cha Thrat went on. "When we first searched the ship you were able to detect the presence of the unconscious survivor, but not locate it because of the conscious emoting of the others. Now that they are pacified into near-unconsciousness, the situation is the same because our survivor's condition has worsened, and I fear that it will remain the same even when the anesthetic becomes available and the others, too, are deeply unconscious."

"I share that fear," the empath said quietly. "But go on."

"In my ignorance of the finer workings of your empathic faculty," she continued, "I assumed that a weak source of emotional radiation positioned nearby would be more easily detectable than a stronger source at a distance. If there had been any such variation in strength, I'm sure you would have mentioned it."

"I would," Prilicla said, "and you are right in many respects. In others, well, my emphathic faculty has limitations. It responds to the quality and intensity of feelings as well as their proximity. But detection is dependent on factors other than distance. There is the degree of intelligence and emotional sensitivity, the intensity of the emotions being felt, the physical size and strength of the emoting brain, and, of course, the level of consciousness. Normally these limitations can be ignored when I'm searching for just one source and my friends, usually the medical team, move away or control their emotions while I'm searching. That isn't the case here. But you must have reached some conclusions. What are they?"

Choosing her words carefully, Cha Thrat replied, "That, because of its location, the unconscious survivor's radiation is and will remain obscured, and that it is very close to, or surrounded by, the conscious sources. This narrows the volume to be searched to the dormitory deck and perhaps the levels above and below it, and I shall concentrate on that volume only. And you said just now that the physical size of the emoting brain is a factor. Could it be that the survivor is a very small, and young, FGHJ hiding close to the mindless parent?"

"Possibly," Prilicla replied. "But regardless of age or size, it is in very bad shape."

Controlling her growing excitement, she went on. "There must be small storage cabinets, systems inspection centers, and odd holes and corners where a crew member or child would not normally go, but where a barely conscious entity whose injuries caused it to act irrationally might have hidden itself. I feel sure than I will find it soon."

"I know," Prilicla said. "But there is more."

Cha Thrat hesitated, then said, "With respect, Cinrusskins are not a robust species, and for that reason are more sensitive to the risk of physical injury than beings like myself. I can assure you that I have no intention of placing myself at risk, for whatever reason. But if I was to tell you my plan in detail, the possibility exists that you would forbid me to carry it out."

"Would you obey me if I did?" Prilicla asked.

She did not reply.

"Friend Cha," Prilicla said gently, "you have many qualities that I find admirable, including that of moderate cowardice, but you worry me. You have shown yourself reluctant to obey orders that you personally feel to be wrong or unjustified. You have been disobedient in Sector General, on this ship, and, I suspect, on your home world. This is not a quality that people find admirable in a person of subordinate rank. What are we going to do with you?"

Cha Thrat was about to tell the little empath how sorry she felt at causing it mental distress, then realized that it already knew exactly how she felt toward it. Instead she said, "With respect, you could allow me to proceed, and ask the Captain to concentrate the sensors on the reduced search area I have indicated, and report any changes to me at once."

"You know that I was thinking in the longer term," Prilicla said. "But yes, I shall do as you suggest. I share friend Murchison's feelings about this situation. There is something very strange here, and possibly dangerous, but we cannot even guess where the threat, if there is a threat, will come from. Take great care, friend Cha, and guard your mind as well as your body."

Cha Thrat began the search as soon as Prilicla left her, starting with the level above the dormitory deck, then moving to the one below it. But from the start her principal intention had been to enter and search those occupied dormitories, and, as soon as she did so, she knew that there would be a reaction from whoever was watching the sensor displays.

When it came, the voice in her earpiece was that of the Captain itself.

"Technician!" it said sharply. "The sensors show a body of your mass and temperature entering one of the dormitories. Get out of there at once!"

It was possible to argue politely and be circumspect with a gentle little entity like Prilicla, Cha Thrat thought sadly, but not with the Captain. She had just been given a direct order that she had no intention of obeying, so she spoke as if she had not heard it.

"I have entered a dormitory and am moving sideways around the room with my back to the wall," she said calmly. "I am moving slowly so as not to disturb or frighten the occupants, who seem to be half asleep. Two of them have turned their heads to watch me but are making no threatening movements. There is a small door, tight-fitting and mounted flush with the wall, probably a recessed storage cabinet, that might be large enough for an FGHJ to force a way in to hide. I am opening the door now. Inside there are . . ."

"Switch on your vision pickup," Fletcher said angrily, "and save your breath."

". . . shelves containing what appears to be cleaning materials for the waste-disposal facility," she continued. "In case a fast retreat is necessary, I have left the heavier equipment outside and am wearing only a headset. Now I'm moving toward the wall facing the entrance where there is another small door."

"So you *can* hear me," Fletcher said coldly. "And you heard my order."

"I've opened it," she went on quickly, "and the missing survivor isn't there. Beside the door at floor level there is a small, flat, rectangular flap. Possibly it conceals a recessed handle for an upward-opening door. I will have to lie flat on the floor, and try to avoid the body wastes, to examine it."

She heard the Captain make an untranslatable but very unsympathetic sound, then she said, It is a tight-fitting flap, hinged on the top side, and free to move in or out with gentle pressure. There is a layer of sponge around the edges that suggests that it is nearly airtight. I can't get my head close enough to the floor to see inside the flap, but when I open it there is a strong smell that reminds me of the Sommaradvan *glytt* plant.

"I'm sorry," she went on. "Quite apart from the fact that you don't know what a *glytt* plant smells like, one wonders whether the seal is intended to keep the unpleasant smell of FGHJ wastes in or the other smell out. Or maybe it is just an inlet point for some kind of deodorant . . ."

"Friend Cha," Prilicla broke in. "In the short time since you inhaled the odor, has there been any irritation of your breathing passages, nausea, impairment of vision, or dulling of sensation or intellect?"

"What intellect?" Fletcher murmured in a disparaging voice.

"No," she replied. "I am opening the door of the last remaining storage closet to be searched. It is larger than the others, filled with racked tools and what looks like replacement parts for the dormitory furniture, but is otherwise empty. The crew members are still ignoring me. I'm leaving now to search the next dormitory."

"Technician," Fletcher said quietly. "If you can reply to Prilicla I know you can hear me. Now, I'm willing to consider your earlier disobedience as a temporary aberration, a fit of overenthusiasm, and a minor disciplinary matter. But if you continue the search in direct contravention of my orders you will be in major trouble. Neither the Monitor Corps nor the hospital has time for irresponsible subordinates."

"But I take full responsibility for my actions," Cha Thrat protested, "including any credit or discredit that may result from them. I know that I lack the training to investigate an other-species ship properly, but

I am simply opening and closing doors and being very careful while I'm doing it."

The Captain did not reply and maintained its silence even when the sensors must have been showing Cha Thrat entering the second dormitory. It was Prilicla who spoke first.

"Friend Fletcher," the empath said quietly, "I agree that there is a small element of risk in what the technician is doing. But it has discussed some of its ideas with me and is acting with my permission and, well, limited approval."

Ignoring the tranquilized FGHJs and not speaking at all, Cha Thrat was able search the dormitory much more quickly, but with the same negative result. None of the storage cabinets revealed the missing survivor, adult or child, and the narrow, floor-level flap held nothing but the smell of *glytt*, which never had been one of her favorite aromas.

But the Cinrusskin's attempts to divert the Captain's anger from her aroused such a sudden emotional warmth in her that she hoped the empath would feel her gratitude. Without breaking into the conversation, and hoping that Prilicla could not feel her growing disappointment, she began searching the third and last dormitory.

". . . In any case, friend Fletcher," the empath was saying, "the responsibility for whatever happens on the distressed ship until the survivors are treated and evacuated is not yours, but mine."

"I know, I know," the Captain agreed irritably. "On the site of a disaster the medical team leader has the rank. In this situation you can tell a Monitor Corps ship commander like myself what to do, and be obeyed. You can even give orders to a Corps Maintenance Technician Grade Two called Cha Thrat, but I seriously doubt if they would be obeyed."

There was another long silence, broken by the subject of the discussion. She said, "I've finished searching the dormitories. All three contain identical arrangements of fittings and storage compartments, none of which contains the FGHJ we're looking for.

"But the first and second dormitories share a common wall," she went on, trying to sound hopeful, "likewise the second and third. But the first and third are divided by a short corridor leading inboard toward what must be another, fairly large storage compartment whose sides are common to the inner walls of the three dormitories. The missing FGHJ could be there."

"I don't think so," Fletcher said. "The sensors show it as an empty compartment, about half the size of a dormitory, with a lot of low-power circuitry and ducting, probably environmental control lines to the dormitories, mounted on or behind the wall surfaces. By empty we mean that there are no large metal objects in the room, although organic material could be present if it was stored in nonmetal containers. But a piece of organic material of the body mass and temperature of a living FGHJ, whether moving or at rest, would show very clearly."

"All the indications are that it is just another storeroom," the Captain ended. "But no doubt you will search it, anyway."

With difficulty, Cha Thrat ignored Fletcher's tone as she said, "During my first search of this area I looked into this corridor and saw the blank end-wall containing what I mistakenly thought to be a section of badly fitted wall plating. My excuse for making this mistake is that there is no external handle or latch visible. On closer examination I see that it is not a badly fitted plate but an inward-opening door that is very slightly ajar, and the scanner shows that it fastens only from the inside.

"The vision pickup is on," she added. "I'm pushing the door open now."

The place was a mess, she thought, with weightlessness adding to the general disorder so that floating debris made it difficult to see any distance into the room. There was a very strong smell of *glytt*.

"We aren't receiving a clear picture," said Fletcher, "and something close to the lens is blocking most of the view. Have you attached the pickup correctly or are we seeing part of your shoulder?"

"No, sir," she replied, trying to keep her tone properly subordinate. "The compartment is gravity-free and a large number of flat, roughly circular objects are floating about. They appear to be organic, fairly uniform in size, dark gray on one surface and with a paler, mottled appearance on the other. I suppose they could be cakes of preprepared food that escaped from a ruptured container, or they might be solid body waste, similar to that found in the dormitories, which has dried and become discolored. I'm trying to move some of it out of the way now."

With a sudden feeling of distaste, she cleared the visual obstructions from the front of the pickup, using her medial hands because they were the only ones still covered by gloves. There was no response from *Rhabwar*.

"There are large, irregular clumps of spongelike or vegetable material attached to the walls and ceiling," she went on, moving her body so that the pickup's images would let the others see, however unclearly, what she was trying to describe. "So far as I can see, each clump is colored differently, although the colors are subdued, and under each one there is a short length of padded shelf.

"At floor level," she continued, "I can see three narrow, rectangular flaps. Their size and positions correspond to those found in the dormitories. These pancakes, or whatever, are all over the place, but I can see something large floating in a corner near the ceiling . . . It's the FGHJ!"

"I don't understand why it didn't register on the sensors," Fletcher said. It was the kind of Captain who insisted on the highest standards of efficiency from its crew and the equipment in its charge, and treated a mal-function in either as a personal affront.

"Good work, friend Cha," Prilicla said, enthusiastically breaking in. "Quickly now, move it to the entrance for loading into the litter. We'll be with you directly. What is the general clinical picture?"

Cha Thrat moved closer, swatting more obstructions from her path as she said, "I can't see any physical injuries at all, not even minor bruising, or external evidence of an illness. But this FGHJ isn't like the others. It seems to be a lot thinner and less well muscled. The skin appears darker, more wrinkled, and the hooves are discolored and cracked in several places. The body hair is gray. I . . . I think this is a much older FGHJ. It might be the ship ruler. Maybe it hid itself in here to avoid what happened to the rest of its crew . . ."

She broke off, and Prilicla called urgently, "Friend Cha, why are you feeling like that? What happened to you?"

"Nothing happened to me," she replied, fighting to control her disappointment. "I am holding the FGHJ now. There is no need to hurry. It is dead."

"That explains why my sensors didn't register," Fletcher said.

"Friend Cha," Prilicla said, ignoring the interruption, "are you quite *sure?* I can still feel the presence of a deeply unconscious mind."

Cha Thrat drew the FGHJ toward her so that she could use her upper hands, then said, "The body temperature is very low. Its eyes are open and do not react to light. The usual vital signs are absent. I'm sorry, it is dead and . . ." She broke off to look more closely at the creature's head, then went on excitedly. "And I think I know what killed it! The back of the neck. Can you see it?"

"Not clearly," Prilicla replied quickly, obviously feeling her own growing excitement, and fear. "One of those disklike objects is in the way."

"But that's *it,*" she said. "I thought at first that one of them had drifted against the cadaver and stuck to its head. But I was wrong. The thing attached itself deliberately to the FGHJ with those thick white tendrils you can see growing from the edge of the disk. Now that I'm looking for them, I can see that they all have the tendrils and, judging by their length, the penetration into the cadaver's spinal column and rear cranium is very deep. That thing is, or was, alive, and could have been responsible for—"

"Technician," Fletcher broke in harshly, "get out of there!"

"At once," Prilicla said.

Very carefully Cha Thrat released her hold on the dead FGHJ, removed her vision pickup, and attached its magnetic clips to a clear area of wall. She knew that the medical team would want to study this strange and abhorrent life-form that was infesting the ship before deciding how to deal with it. Then she turned toward the entrance, which now seemed to be very far away.

The disks hung thickly like an alien minefield between the door and herself. Some of them were still moving slowly in the air eddies caused by her entry or by the blows with which she had so casually knocked them aside, or perhaps of their own volition. They presented views from every angle—the smooth surface of the mottled side, the gray and wrinkled reverse side, and the edges with their fringe of limp white tendrils.

She had been so busy searching for an FGHJ survivor that she had scarcely looked at the objects she had mistaken for cakes of food or dried wastes floating in the room. She still did not know what they were, only of what they were capable, which was the utter destruction of the highly trained and intelligent minds of their victims to leave them with nothing but the basic and purely instinctive responses of animals.

The thought of a predator who did not eat or physically harm its prey, but gorged itself on the *intelligence* of its victim, made her want to seek refuge in madness. She was desperately afraid of touching one of them again, but there were too many of them for her to avoid doing so. But if any of them got in her way, Cha Thrat decided grimly, she would touch it, hit it, very hard.

The gentle, reassuring voice of Prilicla sounded in her earpiece. It said, "You are controlling your fear well, friend Cha. Move slowly and carefully and don't—"

She winced as a high-pitched, piercing sound erupted from the earpiece, signifying that too many people were talking to her at once and had overloaded her translator. But they realized immediately what was happening because the oscillation wavered and died to become one voice, the Captain's.

"Technician, *behind you!*"

By then it was too late.

All of her attention had been directed ahead and to the sides, where the greatest danger lay. When she felt the surprisingly light touch, followed by a sensation of numbness on the back of her neck, a cool, detached part of her mind thought that it was considerate of the thing to anesthetize the area before inserting its tendrils. She swung an eye to the rear to see what was happening, and instinctively raised her upper hands to push away the disk that had left the dead FGHJ and was attaching itself to her. But the hands fumbled weakly, their digits suddenly powerless, and the arms fell limply away.

Other parts of her body ceased working, or began twitching and bending in the random, uncoordinated fashion of a person with serious brain damage. The calm, detached portion of her mind thought that her condition was not a pleasant sight for friends to see.

"*Fight* it, Cha Thrat!" Murchison's voice shouted from her earpiece. "Whatever it's doing, fight it! We're on our way."

She heard and appreciated the concern in the Pathologist's voice, but her tongue was one of the organs that was not working just then because her jaw was clamped shut. Altogether, she was in a state of considerable physiological confusion as muscles continued to twitch uncontrollably, her body writhed in weightless contortions, and sensations of heat, cold, pain, and pleasure affected random areas of her skin. She knew that the creature was exploring her central nervous system, trying to find out how her Sommaradvan body worked so that it would be able to control her.

Gradually the twitchings and writhings and even her fear diminished and were gone, and her body was able to resume its interrupted journey. The lens of the vision pickup turned to follow her. When she reached the door, she slammed it closed and locked it with fastenings that had suddenly become familiar.

"Technician," Fletcher said sharply, "what are you *doing*?"

It was obvious that she was locking the door from the inside, Cha Thrat thought irritably. Probably the Captain meant why was she doing it. She tried to reply but her lips and tongue would not work. But surely her actions would tell all of them that she, it, both of them, did not wish to be disturbed.

CHAPTER 19

They were all talking at once again. She had to bend the earpiece back to reduce the sudden howl of translator oscillation that was making it difficult to think. The vision pickup was still following her and they must have realized the significance of her action because the babble died quickly and became one voice.

"Friend Cha," Prilicla said, "listen to me carefully. Some kind of parasitic life-form has attached itself to you and the quality of your emotional radiation is changing. Try, try hard to pull it off and get out of there before your condition worsens."

"I'm all right," Cha Thrat protested. "Honestly, I feel fine. Just leave me alone until I can—"

"But your thoughts and feelings aren't your own anymore," Murchison broke in. "*Fight*, dammit! Try to keep control of your mind. At least try to open that door again so we won't waste time burning through it when we get to you."

"No," the Captain said firmly. "I'm very sorry, Technician, they aren't leaving this ship . . ."

The argument that ensued immediately overloaded Cha Thrat's translator again, which made it impossible for her to talk to any of them. But there were parts of it, particularly when Fletcher was speaking in its ruler's voice, that she heard clearly.

The Captain was reminding them, and calling on Prilicla to support it, that the strictest possible rules of quarantine governed this situation. They had encountered a life-form that absorbed the memory, personality, and intelligence of its victims and left them like mindless animals. Moreover, judging by their recent observations of Technician Cha Thrat, the things were capable of adapting to and quickly controlling any life-form.

By then nobody was trying to interrupt Fletcher as it went on. "This could mean that they are not native to the planet of the FGHJs, that they may have come aboard anywhere, and are capable of doing this to the members of every intelligent species in the Federation! I don't know what drives them, why they're content to suck out the intelligence of their victims instead of feeding on the bodies, and I don't even want to think about it. Or about how, or how rapidly, they can reproduce themselves. There are dozens of them in the room with Cha Thrat, and they're so small that more of them could be hidden in odd corners all over the ship.

"Until we get a properly equipped and protected decontamination squad in there," Fletcher went on, "I have no choice but to seal and place a guard on the boarding tube. This is something completely new to our experience, and it may well be that the hospital will advise the complete destruction of the ship, and its contents.

"If you will all think about it for a moment," the Captain ended, sounding very unhappy with itself, "you will realize that we cannot take the slightest risk of that life-form getting onto this ship, or running loose in Sector General."

There was silence for several moments while they thought about it, and Cha Thrat thought about the strange thing that had happened, and was still happening, to her.

While trying to help Khone she had experienced a joining, and with it the shock and disorientation and excitement of having her mind invaded, but not taken over, by a personality that was completely alien to her. The effect had been rendered even stranger and more frightening by the fact that the Gogleskan's mind had also contained material from a previous joining with a mind whose memories were even more confusing, those of the Earth-human Conway. But this sensation was entirely different. The approach and entry was gentle, reassuring, and even pleasant, giving her the feeling that it was a process perfected after a lifetime of experience. But like herself, this invader seemed to be badly confused by the contents of her part-Sommaradvan, part-Gogleskan, and part Earth-human mind and, because of that confusion, it was having trouble controlling her body. She was still not sure of its intentions, but quite certain that she was still herself and that she was learning more and more about it with every passing second.

Murchison was the first to break the silence. It said, "We have protective suits and cutting torches. Why don't we decontaminate that compartment ourselves and burn them all, including the one on the technician's neck, and get Cha Thrat back here for treatment while it still has some of its mind left? The hospital people can finish the decontamination when we—"

"No," the Captain said firmly. "If any of you medics go onto that ship, you won't be allowed back here."

Cha Thrat did not want to join in because speaking would involve a minor mental effort and consequent disruption in an area of her mind that she wished to remain receptive. Instead, she moved her lower arms in the Sign of Waiting, then realizing that it meant nothing to non-Sommaradvans, held up one hand palm forward in the Earth-human equivalent.

"I am confused," Prilicla said suddenly. "Friend Cha is not feeling pain or mental distress. It is wanting something very badly, but the emotional radiation is characteristic of a source trying very hard to maintain calm and to control its other feelings . . ."

"But it isn't in control," Murchison broke in. "Look at the way it was moving its arms about. You're forgetting that its feelings and emotions aren't its own."

"You, friend Murchison, are not the emotion-sensitive here," Prilicla said in the gentlest possible of reproofs. "Friend Cha, try to speak. What do you want us to do?"

She wanted to tell them to stop talking and leave her alone, but she desperately needed their help and that reply would have given rise to more questions, interruptions, and mental dislocations. Her mind was a bubbling stew of thoughts, impressions, experiences, and memories that concerned not only her own past on Sommaradva and Sector General, but those of Healer Khone and Diagnostician Conway. The new occupant was blundering about like an intruder lost in a large, richly furnished but imperfectly lit household, examining some items and shying away from others. This, Cha Thrat knew, was not the time to leave it alone.

But if she answered a few of their questions, said just enough to keep them quiet and make them do what she wanted, that might be the best course.

"I am not in danger," Cha Thrat said carefully, "or in any physical or emotional distress. I can regain full control of my mind and body any time I wish it, but choose not to because I don't want to risk breaking mental contact by talking for too long. As quickly as possible I want Senior Physician Prilicla and Pathologist Murchison to join me. The FGHJs are not important right now. Neither is the anesthetic or the search for the other survivor because—"

"*No!*" Fletcher broke in, sounding as if it was about to be physically nauseous. "Those things are intelligent. Do you see the insidious way they are trying to get the technician to reassure us and then entice us over to them? No doubt when you two are taken over there will be even better reasons for the rest of us to join you, or you to return here and leave *Rhabwar*'s crew in the same condition as the FGHJs. No, there will be no more victims."

Cha Thrat tried not to listen to the interruption because it set off trains of thought in her mind that were unsettling the new occupant and kept it from communicating properly with her. Very carefully she lifted her rear medial arm and bent it so that the large digit was pointing at the thing clinging to the back of her neck.

"This is the survivor," she said, "the only survivor."

Suddenly the stranger in her mind was feeling a measure of satisfaction and reassurance, as if it had at last succeeded in making its need understood, and she found that she could speak without the fear of it going away, fading, and perhaps dying on her.

"It is very ill," she went on, "but it was able to regain mobility and consciousness for a short time when I entered the compartment. That was when it decided to make a last, desperate try to obtain help for its friends and the host creatures in their charge. The first, fumbled attempts to make contact were the reason for my uncoordinated limb movements. Only within the past few minutes has it realized that it is the only survivor."

None of them, not even the Captain, was saying a word now. She continued. "That is why I need Prilicla to monitor its emotional radiation at close range, and Murchison to investigate its dead friends, in the hope of finding out what killed them and finding a cure before its own condition becomes terminal—"

"No," the Captain said again. "It sounds like a good story, and especially intriguing to a bunch of e-t medics, but it could still be a ruse to get mental control of more of our people. I'm sorry, Technician, we can't risk it."

Prilicla said gently, "Friend Fletcher makes a good point. And you yourself know that the Captain's arguments are valid because you observed the mindless condition of the FGHJs after these creatures left them. Friend Cha, I, too, am sorry."

It was Cha Thrat's turn to be silent as she tried to find a solution that would satisfy them. Somehow she had not expected the gentle little empath to be so tough.

Finally she said, "Physically the creature is extremely debilitated and I could quite easily remove it to demonstrate its lack of physical control over me, but such a course might kill it. However, if I was to demonstrate my normal physical coordination by leaving this compartment and descending four levels, where we would be clear of the emotional interference from the FGHJs, and if I were to urge the creature to remain conscious until then, would the Cinrusskin empathic faculty be able to detect whether its emotional radiation was that of a highly intelligent and civilized being, or the kind of mental predator that seems to be *scaring* you out of your wits?"

"Four levels down is just one deck above the boarding tube..." began the Captain, but Prilicla cut it short.

"I could detect the difference, friend Cha," it said, "if I was close enough to the life-form concerned. I'll meet you there directly."

There was another howl of oscillation from her translator. When it faded Prilicla was saying "Friend Fletcher, as the senior medical officer present it is my responsibility to make sure whether the life-form attached to Cha Thrat is the patient and not the disease. However, my species prides itself in being the most timid and cowardly in the Federation, and all possible precautions will be taken. Friend Cha, set the vision pickup to show if any of those life-forms try to leave the compartment and follow you. If any of them do, I shall return at once to *Rhabwar* and seal the boarding tube. Is that understood?"

"Yes, Senior Physician," said Cha Thrat.

"If anything suspicious occurs while I am with you," it went on, "even if I am able to avoid capture and still appear to be my own self, friend Fletcher will seal the tube and put the quarantine procedure into immediate effect.

"We need as much information on this life-form as you can give us," it ended. "Please continue, friend Cha, we are recording. I'm leaving now."

"And I'm going with you," Murchison said firmly. "If this is the ship's only survivor, one of a newly discovered intelligent species and possible future member of the Federation, Thorny will walk on me with all six of its feet if I let it die. Danalta and Naydrad can stay here in case we have need of special equipment and to watch the vision pickup. And in case the little beastie isn't as friendly as Cha Thrat insists it is, I'll add a heavy-duty cutting torch to my instruments so that I can protect your back."

"Thank you, friend Murchison," Prilicla said, "but no."

"But yes, Senior Physician," the Pathologist replied. "With respect, you have the rank but not the muscles to stop me."

Impatiently Cha Thrat said, "if you want to be able to detect any conscious emotional radiation, please hurry. The patient needs urgent attention . . ."

There was an immediate objection from Fletcher regarding her unjustified use of the word "patient." She ignored it and, trying her best to describe the thoughts and images that had been placed with so much effort in her mind, went on to outline the case history of the survivor and the history of its species.

They came from a world that even the Sommaradvan, Gogleskan, and Earth-human components of her mind considered beautiful, a planet so bountiful that the larger species of fauna did not have to struggle for survival and did not, for that reason, develop intelligence. But from the earliest times, when all life was in the oceans, a species evolved capable of attaching itself to a variety of native life-forms. They formed a symbiotic partnership in which the host creature was directed to the best sources of food while the weak and relatively tiny parasite had the protection of its larger mount as well as the mobility that enabled it to seek out its own, less readily available food supply. By the time the host creatures left the oceans to become large and unintelligent land animals, the mutually profitable arrangement continued and the parasite had become very intelligent indeed.

The earliest recorded history told of vain attempts to nurture intelligence in many different species of host creature. The native, six-limbed FGHJ life-form with its ability to work in a wide variety of materials, when a parasite was directing its hands, was favored above all the others.

But more and more they had wished for mind-partners they could not control, beings who would argue and debate and contribute new ideas and viewpoints, rather than creatures who were little more than general-purpose, self-replenishing organic tools with the ability to see, hear, and manipulate to order.

With these tools they built great cities and manufacturing complexes and vessels that circumnavigated their world, flew in the atmosphere above it, and, ultimately, crossed the terrible and wonderful emptiness between the stars. But the cities, like their starships, were functional and unbeautiful because they had been built by and for the comfort and use of beings without any appreciation of beauty, and whose animal needs were satisfied by food, warmth, and regular satisfaction of the urge to procreate. Like valuable tools they had to be properly maintained, and many of them were well loved with the affection that a civilized being feels for a faithful but nonintelligent pet.

But the parasites had their own special needs that in no respect resembled those of their hosts, whose animal habits and undirected behavior were highly repugnant to them. It was vital to their continued mental well-being that the masters escaped periodically from their hosts to lead their own lives—usually during the hours of darkness when the tools were no longer in use and could be quartered where they could not harm themselves. This they did in the small, quiet, private places, tiny areas of civilization and culture and beauty amid the ugliness of the cities, where their families nested and they were separated from the host creatures by everything but distance.

It had long been an accepted fact among them that no creature or culture could avoid stagnation if it did not go outside its family or its tribe or, ultimately, its world. In their continuing search for other intelligent beings like or totally unlike themselves, many extrasolar planets had been discovered and small colonies established on them, but none of the indigenous life-forms possessed intelligence and had become just so many sets of other-species tools.

Because of an intense aversion to allowing themselves to be touched by the proxy hands of a nonintelligent creature, their medical science catered chiefly to the needs of their hosts and did not include surgery. The result was that when one of their own-planet tools contracted a disease that, to it, was mildly debilitating, the effect on the parasite was often lethal.

Cha Thrat paused for a moment and raised one of her upper hands to support the weight of the parasite. Sensation had returned to her neck and she felt that the creature's tendrils were loosening and pulling free. She could hear Prilicla and Murchison on the deck below.

"That is what happened to their ship," she went on. "The host FGHJs caught something that caused a mild, undulant fever, and recovered. The parasites, with this one exception, perished. But before they returned to their own quarters to die, they placed their now-undirected host creatures in places where food was available and they would not injure themselves, in the hope that help would reach the host creatures in time. The survivor, who seemed to have a partial resistance to the disease, rendered the vessel safe and accessible to rescuers, released the distress beacon, and returned to the ship's Nest to comfort its dying friends.

"But the effort to do this work," Cha Thrat went on, talking directly to Prilicla and Murchison who were now coming up the ramp toward her, "was too much for its host, an aging FGHJ of whom it was particularly fond, and the creature had a sudden cardiac malfunction and died inside the Nest.

"The distress signal was answered not by one of their own ships, but by *Rhabwar*," she concluded, "and the rest we know."

Prilicla did not reply and Murchison moved to one side, keeping the thin tube of its cutting torch aimed at the back of Cha Thrat's neck. Nervously the Pathologist said, "I'd need to check it with my scanner, of course, but I'd say physiological classification DTRC. It's very similar to the DTSB symbiotes some FGLIs wear for fine surgical work. In those cases it's the parasite who supplies the digits and the Tralthan the brains, although there are some OR nurses who would argue about that . . ."

It broke off as Cha Thrat said, "I have been trying to relinquish control of my speech centers so that it would be able to talk to you directly through me, but it is much too weak and is only barely conscious, so I must be its voice. It already knows from my mind who you are, and it is Crelyarrel, of the third division of Trennchi, of the one hundred and seventh division of Yau, and of the four hundred and eighth subdivision of the great Yilla of the Rhiim. I cannot properly describe its feelings in words, but there is joy at the knowledge that the

Rhiim are not the only intelligent species in the Galaxy, sorrow that this wonderful knowledge will die with it, and apologies for anxiety it caused us by—"

"I know what it is feeling," Prilicla said gently, and suddenly they were washed by a great, impalpable wave of sympathy, friendship, and reassurance. "We are happy to meet you and learn of your people, friend Crelyarrel, and we will not allow you to die. Let go now, little friend, and rest, you are in good hands."

Still radiating its emotional support, it went on briskly. "Put away that cutting torch, friend Murchison, and go with the patient and friend Cha to the Rhüm quarters. It will feel more comfortable there, and you have much work to do on its dead friends. Friend Fletcher, preparations will have to be made at the hospital to receive this new life-form. Be ready to send a long hypersignal to Thornnastor as soon as we have a clearer idea of the clinical picture. Friend Naydrad, stand by with the litter in case we need special equipment here, or for the transport of DTRC cadavers to *Rhabwar* for investigation—"

"No!" the Captain said.

Murchison spoke a few words of a kind not normally used by an Earth-human female, then went on. "Captain, we have a patient here, in very serious condition, who is the sole survivor of a disease-stricken ship. You know as well as I that in this situation, you do exactly as Prilicla tells you."

"No," Fletcher repeated. In a quieter but no less firm voice it went on. "I understand your feelings, Pathologist. But are they really yours? You still haven't convinced me that that thing is harmless. I'm remembering those crew members and, well, it might be pretending to be sick. It could be controlling, or at least influencing, the minds of all of you. The quarantine regulations remain in force. Until the Diagnostician-in-Charge of Pathology, or more likely the decontamination squad clears it, nothing or nobody leaves that ship."

Cha Thrat was supporting Crelyarrel in three of her small, upper hands. The DTRC's body, now that she knew it for what it was, no longer looked or felt repugnant to her. The control tendrils hung limply between her LF002digits and the color of its skin was lightening and beginning to resemble that of its dead friends in the Rhiim nest. Had it to die, too, she wondered sadly, because two different people held opposing viewpoints that they both knew to be right?

Proving one of them wrong, especially when the being concerned was a ruler, would have serious personal repercussions, and she was beginning to wonder if she had always been as right as she thought she had been. Perhaps her life would have been happier if, on Sommaradva and at Sector General, she had been more doubtful about some of her certainties.

"Friend Fletcher," Prilicla said quietly. "As an empath I am influenced by feelings of everyone around me. Now I accept that there are beings who, by word or deed or omission, can give outward expression to emotions that they do not feel. But it is impossible for an intelligent entity to produce false emotional radiation, to lie with its mind. Another empath would know this to be so, but as a nonempath you must take my word for it. The survivor cannot and will not harm anyone."

The Captain was silent for a moment, then it said, "I'm sorry, Senior Physician. I'm still not fully convinced that it is not speaking through you and controlling your minds, and I cannot risk letting it aboard this ship."

In this situation there was no doubt about who was right or about what she must do, Cha Thrat thought, because a gentle little being like Prilicla might not be capable of doing it.

"Doctor Danalta," she said, "will you please go quickly to the boarding tube and take up a position and shape that will discourage any Monitor Corps officer from sealing, dismantling, or otherwise closing it to two-way traffic. Naturally, you should try not to hurt any such officer, and I doubt that lethal weapons will be deployed against you, for no other reason than that anything powerful enough to hurt you would seriously damage the hull, but if—"

"Technician!"

Even though the Captain was on *Rhabwar*'s control deck and at extreme range for Prilicla's empathic faculty, the feeling of outrage accompanying the word was making the little Cinrusskin quiver in every limb. Then gradually the trembling subsided as Fletcher brought his anger under control.

"Very well, Senior Physician," it said coldly. "Against my expressed wishes and on your own responsibility, the boarding tube will remain open. You may move freely between there and the casualty deck, but the rest of this ship will be closed to your people and that . . . that thing you insist is a survivor. The matter of Cha Thrat's gross insubordination, with the strong possibility of a charge of incitement to mutiny, will be pursued later."

"Thank you, friend Fletcher," Prilicla said. Then, switching off its mike, it went on. "And you, friend Cha. You have displayed great resourcefulness as well as insubordination. But I am afraid that, even when it is proved that you acted correctly, the Captain's present feelings toward you are of the kind that I have found to be not only unfriendly but extremely long-lasting."

Murchison did not speak until they were in the Rhiim compartment, when it paused in its scanner examination of Crelyarrel to look at her. The expression and tone of voice, Cha Thrat knew from the Earth-human component of her mind, expressed puzzlement and sympathy as it said, "How can one being get into so much trouble in such a short time? What got into you, Cha Thrat?"

Prilicla trembled slightly but did not speak.

CHAPTER 20

Cha Thrat's arrival for her appointment with the Chief Psychologist was punctual to the second, because she had been told that O'Mara considered being too early to be as wasteful of time as being too late. But on this occasion the impunctuality, although indirectly her fault, was on O'Mara's side. The Earth-human Braithwaite, who was the sole occupant of the large outer office, explained.

"I'm sorry for the delay, Cha Thrat," it said, inclining its head toward O'Mara's door, "but that meeting is running late. Senior Physician Cresk-Sar and, in order of seniority, Colonel Skempton, Major Fletcher, and Lieutenant Timmins are with him. The door is supposed to be soundproof, but sometimes I can hear them talking about you."

It smiled sympathetically, pointed to the nearest of the three unoccupied console desks beside it, and said, "Sit there, you should find that one fairly comfortable while we're waiting for the verdict. Try not to worry, Cha Thrat, but if you don't mind, I'd like to get on with my work."

Cha Thrat said that she did not mind, and was surprised when the screen on the desk she was occupying lit up with Braithwaite's work. She did not know what the Earth-human was doing, but while she was trying to understand it the realization came that it was deliberately giving her something to occupy her mind other than the things they were probably saying about her in the next room.

As one of the wizard's principal assistants, Braithwaite was capable of working a few helpful spells of its own.

Since her return to the hospital, Cha Thrat had been relegated to a kind of administrative hyperspace. Maintenance Department wanted nothing to do with her, the Monitor Corps ruler she had so grievously offended on *Rhabwar* seemed to have forgotten her very existence, and the medical training people treated her with sympathy and great care, much as they would a patient who was not expected to be long among them.

Officially there was nothing for her to do, but unofficially she had never been busier in her whole life.

Diagnostician Conway had been very pleased with her work on Goglesk, and had asked her to visit Khone as often as possible because Cha Thrat and itself were the only people that the FOKT would allow within touching distance, although that situation was beginning to change for the better. With behind-the-scenes assistance from the Chief Psychologist and Prilicla, progress was being made toward breaking down the Gogleskan racial conditioning, and Ees-Tawn was working on a miniature distorter, permanently attached to the subject and triggered automatically during the first microseconds of a distress call, which would make it impossible for the wearer to initiate one of the suicidal joinings.

O'Mara had warned them that the final solution to the Gogleskan problem might take many generations, that Khone would never be completely comfortable at the close approach or touch of another person, regardless of species, but that its offspring was already giving indications of being quite happy among strangers.

Thornnastor and Murchison had been successful in isolating and finding a specific against the pathogen affecting Crelyarrel, although they had admitted to Cha Thrat that the principal reason for its survival on the Rhiim ship was its possession of a fair degree of natural resistance. Now the little symbote was going from strength to strength, and was beginning to concern itself about the health and comfort of the FGHJ host creatures. It wanted to know how soon new Rhiim parasites could be brought to Sector General to take charge of them.

Similar questions were being asked by the group of visiting Monitor Corps officers who seemed to be ignorant of, or perhaps disinterested in, her recent insubordination on *Rhabwar*. They were Cultural Contact specialists investigating the ship with a view to gaining as much information as possible about the species who had caused it to be built, including the location of their planet of origin, before making a formal approach to the Rhiim on behalf of the Federation. They badly wanted to talk to the survivor.

Crelyarrel was anxious to cooperate, but the problem was that its people communicated by a combination of touch and telepathy limited to their own species. It was not yet well enough to take full control of a host crew member and, until it was able to do so, the translation computer could not be programmed with the language used by their FGHJ hosts.

Even though it was now generally accepted that the parasitic Rhiim were a highly intelligent and cultured species, none of the hospital staff were particularly eager to surrender their bodies, however temporarily, to DTRC control—and the feeling was mutual. The only person that Crelyarrel would agree to take over and speak through, with her permission, of course, was Cha Thrat.

As a result of these unofficial demands on her time, there had been little of it left for Cha Thrat to worry about her own problems.

Until now.

The muffled sounds of conversation from the inner office had died away into inaudibility, which meant, she thought, that they were either speaking quietly to each other or not speaking at all. But she was wrong, the meeting was over.

Senior Physician Cresk-Sar silently led the way out, its hairy features unreadable. It was followed by Colonel Skempton, who made an untranslatable sound, then *Rhabwar*'s ruler, who neither looked nor spoke, and Lieutenant Timmins, who stared at her for a moment with one eye closed before leaving. She was rising from her seat to enter the inner office when O'Mara came out.

"Sit where you are, this won't take long," it said. "You, too, Braithwaite. Sommaradvans don't mind having their problems discussed before concerned witnesses, and this one certainly has a problem. Is that deformed bird-cage you're sitting on comfortable?

"The problem," it went on before she could reply, "is that you are an oddly shaped peg who doesn't quite fit into any of our neat little holes. You are intelligent, able, strong-minded yet adaptable, and have experienced, seemingly without any permanent ill effects, the levels of mental trauma and disorientation that would cause many beings severe psychological damage. You are well regarded, even respected, by some very important people here, by many with no influence at all, and disliked by a few. The latter group, chiefly Monitor Corps personnel and a few of the medical staff, feel very unsure of who or what you are, and who has the seniority, while working with you.

"Sometimes," Cha Thrat said defensively, "I'm not sure who or what I am myself. When I am thinking like a senior person I can't help behaving like a . . ." She stopped herself before she said too much.

"Like a Diagnostician," O'Mara said drily. "Oh, don't worry, this department never reveals anyone's deep, dark, and, in your case, peculiar secrets. Prilicla, when it wasn't enthusing over your behavior immediately preceding and during Khone's delivery and on the Rhiim ship, told me about the joining it feels you underwent on Goglesk. Being Prilicla, it is anxious to avoid any painful and embarrassing incidents between its friends Conway, Murchison, and yourself, and so are we.

"But the fact remains," the Chief Psychologist went on, "that you shared minds with Khone who, because of an earlier sharing with Conway, gave you much of the knowledge and experience of a Sector General Diagnostician as well as a Gogleskan healer. You also became deeply involved on the mental level with one of the Rhiim parasites, not to mention some earlier prying into the mind of your Chalder friend, AUGL-One Sixteen. I'm not surprised that there are times when you aren't quite sure who or what you are. Is there any doubt about that at present?"

"No," she replied, "you are talking only to Cha Thrat."

"Good," O'Mara said, "because it is Cha Thrat's problematical future that we must now consider. Since the business on *Rhabwar*, when you were not only insubordinate but completely right, the option of a career in Maintenance, even though Timmins speaks highly of you, is closed, as is any hope you may have had of service as a ship's medic with the Monitor Corps. Shipboard discipline is often invisible, but it is there and it is strict, and no ship commander would risk taking on a doctor with a proven record of insubordination.

"The Cultural Contact people you've been helping with the Rhiim parasite," it continued, "are less discipline-oriented than the others, and they are impressed with you and are grateful enough to offer you a spot on your home planet, after the disciplinary dust has had a chance to settle, of course. What would you say to returning to Sommaradva?"

Cha Thrat made an untranslatable sound and O'Mara said drily, "I see. But the medical and surgical options are also closed to you. In spite of the respect in which are held by many of the senior staff, nobody wants a know-it-all trainee nurse on their wards who is likely to say or do something that will suggest that its Charge Nurse or doctor on duty are, well, clinically incorrect. And while you have influence in high places, that also could disappear if the truth about your Gogleskan mind-swap became common knowledge."

Cha Thrat was wondering if there was anything she could do or say that would halt the relentless closing down of her options, when Braithwaite looked up from its display.

"Excuse me, sir," it said. "But from my knowledge of the personalities involved, Conway, Khone, and Prilicla are unlikely to discuss it among anyone but themselves, and Murchison, who is a very intelligent entity indeed, will do likewise when she realizes the truth or learns it from her life-mate. Her psych profile indicates the presence of a well-developed sense of humor, and it might well be that the thought of an other-species entity, and another female at that, looking upon her with the same libidinous feelings as those of her life-mate, Conway, would be funnier than it was embarrassing. Naturally, I would not suggest that any of these misdirected feelings would be translated into action, but certain entertaining sexual fantasies could arise that would illuminate the whole area of interspecies—"

"Braithwaite," O'Mara said quietly, "it is talk like that which gives people the wrong impression about e-t psychologists.

"As for you, Cha Thrat," it went on, "I decided a long time ago that there was only one position here that suited your particular talents. Once again you will start as a trainee, at the bottom, and advancement will be slow because your chief is very hard to please. It is a difficult and often thankless job that will cause irritation to most people, but then you've become used to that. You will have a few compensations, like being able to poke your olfactory orifices into everyone else's business whenever you think it necessary. Do you accept?"

Suddenly Cha Thrat's pulse was clearly audible to her and she was finding it difficult to breathe. "I—I don't understand," she said.

O'Mara took a deep breath, then exhaled through its nose and said, "You *do* understand, Cha Thrat. Don't pretend to be stupid when you aren't."

"I do understand," she agreed, "and I am most grateful. The delay was due to a combination of initial disbelief and consideration of the implications. You are saying that I am to learn the skills of nonmaterial healing, the casting of spells, and that I am to become a trainee wizard."

"Something like that," the Chief Psychologist said. It glanced at the display on her desk and added, "I see that you've already been exposed to the senior staff psych chart amendment procedure. It is routine, unexciting but very necessary work. Braithwaite has been trying to unload the job on someone for months."

THE
GENOCIDAL
HEALER

TO JEFF
AKA JEFFREY MCLLWAIN, MD, FRCS
WHO IS ALSO GREAT WITH SICK
REFRIGERATORS;
IN APPRECIATION

CHAPTER 1

They had assembled in a temporarily unused compartment on the hospital's eighty-seventh level. The room had seen service at various times as an observation ward for the birdlike Nallajims of physiological classification LSVO, as a Melfan ELNT operating theater, and, most recently, as an overflow ward for the chlorine-breathing Illensan PVSJs, whose noxious atmosphere still lingered in trace quantities. For the first and only time it was the venue of a military court and, Lioren thought hopefully, it would be used to terminate rather than extend life.

Three high-ranking Monitor Corps officers had taken their seats facing a multispecies audience that might be sympathetic, antagonistic, or simply curious. The most senior was an Earth-human DBDG, who opened the proceedings.

"I am Fleet Commander Dermod, the president of this specially convened court-martial," it said in the direction of the recorder. Then, inclining its head to one side and then the other, it went on. "Advising me are the Earth-human Colonel Skempton of this hospital, and the Nidian, Lieutenant-Colonel Dragh-Nin, of the Corps's other-species legal department. We are here at the behest of Surgeon-Captain Lioren, a Tarlan BRLH, who is dissatisfied with the verdict of a previous Federation civil-court hearing of its case. The Surgeon-Captain is insisting on its right as a serving officer to be tried by a Monitor Corps military tribunal.

"The charge is gross professional negligence leading to the deaths of a large but unspecified number of patients while under its care."

Without taking its attention from the body of the court, and seeming deliberately to avoid looking at the accused, the fleet commander paused briefly. The rows of chairs, cradles, and other support structures suited to the physiological requirements of the audience held many beings who were familiar to Lioren: Thornnastor, the Tralthan Diagnostician-in-Charge of Pathology; the Nidian Senior Tutor, Cresk-Sar; and the recently appointed Earth-human Diagnostician-in-Charge of Surgery, Conway. Some of them would be willing and anxious to speak in Lioren's defense, but how many would be as willing to accuse, condemn, and punish?

"As is customary in these cases," Fleet Commander Dermod resumed gravely, "the counsel for the defense will open and the prosecution will have the last word, followed by the consultation and the agreed verdict and sentence of the officers of this court. Appearing for the defense is-the Monitor Corps Earth-human, Major O'Mara, who has been Chief of the Department of Other-Species Psychology at this hospital since it first became operational, assisted by the Sommaradvan, Cha Thrat, a member of the same department. The accused, Surgeon-Captain Lioren, is acting for and is prosecuting itself.

"Major O'Mara, you may begin."

While Dermod had been speaking, O'Mara, whose two eyes were recessed and partially hidden by thin flaps of skin and shadowed by the gray hair which grew in two thick crescents above them, had looked steadily at Lioren. When it rose onto its two feet, the prompt screen remained unlit. Plainly the Chief Psychologist intended speaking without notes.

In the angry and impatient manner of an entity unused to the necessity for being polite, it said, "May it please the court, Surgeon-Captain Lioren stands accused, or more accurately stands self-accused, of a crime of which it has already been exonerated by its own civil judiciary. With respect, sir, the accused should not be here, we should not be here, and this trial should not be taking place."

"That civil court," Lioren said harshly, "was influenced by a very able defender to show me sympathy and sentiment when what I needed was justice. Here it is my hope that—"

"I will not be as able a defender?" O'Mara asked.

"I *know* you will be an able defender!" Lioren said loudly, knowing that the process of translation was removing much of the emotional content from the words. "That is my greatest concern. But why are you defending me? With your reputation and experience in other-species psychology, and the high standards of professional behavior you demand, I expected you to understand and side with me instead of—"

"But I am on your side, dammit—" O'Mara began. He was silenced by the distinctively Earth-human and disgusting sound of the fleet commander clearing its main breathing passage.

"Let it be clearly understood," Dermod said in a quieter voice, "that all entities having business before this court will address their remarks to the presiding officer and not to each other. Surgeon-Captain Lioren, you will have the opportunity to argue your case without interruption when your present defender, be he able or inept, has completed his submission. Continue, Major."

Lioren directed one eye toward the officers of the court, another he kept on the silent crowd behind him, and a third he fixed unwaveringly upon the Earth-human O'Mara, who, still without benefit of notes, was describing in detail the accused's training, career, and major professional accomplishments during his stay at Sector Twelve General Hospital. Major O'Mara had never used such words of praise to or about Lioren in the past, but now the things it was saying would not have been out of place in a eulogy spoken over the mortal remains of the respected dead. Regrettably, Lioren was neither dead nor respected.

As the hospital's Chief Psychologist, O'Mara's principal concern was and always had been the smooth and efficient operation of the ten-thousand-odd members of the medical and maintenance staff. For administrative reasons, the entity O'Mara carried the rank of major in the

Monitor Corps, the Federation's executive and law-enforcement arm, which was also charged with the responsibility for the supply and maintenance of Sector General. But keeping so many different and potentially antagonistic life-forms working together in harmony was a large job whose limits, like those of O'Mara's authority, were difficult to define.

Given even the highest qualities of tolerance and mutual respect among all levels of its personnel, and in spite of the careful psychological screening they underwent before being accepted for training in the Galactic Federation's most renowned multienvironment hospital, there were still occasions when serious interpersonal friction threatened to occur because of ignorance or misunderstanding of other-species cultural mores, social behavior, or evolutionary imperatives. Or, more dangerously, a being might develop a xenophobic neurosis which, if left untreated, would ultimately affect its professional competence, mental stability, or both.

A Tralthan medic with a subconscious fear of the abhorrent little predators which had for so long infested its home planet might find itself unable to bring to bear on one of the physiologically similar, but highly civilized, Kreglinni the proper degree of clinical detachment necessary for its treatment. Neither would it feel comfortable working with or, in the event of personal accident or illness, being treated by a Kreglinni medical colleague. It was the responsibility of Chief Psychologist O'Mara to detect and eradicate such problems before they could become life- or sanity-threatening or, if all else failed, to remove the potentially troublesome individuals from the hospital.

There had been times, Lioren remembered, when this constant watch for signs of wrong, unhealthy, or intolerant thinking which the Chief Psychologist performed with such dedication made it the most feared, distrusted, and disliked entity in Sector General.

But now O'Mara seemed to be displaying the type of uncharacteristic behavior that it had always considered as a warning symptom in others. By defending this great and terrible crime of negligence against an entire planetary population, a piece of wrong thinking without precedent in Federation history, it was ignoring and reversing the professional habits and practices of a lifetime.

Lioren stared for a moment at the entity's head fur, which was a much lighter shade of gray than he remembered, and wondered whether the confusions of advancing age had caused it to succumb to one of the psychological ills from which it had tried so hard to protect everyone else. Its words, however, were reasoned and coherent.

". . . At no time was it suggested that Lioren was promoted beyond its level of competence," O'Mara was saying. "It is a Wearer of the Blue Cloak, the highest professional distinction that Tarla can bestow. Should the court wish it I can go into greater detail regarding its total dedication and ability as an other-species physician and surgeon, based on observations made during its time in this hospital. Documentation and personal affidavits provided by senior and junior Monitor Corps officers regarding its deservedly rapid promotion after it left us are also available. But that material would be repetitious and would simply reinforce the point that I have been making, that Lioren's professional behavior up to and, I submit, while committing the offense of which it is charged, was exemplary.

"I believe that the only fault that the court will find in the accused," O'Mara went on, "is that the professional standards it has set itself, and until the Cromsag Incident achieved, were unreasonably high and its subsequent feelings of guilt disproportionately great. Its only crime was that it demanded too much of itself when—"

"But there *is* no crime!" O'Mara's assistant, Cha Thrat, broke in loudly. It rose suddenly to its full height. "On Sommaradva the rules governing medical practice for a warrior-surgeon are strict, stricter by far than those accepted on other worlds, so I fully understand and sympathize with the feelings of the accused. But it is nonsense to suggest that strict self-discipline and high standards of professional conduct are in any sense bad, or a crime, or even a venial offense."

"The majority of the Federation's planetary histories," O'Mara replied in an even louder voice, the deepening facial color showing its anger at this interruption from a subordinate, "contain many instances of fanatically good political leaders or religious zealots which suggest otherwise. Psychologically it is healthier to be strict in moderation and allow a little room for—"

"But surely," Cha Thrat broke in again, "that does not apply to the truly good. You seem to be arguing that good is . . . is *bad!*"

Cha Thrat was the first entity that Lioren had seen of the Sommaradvan DCNF classification. Standing, it was half again as tall as O'Mara, and its arrangement of four ambulatory limbs, four waist-level heavy manipulators, and a further set for food provision and fine work encircling the neck gave it a shape that was pleasingly symmetrical and stable—unlike that of the Earth-humans, who always seemed to be on the point of falling on their faces. Of all the beings in the room, Lioren wondered if this entity would be the one who best understood his feelings. Then he concentrated his mind on the images coming from the eye that was watching the officers of the court.

Colonel Skempton was showing its teeth in the silent snarl Earth-humans gave when displaying amusement or friendship, the Nidian officer's features were unreadable behind their covering of facial fur, and the fleet commander's expression did not change at all when it spoke.

"Are the counsels for the defense arguing among themselves regarding the guilt or otherwise of the accused," it asked quietly, "or simply interrupting each other in their eagerness to expedite the case? In either event, please desist and address the court one at a time."

"My respected colleague," O'Mara said in a voice which, in spite of the emotion-filtering process of translation, sounded anything but respectful, "was speaking in support of the accused but was a trifle overeager. Our argument will be resolved, in private, at another time."

"Then proceed," the fleet commander said.

Cha Thrat resumed its seat, and the Chief Psychologist, its face pigmentation still showing a deeper shade of pink, went on, "The point I am trying to make is that the accused, in spite of what it believes, is not totally responsible for what happened on Cromsag. To do so I shall have to reveal information normally restricted to my department. This material is—"

Fleet Commander Dermod was holding up one forelimb and hand, palm outward. It said, "If this material is privileged, Major, you cannot use it without permission from the entity concerned. If the accused forbids its use—"

"I forbid its use," Lioren said firmly.

"The court has no choice but to do the same," Dermod went on as if the Surgeon-Captain had not spoken. "Surely you are aware of this?"

"I am also aware, as, I believe, are you, sir," said O'Mara, "that if given the chance the accused would forbid me to say or do anything at all in its defense."

The fleet commander lowered its hand and said, "Nevertheless, where privileged information is concerned, the accused has that right."

"I dispute its right to commit judicial suicide," said O'Mara, "otherwise I would not have offered to defend an entity who is so highly intelligent, professionally competent, and completely stupid. The material in question is confidential and restricted but not, however, privileged since it was and is available to any accredited authority wishing for complete psychological data on a candidate before offering to employ it in a position of importance, or advancement to a level of greater responsibility. Without false modesty I would say that my department's psych profile on Surgeon-Captain Lioren was what gained its original commission in the Monitor Corps and probably its last three promotions. Even if we had been able to monitor closely the accused's psych profile following its departure from the hospital there is no certainty that the Cromsag tragedy could have been averted. The personality and motivations of the entity who caused it were already fully formed, stable, and well integrated. To my later regret I saw no reason to alter them in any way."

The Chief Psychologist paused for a moment to look at the beings crowding the room before returning its attention to the officers of the court. Its desk screen came to life, but O'Mara barely glanced at the upward march of symbols as it continued speaking.

"This is the psych record of a being with a complete and quite remarkable degree of dedication to its profession," the major said. "In spite of the presence of fellow Tarlans of the female sex at that time, there are no social or sexual activities listed or, indeed, any indication that it wished to indulge in either. Self-imposed celibacy is undertaken by members of several intelligent species for various personal, philosophical, or religious reasons. Such behavior is rare, even unusual, but not unsane.

"Lioren's file contains no incidents, behavior, or thinking with which I could find fault," O'Mara went on. "It ate, slept, and worked. While its colleagues were off duty, relaxing or having fun, it spent its free time studying or acquiring extra experience in areas which it considered of special interest. When promotion came, it was intensely disliked by the subordinate medical and environmental maintenance staff on its ward because it demanded of them the same quality of work that it required of itself, but fortunate indeed were the patients who came under its care. Its intense dedication and inflexibility of mind, however, suggested that it might not be suitable for the ultimate promotion to Diagnostician.

"This was not the reason for it leaving Sector General," O'Mara said quickly. "Lioren considered many of the hospital staff to be lax in their personal behavior, irresponsible when off duty, and, by its standards, nonserious to a fault, and it wished to continue its work in an environment of stricter discipline. It fully deserved its Corps promotions, including the command of the rescue operation on Cromsag that ended in disaster."

The Chief Psychologist looked down at its desktop, but it was not seeing the prompt screen, because for some reason it had closed its eyes. Suddenly it looked up again.

"This is the psych profile of an entity who had no choice but to act as it did," O'Mara resumed, "so that its actions in the circumstances were proper. There was no carelessness on its part, no negligence, and therefore, I submit, no guilt. For it was only after the few survivors had been under observation here for two months that we were able to unravel the secondary endocrinological effects of the disease Lioren had been treating. If any offense was committed, it was the minor one of impatience allied to Lioren's firm belief that its ship's medical facilities were equal to the task demanded of them.

"I have little more to say," the major continued, "except to suggest to the court that its punishment should be in proportion to the crime and not, as the accused believes and the prosecution will argue, the results of that crime. Catastrophic and horrifying though the results of the Surgeon-Captain's actions have been, the offense itself was a minor one and should be treated as such."

While O'Mara had been speaking, Lioren's anger had risen to a level where it might no longer be controllable. Brown blotches were appearing all over his pale, yellow-green tegument, and both sets of outer lungs were tightly distended to shout a protest that would have been too loud for proper articulation and would probably have damaged the sound sensors of many of those present.

"The accused is becoming emotionally distressed," O'Mara said quickly, "so I shall be brief. I urge that the case against Surgeon-Captain Lioren be dismissed or, failing that, that the sentence be noncustodial. Ideally the accused should be confined to the limits of this hospital, where psychiatric assistance is available when required, and where its considerable professional talents will be available to our patients while it is—"

"*No!*" Lioren said, in a voice which made those closest to him wince and the translator squawk with sound overload. "I have sworn, solemnly and by Sedith and Wrethrin the Healers, to forgo the practice of my art for the rest of my worthless life."

"Now that," O'Mara replied, not quite as loudly as Lioren, "would indeed be a crime. It would be a shameful and unforgivable waste of ability of which you would be inarguably guilty."

"Were I to live a hundred lifetimes," Lioren said harshly, "I could never save a fraction of the number of beings I caused to die."

"But you could *try*—" O'Mara began, and broke off as once again the fleet commander raised his hand for silence.

"Address your arguments to the court, not each other," Dermod said, looking at them in turn. "I shall not warn you again. Major O'Mara, some time ago you stated that you had little more to say. May the court now assume that you have said it?"

The Chief Psychologist remained standing for a moment; then it said, "Yes, sir" and sat down.

"Very well," the fleet commander said. "The court will now hear the case for the prosecution. Surgeon-Captain Lioren, are you ready to proceed?"

Lioren's skin showed an increasing and irregular discoloration caused by the deep emotional distress that even the earliest and innocent memories evoked, but his surface air sacs had deflated so that he was able to speak quietly.

"I am ready."

CHAPTER 2

The Cromsag system had been investigated by the Monitor Corps scout ship *Tenelphi* while engaged on a survey mission in Sector Nine, one of the embarrassing three-dimensional blanks which still appeared in the Federation's charts. The discovery of a system containing habitable planets was a pleasant break in the boring routine of counting and measuring the positions of a myriad of stars, and when they found one displaying all the indications of harboring intelligent indigenous life, their pleasure and excitement were intense.

The pleasure, however, was short-lived.

Because a scout ship with a complement of only four entities did not have the facilities to handle a first-contact situation, the regulations forbade a landing, so the crew had to content themselves with conducting a visual examination from close orbit while trying to establish the natives' level of technology by analyzing their communications frequencies and any other electromagnetic radiation emanating from the planet. As a result of their findings, *Tenelphi* remained in orbit while it recklessly squandered its power reserves on the ship's energy-hungry sub-space communicator on increasingly urgent distress messages to base.

The Monitor Corps's specialized other-species contact vessel, *Descartes*, which normally made the initial approach to newly discovered cultures, was already deeply involved on the planet of the Blind Ones, where communications had reached the stage where it was inadvisable to break off. But the situation on the new planet was not a problem of First Contact but of insuring that enough of the natives would survive to make any kind of contact possible.

The Emperor-class battleship *Vespasian*, which was more than capable of waging a major war although in this instance it was expected to end one, was hastily converted to disaster-relief mode and dispatched to the region. It was under the command of the Earth-human Colonel Williamson, but in all matters pertaining to relief operations on the surface it was the Tarlan subordinate, Surgeon-Captain Lioren, who had the rank and the sole responsibility.

Within an hour of the two vessels matching orbits, *Tenelphi* had docked with *Vespasian* and the scout ship's captain, the Earth-human Major Nelson, and its Nidian medical officer, Surgeon-Lieutenant Dracht-Yur, were in the operations room giving the latest situation report.

"We have recorded samples of their radio signals," Major Nelson reported briskly, "even though the volume of traffic is unusually small. But we were unable to make any sense of it because our computer is programmed for survey work with just enough reserve capacity to handle the translation requirements of my crew. As things stand, we don't even know if they know we are here—"

"*Vespasian's* tactical computer will translate the surface traffic from now on," Colonel Williamson broke in impatiently, "and the information will be passed to you. We are less interested in what you did not hear than in what you saw. Please go on, Major."

It was unnecessary to mention a fact known to everyone present, that while Williamson's tremendous capital ship had the bigger brain, Nelson's tiny and highly specialized survey vessel had eyes that were second to none.

"As you can see," Nelson went on, tapping the keys that threw the visuals onto the room's enormous tactical display screen, "we surveyed the planet from a distance of five diameters before moving in to map in more detail the areas that showed signs of habitation. It is the third planet, and so far as we know the only life-bearing one, of a system of eight planets. Its day is just over nineteen hours long, surface gravity one and one-quarter Earth-normal, the atmospheric pressure in proportion, and its composition would not seriously inconvenience the majority of our warm-blooded oxygen-breathers.

"The land surface is divided into seventeen large island continents. All but the two at the poles are habitable, but only the largest equatorial continent is presently inhabited. The others show signs of habitation in the past, together with a fairly high level of technology that included powered surface and air transport, with radiation traces suggesting that they had fission-assisted electricity generation. Their towns and cities now appear to be abandoned and derelict. The buildings are undamaged, but there are no indications of industrial or domestic wastes either in atmosphere or on the ground, no evidence of food cultivation, and the road surfaces, street paving, and a few of the smaller buildings have been broken up and damaged due to the unchecked growth of plant life. Even in the inhabited areas of the equatorial continent there is similar evidence of structural and agrarian neglect with the associated indications of—"

"Obviously a plague," Lioren said suddenly, "an epidemic for which they have little natural immunity. It has reduced the planetary population to the extent that they can no longer fully maintain all their cities and services, and the survivors have collected in the warmer and less power-hungry cities of the equator to—"

"To fight a bloody war!" the scout ship's medic, Dracht-Yur, broke in, its snarling Nidian speech making an angry accompaniment to the emotionless translated words. "But it is a strange, archaic form of warfare. Either they love war, or hate each other, very much. Yet they seem to have an inordinate respect for property. They don't use mass-destruction weapons on each other; there is no evidence of aerial bombing or artillery, even though they still have large numbers of ground and atmosphere vehicles. They just use them to transport the combatants to the battleground, where they fight at close quarters, hand to hand and apparently without weapons. It is savage. Look!"

Vespasian's tactical screen was displaying a series of aerial photographs of tropical forest clearings and city streets, sharp and clear despite massive enlargement and the fact that they had been taken from a vertical distance of fifty miles. Normally it was difficult to obtain much information on the body mass and physiological details of a native lifeform from orbit—although a study of the shadow it cast could be helpful—but, Lioren thought grimly, far too many of these creatures had been obliging enough to lie flat on the ground dead.

The pictures shocked but did not sicken the Surgeon-Captain as they did Dracht-Yur, because the Nidian medic belonged to one of those strange cultures who reverenced the decomposing remains of their dead. Even so, the number of recently and not so recently dead lying about in the streets and forest clearings was bound to pose a health risk.

Lioren wondered suddenly whether the surviving combatants were unwilling or simply unable to bury them. A less sharp moving picture showed two of the creatures fighting together on the ground, and so gentle were the blows and bites they inflicted on each other that they might have been indulging publicly in a sexual coupling.

The Nidian seemed to be reading Lioren's mind, because it went on. "Those two look as if they are incapable of seriously damaging each other, and at first I assumed this to be a species lacking in physical endurance. Then other entities were seen who fought strongly and continuously for an entire day. But you will also observe that the bodies of these two show widespread patches of discoloration, while a few of the others have skins without blemish. There is a definite correlation between the degree of physical weakness and the area of discoloration on the body. I think it is safe to assume that these two are seriously ill rather than tired."

"But that," Dracht-Yur ended in an angry growl, "doesn't stop them from trying to kill each other."

Lioren raised one hand slightly from the tabletop, middle digits extended in the Tarlan sign of respect and approval. But the two officers gave no indication of understanding the significance of the gesture, which meant that they had to be complimented verbally.

"Major Nelson, Surgeon-Lieutenant Dracht-Yur," Lioren said, "you have both done very well. But there is more that you must do. Can I assume that the other members of your crew have also had the opportunity of observing the situation below and have discussed it among themselves?"

"There was no way of stopping them—" Nelson began.

"Yes," Dracht-Yur barked.

"Good," Lioren said. "*Tenelphi* is detached from its current survey duty. Transfer its officers to *Vespasian*. They will join the crews of the first four reconnaissance vehicles to go down as advisors since they know more, perhaps only a little more, about the local situation than we do. This ship will remain in orbit until the most effective rescue site has been chosen . . ."

At times like these Lioren was reluctant to waste time on politeness, but he had learned that, where Earth-human senior officers in particular were concerned, time wasted now would help expedite matters later. And Colonel Williamson was, after all, *Vespasian*'s commander and nominally the senior officer.

"If you have any comments or objections so far, sir," Lioren said, "I would be pleased to hear them."

Colonel Williamson looked at Nelson and Dracht-Yur briefly before returning its attention to Lioren. The scout-ship officers were showing their teeth, and a few of the colonel's were also visible as it said, "*Tenelphi* will not be able to resume its survey mission until we have topped up its consumables, and I would be surprised if its officers objected to any break in that deadly dull routine. You are making friends, Surgeon-Captain. Please continue."

"The first priority is to end the fighting," Lioren said, "and only then will it be possible to treat the sick and injured. This forced cessation of hostilities will have to be achieved without inflicting additional casualties or causing too much mental distress among the population. To a culture at the prespaceflight level of technology, the sudden arrival among them of a vessel of the size and power of *Vespasian*, and the visually monstrous entities it contains, would not be reassuring. The first approach will have to be made in a small ship by people who, for psychological reasons, must be of equal or lesser body mass than they are. And it will have to be done covertly, in an isolated area where there are few natives or, ideally, only one whose temporary withdrawal from among its friends will arouse minimum distress . . ."

The vehicle chosen for the mission was *Vespasian's* short-range communications vessel, which was equally capable of space operations or extended aerodynamic maneuvering in atmosphere. It was small but comfortably appointed, Lioren thought, if one happened to be an Earth-human, but at present it was overloaded and overcrowded.

They descended steeply out of the orange light of sunrise into an uneven blanket of dark, predawn cloud, thrusters shut down and velocity reduced so that they would not cause unnecessary distress by dragging a sonic shock wave in their wake, and the ship was darkened except for the radiation from its infrared sensors, which the natives might or might not be able to see.

Lioren stared at the enhanced picture of the forest clearing with its single, low-roofed dwelling and outbuildings rushing up at them. Without power their ship was gliding in too steeply and much too fast and with the flight characteristics, it seemed, of an aerodynamically clean lump of rock. Then three small areas of vegetation were flattened suddenly and driven downward into shallow craters as the ship's pressor beams reached out to support it on immaterial, shock-absorbing stilts. The touchdown was silent and sudden but very gentle.

Lioren turned a disapproving eye toward the pilot, wondering, not for the first time, why some experts felt it necessary to display their expertise so dramatically; the boarding ramp slid out before he could think of words that were both complimentary and critical.

They wore heavy-duty space suits with the air tanks and helmet visors removed, confident that this makeshift body armor would protect them against any bare-handed attack by an intelligent life-form that used only natural weapons. The five Earth-humans and three Orligians in the party ran to search the outbuildings while Dracht-Yur and Lioren moved quickly toward the house, which, in spite of the early hour, had its internal lighting switched on. They circled the house once, keeping below the level of the closed and uncurtained windows, to stop at the building's only entrance.

Dracht-Yur focused its scanner on the door mechanism and the life-sensor on the spaces beyond; then it used the suit radio to say quietly, "Beyond the door there is a large room, presently unoccupied, and three smaller compartments opening off it. The first is empty of life, the second contains traces which are not moving and positioned so closely together that I can't be sure whether there are two or three entities, who are making the low, untranslatable noises characteristic of sleep. Maybe they are sick or wounded. The third room contains one being whose movements appear slow and deliberate, and the sounds from that compartment are quiet but distinct, like the intermittent contact between cooking utensils. The overall indication is that the occupants are unaware of our presence.

"The door mechanism is very basic," the Nidian medic continued, "and the large metal bar on the inside has not been engaged. You can simply lift the latch and walk in, sir."

Lioren was relieved. Breaking down the door would have made the job of convincing these people of his good intentions much more difficult. But with anything up to four natives in the house and only one overeager but diminutive Nidian in support, Lioren was unwilling to enter just then. He remained silent until the others arrived to report that the outhouses contained only agricultural implements and nonsapient farm animals.

Quickly he described the layout of the house, then went on. "The greatest risk to us is the group of three or four beings occupying the room directly opposite this entrance, and they must not be allowed to leave it until the situation has been explained to them. Four of you guard the interior door and four the window in case they try to escape that way. Dracht-Yur and myself will talk to the other one. And remember, be quiet, careful, and nonaggressive at all times. Do not damage furniture or artifacts, and especially not the beings themselves, or do anything to suggest that we are not their friends."

He unlatched the door quietly and led the way inside.

An oil-burning lamp hung from the center of the ceiling, illuminating walls hung with a few pictorial carvings and what seemed to be displays of dried, aromatic vegetation, although to his Tarlan olfactory sensors the aroma was anything but pleasant. Against the facing wall there was a long dining bench with four high-backed chairs pushed under it. A few smaller tables and larger, more heavily padded chairs were visible, plus a large bookcase and other items which he could not immediately identify. The majority of the furniture was of wood and strongly but not expertly built, and a few of the items showed signs of being mass-produced. Plainly they were the very old, scratched, and dented legacies of better times. The middle of the room was uncluttered and covered only by a thick carpet of some fabric or vegetable material that deadened the sound of their feet as they crossed it.

All three of the internal doors had been left ajar, and from the room occupied by the single native the quiet noises of cooking utensils making contact with crockery were accompanied by a soft, wailing sound that was untranslatable. Lioren wondered if the entity was in pain from illness or wounds, or was perhaps indulging in its version of mouth music. He was about to move in to confront the native when Dracht-Yur grasped one of his medial hands and pointed toward the door of the other occupied room.

One of the Earth-humans had been gripping the door mechanism tightly to prevent it being opened from within. Now it held out its free hand waist high with three digits extended, then lowered it palm downward to show two digits at hip level, and brought it down almost to its knee joint before showing one digit. For an instant it released the door handle, pressed both palms together and brought its hands to one side of its face, then inclined its head and closed both of its eyes.

For a moment Lioren was completely baffled by the gestures until he remembered that the Earth-human DBDG classification, and quite a few other life-forms, adopted this peculiar position while asleep. The rest of the hand signals could only mean that the room contained three children, one of whom was little more than an infant, and that they were all asleep.

Lioren dipped his head Earth-human fashion in acknowledgment, relieved that the children could be easily contained in their room so that there would be no possibility of uninformed and terrified escapees spreading panic throughout the area. Feeling pleased and much more confident, he moved forward to open communication with what, judging by the sounds emanating from the food-preparation room, was almost certainly the only adult in the house.

The entity had its back turned toward the entrance, showing him a three-quarters rear profile as it busied itself with some task that was concealed by its upper torso. Because of the absence of individually mobile eye mountings in its cranium and the consequent loss of all-around vision, Lioren was able to watch it for a moment without it being able to see him.

Its bodily configuration more closely resembled Lioren's own than those of the Earth-humans, Nidians, or Orligians accompanying him, which should greatly reduce the visual shock of first contact. Except for the possession of three sets of limbs—two ambulators, two medial heavy manipulators, and two more at neck level for eating and to perform more delicate work, rather than the Tarlan's three sets of four—and a cranium covered by thick, blue fur that continued in a narrow strip along the spine to the vestigial tail, the general physical characteristics were remarkably similar. Its skin showed areas of pale yellow discoloration that were symptomatic of the plague that, with the savage and barbaric war, was threatening to sweep its planet free of intelligent life. The creature's physiological classification was DCSL, and curing its medical condition, at least, would be relatively simple once he obtained its cooperation.

Gently at first but with increasing firmness Lioren began clapping two of his guantleted, medial hands together to attract its attention, and when it swung around suddenly to face him, Lioren said, "We are friends. We have come to—"

It had been supporting a large bowl partially filled with a pale gray semiliquid material between its body and one medial hand, while the other medial hand was holding and pouring the contents of a smaller bowl into the first. Both containers, Lioren had time to note, were thick-walled and seemed to be made of a hard but very brittle ceramic, as was proved by the way they shattered when dropped onto the floor. The noise was loud enough to waken the three youngsters in the other room, and one of them, probably the infant, began making loud, frightened sounds which did not translate.

"We will not harm you," Lioren began again. "We have come to help cure you of the terrible disease which—"

The creature made a high-pitched gobbling sound which translated as, "The children! What have you done to the children?" and hurled itself at Lioren and Dracht-Yur.

It was not a bare-handed attack.

From the number of kitchen implements lying on the tabletop nearby it had snatched up a knife, which it swung at Lioren's chest. The blade was long and pointed, serrated along one edge and sharp enough to leave a deep scratch in the fabric of Lioren's heavy-duty space suit. But the creature was a quick learner, because the second blow was a straight-armed jab which might have penetrated if Lioren had not grasped the creature's wrist in two medial hands and used a third to prise the weapon from its fingers, taking a small, incised wound to one of his own digits in the process, while at the same time holding off its two upper hands, which seemed intent on tearing holes in his face.

The violence of its attack sent Lioren staggering backward into the other room, and he had a glimpse of the diminutive Dracht-Yur diving at the creature's legs and wrapping its short, furry arms tightly around them. The creature overbalanced and all three of them crashed to the floor.

"What are you waiting for, immobilize it!" Lioren said sharply. Then with a sudden feeling of concern for the being, he said, "As yet I am unfamiliar with your internal physiology, and I trust that the weight of my body against your lower thorax is not causing damage to underlying organs."

The creature's response was to struggle even harder against the Earth-human, Orligian, and Tarlan hands holding it down, and only a few of the sounds it was making were translatable. Looking at the obviously confused and terrified being, Lioren spoke silent and highly critical words to himself. This, his first contact with a member of a newly discovered intelligent species, had not been handled well.

"We will not harm you," Lioren said, trying to sound reassuring in a voice louder than that of the creature and those of the three children in the other room, all of whom were awake and contributing their own untranslatable sounds. "We will not harm your children. Please calm yourself. Our only wish is to help you, all of you, to live out your lives free of war and the disease which is affecting you . . ."

It must have understood his translated words, because it had grown silent as he was speaking, but its struggle to free itself continued.

"But if we are to find a cure for this disaster," Lioren went on in a quieter voice, "we will have to isolate and identify the pathogen within your body causing it, and to do this we require specimens of your blood and other body fluids . . ."

They would also be needed to prepare large quantities of safe anesthetics, tranquilizing gases and synthetic food suited to the species metabolism if the war as well as the disease was to be checked with minimum delay and loss of life. But this did not seem to be the right moment to tell it all of the truth, because its efforts to break free had intensified.

Lioren looked at Dracht-Yur and indicated one of the native's medial arms where muscle tension and elevated blood pressure had caused one of the veins to distend, making it an ideal site for withdrawing blood samples.

"We will not harm you," Lioren repeated. "Do not be afraid. And please stop moving your arm."

But the large, glittering, and multibarreled instrument that the Nidian medic had produced, while absolutely painless in use, was not an object to inspire confidence. If their positions had been reversed, Lioren knew, he would not have believed a single word he was saying.

·

CHAPTER 3

With a few violent exceptions, the subsequent contacts with the planet's natives, whose name for their world was Cromsag, went more easily. This was because *Vespasian*'s transmitter had matched frequencies with the Cromsaggar broadcast channels to explain in greater detail who the off-world strangers were, where they had come from, and why they were there. And when the great capital ship landed and began to disgorge and erect prefabricated hospitals and food-distribution centers for the war's survivors, the verbal reassurances were given form and substance and all hostility against the strangers ceased.

But that did not mean that they became friends.

Lioren was sure that he knew everything about the Cromsaggar, with the exception of how their minds worked. From recently dead cadavers abandoned in the war zones he had obtained a complete and accurate picture of their physiology and metabolism. This had enabled their injuries to be treated with safe medication and their war to be ended ingloriously under blankets of anesthetic gas. The scout ship *Tenelphi* had been pressed into service as a fast courier vessel plying between Cromsag and Sector General. It carried specimens requiring more detailed study in one direction and the findings of Head of Pathology Thornnastor, which more often than not agreed with Lioren's own, in the other.

But the Cromsaggar disease was proving difficult for even Diagnostician Thornnastor to isolate and identify. Living rather than dead specimens were required for study, if possible displaying the symptomology from onset to the preterminal stage of the condition, and *Rhabwar*, the hospital's special ambulance ship, was dispatched to obtain them. And even more baffling than the plague, to which the victims invariably succumbed before reaching middle age, was their mental approach to it.

One plague victim had agreed to talk to Lioren about itself, but its words had merely added to the Surgeon-Captain's confusion. He knew the patient only by its case file number, because the Cromsaggar considered their written and spoken symbol of identity to be the most important of personal possessions, and even though this one was close to termination it would not divulge its name to a stranger. When Lioren asked it why many of the Cromsaggar had attacked off-worlders with any weapon that came to hand, but fought among themselves only with teeth, hands and feet, it said that there was no honor or gain in killing a member of one's own race unless it was with great effort and extreme personal danger. For the same reason they always stopped short of killing a very sick, severely weakened, or dying adversary.

Taking the life of another intelligent entity, Lioren firmly believed, was the most dishonorable act imaginable. In his position he should respect the beliefs of others, regardless of how strange or shocking they might be to one of his strict Tarlan upbringing, but he could not and would not respect this one.

Changing the subject quickly, he asked, "Why is it that after you fight, the injured are taken away to be cared for while the dead remain untouched where they fall? We know that your people have some knowledge of medicine and healing, so why do you allow the dead to remain unburied, to risk the spread of further pestilence into your already plague-ridden population? Why do you expose yourselves to this totally unnecessary danger?"

The ravages of the disease, which had covered the entire epidermis in patches of livid camouflage, had left the patient very weak, and for a moment Lioren wondered if it was able to reply, or even if it had heard the questions. But suddenly it said, "A decomposing corpse is indeed a fearful risk to the health of those who pass nearby. The danger and the fear are necessary."

"But *why?*" Lioren asked again. "What do you gain by deliberately subjecting yourselves to fear and pain and danger?"

"We gain strength," the Cromsaggar said. "For a time, for a very short time, we feel strong again."

"In a very short time," Lioren said with the confidence of a healer backed by all the resources of Federation medical science, "we will make you feel well and strong without the fighting. Surely you would prefer to live on a world free of war and disease?"

From somewhere within its wasted body the patient seemed to gather strength. It said loudly, "Never in the memories of those alive, or in the memories of their ancestors, has there been a time without war and disease. The stories told of such times, when the planetwide ruins of towns and cities were populated by healthy and happy Cromsaggar, are stories told only to comfort small and hungry children, children who soon grow large enough to fight and to disbelieve these stories.

"You should leave us, stranger, to survive as we have always survived," it went on, straining to raise itself from the litter. "The thought of a world without war is too frightening to contemplate."

He asked more questions, but the patient, although fully conscious and displaying a slight improvement in its clinical condition, would not speak to him.

There was no doubt in Lioren's mind that a medical cure would quickly be discovered for the condition affecting the ten thousand-odd surviving Cromsaggar. But he was less sure whether a species which fought wars using only the natural weapons provided by evolution, because that made them feel good for a while, was worth saving. The strict rules of engagement that governed the fighting did not make the situation any less barbaric. They did not fight weaker opponents or children or the very few who were advanced in years, but only because the element of personal risk, and presumably the emotional reward, was reduced. He was glad that his only responsibility was the return of the plague sufferers to bodily health and not the curing of what appeared to be the even more diseased minds inhabiting those bodies.

And yet there had been occasions when, in an effort to give his patients something other than their own distressing clinical condition to think about, he had tried to explain star travel and the Galactic Federation to them. He had described the bewildering variety of shapes and sizes that intelligent life could take, and tried to make them understand that they lived on one inhabited world of many hundreds. He found those frightening and inexplicable minds of theirs had displayed an agility and a level of intelligence, although not the degree of education and knowledge, that was almost the equal of his own.

At those times there had been a small and transient improvement in their clinical condition, and that had made Lioren wonder if their craving for the danger and emotional excitement of war and single combat might not someday be fulfilled by the many and even more difficult challenges of peace. But they refused, or perhaps were psychologically unable because of cultural conditioning, to divulge personal information about their social behavior, moral strictures, or feelings on any subject unless, as in the present case, the patient was gravely ill and its mental resistance low.

The truth was that Lioren did not know how his patients felt, about themselves or anyone or anything else, and the stock question of the attending physician, "How do you feel?," was never answered.

Rhabwar was due in two days' time, and he decided that this particular patient would be among those transferred to the ambulance ship for investigation and treatment at Sector General, and that he would ask for a consultation with the vessel's senior medical officer.

Doctor Prilicla was a Cinrusskin, and, as a member of the Federation's only empathic species, it knew how everyone felt.

Lioren asked that the meeting take place on *Rhabwar*'s casualty deck, rather than summoning Prilicla to the overcrowded sick bay of *Vespasian*, for reasons both practical and personal. The level of background emotional radiation from patients was much higher on *Vespasian* and would doubtless have distressed his visitor—it did no harm to show consideration to a professional colleague. On the ambulance ship there was less likelihood of his uncertainties regarding the Cromsaggar becoming known to his subordinates. It was his firm belief that a leader should display certainty at all times to the led if he was to receive their respect and total obedience.

Perhaps the empath held the same belief, but it was more likely that Prilicla had detected Lioren's emotional radiation at a distance, correctly analyzed it, and insured that their meeting would be private. He was grateful but not surprised. It was in the other's own selfish interest to minimize the generation of unpleasant emotional radiation around it, because to do otherwise would be to expose itself to exactly the same degree of unpleasantness.

The Cinrusskin positioned itself at eye level above one of the treatment tables, an enormous, incredibly fragile flying insect rendered small only by Lioren's greater body mass. From its tubular, exoskeletal body there projected six pencil-thin legs, four even more delicately fashioned manipulators, and four sets of wide, iridescent, and almost transparent wings that were beating slowly as, with the aid of the gravity nullifiers strapped to its body, it maintained a stable hover. Only on Cinruss, with its thick atmosphere and gravitational pull of one-eighth standard G, could a species of flying insect have evolved intelligence, civilization, and star travel, and Lioren knew of no race within the Federation who did not consider them to be the most beautiful of all intelligent life-forms.

From one of the narrow openings in the delicate, convoluted egg-shell that was its head came a series of musical trills and clicks which translated as "Thank you, friend Lioren, for the complimentary feelings you are harboring, and for the pleasure of meeting you in person for the first time. I also detect strong emotional radiation which suggests that the purpose of our meeting is professional and urgent rather than social.

"I am an empath, not a telepath," it ended gently. "You will have to tell me what is troubling you, friend Lioren."

Lioren felt sudden irritation at the other's continuing use of the word "friend." He was, after all, the medical and administrative director of the disaster relief operation on Cromsag, and a Surgeon-Captain in the Monitor Corps, while Prilicla was a civilian Senior Physician at Sector General. His irritation was making the empath's whole body tremble and causing its hovering flight to become less stable. He suddenly realized that he was attacking a being with a weapon, his feelings, against which it had no defense.

Even the pathologically warlike Cromsaggar would scorn to attack such a weak and defenseless enemy.

Lioren's irritation quickly changed to shame. This was a time to forget the feelings of justified pride in his high rank and in the many professional accomplishments that had earned it. Instead he should try, as he had often done in the past, to make the most effective use of the abilities of a subordinate whose feelings were easily hurt, and to control his emotions.

"Thank you, friend Lioren, for the mental self-discipline you have just displayed," Prilicla said before he could speak. It settled like a feather onto the top of the examination table, no longer trembling, and added, "But I detect strong background emotional radiation that you are finding more difficult to control and that, I feel sure, concerns the Cromsaggar. My own feelings of concern over the situation here are strong, perhaps as strong as yours, and shared feelings about other persons or situations cause me lesser discomfort. So if there is some way that I can help you please do not hesitate to speak."

Lioren felt renewed irritation at being given permission to discuss the Cromsaggar when his only purpose in coming here had been to do so, but the feeling was faint and transient. As he began to speak, the Surgeon-Captain knew that he was briefly verbalizing his latest report, copied to his Monitor Corps superiors and to Prilicla itself, that *Rhabwar* would be carrying back to Thornnastor, but it was necessary that the empath be acquainted with the current position if it was to understand the importance of the later questions.

He described the continually expanding search that had brought back data fit only for industrial archeologists. There were no recent life signs. Many of the abandoned cities and mining and manufacturing complexes in the north and south temperate regions were many centuries old, and so well constructed that only a moderate effort would be required to restore them because the mineral wealth of the planet was far from exhausted. But the effort had not been made because the race's energies had been directed into fighting, so much so that many of them no longer grew food or had the strength to forage for that which grew wild, and the population had contracted into one region so that they could continue fighting without having to travel far to do so.

"When we stopped the war," Lioren went on, "or rather, when our sleep bombs halted the hundreds of small gang and two-person conflicts, there was an estimated surviving population of just under ten thousand entities, a number which included all the adults, their young, and a few newly born infants. But recently they have begun dying at the rate of about one hundred every day."

Prilicla had begun to tremble again. Lioren was unsure whether it was in response to his emotional radiation or its own reaction to the news of the increasing number of fatalities. He tried to make his mind as well as his voice calm and clinical as he continued.

"In spite of our supporting them with shelters, clothing, and synthetic nutrient, even going so far as to gather supplies of local food that they were too weak to harvest for themselves, the deaths continue. Adult fatalities are invariably due to the plague, sometimes expedited by the debilitating effect of war injuries, and the children succumb to other diseases for which we have no specifics as yet. The Cromsaggar accept our help and our food, but only their young appear grateful for it. They show no interest in what we are trying to do for them. I feel that the adults tolerate us as an additional and unwelcome burden that they can do nothing about. My own feeling is that they are disinterested in their own survival and want to be left alone to commit racial suicide in the bloodiest fashion possible, and there are times when I feel that such a warlike and individually violent race should not be restrained from doing so. I do not know what they themselves feel, about anything."

"And you would like me to use my empathic faculty," Prilicla asked, "to tell you what they feel?"

"Yes," Lioren said, with so much feeling that the Cinrusskin trembled for a moment. "I hoped that you, Doctor, might have detected urges, instincts, feelings about themselves, their offspring, or their present situation. My ignorance regarding their thinking and motivations is total. I would like to be able to do or say something to them that, as with an emotionally disturbed entity about to jump from a high building, would make them want to live instead of die. What is it that they fear, or need, that would make them want to survive?"

"Friend Lioren," Prilicla said without hesitation, "they fear death, like every other self-aware creature, and they want to survive. There were no indications, even in the most serious cases, of a wish for individual death or racial self-destruction, and they should not be—"

"I am sorry," Lioren broke in. "My earlier remark about allowing them to commit racial suicide—"

"They were words spoken because of helplessness and frustration, friend Lioren," Prilicla said, in the gentlest of interruptions, "that were completely contradicted by your underlying emotional radiation at the time. There was no need for an apology then or for your embarrassment now.

"And I had been about to say," it went on, "that the Cromsaggar should not be criticized for their lack of cooperation, and the strong feelings of ingratitude until we know why they feel so ungrateful. These feelings were strongly present in all of the adult patients I monitored during transportation to Sector General and while I was present at the subsequent attempts to question them. They know we are trying to help them, but will not help us with clinical or personal information about themselves. When the interrogation was intensified they became agitated and fearful, and a marked if temporary remission of symptoms was observed at these times."

"I have made the same observation," Lioren said, "and assumed that it was the transfer of focus from a material condition to an immaterial one, the psychological mechanism which can sometimes make faith healing effective. I did not consider it an important datum."

"You are probably correct," Prilicla said. "But Chief Psychologist O'Mara is of the opinion that the marked remission due to the fear stimulus, combined with their fanatical refusal to communicate with us beyond the exchange of a few words, indicates the presence of an extremely strong and deep-rooted conditioning about which the Cromsaggar, as individuals, may be unaware. Friend O'Mara likens it to the racial group psychoses afflicting the Gogleskans, and says that it is trying to probe a very sensitive area that is surrounded by a very thick wall of mental scar tissue, and advises everyone concerned to proceed slowly and carefully."

The Gogleskan psychosis forced them into avoiding direct physical contact with each other for the greater part of their adult lives, which was certainly not the problem with the Cromsaggar. Trying to control his feelings of impatience, Lioren said, "If we do not quickly find a cure for this plague, your Chief Psychologist will run out of subjects for his slow and careful investigation. What progress has been made since your last visit?"

"Friend Lioren," Prilicla said gently, "significant progress has been made. However, I sense and wholly agree with your need to avoid wasting time, so I suggest that Pathologist Murchison makes its report to you in person rather than having it relayed through myself, since you will doubtless have questions and I, because of my selfish need to surround myself with pleasant emotional radiation, have the unfortunate habit of accentuating the positive aspects of any situation."

Lioren's original reason for wanting a private meeting with Prilicla no longer seemed valid, and he could not reject the other's suggestion without seriously embarrassing both himself and the empath. He had the feeling, which was no doubt shared by the empath, that somehow he had lost the initiative.

Pathologist Murchison was a warm-blooded oxygen-breather of physiological classification DBDG with a body that, although considerably shorter and less massive than Lioren's own, had the soft, lumpy and top-heavy aspect of many of the Earth-human females. It was Thornnastor's principal assistant, when not required for special ambulance-ship duty, and its words were clear and concise and its manner respectful without being subservient. It also had the slightly irritating habit of answering questions before Lioren could ask them.

The identification, isolation, and neutralization of other-species pathogens, Pathologist Murchison said, was a routine procedure for Thornnastor's department, but the behavioral characteristics of the Cromsaggar virus—its mechanisms of transmission, infection, incubation, and propagation—remained undetectable to all of the normal investigative techniques. It was only in recent days, when the discovery had been made that the virus was either inherited at conception or transmitted by the mother prior to birth, that some progress had been made.

"The effects on the adult Cromsaggar are known to you," Murchison went on, "and the present indications are that every member of the species is infected. In the preterminal stage there is a livid rash and skin eruptions covering most of the body, accompanied by progressive and massive debilitation and lassitude which is sometimes overcome, temporarily, by strong emotional stimuli such as fear and danger. The effects on the children are less apparent and this led to the initial assumption that the young were immune, which they are not.

"We have since discovered," it continued, "that severe debility and lassitude are also present in the young, although it is difficult to be precise since we have no idea of how active a young, noninfected Cromsaggar should be. And, incredible though it might seem, neither can we be precise about the ages of these child patients. There is physiological and verbal evidence which suggests that many of them are not nearly as young as they appear, and that our age estimates should be extended by a factor of two or three because, in addition to its general debilitating effect, the plague retards the overall physiological development and greatly delays the onset of puberty. Probably there are psychological effects, as well, which might explain their grossly antisocial adult behavior, but again, this must remain speculative since you have yet to find a normal, disease-free Cromsaggar."

"I doubt whether such an entity exists," Lioren said. "But you spoke of having verbal as well as physiological evidence. These people absolutely refuse to give information about themselves. How was it obtained?"

"A large proportion of the cases you sent us were young or, as we now know, not yet physically mature," Murchison replied. "The adult patients remain completely uncooperative, but O'Mara was able to open dialogue with a few non-adults, who were much less reticent about themselves. Because of this immature viewpoint, adult motivations still remain unclear, and the picture of the Cromsaggar culture that is emerging is confusing and fraught with—"

"Pathologist Murchison," Lioren interrupted, "my interest is in the clinical rather than the cultural picture, so please confine yourself to that. My reason for asking *Rhabwar* to transfer so many young or not so young patients to the hospital was that they were among the large numbers left parentless or without adults to care for them. As well as suffering from undernourishment or exposure, conditions which are treatable, they displayed symptoms of respiratory distress associated with elevated temperature, or a wasting disease affecting the peripheral vascular and nervous systems. If Thornnastor's investigation into the plague is showing no results, what of these other and, I would think, clinically less complex conditions which seem to affect only the young?"

"Surgeon-Captain Lioren," the pathologist said, using Lioren's name and rank for the first time, "I did not say that no progress is being made.

"All of the non-adult cases are being investigated and significant progress is being made," it went on quickly. "In one of them, the condition presenting respiratory distress symptoms, there has been a minor but positive response to treatment. But the main effort is being directed toward finding a specific for the adult condition, because it has become evident that if the massive debilitation and growth-retarding effects of the plague were removed, the diseases currently afflicting the pre-adult

Cromsaggar would be countered by their bodies' natural defense mechanisms and would no longer be life-threatening."

If that much was known, Lioren thought, then progress was indeed being made.

"The trials conducted so far," Murchison continued, "have been inconclusive. Initially the medication was introduced in trace quantities and the patients' condition monitored routinely for fifty standard hours before the dosage was increased, until on the ninth day, within a few moments of the injection being given, both patients lost consciousness."

It paused for a moment to look at Prilicla then, seeming to receive a signal undetectable by Lioren, resumed. "Both patients were placed in isolation some distance from the others and each other. This was done so as to minimize same-species interference in their emotional radiation. Doctor Prilicla reported that the level of unconsciousness was extraordinarily deep, but that there was no sign of the subconscious distress that would have been present had they been drifting into termination. It suggested that the unconsciousness might be recuperative since it had many of the characteristics of sleep following a lengthy period of physical stress and that nutrient should be given intravenously. A few days after this was done there was a minor remission of symptoms in both cases, and evidence of slight tissue regeneration, although both patients remained deeply unconscious and in a critical condition."

"Surely that means—!" Lioren began, and broke off as Murchison held up one hand as if it and not himself had the rank. But suddenly he was too excited to verbally tear its insubordinate head off as he should.

"It means, Surgeon-Captain," Murchison said, "that we must proceed very carefully and, if the first two test subjects regain consciousness rather than drifting into termination, we must closely monitor their clinical and psychological condition before the trial is extended to the other patients. Diagnostician Thornnastor and everyone in its department believes, and Doctor Prilicla feels sure, that we are on the way to finding the cure. But until we are certain we must exercise patience for a time until—"

"How much time?" Lioren demanded harshly.

Prilicla's fragile body was shaking as if a strong wind was blowing through the casualty deck, but Lioren could no more have controlled the emotional storm of impatience, eagerness, and excitement that raged within him than he could have flown on the empath's fragile wings. He would apologize to Prilicla later, but now all that he could think of was the steadily dwindling number of Cromsaggar who still clung to life on this plague world, and who might now have a chance to remain alive. More quietly, he asked, "How long must I wait?"

"I don't know, sir," the pathologist said. "I only know that *Tenelphi* has been ordered to remain at flight readiness at Sector General until the medication has been approved for general use, so as to bring you the first production batch without delay."

CHAPTER 4

*R*habwar* departed with its casualty deck filled principally with non-adult Cromsaggar. There were many adult cases in *Vespasian*'s sick bay—and in the widely dispersed medical stations that Lioren visited every day—who were in a much more serious condition, but the future survival of any species lay with its young, and those fortunate enough to be under the care of Thornnastor would be the first to be cured.

He ignored the polite but increasingly sarcastic messages from Colonel Skempton, the administrative head of Sector General, reminding him that the hospital was unable to accept the entire Cromsag population, depleted though it might be, for hospitalization, and that they had already received more than enough members of that species for the purposes of clinical investigation. The entire *Rhabwar* crew would have been aware of Skempton's uncoded messages and the pressure on ward accommodation that had prompted them, but Prilicla had raised no objections to transporting the additional twenty patients.

Prilicla must be the least objectionable entity in the known galaxy, Lioren thought, unlike the Cromsaggar, who were his patients but who would never be his friends—unless there was a species-wide personality reconstruction by the Galactic Federation's many deities, of whose existence he had the gravest doubts.

Nevertheless, he spent all of his time, when he was not engaged in eating or sleeping, visiting the worst of his massively unlikable patients or encouraging the two hundred Corps medics and food technicians scattered across the continent who were trying, not always with success, to keep them alive. Always he hoped for a change of attitude, a willingness to talk to him and give information that would enable him to help them or that a tiny crack would show in their impenetrable wall of noncooperation, but in vain. The Cromsaggar, adult and young alike, continued dying at a steadily increasing rate because, like Sector General, he did not have the facilities to feed intravenously the entire population.

Occasionally, and in spite of the surface and orbital surveillance, they managed to die at each others' hands.

It had happened while he had been flying over one of the forest settlements that had long since been searched and declared empty of intelligent life, but that must have been because the occupants had taken to the trees to elude the searchers. Lioren spotted the small-scale war being waged by six of them in a grassy clearing between two buildings. By the time the flier, which would have carried a crew of four Nidians had it not been for his long Tarlan legs, had circled back to land and Dracht-Yur had helped him extricate himself from the tiny vessel's seating, the hand-to-hand fighting was over and four Cromsaggar lay still on the ground.

In spite of the numerous bites and digitally inflicted wounds covering the bodies, they were able to identify them as three dead males and one female whose life expectancy would be measured in seconds. Dracht-Yur pointed suddenly to the ground nearby where two separate trails of crushed and blood-spattered grass converged toward the open door of one of the buildings.

The advantage of a longer stride meant that Lioren went through the entrance seconds ahead of the Nidian, and his first sight of the two writhing, bloody bodies locked together in mortal combat on the floor reinforced the anger and disgust he felt at such animal behavior between supposedly intelligent beings. Moving forward, he quickly interposed his medial arms between the tightly pressed bodies and tried to push them apart. Only then did he make the disconcerting discovery that they were not, as he had first thought, two males fighting each other to the death but a male and female indulging in a sexual coupling.

Lioren released them and backed away quickly, but suddenly they broke apart and launched themselves at him just as Dracht-Yur arrived and blundered into his rear legs. The weight of the combined attack toppled him over backward so that he sprawled flat on the floor with the two Cromsaggar on top of him and the Nidian somewhere underneath. Within moments he was fighting for his life.

After the first few days on Cromsag had shown the natives to be too severely weakened by the plague to warrant the use of heavy protective suits, all Corps personnel had taken to wearing their cooler and less restrictive shipboard coveralls, which gave protection only against the sun, rain, and insect bites.

It was with a sense of outrage that Lioren realized that for the first time in his life the hands—not to mention the feet, knees, and teeth—of another person had been raised in anger against him. On Tarla disputes were not settled in this barbaric fashion. And even though the number of his limbs equaled the total of theirs, they did not behave like plague-weakened Cromsaggar. They were inflicting serious damage to his body and causing him more pain than he had ever thought it possible to feel.

As he fended off the more disabling body blows and tried desperately to keep the two Cromsaggar from pulling off his dirigible eye-supports, Lioren was aware of Dracht-Yur wriggling from underneath him and crawling toward the door. He was pleased when his attackers ignored it, because the Nidian's small, furry limbs had neither the muscle power nor the reach to make a useful contribution to the struggle. A few seconds later he caught a glimpse of the Nidian's head enclosed by a transparent envelope, heard the expected soft explosion of a bursting sleep-gas bulb, and felt the bodies of his attackers go suddenly limp and collapse on top of him before rolling slowly onto the floor.

For the few moments that the bodies, covered as they were by livid patches of discoloration and the oozing sores characteristic of preterminal plague victims, made heavy and almost intimate contact with him,

it was a great relief to remember that one world's pathogens were ineffective against the members of off-planet species.

Designed as it was for maximum effect on the Cromsaggar metabolism, the anesthetic gas produced similar if less immediate results on
other warm-blooded oxygen-breathers. Lioren was unable to move, but
he was aware of the Nidian growling and barking urgently into its headset while it applied dressings to the worst of his wounds. Presumably it
was telling the pilot of their flier to send for medical assistance, but his
own translator pack had been damaged in the struggle and he could not
understand a word. This did not worry him unduly, because the intense
discomfort of his many injuries had faded to the mildest of irritations
and the hard floor beneath him felt like the softest of sleeping pits. But
his mind was clear and seemed unwilling to follow his body into sleep.

Interrupting the two Cromsaggar in the sex act had been a serious
mistake, but an understandable one because none of his people had
witnessed the occurrence of anything like a sexual coupling since arriving on Cromsag, and everyone, himself included, had assumed that the
species had become too physically debilitated by the plague to make
much of such activity possible. And their reaction, the sheer strength
and ferocity of their attack, had surprised and shocked him.

During the very short breeding season on Tarla such activity, especially among the aging who had been lifemates for many years, was
a cause for celebration and public display rather than a matter for con-
cealment—although he knew that many species within the Federation,
races who were otherwise highly intelligent and philosophically advanced, considered the mating process to be a private matter between
the beings concerned.

Naturally, Lioren had no personal experience in this area, since his
dedication to the healing arts precluded him indulging in any pleasure
which would allow emotional factors to affect the clinical objectivity of
his mind. If he had been an ordinary Tarlan male, an artisan or a member of one of the noncelibate professions interrupted in similar circumstances, there would have been a verbal impoliteness, but certainly not
violence.

Distressing and distasteful as the incident had been, Lioren's mind would not rest in its search to find a reason for such an unreasonable reaction, however alien or uncivilized that reason might be. Could it be that, gravely ill and seriously injured as they had been in the fighting outside, they had crawled into the house to seek a moment of mutual pleasure together before dying? He knew that the coupling must have been by mutual agreement, because the Cromsaggar mechanics of reproduction were physiologically too complicated for the attentions of one partner to be forced on another.

That did not rule out the possibility that the coupling was the end result of the fighting, the bestowal of a female's favor on a warrior victorious in battle. There were many historical precedents for such behavior, although not, thankfully, in the history of Tarla. But that reason was unsatisfactory because both male and female Cromsaggar fought, although not each other.

Lioren made a mental note to prepare a detailed report of the incident for the cultural contact specialists who would ultimately have to produce a solution to the Cromsaggar problem, if any of the species survived and it was invited to join the Federation.

The four separate images of the room, including the one of Dracht-Yur working on the other casualties, that his immobilized eyes were still bringing him dimmed suddenly into blackness, and he remembered a feeling of mild irritation before he fell asleep in midthought.

Dracht-Yur confined him to the sick bay on *Vespasian* until the worst of his injuries healed, reminding him, as only a hairy, small-minded, and sarcastic dwarf of a Nidian could, that until then the relationship between them was one of doctor and patient and that in the present situation it was the Surgeon-Lieutenant who had the rank.

It could not, however, no matter how often it stressed the advisability of post-trauma rest and mental recuperation, bind Lioren's jaw closed or keep him from setting up a communication system by his bedside.

Time passed like a pregnant *strulmer* climbing uphill, and the medical situation on Cromsag worsened until the daily death rate climbed from one hundred to close on one-fifty, and still *Tenelphi* did not come. Lioren sent a necessarily brief hyperspace radio signal to Sector General, prerecorded and repeated many times so that its words could be reconstructed after fighting their way through the interference of the intervening stars, requesting news. He was not surprised when it was ignored, because the expenditure of power needed for a lengthy progress report would have been wasteful indeed. All that he was telling them was that he and the medical and support personnel on Cromsag were beginning to feel so helpless and angry and impatient that the condition verged on the psychotic, but the hospital probably knew that already.

Five days later he received a reply stating that *Tenelphi* had been dispatched and was estimating Cromsag in thirty-five hours. It was carrying medication, as yet incompletely tested for long-term effects, which was a specific against the grosser, more life-threatening symptoms of the plague, and that the details of the pathological investigation and directions for treatment accompanied the medication.

During the excitement that ensued Lioren went over his plans for fast distribution. Dracht-Yur relented to the extent of allowing him to transfer from sick bay to the communications center of *Vespasian*, but not to risk compounding his injuries by traveling the air or surface of Cromsag in vehicles totally unsuited to the Tarlan physiology. But the general feeling of relief and euphoria lasted only until the arrival of *Tenelphi*.

The scout ship carried more than enough of the antiplague specific, which required only a single, intravenous application, to treat every Cromsaggar on the planet, but Lioren was forbidden to use it until additional field trials had been carried out.

According to Chief Pathologist Thornnastor, the physiological results following a minimum dosage had been very good, but there were indications of possibly damaging side effects. Symptoms of mental confusion and periods of semiconsciousness had been observed. These might prove to be temporary, but further investigation was required.

The single injection was followed by a slight but continuing reduction in symptoms, a slow improvement in the vital signs, and evidence of tissue and organs regeneration throughout the body in the days which ensued. During the periods of semiconsciousness the test subjects had requested and consumed food in quantities which, considering stomach size and the clinical condition of the patients involved, seemed unusually large. There was a steady increase in body weight.

The non-adult subjects had responded in similar fashion, including the periods of unconsciousnessness interspersed with episodes of semiconsciousness and mental confusion, except that with the young the food demand in relation to their smaller size had been greater. Daily measurement had shown a steady increase in growth, both in body mass and limb dimensions.

It was thought probable that with the gradual remission of the condition the non-adult patients, whose physical growth had been retarded by the plague, were returning to optimum size for their ages. The periods of unconsciousness and impaired thinking were in response to a demand by the body for maximum rest during these periods of regeneration and were of little clinical importance. The medication was being used in minimum quantities, but a very small increase in the dosage of one test subject resulted in a strengthening and acceleration of the effects already noted. In spite of the excellent physiological results so far, the associated episodes of mental confusion were cause for concern lest a side effect of the medication led to long-term brain damage.

Thornnastor apologized for sending medication that it had not completely cleared for use, but said that Lioren's hyperspace radio signals had emphasized the urgency of the situation, and in order to save a few days' transit time between the medication's approval and its administration to the patients the final tests should be made concurrently on Cromsag and in Sector General.

"I have been instructed to conduct tests on a maximum of fifty Cromsaggar," Lioren said, when he was relaying Thornnastor's report to his senior medical officers. "The subjects are to include the widest possible variation in age and clinical condition, as well as minor variations in the dosage administered within that number. We are to pay particular attention to the mental state of these subjects during their periods of semiconsciousness, in the hope that their degree of confusion will be lessened when they are on their home world among others of their kind rather than in the strange and doubtless unsettling environment of Sector General. The initial test period will require ten days, followed by a further—"

"In ten days we would lose a quarter of the remaining population," Dracht-Yur broke in suddenly, its barking speech sounding angry even through the translator, "which has already shrunk to two-thirds of the number alive when *Tenelphi* found this Crutath-accursed planet. They're dying out there like, like . . ."

"That was my thought exactly," Lioren said, omitting the reprimand the Nidian deserved for its bad manners, and making a mental note to check on the meaning of the word "Crutath." "It is a thought which all of you share. But it is not because of our common feelings that I will disobey Thornnastor and ignore its recommendations. The decision is not yours. I will, of course, listen to your professional advice and accept it if it has merit, but the instruction to proceed and the responsibility for everything that ensues as a result will be entirely mine.

"This is what I am planning to do . . ."

There was no criticism of his plan because he had formulated it with great care and attention to detail, and—strangely, since it was coming from subordinates to a superior—the advice offered by many of them was personal rather than professional. They advised that he obey Thornnastor, but compromise by testing a few hundred, perhaps a thousand subjects instead of a mere fifty, saying that the course he was advocating would do nothing for any hopes he might have for future advancement. Lioren felt a strong temptation to do as they suggested, if only out of respect for the words of an entity said to be the foremost pathologist in the Federation rather than out of any selfish concern over his future career, but he was not sure that Diagnostician Thornnastor fully appreciated the urgency of the Cromsaggar problem. The hospital's Chief of Pathology was a perfectionist who would never allow imperfect work to leave its department, and giving Lioren permission to assist with the test program was probably the only compromise that it was capable of making. But a great, hulking Tralthan whose data-crammed mind, it was said, permanently accommodated the brain recordings of at least ten other-species medical authorities could be forgiven for a certain amount of mental confusion.

The Cromsaggar death rate was climbing steadily toward two hundred a day, and treating a mere fifty of them with an unnecessary degree of caution when virtually the entire population could be given the chance to live instead of dying in a lingering and painful manner was, to Lioren's mind, a great and a cowardly and a completely unacceptable wrong.

In this desperate situation he could accept imperfections even if Thornnastor's department could not. The psychological effects that accompanied the cure might be temporary, and even if they were not then they, too, might be curable in time. But if the worst should happen and permanent mental harm was the result, it was highly unlikely that the condition would be transmitted to an offspring, because O'Mara itself had stated that the damage was nonphysical. Any Cromsaggar child born of cured but mentally deficient parents would grow up healthy and sane.

Or as sane, Lioren thought, as it was possible for any member of this bloodthirsty race to be.

He had told his staff that it must be an operation combining maximum effort with maximum urgency, and that every single Cromsaggar on the planet must be treated for effect rather than submitting them to time-wasting trials, and within an hour of the meeting's end the plan was being implemented. On foot to the patients who were being housed close to the grounded *Vespasian*, and by surface or air transport to the more distant shelters, the medication and supplies of synthetic nutrient were being distributed by every Monitor Corps entity available, which meant all but the capital ship's watch-keeping and communications officers and those charged with the maintenance of the air and surface vehicles. Lioren, whose injuries were still hampering his mobility, divided his attention between communications and the sick bay, where he was the only medic on duty.

The dosage administered varied in proportion to the age, body mass, and clinical condition of the patients. With the very young it was triple that recommended for trial purposes by Thornnastor, and, making due allowance for the potency of the medication, for those close to termination it was massive. Priority should have been given to the more serious cases, but there was so much variation in the degree of illness within small groups that it saved time if everyone was treated as and when they were encountered.

It quickly developed into a routine that was too frenetic to be described as boring. A few words of explanation and reassurance would be given, the single injection administered, and food and water placed within easy reach of the patient, who was usually too ill to make anything but a verbal objection; then it would be on to the next one.

By the end of the third day the entire population had been treated and the second phase began, that of visiting the patients, on a daily basis if possible, to replenish the consumables and observe and report on any change in their clinical condition. The medical and support staff worked day and night, eating infrequently of the same bland, synthetic food supplied to their patients and sleeping hardly at all. Increasing fatigue caused a forced landing and two ground-vehicle accidents, none of which involved fatalities, so that the ship's hospital no longer held only plague victims.

On the fourth day one of his adult Cromsaggar in sick bay terminated, but the number of deaths outside the ship went down to one hundred and fifteen. On the fifth day the figure had dropped to seven, and there were no fatalities reported on the sixth day.

Except for the difference in scale and the continuing effort needed to keep the widely dispersed patients supplied with food, the situation in sick bay reflected the clinical conditions outside.

As Thornnastor had predicted, a gradual remission in external symptoms was apparent and the food requirement of the adult patients had increased, and the fact that all of the food had been synthesized made no difference to their appetites. Much as he wanted to monitor their progress internally, they would not cooperate and refused to allow him to so much as touch them. With all of his medical staff and the majority of the ship's crew scattered across the continent, he thought it better not to force the issue, especially as the patients were growing stronger with every day that passed. In spite of the differences in body mass, the young were eating more than the adults, and, as Thornnastor had also observed, their rate of physical growth was phenomenal.

It was obvious that, in order to cause such a massive retardation of growth, the disease, which the Cromsaggar had acquired prenatally, must have involved the entire endocrine system. Now that the process was being reversed and they were not only growing but maturing, another, nonclinical change was occurring. The young patients who, once their initial fear had given way to curiosity and they had grown accustomed to his strange body and multiplicity of limbs, had spoken to him freely and with the unguarded enthusiasm of children were becoming increasingly reticent.

They were speaking to him less because, Lioren observed, their recovering elders were talking to them more. And they talked only when he was not present.

By then his Monitor Corps patients had been well enough to be discharged to continue their recuperation in their own quarters, so he did not know what the Cromsaggar talked about until one day, after replenishing the food supply and his few words of friendship and reassurance had been ignored, he deliberately left one of the sick-bay senders switched on Transmit so that he would be able to listen to them from his own quarters.

In the manner of all eavesdroppers, he fully expected to overhear unkind things about himself and the bad dreams from the sky, which was the literal translation of the Cromsaggar name for their rescuers. But he was completely wrong. Instead, they talked and chanted and sang together so that his translator was unable to separate the individual voices. It was only when a single Cromsaggar spoke out alone, an adult addressing one or more of the young, that Lioren realized what he was hearing.

It was part of an initiation ceremony, a preparation and formalized sex instruction given to the newly mature before entry into adult life, including the behavior expected of them thereafter.

Lioren broke the connection hastily. The rite of passage into adulthood was a highly sensitive area in the cultures of many intelligent species, and one into which he was not qualified to delve. If he were to continue listening out of mere lascivious curiosity, he might find that he no longer respected himself.

He was relieved, nevertheless, that with the exception of two very small children who were little more than infants, the sick bay held only male Cromsaggar.

During the days that followed there were no organic fatalities reported, but the air and surface vehicles, which had been in continuous operation over eight days and nights, had not fared so well. The food synthesizers on *Vespasian* and in the outlying medical stations were running at maximum safe overload, a condition that was not recommended for more than a few hours at a time. All of the organic components were displaying signs of stress and severe fatigue but were operating at close to optimum efficiency, even though they rarely talked to each other and seemed to be asleep on their feet. It was becoming clear to everyone concerned that the operation was a success and that no member of the patient population was about to die, and that knowledge was both the fuel and the lubrication which kept them working.

It was irritating to all of them, but not important, that the Cromsaggar showed no gratitude for what was being done for them apart from demolishing the previous day's food supply. The brief explanation of the treatment and reassurance regarding their ultimate cure that was given at every visit to replenish stores was ignored. The patients were not actively hostile, unless one of the medics tried to check on their vital signs or obtain a blood sample, whereupon they reacted violently toward the person concerned.

An ungrateful and unlikable race, Lioren thought, not for the first time. But it was their physiology rather than their psychology which was his problem, and the problem was being solved.

From Sector General there was a continuing silence.

He could imagine Thornnastor's slow, careful progress, with its relatively few patients, toward a stage in the treatment which Lioren had already surpassed with the entire planetary population. It was no reflection on the Tralthan pathologist, who was, after all, the entity responsible for producing the cure for the plague. But if Lioren had not ignored its recommendations and risked the displeasure of his superiors, many hundreds of Cromsaggar would have died by now. And without false modesty on his part, the solution he had devised for the problem had been truly elegant.

His calculated variation in the dosage administered, based as it had been on age, body mass, and clinical factors, had insured that the young and old alike were progressing toward a complete cure at the same time. In spite of his insubordination, he was sure that his action would merit praise rather than censure.

Early on the following day he sent a brief message to the Monitor Corps base on Orligia, and copied to Sector General, requesting additional food synthesizers and spares for the air and ground transport units, adding that there had been no Cromsaggar fatalities for eight days and that a full report accompanied by a medical officer with firsthand experience of the situation was being sent with *Tenelphi* to the hospital. The request for synthesizers combined with the sudden drop in the death rate would tell Thornnastor what Lioren had done, and the scout ship's medical officer would be able to fill in the details.

Dracht-Yur had been working well and very hard, and ordering its return to normal duties on *Tenelphi* would be both a rest and a well-deserved reward for its efforts. It would also remove the Surgeon-Lieutenant from the scene and thereby make it possible for Lioren, whose injuries were healing well, to escape the little Nidian's irksome medical quarantine.

Before retiring that night Lioren posted the usual guard outside the sick bay, an unnecessary precaution because none of the Cromsaggar had shown any interest in what lay beyond the entrance, but necessary in Captain Williamson's opinion in case one of the young ones decided to go exploring and injured itself on ship equipment. Tomorrow he would fly to the outlying medical shelters and, for the first time since his embarrassing mishap with the mating Cromsaggar, view the situation for himself.

He would be seeing, Lioren told himself with mixed feelings of pleasure, pride, and self-congratulation, the final stages of the cure of Cromsag.

Before he was due to board his flier next morning he visited sick bay to check on the condition of his patients, only to find the deck and walls splattered with Cromsaggar blood and all of the adults dead. The entrance guard, after succumbing to a violent attack of nausea, reported hearing quiet voices and chanting that had continued far into the night, followed by a period of unbroken silence which it had attributed to them being asleep. But from the condition of the bodies it was clear now that they had instead been fighting and silently kicking, biting, and tearing the lives out of each other until only two of the female infants survived.

Lioren was still trying to recover from the shock, and make himself believe that he was not asleep and having a particularly horrendous dream, when the wall speaker beside him came to sudden, noisy life. It said that he should go at once to the communications center and that the bloody, self-inflicted massacre in sick bay had been repeated all over Cromsag.

Very soon it became clear that Surgeon-Captain Lioren was responsible not for curing but for killing a planetary population.

CHAPTER 5

When Lioren finished speaking there was complete stillness in the room. Even though all present were already aware of every harrowing detail of the Cromsag Incident and his responsibility for it, the mere repetition was enough to shock any civilized being into silence.

"The guilt in this matter is entirely mine," Lioren resumed, "and lest there be any doubt about this in anyone's mind, I ask Thornnastor, the Diagnostician-in-Charge of Pathology, to give its evidence."

The Tralthan lumbered forward on its six elephantine feet to take the witnesses position, and, fixing one eye each on the president of the court, Lioren, O'Mara, and its printed notes, it began to speak. Within a few minutes Fleet Commander Dermod was holding up one hand for silence.

"The witness is not obliged," it said, "to relate its evidence in such clinical detail. No doubt its medical colleagues would find it interesting but it is not understandable by the court. Please simplify your language, Diagnostician Thornnastor, and go to the explanation of why the Cromsaggar acted as they did."

Thornnastor stamped its two medial feet in a gesture which suggested impatience, but whose exact significance would have been clear only to another Tralthan, and said, "Very well, sir . . ."

Because of the more cautious approach to the trial program at Sector General and the consequently slower progress toward a complete cure, Thornnastor explained, the hypersignal from *Vespasian* was received in time to prevent a repetition of the catastrophe that had occurred on Cromsaggar. All of the Cromsaggar had been dispersed and confined to single quarters, and the Department of Other-species Psychology had intensified its efforts to overcome the fanatical noncooperation of the patients so that they would answer questions about themselves.

It was only when the decision had been made, very reluctantly and only after lengthy consideration of possible psychological damage, to tell the patients the whole truth of what had happened on their home planet, including the fact that they were the sole surviving adult members of their race, that they began to talk about themselves. There was much anger and recrimination, understandably, but enough information was provided to make possible the formation of a theory which was supported by the archeological evidence.

The best estimate was that the plague had made its first appearance just under one thousand years ago, when the Cromsaggar level of technological and philosophical advancement included atmospheric flight and a culture that no longer practiced war. No information was available regarding the origin and evolution of the disease other than that it was transmitted by either parent during sexual coupling and, in the beginning, its effects had been mild and embarrassing rather than life-threatening. The majority of the Cromsaggar did not travel widely, and they took their sexual bondings, once formed, very seriously and did not stray in this respect, either. A number of the more farsighted Cromsaggar formed communities that were plague-free, but the mating process depended on emotional rather than medical factors and eventually the disease broached this immaterial defense. Another three centuries were to pass before the plague spread unchecked across all of Cromsag to infect every member of the population, adult and child alike. By that time it had increased in virulence, and deaths in middle age were becoming common.

The continuing efforts of the medical scientists were of no avail, and by the end of the following century their civilization had receded to pretechnology levels with no hope of a revival, and it was rare for anyone to live more than a decade past maturity. As a race, the Cromsaggar were facing extinction, a very early extinction because of the effect of the plague on the birth rate.

"The complete symptomology of the disease," Thornnastor said, "including the endocrinological involvement with its effect on the sufferers' rate of growth and maturation, has already been studied and can be discussed at length, but I shall summarize and simplify for the benefit of the court.

"Among the adults of both sexes," it went on, "the visually and tactually unpleasant skin condition was one factor in the reducing birth rate, but it was a minor one. Even if the tegument of both partners was flawless and aesthetically pleasing, the greatly reduced performance of the endocrine system is such that the act of sexual coupling and conception is impossible without an abnormal level of prior emotional stimulation."

Thornnastor paused. It did not possess the kind of features which could change expression, but it was as if the mind-pictures it was seeing inside its great, immobile dome of a head had made further speech impossible for a moment. Then it went on. "Efforts were made to circumvent this difficulty by medical means, and by the use of substances derived from naturally occurring vegetation which heightened the senses or had hallucinatory effects. These methods proved ineffective and were discarded because of problems of irreversible addiction, death from overdose, and seriously deformed and nonviable offspring. The solution that was ultimately found was nonmedical and involved a deliberate regression in social behavior to the dark ages of their history.

"The Cromsaggar went to war . . ."

It was not a war fought for reasons of territorial expansion or trade advantage, and neither was it fought at a distance from fortified positions or by warriors acting in concert or protected by armored machines or equipment, and it was a war not waged to the death because there was no intention on either side of killing an opponent who might very well be a family member or a friend. In fact, there were no sides because it was fought hand to hand between pairs of unarmed individuals, and it was a war whose sole purpose was to cause the maximum of fear, pain, and danger, but if possible, not death to the combatants. There was no threat or danger from a beaten and seriously wounded opponent and, even though they had been trying desperately to kill each other moments before, the vanquished were left where they lay, hopefully to recover from their wounds to fight and instill fear in an opponent another day.

Life was rare and precious to the Cromsaggar, rarer and more precious with every dwindling generation that passed; otherwise they would not have tried so hard to keep their race alive.

For it was only by overloading the sensorium with pain and intense muscular effort and subjecting themselves to the highest possible levels of emotional stress that endocrine systems rendered dormant by the effects of the plague could be roused into something like normal activity, and remain so, aside from the wounds that had been sustained, for the time necessary for a successful coupling and procreation to take place.

But in spite of the terrible solution that had been found, adult deaths from the plague continued to rise and the birth rate to fall. The population contracted in numbers and territory occupied, moving to one continent so as to conserve what little was left of their civilization and resources and to be within easy fighting distance of each other. There was archeological evidence to suggest that in the beginning the Cromsaggar were not warlike, but the need to fight and often kill each other so that their race as a whole could survive made them so, and by the time *Tenelphi* discovered them, the practice of hand-to-hand combat among all adults had been conditioned into the race for many centuries.

"Even though the decision was taken for the best of all clinical reasons, that of saving many lives," Thornnastor went on, "without prior knowledge of this conditioning, the effect of introducing a complete and short-duration cure for the plague could not have been foreseen. It is probable, and Chief Psychologist O'Mara agrees with me in this, that the Cromsaggar who had been treated were aware of feeling better and stronger than they had ever felt before, and subconsciously they must have realized that it was no longer necessary for them to fight and place themselves in the greatest possible danger in order to achieve sexual arousal. But for many centuries they had been taught from an early age that single combat between members of one's own sex invariably preceded coupling with one of the opposite, a level of conditioning with the strength of an evolutionary imperative. And so, the more their clinical condition improved the greater was their urge to fight and procreate. The many young, whose physical development had been retarded by the effects of the plague and who had suddenly come to maturity, felt the same compulsion to fight.

"But the real tragedy," the Tralthan continued, "lay in the fact that individually and as a group they were fully cured, and stronger than any Cromsaggar had been since the coming of the plague. Previously they had been weak, diseased, and able to expend only a small fraction of the physical effort of which they were now capable. Their newfound strength reduced the personal fear of pain and death, and made it difficult to calibrate the levels of damage inflicted on and by opponents who were so strong and evenly matched. The result was that they killed each other, every single adult on Cromsag, leaving only the infants and children alive.

"Briefly and simply," Thornnastor ended, "that is the background to the Cromsag Incident."

The silence that followed Thornnastor's words lengthened and deepened until the faint, bubbling sound made by the refrigerated life-support system of an SNLU in the audience seemed loud. It was like the Tarlan Silence of Remembrance after the passing of a friend, except here it was the population of a world that had died and it seemed that no person present was going to break it.

"With respect to the court," Lioren said suddenly, "I ask that the trial be ended here and now, without further argument and waste of time. I stand accused of genocide through negligence. I am guilty without doubt or question and the responsibility and the guilt are entirely mine. I demand the death penalty."

O'Mara rose to his feet before Lioren had finished speaking. The Chief Psychologist said, "The defense would like to correct the accused on one very important point. Surgeon-Captain Lioren did not commit genocide. When the incident occurred it reacted quickly and correctly in the circumstances, by warning the hospital and organizing the rescue and care of the newly orphaned Cromsaggar children, this in spite of the fact that many of its own people had been so taken by surprise that they were unable to use the gas in time, and who were seriously injured in attempts to stop the fighting. During this period the Surgeon-Captain's behavior was exemplary and, although the witnesses are not here present, their evidence was presented to and accepted by the civil court on Tarla and is on record—"

"The evidence is not disputed," Lioren broke in impatiently. "It is not relevant."

"As a result of this timely warning and subsequent actions," O'Mara continued, ignoring the interruption, "the adult Cromsaggar under treatment here were separated before they could attack each other, and the young, both here and on Cromsag, were saved. Altogether thirty-seven adults and two hundred and eighty-three children, with a roughly equal distribution of sex, are alive and well. I have no doubt that, after a lengthy period of reeducation, resettlement, and specialized assistance in breaking their conditioning, Cromsag will be repopulated, and, now that the plague has been removed, its people will return to living together in peace.

"It is understandable that the accused should feel an overwhelming guilt in this matter," the psychologist went on in a quieter voice. "Had that not been so, it would not have caused this court-martial to be convened. But it is possible that the great guilt that it feels over the Cromsag Incident, together with its urgent need to discharge that guilt and its impatience to receive punishment for the alleged crime, has caused it to exaggerate its case. As a psychologist I can understand and sympathize with its feelings, and with its attempts to escape the burden of its guilt. And I am sure that there is no need to remind the court that, among the sixty-five intelligent species who make up the Galactic

Federation, not one of them practices judicial execution or physical chastisement during confinement."

"You are correct, Major O'Mara," the fleet commander said. "The reminder is unnecessary and time-wasting. Make your point briefly."

The color of O'Mara's facial skin deepened slightly, and it said, "The Cromsaggar are not extinct, and they will continue to survive as a race. Surgeon-Captain Lioren is guilty of exaggeration, but not genocide."

All at once Lioren felt anger, despair, and a terrible fear. He kept one eye on O'Mara and directed the other three individually toward the officers of the court and forced calmness and clarity onto his mind as he said, "The exaggeration, this small inaccuracy that was intended only as a simplification of a terrible truth, is unimportant because the enormity of my guilt is beyond measure. And I should have no need to remind Major O'Mara of the punishment, the destruction of a medic's professional future rather than life, which is meted out to any member of the staff whose carelessness or lack of observation leads to the clinical deterioration or death of a patient.

"I am guilty of negligence," Lioren went on, wishing that the translator could reproduce the desperation in his voice, "and the defense counsel's attempt to belittle and excuse what I have done is ridiculous. The fact that others, including the hospital personnel concerned with the trials of the medication, were also surprised by the Cromsaggar behavior is not an excuse. I should not have been surprised, because all the information was available to me, all the clues to the puzzle were there if I had correctly read the signs. I did not read them because I was blinded by pride and ambition, because a part of my mind was thinking that a rapid and total cure would enhance my professional reputation. I did not read them because I was negligent, unobservant, and mentally fastidious in refusing to listen to patients' conversations relating to Cromsaggar sex practices which would have given a clear warning of what was to happen, and because I was impatient of superiors who were advocating caution—"

"Ambition, pride, and impatience," O'Mara said, rising quickly to its feet, "are not crimes. And surely it is the degree of professional negligence, if any, that the court must punish, not the admittedly terrible and far-reaching effects of what is at most a minor transgression."

"The court," Fleet Commander Dermod said, "will not allow counsel to dictate to it, nor will it allow another such interruption of the prosecution's closing statement. Sit down, Major. Surgeon-Captain Lioren, you may proceed."

The guilt and the fear and the desperation were filling Lioren's mind so that the finely reasoned arguments he had prepared were lost and forgotten. He could only speak simply of how he felt and hope that it would be enough.

"There is little more to add," he said. "I am guilty of a terrible wrong. I have brought about the deaths of many thousands of people, and I do not deserve to live. I ask the court for mercy, and for the death sentence."

Again O'Mara rose to its feet. "I am aware that the prosecution is allowed the last word. But with respect, sir, I have made a detailed submission regarding this case to the court, a submission which I have not had the opportunity of introducing for discussion."

"Your submission was received and has been given due consideration," the fleet commander said. "A copy was made available to the accused, who, for obvious reasons, chose not to introduce it. And may I remind defense counsel that it is I who will have the last word. Please sit down, Major. The court will confer before passing sentence."

The misty gray hemisphere of a hush field appeared around the three officers of the court, and it seemed that everyone else might have been enclosed in the same zone of silence as their eyes turned on Lioren. In spite of it being at extreme range for an empath, at the rear of the audience he could see Prilicla trembling. But this was not a time when he could control his emotional radiation. When he remembered the contents of O'Mara's submission to the court, he felt the most dreadful extremes of fear and despair overwhelming his mind and, for the first time in his life, an anger so great that he wanted to take the life of another intelligent being.

O'Mara saw one of his eyes looking in its direction and moved its head slightly. It was not an empath, Lioren knew, but it must be a good enough psychologist to know what was in Lioren's mind.

Suddenly the hush field went down and the president of the court leaned forward in its chair.

"Before pronouncing sentence," the fleet commander said, looking toward O'Mara, "the court wishes clarification and reassurance from defense counsel regarding the accused's probable behavior in the event of a custodial rather than the death sentence being imposed. Bearing in mind Surgeon-Captain Lioren's present mental state, isn't it likely that either sentence would quickly result in the accused's death?"

O'Mara rose again. Its eyes were on Lioren rather than the fleet commander as it said, "In my professional opinion, having observed the accused during its training here and studying its behavior subsequent to the Cromsag Incident, it would not. The Surgeon-Captain is an ethical and highly moral being who would consider it dishonorable to escape what it will consider to be a justly imposed punishment for its crime by means of suicide, even though a custodial sentence would be the harshest, in terms of continued mental distress, that could be imposed. However, as the court will recall from my submission, I prefer the term 'remedial' to 'custodial.' To reiterate, the accused would not kill itself but it would, as you have already gathered, be most grateful if the court would do the job for it."

"Thank you, Major," the fleet commander said; then it turned to face Lioren.

"Surgeon-Captain Lioren," it said, "this court-martial upholds the earlier verdicts of your own civil and medical courts on Tarla, your home world, and finds you guilty of an excusable error in observation and judgment which led, regrettably, to a major catastrophe. Although it would be kinder in the circumstances to do so, we will not depart from Federation judicial practice of three centuries, or waste a potentially valuable life should the therapy prove successful, by imposing the death sentence that you so plainly desire. Instead you are to be given a custodial and remedial sentence of two years, stripped of your Monitor Corps and medical rank, and forbidden to leave this hospital, which is an establishment large enough for your confinement not to prove irksome. For obvious reasons you are also forbidden access to the Cromsaggar ward. You will be placed in the charge and under the direction of Chief Psychologist O'Mara. In that time the major expects to bring about a psychological and emotional readjustment which will enable you to begin a new career.

"You have the court's deepest sympathy, ex-Surgeon-Captain Lioren, and its best wishes."

CHAPTER 6

L ioren stood on the clear area of floor in front of O'Mara's desk, surrounded on three sides by the strangely shaped furniture designed for the comfort of physiological classifications other than his own, and stared down at the psychologist with all of his eyes. Since the imposition of the sentence and a regimen that nothing in his power could change, the intensity of his feelings toward the stocky little biped with its gray head fur and eyes that never looked away had diminished from a life-threatening hatred to a level of dislike so deeply etched into Lioren's mind that he did not believe that it could ever be erased.

"Liking me is not a prerequisite of the treatment, fortunately," O'Mara said, seeming to read Lioren's mind; "otherwise Sector General would be without its medical staff. I have made myself responsible for you and, having read a copy of my written submission to the court-martial, you are aware of my reasons for doing so. Need I restate them?"

O'Mara had argued that the principal reason for what had happened on Cromsag had been due to certain character defects in Lioren, faults which should have been detected and corrected during its other-species medical training at Sector General, and this was an omission for which the Psychology Department was entirely to blame. That being the case, and bearing in mind the fact that Sector General was not a psychiatric hospital, Lioren could be considered as a trainee who had not satisfactorily completed his training in other-species relations rather than a patient, and be attached to the Psychology Department under O'Mara's supervision. In spite of his proven medical and surgical ability with many life-forms, as a trainee he would have less status than a qualified ward nurse.

"No," Lioren said.

"Good," O'Mara said. "I dislike wasting time, or people. At present I have no specific orders for you other than that you will move freely within the hospital, initially with an escort from this department, or, if there are times when this causes an unacceptable level of embarrassment or distress, you will perform routine office tasks. These will include you familiarizing yourself with the work of the department and the medical staff psych files, most of which will be opened to you for study. Should you uncover any evidence of unusual behavior, uncharacteristic reactions toward other-species staff members, or unexplained reductions in professional standards, you will report it to me, having first discussed it with one of your department colleagues to insure that it is worth my attention.

"It is important to remember," the psychologist went on, "that with the exception of a few of the most gravely ill patients, everyone in the hospital knows all about your case. Many of them will ask questions, polite and considerate questions for the most part, except the Kelgians, who do not understand the concept of politeness. You will also receive many well-intentioned offers of help and encouragement and much sympathy."

O'Mara paused for a moment; then, in a softer voice, it continued. "I shall do everything that I can to help you. Truly, you have suffered and are suffering a great mental anguish, and laboring under a burden of guilt greater than any I have encountered in the literature or in my own long experience; a load so heavy that any other mind but yours would have been utterly destroyed by it. I am greatly impressed by your emotional control and horrified at the thought of your present level of mental distress. I shall do everything possible to relieve it and I, too, who am in the best position of anyone other than yourself to understand the situation, offer you my sympathy.

"But sympathy," it went on, "is at best a palliative treatment, and one which diminishes in effect with repeated application. That is why I am applying it on this one and only occasion. Henceforth, you will do exactly as you are told, perform all the routine, menial, boring tasks set you, and you will receive no sympathy from anyone in this department. Do you understand me?"

"I understand," Lioren said, "that my pride must be humbled and my crime punished, for that is what I deserve."

O'Mara made an untranslatable sound. "What you think you deserve, Lioren. When you begin to believe that you might *not* deserve it, you will be well on the way to recovery. And now I will introduce you to the staff in the outer office."

As O'Mara had promised, the work of the office was routine and repetitious, but during the first few weeks it was still too new for him to find it boring. Apart from the periods spent sleeping, or at least resting, or using his room's food dispenser, Lioren had not left the department, nor had he exercised anything but his brain. His concentration on the new duties was total, and as a result the quality, quantity, and his understanding of the work increased to the point where it drew praise from both Lieutenant Braithwaite and Trainee Cha Thrat, although not from Major O'Mara.

The Chief Psychologist never praised anyone, it had told him, because its job was to shrink heads, not swell them. Lioren could not make any clinical or semantic sense of the remark and decided that it must be what the Earth-human DBDGs called a joke.

Lioren could not ignore his growing curiosity about the two beings with whom he was spending so much time, but the psych files of departmental personnel were closed to each other, and they neither asked personal questions nor answered any about themselves. Possibly it was a departmental rule, or O'Mara had told them to keep a rein on their natural curiosity out of consideration for Lioren's feelings, but then one day Cha Thrat suggested that the rule did not apply outside the office.

"You should forget that display screen for a while, Lioren," the Sommaradvan said as it was about to leave for its midday meal, "and rest your mind from Cresk-Sar's interminable student progress reports. Let's refuel."

Lioren hesitated for a moment, thinking about the permanently crowded dining hall for the hospital's warm-blooded oxygen-breathers and the people he would have to meet in the busy corridors between. Lioren was not sure if he was ready for that.

Before he could reply, Cha Thrat said, "The catering computer has been programmed with a full Tarlan menu, synthetic, of course, but much better than that tasteless stodge the room dispensers dish out. That computer must be feeling hurt, aggrieved, even insulted at being ignored by the only Tarlan on the staff. Why not make it happy and come along?"

Computers did not have feelings, and Cha Thrat must know that as well as he did. Perhaps it was making a Sommaradvan joke.

"I will come," Lioren said.

"So will I," Braithwaite said.

It was the first time in Lioren's experience that the outer office had been left unattended, and he wondered if one or both of them were risking O'Mara's displeasure by doing so. But their behavior on the way to the dining hall, and the firm but unobtrusive manner in which they discouraged any member of the medical staff who seemed disposed to stop him and talk, made it plain that they were acting with the Chief Psychologist's approval. And when they found three vacant places at a table designed for the use of Melfan ELNTs, Braithwaite and Cha Thrat made sure that he remained between them. The other occupants, five Kelgian DBLFs noisily demolishing the character of some unnamed Charge Nurse as they were rising to leave, could not be avoided. Nothing was proof against Kelgian curiosity.

"I am Nurse Tarsedth," one of them said, turning its narrow, conical head to point in Lioren's direction. "Your Sommaradvan friend knows me well, since we trained together, but does not recognize me because it insists that, in spite of having four eyes, it cannot tell Kelgians apart. But my questions are for you, Surgeon-Captain. How are you feeling? Does your guilt manifest itself in bouts of psychosomatic pain? What therapy has O'Mara devised for you? Is it effective? If not, is there anything I can do to help?"

Suddenly Braithwaite started making untranslatable sounds, and its facial coloring had changed from pinkish yellow to deep red.

Tarsedth looked at it briefly, then said, "This often happens when the food and air passages share a common entrance channel. Anatomically, the Earth-human DBDG life-form is a mess."

Anatomically, Lioren thought as he tried hard to concentrate on the questioner in an attempt to avoid the pain that its questions were causing, the Kelgian was beautiful. It was physiological classification DBLF, warm-blooded, oxygen-breathing, multi-pedal, and with a long, flexible cylindrical body covered overall by highly mobile, silvery fur. The fur moved continually in slow ripples from its conical head right down to the tail, and with tiny cross-eddies and wavelets appearing as if the incredibly fine pelt were a liquid stirred by an unfelt wind. It was that fur which explained, and excused, the other's rude and direct approach to what it must know to be a sensitive subject.

Because of inadequacies in the Kelgian speech organs, their spoken language lacked modulation, inflection, and any emotional expression, but they were compensated by the fur, which acted, so far as another Kelgian was concerned, as a perfect but uncontrollable mirror of the speaker's emotional state. As a result the concept of lying or being diplomatic, tactful, or even polite was completely alien to them. A Kelgian said exactly what it meant or felt because its fur revealed its feelings from moment to moment, and to do otherwise would have been considered a stupid waste of time. The opposite also held true, because politeness and the verbal circumlocutions used by many other species simply confused and irritated them.

"Nurse Tarsedth," Lioren said suddenly, "I am feeling very unwell, but on the psychological rather than the physical level. The therapy O'Mara is using in my case is not yet clear to me, but the fact that I have visited the dining hall for the first time since the trial, even though accompanied by two protectors, suggests that it is beginning to work, or that my condition may be improving in spite of it. If your questions are prompted by more than mere curiosity and the offer of help intended to be taken as more than a verbal kindness, I suggest that you ask for details of the therapy and its progress, if any, from the Chief Psychologist."

"Are you stupid?" the Kelgian said, its silvery pelt tufting suddenly into spikes. "I would not dare ask a question like that. O'Mara would tear my fur off in small pieces!"

"Probably," Cha Thrat said as Tarsedth was leaving, "without benefit of anesthetic."

Their food trays slid from the table's delivery recess to the accompaniment of an audible signal that kept him from hearing the Kelgian's reply. Braithwaite said, "So that's what Tarlans eat," and thereafter kept its eyes averted from Lioren's platter.

In spite of having to eat and speak with the same orifice, the Earth-human kept up a continuous dialogue with Cha Thrat, during which they both left conversational gaps enticingly open so that Lioren could join in. Plainly they were doing their best both to put him at ease and keep his attention from the nearby tables where everyone was watching him, but, with a member of a species who had to make a conscious mental effort *not* to look in every direction at once, they were having little success. It was also plain that he was undergoing psychotherapy of a not very subtle form.

He knew that Cha Thrat and Braithwaite were fully informed about his case, but they were trying to make him repeat the information verbally so as to gauge his present feelings about himself and those around him. The method they were using was to exchange what appeared to be highly confidential and often personal information about themselves, their past lives, their personal feelings about the department and toward O'Mara and other entities on the hospital staff with whom they had had pleasant or unpleasant contact, in the hope that Lioren would reciprocate. He listened with great interest but did not speak except in answer to direct questions from them or from staff members who stopped from time to time at their table.

Questions from the silver-furred Kelgians he answered as simply and directly as they were asked. To the shy well-wishings of a massive, six-legged Hudlar whose body was covered only by a recently applied coat of nutrient paint and the tiny ID patch of an advanced student nurse he replied with polite thanks. He also thanked an Earth-human called Timmins, wearing a Monitor Corps uniform with Maintenance insignia, who hoped that the Tarlan environment in his quarters had been properly reproduced, and said that if there was anything else that would make him feel more comfortable he should not hesitate to ask for it. A Melfan wearing the gold-edged band of a Senior Physician on one crablike arm stopped to say that it was pleased to see him making use of the dining hall, because it had wanted to speak to the Tarlan but that, regrettably on this occasion, it was due in ELNT Surgery. Lioren told it that he intended using the dining hall regularly in the future and that there would be other opportunities to talk.

That reply seemed to please Braithwaite and Cha Thrat, and when the Melfan Senior left them they resumed the conversation whose gaps Lioren steadfastly refused to fill. If he had chosen to speak and reveal his feelings just then, it would have been to say that, having been condemned to live for the terrible crime he had committed, he must accept as part of the punishment these constant reminders of his guilt.

He did not think they would be pleased to hear that.

The members of the Psychology Department, Lioren discovered, were free to move anywhere within the hospital and talk to or question, at any time which did not adversely affect the performance of the individual's professional duties, everyone from the lowest trainee nurse or maintenance person up to the near godlike Diagnosticians themselves, and it came as no surprise that their authority to pry into everyone else's most private and personal concerns made them very few friends among the staff. The surprises were the manner in which these multispecies psychologists were recruited and their prior professional qualifications, if any.

O'Mara had joined Sector General shortly before it had been commissioned, as a structural engineer, and the work it had done among the original staff and patients that resulted in its promotion to major and Chief Psychologist was no longer open for study, although there was a rumor that it had once wet-nursed an orphaned infant Hudlar unaided and without benefit either of heavy-lifting machinery or translation devices, but that story Lioren considered to be too wildly improbable to have any basis in fact.

From the words spoken and unspoken it seemed that Lieutenant Braithwaite's career had begun in the Corps's Other-Species Communications and Cultural Contact Division, where initially it had shown great promise and an even greater impatience with its superiors. It was enthusiastic, dedicated, self-reliant, and intuitive where its work was concerned, and whether its intuition proved trustworthy, as happened in the majority of cases, or unsafe, the result was deeply stressful to those in authority. Its attempt to expedite the First Contact procedure on Keran by circumventing the philosophically conservative priesthood caused a citywide religious riot in which many Keranni were killed and injured. Thereafter it was disciplined before being transferred to a number of subordinate administrative positions, none of which proved suitable either to Braithwaite or its superiors, before coming to Sector General. For a short time it was attached to the Maintenance Department's internal-communications section until, in an attempt to rewrite and simplify the multispecies translation program, it knocked down the main computer and left the entire hospital staff and patients unable to do anything but bark, gobble, or cheep unintelligibly at each other for several hours. Colonel Skempton had been less impressed by what Braithwaite had hoped to do than by the havoc it had caused, and was about to banish it to the loneliest and most distant Monitor Corps outpost in the Federation when O'Mara had intervened on its behalf.

Similarly, Cha Thrat's career had been beset by personal and professional difficulties. It was the first and so far only Sommaradvan female to qualify and practice as a warrior-surgeon, a position of great eminence in a profession which was otherwise exclusively male. Lioren was unsure of what a warrior-surgeon of that planet was supposed to be or do, but it had been able to treat successfully a member of an off-planet species, an Earth-human Monitor Corps officer very seriously injured in a flier crash, that Cha Thrat had encountered for the first time. Impressed by its surgical skills and flexibility of mind, the Corps had offered it the opportunity of training in multispecies surgery at Sector Twelve General Hospital. Cha Thrat had accepted because, unlike on its home world, the other-species doctors there would judge it on professional merit without caring whether it was male or female.

But the intense dedication and rigorous clinical disciplines of a warrior-surgeon of Sommaradva, which in many respects resembled those of Lioren's own Tarlan medical fraternity, were not those of Sector General. Cha Thrat did not go into the details of its misdemeanors, suggesting instead that any member of the staff would be eager to satisfy Lioren's curiosity in the matter, but the impression given was that as a trainee it had exercised its clinical initiative too freely, and too often proved its nominal superiors wrong. After one particular incident during which it had temporarily lost one of its own limbs, no ward in the hospital would accept it for training and it, like Braithwaite, had been transferred to Maintenance until a major act of insubordination warranted by the clinical situation at the time brought about its dismissal. And, again like Braithwaite, it was O'Mara who had kept Cha Thrat from leaving the hospital by recruiting it for the department.

As the conversation that was designed both to inform and to draw him out continued, Lioren felt a growing sympathy for these two entities. Like himself they had been cursed with too much intelligence, individuality, and initiative and had suffered grievously thereby.

Naturally, their crimes were insignificant compared with Lioren's own, because they were psychologically flawed misfits rather than criminals and not fully responsible for the wrongs they had done. But were they confessing those misdeeds to him in the form of an apparently unimportant exchange of gossip, ostensibly so that he would better understand them and the situation within the department? Or was it an attempt to assuage their own guilt by trying to help him? He could not be sure because they were concealing their true feelings, unlike himself, by talking too much rather than by remaining silent. The thought that they might not be suffering at all, that their efforts to help Lioren and their other department duties made them forget their past misdeeds came to trouble him, but he dismissed the idea as ridiculous. One could no more forget a past crime than one's own name.

"Lioren," Braithwaite said suddenly. "You are not eating and neither are you talking to us. Would you prefer to return to the office?"

"No," Lioren said, "not immediately. It is clear to me that this visit to the dining hall was a psychological test and that my words and behavior have been closely observed. You have also, almost certainly as part of the test, been answering questions about yourselves without my having to ask them, some of them personal questions which I would have considered it most impolite to ask. Now I will ask one question directly of you. As a result of these observations, what are your conclusions?"

Braithwaite remained silent, but with a small movement of its head indicated that Cha Thrat was to answer.

"You have heard and will understand," the Sommaradvan said, "that I am a warrior-surgeon forbidden to practice my true art and am not yet a fully-qualified wizard. For this reason the spells that I cast lack subtlety, as your words have already shown, and are quite transparent. There is a risk that my observations and conclusions, too, may be oversimplified and inaccurate. They are that my spell aimed at bringing you out of the seclusion of the office and your quarters to the dining hall was unsuccessful in that you reacted calmly and with no apparent emotional distress to the entities who approached you. It was unsuccessful in that it did not overcome your unwillingness to reveal personal feelings, which was another and more important purpose of the test. My conclusion is that any future visits to the dining hall should be unaccompanied unless the accompaniment be for social rather than therapeutic reasons."

Braithwaite nodded its head in the Earth-human gesture of silent agreement. "As the subject of this partially successful test, Lioren, what are your own conclusions about it? Express your feelings about that, at least, freely as would a Kelgian, and do not spare ours."

Lioren was silent for a moment, then said, "I feel curious as to why, in this age of advanced medicine and technology, Cha Thrat considers itself to be a wizard, unqualified or otherwise. I also feel surprise and concern regarding the personal information you have revealed to me. At the risk of being grossly offensive, I can only conclude that . . . Is the Psychology Department staffed with insubordinate misfits and entities with a history of emotional disturbance?"

Cha Thrat made an untranslatable sound and the Earth-human barked softly.

"Without exception," Braithwaite said.

CHAPTER 7

Never in all his long years as a student on Tarla and during his advanced training at Sector General had Lioren been given such a woolly-minded and imprecise set of instructions.

Surely Major O'Mara, who was reputed to possess one of the finest and most analytical minds in the hospital, should not be capable of issuing such instructions. Not for the first time Lioren wondered if the Chief Psychologist, charged as it was with the heavy responsibility of maintaining the mental health of close on ten thousand medical and maintenance staff belonging to sixty-odd different species, had been affected by one of the nonphysical physical maladies it was expected to treat. Or was it simply that Lioren, as the department's most recent and least knowledgeable recruit, had misunderstood the other's words?

"For my own mental clarification and to reduce the possibility of misunderstanding," Lioren said carefully, "may I repeat my instructions aloud?"

"If you think it necessary," the Chief Psychologist replied. From Lioren's growing experience of reading Earth-human voice sounds and the expressions on their flabby, yellow-pink faces, he knew that O'Mara was losing patience.

Ignoring the nonverbal content of the response, Lioren said, "I am to observe Senior Physician Seldal, for as long and as often as the subject's duty schedule and my other work allows, without drawing attention to the fact that it is under observation. I am to look for evidence of abnormal or uncharacteristic behavior even though you are aware that, to a Tarlan BRLH like myself, normal and characteristic behavior in a Nallajim of physiological classification LSVO would appear equally strange to me. I am to do this without any prior indication of what it is that I am to look for or, indeed, if there is anything to look for in the first place. If I am able to detect such behavior, I should try, covertly, to discover the reason for it, and my report should include suggestions for remedial treatment.

"But what," he went on when it was clear that the other was not going to speak, "if I cannot detect any abnormality?"

"Negative evidence," O'Mara said, "can also be valuable."

"Is it your intention that I proceed in complete ignorance," Lioren asked, anger making him forget for a moment the deference due to a nominal superior, "or will I be allowed to study the subject's psych file?"

"You may study it to your heart's content," O'Mara said. "And if you have no further questions, Charge Nurse Kursenneth is waiting."

"I have an observation and a question," Lioren said quickly. "This seems to me to be a particularly imprecise method of briefing a trainee on his first case. Surely I should be given some indication of what is wrong with Seldal. I mean, what did the Senior Physician do to arouse your suspicions in the first place?"

O'Mara exhaled noisily. "You have been assigned the Seldal case, and you have not been told what to do because I don't know what to do with it, either."

Lioren made a surprised sound which did not translate and said, "Does the possibility exist that the most experienced other-species psychologist in the hospital is faced with a case that it is incapable of solving?"

"Other possibilities you might consider," O'Mara said, leaning back into its chair, "is that the problem does not exist. Or that it is a minor one and so unimportant that no serious harm will result if it was to be mishandled by a trainee. It is also possible that more urgent problems are claiming my attention and this is the reason why you have been given this small and nonurgent one.

"For the first time you are being given access to the psych file of a Senior Physician," it went on before Lioren could reply. "It might also be that, as a trainee, you are expected to discover for yourself what it was that aroused my suspicions, and in the light of your subsequent investigation to decide whether or not they were justified."

Embarrassed, Lioren allowed his four medial limbs to go limp so that the fingertips touched the floor, the sign that he was defenseless before the just criticism of a superior. O'Mara would understand the significance of the gesture, but the Earth-human chose to ignore it and went on, "The most important part of our work here is to be constantly on the lookout for abnormal or uncharacteristic behavior in each and every member of the staff, whatever the species or circumstances, and ultimately to develop an instinct for detecting the cause of such trouble before it can seriously affect the being concerned, other staff members or patients. Are your objections based on an unwillingness to speak at length, rather than the necessarily brief conversations held in the dining hall, because the subject of your past misdeeds would be sure to come up and this would cause you severe emotional distress?"

"No," Lioren said firmly. "Any such discomfort would be as nothing compared with the punishment I deserve."

O'Mara shook its head. "That is not a good response, Lioren, but for now I shall accept it. Send in Kursenneth as you leave."

The Kelgian Charge Nurse undulated rapidly into the inner office, its silvery fur rippling with impatience, as Lioren closed the door behind him and dropped into his work position with enough force to make the support structure protest audibly. The only other person in the outer office was Braithwaite, whose attention was focused on its visual display. Muttering angrily, he bent over the console to key in his personal ID and departmental authorization with the request for the Seldal material, optioning for the printed rather than the Tarlan audio translation.

"Are you addressing me or yourself?" Braithwaite asked, looking up suddenly from its work and displaying its teeth. "Either speak a little louder so I can hear you, or more quietly so I can't."

"I am not addressing anyone," Lioren said. "I am thinking aloud about O'Mara and its unreasonable expectations of me. Mistakenly I assumed that I was speaking in an undertone, and I apologize for distracting you from your work."

Braithwaite sat back in its chair, looked at the closely printed sheets that were piling up on Lioren's desktop and said, "So he gave you the Seldal case. But there is no need to agitate yourself. If you can produce a result at all, you would not be expected to do so overnight. And if you should tire of delving into the not very murky recesses of a Nallajim Senior's mind, the latest batch of trainee progress reports from Cresk-Sar are on your desk. I would like you to update the relevant personnel files before the end of next shift."

"Of course," Lioren said. Braithwaite showed its teeth again and returned to its work.

Senior Physician Cresk-Sar had been his clinical tutor during his first year at the hospital and it was still a person totally impossible to please. Reading its characteristically pessimistic report on the apparent lack of progress of the current intake of student nurses, Lioren wondered for a moment whether he should give priority to the deadly dull but important material from the Senior Tutor or to the more interesting but probably less productive psych file on Seldal. Dutifully, as befitted the most junior member of the department, he decided on the former.

A few moments later, while he was reading the clinical competence appraisal and promotion options for a Kelgian student nurse whose name was familiar to him, he abruptly changed his mind and called up the Seldal file. He began studying it so closely that he scarcely noticed the departure of Kursenneth and the arrival of a Tralthan intern who lumbered into the inner office on its six massive feet. But the noise had caused Braithwaite to look up, and Lioren made a polite, untranslatable sound designed to attract the lieutenant's attention.

"This is interesting," he said, "but the only parts that I fully understand are the LSVO physiological and environmental data. I don't know enough about Nallajim interpersonal behavior in general and Seldal in particular to be able to detect any abnormality. It would be better if I was to observe Seldal directly for a period, and talk to it if this can be done without arousing its suspicions, so that I will have a clearer idea of the entity I am investigating."

"It's your case," Braithwaite said.

"Then that is what I shall do," Lioren said, securing the Seldal and Cresk-Sar material and preparing to leave.

"And I agree," the lieutenant said, returning to its work, "that doing anything else is preferable to wading through Cresk-Sar's god-awful boring progress reports . . ."

A quick reference to the senior staff duty roster told Lioren that Seldal would be in the Melfan OR on the seventy-eighth level. Allowing for traffic density in the intervening corridors and a delay while changing into a protective envelope before taking the shortcut through the level of the chlorine-breathing Illensan PVSJs, he should be able to see the Senior Physician before it left for its midday meal.

As yet Lioren had no clear idea of what he would do or say when he was confronted with his first nonsurgical case, and on the way there was no opportunity to think of anything other than avoiding embarrassment or injury by tripping over or colliding violently with staff members.

Theoretically the entities possessing the greater medical seniority had the right of way, but not for the first time he saw a Senior belonging to one of the smaller physiological classifications take hasty evasive action when a six-limbed Hudlarian FROB Charge Nurse with eight times the body mass and an urgent task to perform bore down on it. In such cases it was reassuring to see that the instinct for survival took precedence over rank, although the ensuing contact was verbally rather than physically violent.

With Lioren, however, there was no problem. His trainee's armband indicated that he had no rank at all and should get out of everyone's way.

Two crablike Melfan ELNTs and a chlorine-breathing Illensan PVSJ chittered and hissed their displeasure at him as he dodged between them at an intersection; then he jumped aside as a multiply absentminded Tralthan Diagnostician lumbered heavily toward him, and in so doing accidentally jostled a tiny, red-furred Nidian intern, who barked in reproof.

Even though their physiological classifications varied enormously, the majority of the staff were warm-blooded oxygen-breathers like himself. A much greater hazard to navigation were the entities traversing what was to them a foreign level in protective armor. The local protection needed by a TLTU doctor, who breathed superheated steam and whose pressure and gravity requirements were many times greater than the environment of the oxygen levels, was a great, clanking juggernaut which had to be avoided at all costs.

In the PVSJ transfer lock he donned a lightweight envelope and let himself into the yellow, foggy world of the chlorine-breathers. There the corridors were less crowded, and it was the spiny, membranous, and unadorned denizens of Illensa who were in the majority while the Tralthans, Kelgians, and a single Tarlan, himself, wore or in some cases drove protective armor.

The greatly reduced volume of pedestrian traffic gave Lioren a chance to think again about his strangely imprecise assignment, his department, and the work that he had been sentenced to perform.

Even if he was able to prove that O'Mara's suspicions were unfounded, investigating Seldal would be a unique experience for him. He would take the case very seriously indeed, regardless of its probable minor nature, and if his observations showed that Seldal really had a problem . . .

Lioren raised his four eyes briefly to offer up a prayer to his light-years-distant God of Tarla, in whose existence he no longer believed, pleading for guidance as to what was or was not abnormal behavior in one of the highly intelligent, three-legged, nonflying birdlike natives of Nallaji. He lowered his eyes in time to flatten himself against the wall as the mobile refrigerated pressure envelope belonging to an ultra-low-temperature SNLU rolled silently toward him from a side corridor. Irritated at his momentary lapse of attention, Lioren resumed his journey.

Until now the only abnormal and dangerous behavior he had identified, and it was a type all too prevalent in the hospital, was careless driving.

CHAPTER 8

Lioren moved along the Melfan surgical ward at a pace which suggested that he knew where he was going and what he intended doing when he got there. The Illensan Charge Nurse on duty looked up from its desk, stirred restively within its protective envelope, but otherwise ignored him, and the other nurses were too busy attending to the post-op ELNTs even to notice his passing. But as he walked between the double line of padded support frames which were the Melfan equivalent of surgical beds it became clear that Senior Physician Seldal, in spite of its name appearing on the ward's staff-on-duty board, was not present. Neither was Student Nurse Tarsedth.

Among the Illensan, Kelgian, and Tralthan nurses working all around him a Nallajim would have been hard to miss, which meant that it must still be in the operating theater adjoining the ward. Lioren climbed the ascending ramp to the observation gallery—a large number of the medical staff were physiologically incapable of mounting stairs—and saw that he had guessed right. He also discovered that there were two other observers in the gallery. As he had hoped and half expected, one of them was Tarsedth, the Kelgian DBLF who had spoken to him during his first visit to the dining hall several days earlier.

"What are *you* doing here?" the Kelgian asked, its fur rippling with erratic waves of surprise. "After that mess you made on Cromsag they told us that you would be having nothing to do with other-species bloodletting."

Lioren thought that it was a particularly dishonorable thing to lie to a member of a species that was totally incapable of lying, so he decided on the compromise of not telling all of the truth.

"I still retain my interest in other-species surgery, Nurse Tarsedth," he said, "even though I am forbidden to practice it. Is the case interesting?"

"Not to me," Tarsedth said, returning its attention to the scene below them. "My principal interest here is in the OR staff procedure, artificial gravity controls, patient presentation, and instrument deployment, not all this surgical pecking at some hapless Melfan's innards."

The other occupant of the gallery, an FROB, vibrated its speaking membrane in the Hudlar equivalent of clearing its throat, and said, "I am interested in the surgery, Lioren. As you can see, the operation is nearing completion. But if there is any aspect of the earlier work of particular interest to you, I would be pleased to discuss it."

Lioren turned all of his eyes on the speaker but was unable, as were the majority of the hospital staff, to tell one Hudlar from another. The transparent eye casings were featureless, as were the squat, heavy body and the six tapering, immensely strong tentacles which supported it. The skin, which in appearance and texture resembled a seamless covering of flexible armor, was discolored by patches of dried-out, exhausted food, indicating that the being was urgently in need of respraying with nutrient. But it seemed to know Lioren, or knew of him. Was it possible that this friendly Hudlar, like Tarsedth, had spoken to him earlier?

"Thank you," Lioren said. Choosing his words carefully, he went on, "I am interested in Nallajim surgical procedure, and in particular how this one—"

"I thought all you Psychology people knew everything about everybody," Tarsedth broke in, strong emotion agitating its fur. "You've read Cresk-Sar's reports on us, so you know I am here, spending free time trying to familiarize myself with other-species OR procedures. You know that I'm trying to impress our noxious little Nidian tutor with my knowledge and interest in the subject so that it will approve my request for a posting to the new ELNT theater on fifty-three, and the early promotion that it would bring. I wouldn't be surprised if you were sent here by O'Mara or Cresk-Sar.

"You know everything," Tarsedth ended, its pelt spiking into worried peaks, "but Psychology people say nothing."

Lioren controlled his anger by reminding himself once again that the Kelgian could not help expressing its true feelings, and his reply, so far as it went, was equally blunt and honest.

"I came here to watch Seldal at work," he said, "and I have no interest in your future plans or your method of furthering them. Cresk-Sar's latest report came in this morning, and from reading it and earlier reports I have been made aware of your progress in the most meticulous and boring detail. I am also aware that the material in your file is confidential to my department and must not be discussed with anyone outside it. However, I will say that you are—"

The Hudlar's speaking membrane vibrated suddenly as it said, "Lioren, be careful. If you have information which should not be divulged, even though the reasons appear to you to be unreasonable or administrative rather than therapeutic, please remember that you are once again a trainee and your future depends, like ours, in keeping our department heads happy or, at very least, not actively antagonistic toward us because of disobedience or insubordination.

"Tarsedth is trying very hard for this promotion," it went on quickly, "and it is irritated by what it considers to be the unnecessary secrecy regarding its chances. But it would not wish reassurance or otherwise if the information you gave it was to lead to your dismissal. Like the other nurse trainees, all of whom have discussed you at great length, Tarsedth believes that your only hope of coming to terms with your terrible problem is to remain within the hospital.

"Lioren," it ended, "please guard your tongue."

For a moment a sudden engagement of his emotions made it impossible for Lioren's speech centers to function. It seemed that the dislike of the medical staff for Psychology Department members was not general. But he must not forget that his purpose in coming here was to collect information on Seldal, and the best way of doing that might be to place these two entities under an obligation to him.

"As I was about to say," Lioren resumed, "I am forbidden to discuss restricted material, whether it refers to the inner workings of the mind of a nurse-in-training or that of the able and highly respected Senior Physician Cresk-Sar . . ."

Tarsedth made a sound which did not translate, but the uneven ruffling of its fur made it plain what the Kelgian thought of its principal tutor.

"However," he went on, "that does not preclude the discussion of such matters between yourselves, or of you producing theories regarding your possible future behavior based on past, firsthand knowledge of the entity concerned. You might begin by considering the fact that, for a great many years, Cresk-Sar has been noted for being the most dedicated, meticulous, professionally uncompromising, and personally unpleasant tutor on the staff. And that its trainees suffer the most extreme mental and emotional discomfort, but rarely fail their examinations. Perhaps because of the fear that they will disappoint it by failing to achieve their full potential, the most promising students are made to suffer the worst unpleasantness. You might also remember that Cresk-Sar is so single-minded about its teaching duties that it frequently interrupts and questions trainees regarding their progress during off-duty periods. You might also consider the probable effect on such a tutor of a hypothetical trainee who seems to be ambitious, dedicated, or stupid enough to spend free time, and even forgo a meal as you are doing, in furthering that ambition.

"Having weighed all these factors yourselves," Lioren added, "you might consider that our hypothetical trainee had nothing to worry about, and hypothetically I would be forced to agree with you."

"Lioren," Tarsedth said, its fur settling into slow, relieved waves, "you are breaking, or at least seriously deforming, the rules. And ambitious I may be but stupid I am not; I packed a lunch box. But this one—" It pointed its head in the Hudlar's direction. "—came away without its nutrient supply. It will have to be very polite and apologetic, whatever that means, to the Charge Nurse and ask for a quick spray, or it won't make our next lecture."

"I'm always polite and apologetic," the Hudlar said, "especially to Charge Nurses, who must grow a little tired of forgetful, starving FROBs turning up at odd times looking for a handout. It will be critical toward me, perhaps personally abusive, but it won't refuse. After all, a Hudlar collapsing from malnutrition in the middle of its ward would make the place look untidy."

He looked closely at the Hudlar, whose smooth and incredibly dense body was beginning to sag in spite of its six widely spaced tentacles. The FROB classification were native to a very heavy-gravity planet with proportionately high atmospheric pressure. The world's atmosphere resembled a thick, semiliquid soup laden with tiny, airborne food particles, which were ingested by an absorption mechanism covering its back and flanks, and, because the Hudlars were intensely energy-hungry creatures, the process was continuous. In other-world environments and at the hospital it had been found more convenient to spray them at frequent intervals with nutrient paint. It was possible that this one had found Seldal's procedure so interesting that it had allowed its energy reserves to run dangerously low.

"Wait here," Lioren said briskly, "while I ask Charge Nurse for a sprayer. It would be less troublesome for all concerned if you made the observation gallery untidy instead of collapsing in the main ward. And up here we won't risk spraying your smelly Hudlar nutrient onto its nice clean floor and patients."

By the time he returned with the nutrient tank and sprayer, the Hudlar's body had settled to the floor with its tentacles twitching feebly and only soft, untranslatable sounds coming from its speech membrane. Lioren used the sprayer expertly and accurately—in common with his fellow Monitor Corps officers, he had been taught to perform this favor for FROB personnel engaged in construction work in airless conditions—and within a few minutes it was fully recovered. Below them

Seldal and its patient were no longer visible and the theater was emptying of its OR staff.

"That particular act of charity caused you to miss the end of the operation," Tarsedth said, ruffling its fur disapprovingly at the Hudlar. "Seldal has left for the dining hall and won't return until—"

"Your pardon, Tarsedth," the Hudlar broke in, "but you are forgetting that I recorded the procedure in its entirety. I would be happy to have both of you view a rerun in my place after lectures."

"No!" Tarsedth said. "Hudlars don't use beds or chairs and there would be nowhere for a soft body like mine, or even Lioren's, to relax. And my place is far too small to allow a couple of outsize *thrennigs* like you two inside. If it is that interested, Lioren can always borrow your tape sometime."

"Or both of you could come to my room," Lioren said quickly. "I have never seen a Nallajim surgeon perform and any comments you might make would be helpful to me."

"When?" Tarsedth said.

He had arranged a time suitable for all three of them when the Hudlar said quietly, "Lioren, are you sure that talking about other-species surgery will not cause you emotional distress or that gossiping, for that is what we will be doing, with people outside your department will not get you into trouble with O'Mara?"

"Nonsense!" Tarsedth said. "Gossiping is the most satisfying nonphysical activity between people. We'll see you then, Lioren, and this time I'll make sure my overweight friend here remembers to bring a spare nutrient tank."

When they had gone, Lioren returned the exhausted tank to the Charge Nurse, who needed to be reassured that the nutrient spray had not smeared the transparent wall of the observation gallery. He had often wondered why every ward's Charge Nurse, regardless of size, species, or environmental requirements, was so fanatically insistent that its medical domain was kept at all times neat, orderly, and scrupulously clean. But only now had he begun to realize that, regardless of what the subordinate nursing staff might think of it personally, the ward of a

Charge Nurse who demanded perfection in the minor details was particularly well suited to dealing with major emergencies.

Lioren felt symptoms of a minor and nonpainful discomfort in his stomach that was usually attributable to excitement, nonphysical pleasure, or hunger—on this occasion he thought that it might be a combination of all three. He plotted a course that would take him as quickly as possible to the dining hall, intent on eliminating one of the possible causes, but he did not expect the symptoms to be entirely relieved, because he was thinking about his first nonsurgical case.

Abasing himself to the professional level of a couple of trainee nurses—and him a former Surgeon-Captain in the Monitor Corps—had not been as difficult as he had thought, nor had it shamed him to the degree he had expected and deserved. He was even pleased with himself for correctly deducing from Cresk-Sar's report that Tarsedth would be observing Seldal's operation. After lunch, in order to keep the entity Braithwaite happy, he would return to the office and deal with the remainder of the Senior Tutor's report.

Altogether it promised to be a long, busy day and an even longer evening, during which he would view the recording of Seldal's operation and discuss the Nallajim's procedure at length. Having been told of Lioren's abiding interest in other-species surgery, the two nurses would be expecting many questions from him. In the circumstances it would be natural for the conversation to wander from the operation to the personality, habits, and behavior of the surgeon performing it. Everyone liked to gossip about their superiors, and the quantity of highly personal information available usually increased in direct proportion to the rank of the individual concerned. If he was careful, this information could be abstracted in such a way that neither his informants nor his case subject would be aware of what was happening.

As the beginning of a covert investigation, Lioren thought with a little shiver of self-congratulation, it was faultless.

CHAPTER 9

"W ith Nallajims," Tarsedth said while they were reviewing the Seldal operation late that evening, "I can never make up my mind whether I'm watching surgery or other-species cannibalism."

"In their early, precurrency days," the Hudlar said, the modulation of its speaking membrane suggesting that its words were not to be taken seriously, "that was the only way a Nallajim doctor could obtain its fee from a patient."

"I am filled with admiration," Lioren said, "that a life-form with three legs, two not-quite atrophied wings, and no hands at all could become a surgeon in the first place. Or, for that matter, perform any of the other delicate manipulatory functions which led to the evolution of intelligence and a technology-based culture. They began with so many serious physiological disadvantages that—"

"They do it by poking their noses into the most unlikely places," Tarsedth said, its fur rumpling with impatience. "Do you want to watch the operation or talk about the surgeon?"

Both, Lioren thought, but he did not speak the word aloud.

The LSVO physiological classification to which Seldal belonged was a warm-blooded, oxygen-breathing species which had evolved on Nallaji, a large world whose high rotational velocity, dense atmosphere, and low gravity in the intensely fertile equatorial regions had combined to provide an environment suited to the proliferation of avian life-forms. It had been an environment which enabled airborne predators to evolve which were large both in variety and size, but so heavily armed and armored that they had gradually rendered themselves extinct. Over the millennia while this incredibly violent process was working itself out, the relatively tiny LSVOs had been forced out of the skies and their high, vulnerable nests and had taken to the shelter of the trees, deep gullies, and caves.

Very quickly they had to adapt to sharing the ground with the small animals and insects which had formerly been their prey.

Gradually the Nallajim had lost the ability for sustained flight, and as a species they had progressed too far along the evolutionary path for their wings to become arms, or even for their wingtips to subdivide into the digits suitable for the fabrication of tools or weapons. But it was the savage, mindless, and continuing threat from insects large and small who infested, and by their sheer numbers dominated, the land as the giant avians interdicted the air that brought about the minor changes in bone structure and musculature of the beak that caused the Nallajim to develop intelligence.

Handless but no longer helpless, they had been forced to use their heads.

On Nallaji, the winged insects that swarmed and stung their prey to death were outnumbered by those that burrowed and laid eggs deep within the sleeping bodies of their victims. The only way these burrowing insects could be removed was by pecking them out with the long, thin, flexible Nallajim beak.

From being a simple family and tribal debugging device, the LSVO beak progressed to a stage where it was capable of fabricating quite complex insect-proof dwellings, tools, insect-killing weapons, cities, and ultimately starships.

"Seldal is *fast*," Lioren said admiringly, after one particularly delicate piece of deep surgery, "and it gives remarkably few instructions to its OR staff."

"Use your eyes," Tarsedth said. "It doesn't have to talk to them because the staff are engaged in supporting the patient more than the surgeon. Look at the way its beak jabs all over that instrument rack. By the time it gave directions to a nurse and the correct instrument was stuck onto its beak, Seldal could have obtained the instrument unaided, completed the incision, and been ready for the next stage.

"With this surgeon," the Kelgian went on, "it is the choice and disposition of the racked instruments that is important. There is no juggling with clamps and cutters, no verbal distractions, no tantrums because an OR nurse is slow or misunderstands. I think I'd like to work with this birdbrained Senior Physician."

The conversation, Lioren thought, was moving away from Seldal's operation to the subject of Seldal itself, which was exactly what he had been hoping would happen. But before he could take advantage of the situation, the Hudlar, who was plainly another enthusiast where Nalla-jim surgery was concerned, tried to be helpful while displaying its own expertise.

"Its procedure is very fast and may seem to be confusing to you, Lioren," it said, "especially since you have told us that you have no prior surgical experience with Melfan ELNTs. As you can see, the patient's six limbs and all of the body are exoskeletal. The vital organs are housed within that thick, osseous carapace and are so well protected that trau-matic injury rarely occurs although these organs are, unfortunately, sub-ject to a number of dysfunctions which require surgical intervention . . ."

"You," Tarsedth broke in, its fur spiking with irritation, "are begin-ning to sound like Cresk-Sar."

"I'm sorry," the Hudlar said. "I only meant to explain what Seldal was doing, not bring back unpleasant memories of our tutor."

"Do not trouble yourself," Lioren said. The Hudlar FROBs were acknowledged to be the physically strongest life-forms of the Galactic Federation and with the least-pervious body tegument, but emotionally their skins were extremely thin. He added, "Please continue, so long as you don't ask questions afterward."

The Hudlar's membrane vibrated with an untranslatable sound. "I won't. But I was trying to explain why speed is so important during

Melfan surgery. The major internal organs float in a shock-absorbent fluid and are only tethered loosely to the interior walls of the carapace and underside. When the fluid is removed temporarily prior to surgery, the organs are no longer supported and they sink onto each other with consequent compression and deformation effects which include restriction of the blood supply. Irreversible changes take place which could result in termination of the patient if the situation is allowed to continue for more than a few minutes."

With an intensity that shocked his sensorium like a traumatic injury, Lioren found himself wishing suddenly for the impossible, for a recent past that had taken a different turning and would have allowed him to share this trainee's enthusiasm for other-species surgery rather than a demeaning and probably unproductive interest in the surgeon's mind. The thought that the pain, no matter how severe or often it came, would always be less than he deserved brought little comfort.

"Normally an ELNT surgical procedure requires a large operative field and many assistants," the Hudlar went on, "whose principal purpose is to support these no-longer-floating organs on specially shaped pans while the surgeon-in-charge performs the operation proper. This procedure has the disadvantages of requiring an unnecessarily large opening in the carapace to allow entry of the supporting instruments, and the healing of such a wound is slow and sometimes leads to unsightly scarring and discoloration where the section of carapace was temporarily removed. This can lead to severe emotional trauma in the patient because the carapace, the richness and graduations of its color and individuality in pattern, plays an important part in the courtship process. With a single Nallajim operating, however, the greater speed of this procedure combined with the smaller entry wound reduces both the size and the possibility of a disfigurement occurring postoperatively."

"A good thing, too," Tarsedth said, its fur rippling in vehement sympathy. Kelgian DBLFs had the same feelings about their mobile, silvery fur as the Melfan ELNTs about their beautifully marked carapaces. "But would you look at the way it is pecking at the operative field, sometimes with its naked beak, like a bloody astigmatic vulture!"

Seldal's instrument rack was suspended vertically just beyond the operative field, within easy reach of the surgeon's beak. Each recess contained specialized instruments with hollow, conical grips that enabled the Nallajim's upper, lower, or entire beak to enter and grasp, use, replace, or discard them with bewildering rapidity. Occasionally Seldal went in with nothing but the two, long, cylindrical lenses that extended from its tiny eyes almost to the tip of its beak—which had been strapped in position for the duration of the operation—to correct its avian tendency for long-sightedness. Its three claws were wrapped tightly around the perch attached to the operating frame, and the stubby wings fluttered constantly to give it additional stability when it jabbed with its beak.

"In early times," the Hudlar said, "both the eggs and the egg-laying insects which had to be removed from the patients were edible, and it was considered proper for the surgeon to ingest them. Melfan tissue would not be harmful to a Nallajim, and you will remember from basic training that any ELNT pathogens it contained would not affect or infect an entity who had evolved on a different world. But in a multispecies hospital like Sector General eating parts of a patient, however small, can be emotionally disturbing to onlookers, so you will note that all such material is discarded.

"The operation," the Hudlar went on, "is to remove—"

"It surprises me," Lioren broke in, again trying to guide the conversation back to the surgeon rather than its work, "that a same-species surgeon, Senior Physician Edanelt, for example, was not assigned to the case instead of a life-form who requires a Melfan Educator tape to—"

"That," Tarsedth said, "would be like expecting Diagnostician Conway to forgo all other-species surgery until it had first treated the Earth-human DBDGs in the hospital. Don't be stupid, Lioren. Operating on an other-species patient is far more interesting and exciting than one of your own kind, and the more physiological differences there are the greater the professional challenge. But you know all this already. On Cromsag you treated—"

"There is no need to remind me of the results," Lioren said sharply, irritated in spite of knowing that the other could not help being irritating. "I was about to say that Seldal, who has a beak and no arms, is showing no signs of mental confusion while its mind is partially under the control of a being accustomed to using six limbs all of which are capable of various degrees of manipulation. The psychological and emotional pressure, not to mention the input from its mind-partner's involuntary muscle system, must be considerable."

"Yes," the Hudlar said. "Obviously it has good control of both minds. But I wonder how I, another six-limbed being, would feel if I had to take a Nallajim tape. I don't have a beak equivalent or even a mouth."

"Don't waste time worrying about it," Tarsedth said. "Educator tapes are only offered to those studious, highly intelligent, and emotionally stable types who are being considered for promotion to Senior Physician or higher. The way Cresk-Sar criticizes our work, can you imagine one of us ever being offered an Educator tape?"

Lioren did not speak. Much stranger things had happened in Sector General—the staff records showed that Thornnastor's principal assistant, the DBDG Earth-human Pathologist Murchison, had joined the hospital as a trainee nurse—but it was a strict rule of the department that the subject of a long-term promotion should not be discussed with trainees who were being considered for it nor, except in the most general terms, any of the problems associated with the Educator-tape system.

The major problem from which all the others stemmed was that, while Sector General was equipped to treat every known form of intelligent life, no single entity could hold in its mind even a fraction of the physiological data necessary for this purpose. Surgical dexterity was a product of aptitude, training, and experience, but the complete information covering the physiology of a given patient could only be transferred artificially by Educator tape, which was the brain record of some great medical authority belonging to the same species as that of the patient to be treated.

If a Melfan doctor was assigned to a Kelgian patient, it was given a DBLF tape until the treatment was complete, after which the mind recording was erased. The exceptions to this rule were the Senior Physicians of proven emotional stability such as Seldal, and the Diagnosticians.

The Diagnosticians were those rare beings whose minds were stable enough to retain permanently six, seven, and in one case up to ten physiology tapes simultaneously. To these data-crammed minds were given the initiation and direction of original research in xenological medicine in addition to the practice and teaching of their considerable art.

The tapes, however, imparted not only the physiological data required for treatment, but the entire memory and personality of the donor entity as well. In effect a Diagnostician, and to a lesser extent a Senior Physician, subjected itself voluntarily to an extreme form of multiple schizophrenia. The donor entities apparently sharing the host doctor's mind could be aggressive, unpleasant individuals—geniuses were rarely nice people—with all sorts of pet peeves and phobias. Normally these would not become apparent during the course of an operation or treatment because both host and donor minds were concentrating on the purely medical aspects of the work. The worst effects were felt when the possessor of the tape was sleeping.

Alien nightmares, Lioren knew from a few of his own tape experiences, were really nightmarish. And alien sexual fantasies were enough to make the host mind wish, if it was capable of wishing coherently for anything at the time, that it was dead. He could not even imagine the physical and emotional effect of the sensorium of an enormous, intelligent crustacean on the mind of a ridiculously fragile but equally intelligent bird.

He continued to watch the frenetically active Seldal while recalling the saying often repeated among the hospital staff that anyone who was sane enough to practice as a Diagnostician was mad, a remark reputed to have originated with O'Mara itself.

"Seldal's ELNT procedure fascinates me," Lioren said, firmly returning to the subject of his investigation. "It shows no hesitation whatever, no pauses for thought or reconsideration, none of the too-careful movements one sees with Educator-tape work. Is it like this with other life-forms?"

"With respect, Lioren," the Hudlar said, "at the speed it works would you notice an awkward pause if you saw one? We have watched it perform an Earth-human gastrectomy and, among others, do something to a DBLF that Tarsedth had better explain to you since the Kelgian reproductive mechanism is proving difficult for me to understand—"

"You should talk!" Tarsedth broke in. "Every time a Hudlar mother produces offspring it changes to male mode. That's—that's *indecent!*"

"Presumably these patients required only short-duration Educator taping," the Hudlar went on, "but Seldal accommodated itself to them without apparent difficulty. For the past six weeks it has been engaged principally on Tralthan surgery and says that it finds the work most interesting, stimulating, and comfortable, next to working on another Nallajim—"

"Another female Nallajim, it means," Tarsedth said, ruffling its fur in disapproval, or perhaps envy. "Do you know that in the three years that Seldal has been here it has been nested by nearly every female LSVO on the staff? What they see to ruffle their tail feathers in such a scrawny, self-effacing nonentity is beyond my understanding."

"Is my translator faulty," Lioren asked, trying to hide his excitement at acquiring this new and potentially useful datum, "or am I to understand that Seldal actually discussed its Educator-tape problems with a couple of trainees?"

"The discussion was perfunctory," the Hudlar said before Tarsedth could reply, "and was concerned with personal preferences rather than problems. Seldal is very approachable, for a Senior, and usually invites post-op questions from anyone who has been watching from the observation gallery. There wasn't time this morning or you could have asked questions yourself.

"In any case," it went on, turning itself ponderously to regard Tarsedth, "my interest in Seldal's love life, which seems to have become less gaudy in recent weeks, is at best academic. But even among my own species it is not uncommon for female-mode persons to be attracted to males who have personalities which are as shy and timid as that of Seldal. Such people are frequently more sensitive, unhurried, and interesting as lovers."

It returned its attention to Lioren and continued. "To modify a saying of one of our classmates, which seems to apply to activities associated with same-species reproduction, a faint heart sometimes wins the fair lady."

"It's talking about Hadley," Tarsedth explained, "an Earth-human trainee. It was supposed to have gone into the maintenance tunnels with . . ."

He had not heard that particular item of gossip before, probably because no official notice had been taken of the incident or the grapevine had been already overloaded with even more scandalous material that day. The story of Hadley's misdemeanor was followed by others, many of which had found their way to his department in the form of much less interesting psych-file updates which were, regrettably, free of Tarsedth's creative exaggeration. He was forced to use every verbal strategem he could devise to bring the conversation back to the Nallajim Senior and keep it there.

Lioren was discovering many interesting facts about Seldal's behavior, personality, and interests. It was information which he would not have been able to obtain from the Senior Physician's file. So far as his assignment was concerned, the evening was being spent profitably and, he thought with increasing feelings of guilt, very enjoyably.

CHAPTER 10

The following morning's work period was sufficiently far advanced for his digestive system to begin complaining that it had nothing to engage its attention when Braithwaite walked slowly across to Lioren's desk. Placing its flabby pink hands palms downward on an uncluttered area of the work surface, it bent its arms so that its head was close to his and said quietly, "You haven't spoken a word for more than four hours. Is there a problem?"

Lioren leaned back, irritated by the uninvited close approach of the being, and by the fact that on several previous occasions it had criticized him for talking too much. Even though Braithwaite was showing concern and trying to be helpful, he wished that his immediate superior's behavior would not vacillate so. There were times when he much preferred the approach of O'Mara, who was, at least, consistently nasty.

At the adjacent desk, Cha Thrat was concentrating even more intently on its screen as it pretended not to listen. For some reason Lioren's problems, and some of his suggested solutions, had been a source of considerable amusement over the past few days, but this time it was going to be disappointed.

"The reason for my silence," he replied, "is that I was concentrating on clearing the routine work so as to have more time available for Seldal.

There is no specific problem, merely a discouraging lack of progress in every direction."

Braithwaite removed its hands from his desk and straightened up. Showing its teeth, it asked, "In which direction are you progressing least?"

Lioren made the Gesture of Impatience with two of his medial limbs and said, "It is difficult to quantify negative progress. Over the past few days I have observed Seldal's performance of major surgery and discussed the subject's behavior with other observers, during which information emerged which was not available from its psych file. The new material is based on unsupported gossip and may not be entirely factual. The subject is highly respected and popular among its medical subordinates. This popularity seems to be deserved rather than deliberately sought. I cannot find any abnormality in this entity."

"Obviously that is not your final conclusion," said Braithwaite, "or you wouldn't be trying to free more time for the investigation. How do you plan to spend this time?"

Lioren thought for a moment, then said, "Since it will not always be possible to question observers or its OR staff without revealing the reason for my questions, I shall have to ask—"

"No!" Braithwaite said sharply, the hairy crescents on its face lowering so that they almost hid its eyes. "You must not question the subject directly. If you should discover anything amiss, report it to O'Mara and do or say nothing to Seldal itself. You will please remember that."

"I am unlikely to forget," Lioren said quietly, "what happened the last time I used my initiative."

For a moment there was neither sound nor movement from Cha Thrat or Braithwaite, but the Earth-human's facial pigmentation was deepening in color. Lioren went on. "I was about to say that I would have to question Seldal's patients, discreetly, in the hope of detecting by hearsay any unusual changes in the subject's behavior during its visits before and after surgery. For this I need a list and present locations of Seldal's post-op patients and the timing of its ward rounds so that I can talk to them without meeting the subject itself. To avoid comment by the ward staff concerned it would be better if someone other than myself requested this information."

Braithwaite nodded its head. "A sensible precaution. But what will be your excuse for speaking to these patients and for talking to them about Seldal?"

"The reason I shall give for visiting them," Lioren replied, "will be to ask for any comments or criticism they may have regarding the environmental aspects of their various recovery wards, since this is an important nonmedical aid to recuperation and the department carries out such checks from time to time. I shall not ask the patients about their medical condition or their surgeon. But I have no doubt that both subjects will arise naturally and, while pretending disinterest, I shall gather as much information as I can."

"A finely woven, intricate, and well-concealed spell," Cha Thrat said before Braithwaite could speak. "My compliments, Lioren. Already you show promise of becoming a great wizard."

Braithwaite nodded its head again. "You seem to be covering all eventualities. Is there any other information or help you need?"

"Not at present," Lioren said.

He was not being completely truthful, because he wanted clarification of Cha Thrat's compliment, which, to a highly qualified former medic like himself, had verged on the insulting. Perhaps "spell" and "wizard," which were words that Cha Thrat used frequently, had different meanings on Sommaradva than on Tarla. But it seemed that his curiosity was soon to be satisfied, because the Sommaradvan wanted to see a Tarlan trainee wizard at work.

The choice of the first patient was forced on him because the other two were beginning their rest periods and Psychology Department staff had no authority to intervene during clinical treatment, which included interrupting a patient's sleep. The interview promised to be the most difficult and delicate of the three cases Braithwaite had listed for him.

"Are you sure you want to talk to this one, Lioren?" Cha Thrat asked with the small upper-limb movements that he had learned signified deep concern. "This is a very sensitive case."

Lioren did not reply at once. It was a truism accepted on every inhabited world of the Federation that medics made the worst patients. Not only was this one a healer of the highest professional standing, the interview would have to be conducted with great care because patient Mannen's condition was terminal.

"I dislike wasting time," Lioren said finally, "or an opportunity."

"Earlier today," Cha Thrat said, "you told Braithwaite that you had learned your lesson regarding the too-free use of initiative. With respect, Lioren, it was impatience and your refusal to waste time that caused the Cromsag Incident."

Lioren did not reply.

Mannen was an Earth-human DBDG, of advanced age for that comparatively short-lived species, who had come to Sector General after graduating with the highest honors at its home world's foremost teaching hospital. It had quickly been promoted to Senior Physician and within a few years to the post of Senior Tutor, when its pupils had included such present members of the medical hierarchy as Conway, Prilicla, and Edanelt, until it relinquished the position to Cresk-Sar on its elevation to Diagnostician. Inevitably the time had come when the establishment's most advanced medical and mechanical aids were no longer capable of extending its life, even though its level of mentation remained as sharp and clear as that of a young adult.

Ex-Diagnostician and current-patient Mannen lay in a private compartment off the main DBDG medical ward, with biosensors monitoring its vital signs and the usual life-support mechanisms absent at its own request. Its clinical condition was close to critical but stable, and its eyes had remained closed, indicating that it was probably unconscious or asleep. Lioren had been surprised and pleased when they found the patient unattended, because Earth-humans were numbered among the intelligent species who liked the company of family or friends at ending of life. But his surprise had disappeared when the ward's Charge Nurse informed them that the patient had had numerous visitors who had left or been sent away within a few moments of arrival.

"Let us leave before it awakens," Cha Thrat said very quietly. "Your excuse for being here, to ask if it is satisfied with the room's environmental system, is, in the circumstances, both ridiculous and insensitive. Besides, not even O'Mara can work a spell on an unconscious mind."

For a moment Lioren studied the monitor screens, but he could not recall the values he had learned so long ago regarding the measurement of Earth-human life processes. This room was a quiet and private place, he thought, in which to ask personal questions.

"Cha Thrat," he asked softly, "what precisely do you mean by working a spell?"

It was a simple question that required a long and complicated answer, and the process was neither shortened nor simplified by Cha Thrat breaking off every few minutes to look worriedly toward the patient.

The Sommaradvan culture was divided into three distinct levels of person—serviles, warriors, and rulers—and the medical fraternities responsible for their welfare were similarly stratified.

At the bottom were the serviles, people who were unwilling to strive for promotion and whose work was undemanding, repetitive, and completely without risk because in their daily lives they were protected against gross physical damage. The healers charged with their care were physicians whose treatments were purely medical. The second level, much less numerous than the serviles, were the warriors, who occupied positions of great responsibility and, in the past, considerable physical danger.

There had been no war on Sommaradva for many generations, but the warrior class had kept the name because they were the descendants of the people who had fought to protect their homelands, hunted for food, and raised defenses against predatory beasts while the serviles saw to their physical needs. Now they were the technicians, engineers, and scientists who still performed the high-risk or the most prestigious duties, which included the protection of rulers. For this reason the injuries sustained by warriors had usually been traumatic in nature, requiring surgical intervention or repair rather than medication, and this work was the responsibility of the warrior-surgeons. At the top of Sommar-adva's medical tree were the ruler-healers, who had even greater responsibilities and, at times, much less reward or satisfaction in their work.

Protected against all risk of physical injury, the ruler class were the administrators, academics, researchers, and planners on Sommaradva. They were the people charged with the smooth running of the cities and the world, and the ills which affected them were principally the phantasms of the mind. Their healers dealt only in wizardry, spells, sympathetic magic, and all the other practices of nonphysical medicine.

"Naturally," Cha Thrat said, "as our culture advanced socially and scientifically an overlapping of responsibilities occurred. Serviles occasionally fracture a limb, or the mental stresses encountered while studying for promotion sometimes threaten the sanity of the mind concerned, or a ruler succumbs to a servile digestive upset, all of which necessitates healers practicing above or below their class.

"Since earliest times," the Sommaradvan concluded, "our practitioners of healing have been divided into physicians, surgeons, and wizards."

"Thank you," Lioren said. "Now I understand. It is merely a matter of semantic confusion combined with a too-literal translation. To you a spell is psychotherapy which can be short and simple or long and complicated, and the wizard responsible for it is simply a psychologist who—"

"It is *not* a psychologist!" Cha Thrat said fiercely; then, remembering the patient, it lowered its voice again and went on, "Every non-Sommaradvan I have met makes the same mistake. On my world a psychologist is a being of low status who tries to be a scientist by measuring brain impulses or bodily changes brought about by physical and mental stress, and by making detailed observations of the subject's subsequent behavior. A psychologist tries to impose immutable laws in an area of nightmares and changing internal realities, and attempts to make a science of what has always been an art, an art practiced only by wizards.

"A wizard will use or ignore the instruments and tabulations of the psychologists," the Sommaradvan continued before Lioren could speak, "to cast spells that influence the complex, insubstantial structures of the mind. A wizard uses words, silences, minute observation, and most important, intuition, to uncover and gradually reorient the sick, internal reality of the patient to the external reality of the world. There is a great difference between a mere psychologist and a wizard."

The other's voice had been rising again but the sensors reported no change in the patient's condition.

It was obvious to Lioren that the Sommaradvan had few opportunities to talk freely about its home planet and the few friends it had left there or to relieve its feelings about the intolerance of its professional peers that had forced it to come to Sector General. It went on to relate in detail the disruption its particularly rigid code of professional ethics had caused throughout the hospital until its eventual rescue by the wizard O'Mara, and its own personal feelings and reactions to all these events. Plainly Cha Thrat wanted, perhaps badly needed, to talk about itself.

But confidences invited more confidences, and Lioren began to wonder if he, the one member of the Tarlan species on the hospital staff speaking like this to its only Sommaradvan, did not have the same need. Gradually there was developing a two-way exchange in which the questions and answers were becoming very personal indeed.

Lioren found himself telling Cha Thrat about his feelings during and after the Cromsag Incident, of the guilt that was terrible beyond words or belief, and of his helpless fury at the Monitor Corps and O'Mara for refusing him the death he so fully deserved and for sentencing him instead to the ultimate cruelty of life.

At that point Cha Thrat, who must have sensed his increasing emotional distress, firmly steered the conversation onto O'Mara and the

Chief Wizard's reasons for taking them into its department, and from there to the assignment that had brought him here in the hope of gathering information from a patient who was plainly in no condition to give it.

They were still discussing Seldal and wondering aloud whether they should try talking to Mannen the next day, if it should survive that long, when the supposedly unconscious patient opened its eyes and looked at them.

"I, that is, we apologize, sir," Cha Thrat said quickly. "We assumed that you were unconscious because your eyes remained closed since our arrival and the biosensor readings showed no change. I can only assume that you realized our mistake, and because we were discussing matters of a confidential nature, you maintained the pretense of sleep out of politeness to avoid causing us great embarrassment."

Mannen's head moved slowly from side to side in the Earth-human gesture of negation, and it seemed that the eyes staring up at him were in some clinically inexplicable fashion younger than the rest of the patient's incredibly wrinkled features and time-ravaged body. When it spoke, the words were like the whispering of the wind through tall vegetation and slowed with the effort of enunciation.

"Another . . . wrong assumption," it said. "I am . . . never polite."

"Nor do we deserve politeness, Diagnostician Mannen," Lioren said, forcing his mind and his voice to the surface of a great, hot sea of embarrassment. "I alone am responsible for this visit, and the blame for it is entirely mine. My reason for coming no longer seems valid and we shall leave at once. Again, my apologies."

One of the thin, emaciated hands lying outside the bed covering twitched feebly, as if it would have been raised in a nonverbal demand for silence if the arm muscles had possessed sufficient strength. Lioren stopped speaking.

"I know . . . your reason for coming," Mannen said, in a voice barely loud enough to carry the few inches to its bedside translator. "I overheard everything . . . you said about Seldal . . . as well as yourself. Very interesting it was . . . But the effort of listening to you . . . for nearly two hours . . . has tired me . . . and soon my sleep will not be a pretense. You must go now."

"At once, sir," Lioren said.

"And if you wish to return," Mannen went on, "come at a better time . . . because I want to ask questions as well as listen to you. But the visit should not be long delayed."

"I understand," Lioren said. "It will be very soon."

"Perhaps I will be able to help you . . . with the Seldal business and in return . . . you can tell me more about Cromsag . . . and do me another small favor."

The Earth-human Mannen had been a Diagnostician for many years. Its help and understanding of the Seldal problem would be invaluable, especially as it would be given willingly and without the need of him having to waste time hiding the reason for his questions. But he also knew that the price he would have to pay for that assistance in inflaming wounds that could never heal would be higher than the patient realized.

Before he could reply, Mannen's lips drew back slowly in the peculiar Earth-human grimace which at times could signify a response to humor or a nonverbal expression of friendship or sympathy.

"And I thought I had problems," it said.

CHAPTER 11

Lioren's subsequent visits were lengthier, completely private, and not nearly as painful as he had feared.

He had asked Hredlichi, the Charge Nurse on Mannen's ward, to inform him immediately whenever the patient was conscious and in a condition to receive visitors, regardless of the time of the hospital's arbitrary day or night that should be. Before agreeing, Hredlichi had checked with the patient, who hitherto had refused visits from everyone except for the ward rounds of its surgeon, and been greatly surprised when Mannen agreed to receive nonmedical visits only from Lioren.

Cha Thrat had explained it was insufficiently motivated to be willing to interrupt its sleep or drop other, more urgent work at a moment's notice to pursue the Seldal investigation—which was, after all, Lioren's responsibility—although it would continue to assist Lioren in any other way which did not involve major personal inconvenience. As a result, the first visit to Mannen had been the only one at which the Sommaradvan had been present.

By the third visit, Lioren was feeling relieved that Mannen did not want to talk exclusively about the Cromsaggar, disappointed that his understanding of Seldal's behavior was no clearer, and embarrassed that the patient was spending an increasing proportion of each visit talking about itself.

"With respect, Doctor," Lioren said after one particularly argumentative self-diagnosis, "I am not in possession of an Earth-human Educator tape which would enable me to give an opinion in your case nor, as a member of the Psychology Department, am I allowed to practice medicine. Seldal is your physician-in-charge and it—"

"Talks to me as if . . . I was a drooling infant," Mannen broke in. "Or a frightened, terminal patient. At least you don't . . . try to administer . . . a lethal overdose . . . of sympathy. You are here to . . . obtain information about Seldal and, in return, to satisfy my curiosity . . . about you. No, I am not so much afraid of dying . . . as having too much time to think about it."

"Is there pain, Doctor?" Lioren asked.

"You know there is no pain, dammit," Mannen replied in a voice made stronger by its anger. "In the bad old days there might have been pain, and inefficient painkilling medication that so depressed the functioning of the involuntary muscle systems that . . . the major organs went into failure and the medication killed the patient as well as its pain . . . so that its medic escaped with the minimum of ethical self-criticism and . . . its patient was spared a lingering death. But now we have learned how to negate pain without harmful side effects . . . and there is nothing I can do but wait to see which of my vital organs . . . will be the first to expire from old age.

"I should not," Mannen ended, its voice dropping to a whisper again, "have allowed Seldal loose in my intestines. But that blockage was . . . really uncomfortable."

"I sympathize," Lioren said, "because I, too, wish for death. But you can look back with pride and without pain to your past and to an ending that will not be long delayed. In my past and future lies only guilt and desolation that I must suffer until—"

"Do you really feel sympathy, Lioren?" Mannen broke in. "You impress me as being nothing but a proud and unfeeling . . . but very efficient organic healing machine. The Cromsag Incident . . . showed that the machine had a flaw. You want to destroy the machine . . . while O'Mara wants to repair it. I don't know which of you will succeed."

"I would never," Lioren said harshly, "destroy myself to avoid just punishment."

"To an ordinary member of the staff," Mannen went on, "I would not say such . . . personally hurtful things. I know you feel you deserve them . . . and worse . . . and you expect no apology from me. But I do apologize . . . because I am hurting in a way that I did not believe possible . . . and am striking out at you . . . and I ignore my friends when they visit me in case they discover . . . that I am nothing but a vindictive old man."

Before Lioren could think of a reply, Mannen said weakly, "I have been hurtful to a being who has not hurt me. The only recompense I can make is by helping you . . . with information on Seldal. When it visits me tomorrow morning . . . I shall ask it specific and very personal questions. I shall not mention . . . nor will it suspect your connection."

"Thank you," Lioren said. "But I do not understand how you can ask—"

"It is very simple," Mannen said, its voice strengthening again. "Seldal is a Senior Physician and I was, until my summary demotion to the status of patient, a Diagnostician. It will be pleased to answer all my questions for three reasons. Out of respect for my former rank, because it will want to humor a terminal patient who wants to talk shop for what might well be the last time, and especially because I have not spoken a word to it since three days before the operation. If I cannot discover any helpful information for you after that exercise, the information does not exist."

This terminally ill entity, in what might well be the last constructive act of its life, was going to help him with the Seldal assignment as no other person was capable of doing, simply because it had used a few impolite words to him. Lioren had always considered it wrong to become emotionally involved in a case, however slightly, because the patient's interests were best served by the impersonal, clinical approach— and Mannen was not even his patient. But somehow it seemed that the investigation into the Nallajim Senior's behavior was no longer his only concern.

"Thank you again," Lioren said. "But I had been about to say that I cannot understand why you are hurting in ways that you did not believe possible when your medication should render you pain-free. Is it a nonmedical problem?"

Mannen stared up at him unblinkingly for what seemed a very long time in silence, and Lioren wished that he was able to read the expression on its wasted and deeply wrinkled features. He tried again.

"If it is nonmedical, would you prefer I send for O'Mara?"

"No!" Mannen said, weakly but very firmly. "I do not want to talk to the Chief Psychologist. He has been here many times, until he stopped trying to talk to a person who pretended to be asleep all the time and, like my other friends, stayed away."

It was becoming clear that Mannen wanted to talk to someone, but had not yet made the decision to do so. Silence, Lioren thought, might be the safest form of questioning.

"In your mind," Mannen said finally, in a voice which had found strength from somewhere, "there is too much that you want to forget. In mine there is even more that I cannot remember."

"Still I do not understand you," Lioren said.

"Must I explain it as if you were a first-day trainee?" the patient said. "For the greater part of my professional life I have been a Diagnostician. As such I have had to accommodate in my mind, often for periods of several years, the knowledge, personalities, and medical experience of anything up to ten entities at a time. The experience is of many alien personalities occupying and—because these tape donors were rarely timid or self-effacing people—fighting for control of the host mind. This is a subjective mental phenomenon which must be overcome if one is to continue as a Diagnostician, but initially it seems that the host mind is a battleground with too many combatants warring with each other until—"

"That I do understand," Lioren said. "During my time here as a Senior I was once required to carry three tapes simultaneously."

"The host is able to impose peace and order," Mannen continued slowly, "usually by learning to understand and adapt to and make friends with these alien personalities without surrendering any part of his own mind, until the necessary accommodation can be made. It is the only way to avoid serious mental trauma and removal from the roster of Diagnosticians."

Mannen closed its eyes for a moment, then went on. "But now the mental battlefield is deserted, emptied of the onetime warriors who became friends. I am all alone with the entity called Mannen, and with only Mannen's memories, which includes the memory of having many other memories that were taken from me. I am told that this is as it should be because a man's mind should be his own for a time before termination. But I am lonely, lonely and empty and cared for and completely pain-free while I spend a subjective eternity waiting for the end."

Lioren waited until he was sure that Mannen had finished speaking; then he said, "Terminally aged Earth-humans, indeed the members of the majority of species, find comfort in the presence of friends at a time like this. For some reason you have chosen to discourage such visits, but if you would prefer the company of donor entities who were your friends of the mind, the answer is to reimpress your brain with Educator tapes of your choosing. I shall suggest this solution to the Chief Psychologist, who might—"

"Tear you psychologically limb from Tarlan limb," Mannen broke in. "Have you forgotten that you are supposed to be investigating Seldal, not one of its patients called Mannen? Forget about the tapes. If O'Mara ever found out what you, a psychology trainee, have been trying to do here, you would be in very serious trouble."

"I cannot imagine," Lioren said very seriously, "being in worse trouble than I am now."

"I'm sorry," Mannen said, raising one of its hands a few inches above the covers and then letting it fall again. "For a moment I had forgotten the Cromsag Incident. A tongue-lashing from O'Mara would be insignificant compared to the punishment you are inflicting on yourself."

Lioren did not acknowledge the other's apology because the guilty did not deserve one and said instead, "You are right, reimpressing your

Educator tapes is not a good solution. My knowledge of Earth-human psychology is meager, but would it not be better if at this time your mind was your own, and not filled with others whose mind records were taken before they even knew of your existence, and whose apparent friendship for you was a self-delusion aimed at making their alien presence more bearable? At this time should you not be ordering the contents of your own mind, its thoughts, experiences, right or wrong decisions, and its considerable accomplishments during your own lifetime? This would help to pass your remaining time, and if your friends were no longer discouraged from visiting you, that would also shorten—"

"I have yet to meet an intelligent being," Mannen said, "who did not wish for a long life and an instantaneous death. But such wishes are rarely granted, are they, Lioren? My suffering does not compare with yours, but I will still have a long time to spend in a body deprived of all feeling and with a mind that is empty and alien and frightening because it is my own, a mind I can no longer fill."

The ex-Diagnostician's two recessed eyes were fixed on the one of Lioren's that was closest to it. He returned the patient's stare for several minutes, his mind recalling the words the other had spoken and searching everyone of them for unspoken meanings, but Mannen spoke before he did.

"I have not talked for so long in many weeks," it said, "and I am very tired. Go now, or I will be so discourteous as to fall asleep in the middle of a sentence."

"Please don't," Lioren said quickly, "because I have one more question to ask of you. It is possible that you are thinking that an entity who has already committed the monstrous and multiple crime of genocide would not suffer additional distress if he were to commit a single and, relatively, more venial offense as a favor to a colleague. Are you suggesting that I shorten your time of waiting?"

Mannen was silent for so long that Lioren checked the biosensors to be sure that it had not lost consciousness with its eyelids open; then it said, "If that was my suggestion, what would your answer be?"

Lioren did not wait as long before replying. "The answer would be no. If it is possible, I must try to reduce my guilt, not increase it by however small an amount. The ethical and moral aspects might be argued, but I could not justify such an act on medical grounds because there is no physical distress of any kind. Your distress is subjective, the product of a mind that is empty of all but one occupant, you, who is no longer happy there.

"But the experience is not new to you," Lioren went on, "because it was your normal condition before you became a Senior Physician and then a Diagnostician. I have already suggested that you fill your mind with old memories, experiences or professional decisions which brought you pleasure, or problems which you enjoyed solving. Or would you prefer to continue exercising it with new material?"

What he was about to say would sound callous and selfish and might well anger the patient into total noncooperation, but he said it anyway.

"For example," he added, "there is the mystery of Seldal's behavior."

"Go away," Mannen said in a weak voice, closing its eyes, "go now."

Lioren did not leave until the biosensor readings indicated the changes which told him that on this occasion the patient's sleep was not a pretense.

When he returned to the office next morning, Lioren deliberately concentrated on the routine work so as to avoid having to discuss Mannen with Cha Thrat. He did not think that the words of a terminal patient should be judged too harshly, nor be repeated to others, especially when they had no direct bearing on the Seldal investigation.

Of the other three Seldal post-op patients he questioned, two were willing to talk to him at length—about themselves, the hospital food, the nurses whose ministrations were at times as gentle as the hands of a parent or as insensitive as a kick from a Tralthan's rear leg, but about their Nallajim surgeon scarcely at all. During the little time Seldal spent with them, it listened more than it talked, which was a little unusual in a Senior but was not a character deviation serious enough to worry O'Mara. He was disappointed but not surprised when his general and necessarily vague questions brought no results.

The post-op care of the third patient was the responsibility of Tralthan and Hudlar nurses, who had been forbidden to discuss the case outside the ward. Seldal had likewise forbidden members of any physiological classification less massive than a Hudlar or Tralthan even to approach it. Lioren was curious about this mystery patient and decided to call up its medical record, only to find that the file was closed to him.

He was surprised and pleased when Charge Nurse Hredlichi contacted him to say that Mannen had left instructions that Lioren was to be allowed to visit it at any time. He was even more surprised at the patient's opening words.

"This time," it said, "we will talk about Senior Physician Seldal, your investigation and you yourself, and not about me."

Mannen's voice was slow, weak, and barely hovering above the limit of audibility, but there were no long pauses for breath, and its manner, Lioren thought, was that of an ailing Diagnostician rather than a terminal patient.

It had spoken to the Nallajim during its twice-daily ward round, and on both occasions Seldal had been pleased that the patient was talking to it again and showing interest in events and people other than itself. During the first talk it was obvious that Seldal was humoring its patient by answering Mannen's deliberately nonspecific questions about the latest hospital gossip and its other patients, and the Nallajim Senior had spent much longer with it than was clinically necessary.

"Naturally," Mannen continued, "that was simple professional courtesy extended to the person I once was. However, one of the people we discussed was the new Psychology Department trainee, Lioren, who seemed to be wandering about the hospital with no clear idea of what it was doing."

Lioren's medial limbs jerked outward instinctively into the Tarlan posture of defense, but the threat was removed by the patient's next words.

"Don't worry," Mannen went on, "we talked about you, not your interest in Seldal. Charge Nurse Hredlichi, who has four mouths and cannot keep any of them closed, told it of your frequent visits to me, and it was curious to know why I had allowed them and what we talked about. Not wishing to tell an outright lie this close to my end, I said that we talked about our troubles, and said that your problems made my own seem small by comparison."

Mannen closed its eyes for a moment, and Lioren wondered if the effort of that long, unbroken conversation had exhausted it, but then it opened them again and said, "During its second ward round I asked about its Educator tapes. Stop jerking your arms about like that, you'll knock over something. It is shortly to undergo the medical and psychological examinations for Diagnostician, and I know that any advice coming from an ex-Diagnostician with decades of experience would be welcomed. The questions regarding its methods of accommodating and adapting to its present mind-partners were expected and aroused no suspicion. Whether or not the information given so far will help your investigation I cannot say."

By the time Mannen had finished speaking, its voice was so low that Lioren had collapsed himself awkwardly onto his knees to bring his head close to the other's lips. He did not know if the information was helpful, but it had certainly given him a lot to think about.

"I am most grateful, Doctor," he said.

"I am doing you a favor, Surgeon-Captain," Mannen said. "Are you willing to do one in return?"

Without hesitation, Lioren replied, "Not that one."

"And if I was to . . . withdraw cooperation?" the other asked in a voice which carried only a few inches from its lips. "Or go back to pretending to be asleep? Or if I were to tell Seldal everything?"

Their heads were so close together that Lioren had to extend three of his eyes to cover the full length of the patient's incredibly emaciated body. "Then I would suffer embarrassment, distress, and perhaps punishment," he said. "It would be as nothing to the punishment I deserve. But you are suffering distress, of a kind that I can barely imagine, which is *not* deserved. You say that you find solace neither in the company of friends nor in preterminal contemplation of your past life. It may be that your empty mind is terrifying, not because it is empty but because its only occupant has become a stranger to you. But this mind is a valuable resource, the most valuable resource that was ever in your possession, and it should not be wasted by a premature termination, however accomplished. For as long as possible your mind should be used."

A long exhalation of the patient's breath pressed gently against Lioren's face, and then Mannen said weakly, "Lioren, you are . . . a cold fish."

Within a few minutes it was asleep and Lioren was on the way back to the office. Several times he collided with other life-forms, fortunately without injury on either side, because his mind was on the patient he had left rather than the ever-present problem of corridor navigation.

He was using the remaining hours or days of an emotionally distressed and terminal patient as a means of furthering a simple, unimportant, and nonurgent investigation, as he would use any suitable tool that came to hand which would enable him to complete a job. If in the process he altered or increased the efficiency of the tool, that was not an important consideration. Or was it?

He was remembering that on Cromsag he had been involved in solving a problem. On that occasion, too, he had considered the solution to be more important than any of the individuals involved, and his intellectual pride and his impatience had depopulated a planet. On his native Tarla that pride and high intelligence had been a barrier that none could penetrate, and he had had superiors and subordinates and family but no friends. Perhaps Mannen's singularly inaccurate physiological description, which he had put down to the mental confusion of fatigue, had been correct and Lioren was a cold fish. But it might not be entirely correct.

Lioren thought of the wasted and barely living entity he had just left, the pitiful and fragile tool that was performing exemplary work, and he wondered at the strange feelings of hurt and sadness that arose in him.

Was his first experience of friendship, like his first friend, to be short-lived?

As soon as Lioren entered the office he knew that something was wrong, because both Cha Thrat and Braithwaite swung round to face him. It was the Earth-human who spoke first.

"O'Mara is at a meeting and is not to be disturbed and, frankly, I have no idea how to advise you about this," Braithwaite said in a rapid, agitated voice. "Dammit, Lioren, you were told to be discreet in your enquiries. What have you been saying about your assignment, and to whom? We have just had a message from Senior Physician Seldal. It wants to see you in the Nallajim staff flocking lounge on Level Twenty-three."

Cha Thrat made the Sommaradvan gesture of deep concern, and added, "At once."

CHAPTER 12

Since the Nallajim LSVOs often entertained other-species colleagues, their lounge was spacious enough not to cause Lioren any physical inconvenience, but he wondered at the choice of meeting place. In spite of their fragile, low-gravity physiology, the birdlike species could be as abrasive in their conversational manner as any Kelgian, and if this one had found cause for complaint against Lioren, the expected course would have been for it to present itself in the Psychology Department and demand to see O'Mara.

Of one thing he felt very sure, Lioren thought as he moved between the nestlike couches filled with sleeping or quietly twittering occupants toward Seldal, this would not be a social occasion.

"Sit or stand, whichever is more comfortable for you," the Senior Physician said, lifting a wing to indicate the couch's food dispenser. "Can I offer you anything."

It was wrong, Lioren told himself as he lowered his body into the downy softness of the couch, to feel sure about anything.

"I am curious about you," the Nallajim Senior said, the rapid twittering of its voice making an impatient background to the slower, translated words. "Not about the Cromsag Incident because that has become common knowledge. It is your behavior toward my patient Mannen that interests me. Exactly what did you say to him, and what did he say to you?"

If I told you that, Lioren thought, this meeting would not long remain a social occasion.

Lioren did not want to lie, and he was trying to decide whether it would be better to avoid telling all of the truth or simply remain silent when the Nallajim spoke again.

"Hredlichi tells me," it said, "and I use the Charge Nurse's words as clearly as I can recall them, that two of O'Mara's Psych types, Cha Thrat and yourself, approached it asking permission to interview its patients, including the terminal case, Mannen regarding some planned improvements in ward environment. Hredlichi said that it was too busy to waste time arguing with you, and your physical masses were such that it could not evict you bodily, so it decided to accede where the patient Mannen was concerned knowing that the ex-Diagnostician would ignore you as it had done everyone else who tried to talk to it. But Hredlichi says that you spent two hours with the patient, who subsequently left instructions that you could visit it at any time.

"Ex-Diagnostician Mannen is highly regarded at Sector General," Seldal went on, "and its length of service on the staff is second only to that of O'Mara, who was and is its friend. When I joined the hospital it was in charge of training. It helped me then and on many occasions since so that I, too, consider it to be more than a medical colleague. But until yesterday, when it suddenly acknowledged my presence and began to ask questions which were lucid, general, but more often personal, it would not speak to anyone except you.

"I ask again, Lioren, what transpired between Mannen and yourself?"

"It is a terminal patient," Lioren said, choosing his words with care, "and some of the words and thoughts expressed might not have been those of the entity you knew when it was at the peak of its physical and mental powers. I would prefer not to discuss this material with others."

"You would prefer not . . ." began Seldal, its angry, twittering speech rising in volume so that the sleeping Nallajims around them stirred restively in their nests. "Oh, keep your secrets if you must. Truly, you remind me of the departed Carmody, who was before your time. And you are correct, I would not want to know about it if a great entity like Mannen were to display weakness, even though I once shared my mind with an Earth-human DBDG who believed that feet of clay could sometimes form a most solid foundation."

"Thank you for your forbearance, sir," Lioren said.

"I have learned forbearance," the Senior Physician said, "from a very close friend. I shall not explain that, but instead I shall tell you what I think went on between you."

Lioren was greatly relieved that the other was no longer angry and, seemingly, did not suspect that it was the object of Lioren's investigation rather than Mannen. He was wondering whether the remark about learning from a very close friend was an important datum when the Nallajim resumed speaking.

"When Mannen discovered who you were during your first visit," Seldal went on, "it decided that you might have more problems than it had and became curious about you. This curiosity must have led to personal questions about your reactions to the Cromsag business that were distressing to you, but it was the first time in several weeks that Mannen showed curiosity about anything. Now it seems to be curious about everything. It has talked about you, and closely questioned me, and asked about my other patients, the latest gossip, everything. I am most grateful, Lioren, for the significant improvement your visits have brought about in its condition . . ."

"But the clinical picture—" Lioren began.

"Has not changed," it said, completing the sentence for him. "But the patient is *feeling* better."

"Hredlichi also tells me," Seldal went on, "that you interviewed my other patients about a ward environment improvement scheme, with the exception of my isolation case who is forbidden visitors and all medical contacts not directly involved with its treatment. The case is a young and therefore relatively small member of a macrospecies, so there would be an element of risk involved to any life-form of more or less normal body mass approaching it closely. If you still want to do so, you now have my permission to visit it whenever you wish."

"Thank you, Senior Physician," Lioren said, feeling grateful but even more confused by the way the conversation was going. "Naturally, I am curious about the secrecy surrounding that particular patient—"

"As is everyone else in the hospital," Seldal broke in, "who is not closely involved with its treatment, which, I must admit, is not going well. But I am not merely satisfying your curiosity, I have a favor to ask.

"My recent conversations with Mannen and the way it speaks of you," the Nallajim went on quickly, "make me wonder if the change you brought about in the ex-Diagnostician might be repeated with the young Groalterri patient, whose prognosis is being adversely affected for nonmedical reasons about which it will not speak. My idea is that it, too, may benefit from knowing that its problems are minor when compared with your own. But I will understand if you prefer not to assist me."

"I will be pleased to help you in whatever way I can," Lioren said, controlling his excitement and the volume of his voice with difficulty. "A—a Groalterri, here in the hospital? I have never seen one, and had doubts about their existence . . . Thank you."

"Lioren, you should take more time to consider," the Nallajim said. "As with Mannen, the process of recollection will be distressing for you. But it seems to me that you accept this distress willingly, as a just punishment that you must not avoid. I think this is wrong and unnecessary. At the same time I must accept these feelings, and use you and them as I would any other surgical tool, for the good of my patient. Nevertheless, I am sorry for inflicting this added punishment on you."

There was a little of the psychologist in every being, Lioren thought, and tried to change the subject. "May I also continue my visits to Doctor Mannen?"

"As often as you wish," Seldal replied.

"And discuss this new case with it?" Lioren asked.

"Could I stop you?" Seldal asked in return. "I will not discuss the case further lest my ideas influence your own. The Groalterri patient's medical file will be opened to you, including what little information there is on the species' home world."

It was very strange, Lioren thought as he left the Nallajim lounge, that the Senior Physician should be using him as a tool in the treatment of a difficult patient while he was using the other's patients as tools in his investigation of Seldal itself—not that he was making much progress with that.

He called briefly on Mannen to tell it about this new development and give its too-empty mind something more to think about before returning to the department. Chief Psychologist O'Mara was still absent, and Lieutenant Braithwaite and Cha Thrat were behaving as if they were about to perform a slightly premature Rite for the Dead over him. Lioren told them that he was not in any trouble, that Senior Physician Seldal had asked him for a favor which he was, of course, granting, and as a result of which he would have to copy some material for later study in his quarters.

"The *Groalterri* patient!" Braithwaite said suddenly, and Lioren turned to see that Cha Thrat and the lieutenant were standing behind him reading his display. "We aren't supposed to know that it is even in the hospital, and now you're involved with it. What is Major O'Mara going to think about this?"

Lioren decided that it was what Earth-humans called a rhetorical question and continued with his work.

CHAPTER 13

Since its formation by the original four star-traveling cultures of Traltha, Orligia, Nidia, and Earth, who had formed as its executive and law-enforcement arm the multispecies Monitor Corps, the Galactic Federation had expanded to include the members of sixty-five intelligent species and in population and area of influence had begun to live up to its original and somewhat grandiose name. But not all of the planetary cultures discovered by the Corps survey vessels were opened to full contact, because a few of them would not benefit from it.

These were the worlds whose technical and philosophical development were such that the sudden appearance among them of great ships from the sky, and the strange, all-powerful beings armed with wondrous devices that they contained, would have given the emerging cultures such a racial inferiority complex that their potential for future development would have been seriously inhibited. And there was one world on which the decision for making full contact was not the Galactic Federation's to make.

As befitted a culture that had been old and wise when the natives of Earth and Orligia and Traltha had still been wriggling through their primeval slime, the Groalterri had been very diplomatic about it. But they had let it be known without ambiguity that they would not tolerate the Federation's presence in their adult domain nor allow the maturity and delicacy of their thinking to be upset by a horde of chattering, moronic, other-species children. Both individually and as a race the Groalterri carried enough philosophical and physiological weight to make it so.

They did not have any objection to being observed from space, so the details of their physiological classification and living environment had been obtained by the long-range sensors of an orbiting survey vessel, and this was the only information available.

The Groalterri were the largest intelligent macro life-form so far discovered, a warm-blooded, oxygen-breathing, and amphibious species of physiological classification BLSU who, as individuals, continued to grow in size from their parthenogenetic birth to the end of their extremely long life spans. In common with other extravagantly massive life-forms, intelligent or otherwise, they found difficulty in moving about unaided, so that from the young-adult state onward they avoided potentially lethal gravitic distortion of their bodies by swimming or floating in their individual lakes or communal inland seas, many of which had been produced artificially and contained a level of biotechnology far beyond the understanding of the observers.

Another characteristic they shared with large creatures—the library computer cited the examples of the nonintelligent Tralthan yerrit and the Earth panda—was that the mass of the embryo was so small that often a pregnancy was not suspected until after the birth had taken place. In spite of the vast size and elevated intelligence levels of adult Groalterri, their offspring were relatively tiny and uncivilized in their behavior and remained so into early adolescence.

That was one of the reasons for the nursing attendants being chosen from the heavy-gravity Tralthan FGLI and Hudlar FROB classifications, Lioren thought as he prepared for his first sight of the patient. Another was that the Federation wanted to do the hitherto unapproachable Groalterri a favor, probably in the hope that it might one day be returned, and had dispatched a Monitor Corps transport vessel to move the seriously injured young one to Sector General for treatment. It was the Corps who had insisted on secrecy so as to minimize political and professional embarrassment should the patient terminate.

There were two unarmed but very large Earth-human Corpsmen guarding the entrance to the ward, a converted ambulance dock, to discourage unauthorized visitors and to advise those with authorization to don heavy-duty space suits. The ward atmosphere and pressure was suited to most warm-blooded oxygen-breathers, they explained to Lioren, but the protection might keep the patient from inadvertently killing him.

In his present mental state, the chance of having his life ended traumatically was a fate greatly to be desired, Lioren thought, but did as they advised without demur.

Even though Seldal's notes had prepared him for the young BLSU's body mass and dimensions, the sheer size of the patient came as a shock, and the thought that an adult Groalterri could grow to many hundreds of times as big was too incredible for his mind to accept as a reality. For the patient filled more than three-quarters the volume of the dock, and so large was it that the consequent distortion of perspective kept him from seeing more than a fraction of its surface features until he had used his suit thrusters to tour the vast body.

The dock was being maintained in the weightless condition with the patient lightly restrained by a net whose mesh was sufficiently open to allow medical examination and treatment to be carried out. On the dock's six inner surfaces, wide-focus pressor and tractor beams controlled from the Nurses' Station had been positioned so as to hold the creature suspended and out of contact with the walls.

The patient's overall body configuration, Lioren saw, was that of a squat octopoid with short, thick tentacular limbs and a central torso and head that seemed disproportionately large. The eight limbs terminated alternately in four sets of claws that would with maturity evolve into manipulatory digits while the remaining four ended in flat, sharp-edged, osseous blades that were larger than twice the spread of Lioren's medial arms.

In presapient times those four bone-tipped extremities would have been fearsome natural weapons, Seldal had warned him, and the very young of any species could sometimes revert to their savage past.

Lioren made another tour of the gigantic body, staying as far from the net that enclosed it as the dock walls and deck would allow. This time he studied the hundreds of tiny post-op scars and freshly dressed wounds as well as the areas of pustulating infection that covered half of the creature's upper body surface.

The condition had been caused by a deep penetration of the subdermal tissue by a nonintelligent, hard-shelled, and egg-laying insect lifeform which did not appear to have the physical ability to achieve such depth, but the reason for the multiple traumatic penetration was unknown. In spite of the Groalterri language being held in the hospital's translation computer, so far the patient had refused to give any information about itself or the reason for its condition.

That was why Lioren ended his tour of the body by drifting to a weightless halt above the circular swelling that was the creature's head. There, centered above the four heavily lidded eyes that were equally spaced around the cranium, was the area of tightly stretched skin that served both as the creature's organ of speech and hearing.

Lioren made a quiet, untranslatable sound and said, "If this physical or verbal intrusion gives offense I apologize, for such is not my intention. May I speak with you?"

For a long moment there was no response; then the enormous flap of flesh that was the nearest eyelid opened slowly and Lioren found himself looking into the depths of a dark transparency that seemed to go on forever. Suddenly the tentacle just below him tensed, then curled upward and tore through the restraining net as if it had been the insubstantial structure of a web-spinning insect. The great, bony blade at its tip crashed against the wall behind him, leaving a deep, bright trench in the metal before continuing the swing past Lioren's head, so closely that the push of displaced air could be felt through his open visor.

"Another stupid, half-organic machine," the patient said, just as Lioren was caught by a tightly focused tractor beam and whisked back to the safety of the Nurses' Station.

Reassuringly the Hudlar duty nurse said, "The patient does not mind visual or tactile examinations or even surgery, but reacts in unsocial fashion to attempts at communication. The probability is that it meant to discourage rather than harm you."

"If it had wanted to harm me," Lioren said, remembering how that outsize, organic axe had whistled past his head, "my suit would not have been of much use."

"Nor would my own normally impenetrable Hudlar skin," the nurse said. "Doctor Seldal belongs to a fragile species in which cowardice is a prime survival characteristic but it, too, scorns the use of body armor. The few other visitors who come here are allowed to decide for themselves.

"I have found," the Hudlar went on, "that the patient is more likely to speak to an entity who is not encased in body armor, which it apparently regards as a being who is partly mechanical and of low intelligence. Its words to these uncovered visitors are few and never polite, but it does sometimes speak to them."

Lioren thought of the few words that the patient had spoken after nearly frightening him into premature termination with its pretended attack, and he began unfastening his nonprotective suit. "I am most grateful for your advice, Nurse. Please help me out of this thing and I shall try again. And, Nurse, if there is anything else you wish to say to me I will be pleased to listen."

As the FROB moved forward to assist him, its speaking membrane vibrated with the words, "You do not recognize me, Lioren. But I know you and I, too, am grateful for the helpful words that you spoke to my Kelgian friend, nurse-in-training Tarsedth, before and during our recent visit to your quarters. I am greatly surprised that Seldal allowed you to come here, but if there is anything further that I can do to assist you, you have only to ask."

"Thank you," Lioren said.

He was thinking that the assignment O'Mara had given him to investigate Seldal's behavior, and his unorthodox method of conducting it, was having unforeseen results. For reasons Lioren could not understand he seemed to be collecting friends.

The second time Lioren approached the patient's head he was wearing only his translator pack and a thruster unit to help him navigate in the weightless condition. Again he halted close to one of the enormous, closed eyes and spoke.

"I am not, in whole or in part, a machine," he said. "Again I ask with respect, can I speak to you?"

Once more the eyelid opened slowly like a great, fleshy portcullis, but this time the response was immediate.

"There is no doubt in either of our minds that you have the ability to speak to me," it replied in a voice that accompanied the translated words like a deep, modulated drumroll. "But if your question was carelessly phrased, as is much of the speech in this place, and you are asking whether I will listen and reply, I doubt it."

Below him one of the great tentacles stirred restively inside the torn netting, then became motionless again. "Your shape is new to me, but it is likely that your questions and behavior will be the same as all the others. You will ask questions whose answers should be already known through prior observation. Even the tiny Cutter called Seldal, who pecks at me and fills the wounds with strange chemicals, asks how I am. If it does not know, who does? And they all behave toward me as if they were the Parents with power and authority and I the tiny offspring needing consolation. It is as if insects were pretending to be wiser and larger than a Parent, which is ridiculous beyond belief.

"I speak to you very simply of these things," the BLSU went on, "in the hope that you have the authority to end this ridiculous pretense and that you will leave me undisturbed to die.

"Go," it ended, "at once."

The great eye closed as if to banish him from sight and mind, but Lioren did not move. "Your wishes in this matter will be passed without delay to the others concerned with your treatment, because the words that have passed between us are being recorded for later study by—"

Lioren broke off. All of the creature's tentacles were curling and writhing within the restraining net, which parted loudly in several places before they relaxed again.

"My words," it said, "are an expression of my thoughts that were given to you and earlier to those with whom I spoke. Without my express permission on each and every occasion, these thoughts are not to be shared with entities who are not present and whose minds are likely to misunderstand and distort my meaning. If this is being done, I shall speak no more. Go away."

Still, Lioren did not move. Instead he keyed his translator to the Nurses' Station frequency and prepared to speak once again in the manner of a Surgeon Captain.

"Nurse," he said, "please switch off all recording devices and erase the words spoken since my arrival. Do likewise with the earlier conversations between Doctor Seldal and the patient. Any personal words of the patient that you yourself have heard on this and previous occasions are to be treated as privileged communications and disclosed to no other person. From this moment on, and until the patient itself has given permission for you to do otherwise, you will cease listening in to any conversation that passes between the patient and anyone else, nor will you use your own organic sound sensors to do so. Do you fully understand your instructions, Nurse? Please speak."

"I understand," the Hudlar replied, "but will Senior Physician Seldal?"

"The Senior Physician will understand when I make it aware of the strong feelings of the patient regarding the unauthorized recording of its conversations. In the meantime I assume full responsibility."

"Breaking sound contact," the nurse said.

It was only the sound contact that had been broken, Lioren knew, because the nurse would be continuing to watch and record the proceedings on the clinical monitors as well as watching him even more intently on the visuals in case he had to be pulled out of trouble with the tractors again. He returned his attention to the eye of the patient, which was again closed.

"We may now speak," Lioren said, "without our words being overheard or recorded, and I shall not repeat anything you say without your express permission. Is this satisfactory?"

The patient's gargantuan body remained still, it did not speak, and its eye did not open. Lioren could not help remembering his first visit to ex-Diagnostician Mannen and thought that here, too, the clinical monitors were indicating that the patient was motionless but conscious. Perhaps the BLSU classification did not sleep, for there were several intelligent species in the Federation who had evolved in presapient conditions of extreme physical danger so that a part of their minds remained constantly on watch. Or it might be that the patient, being a member of a species said to be the most philosophically advanced yet discovered, had twice asked him to leave and was now ignoring him because it was too civilized to be capable of physically enforcing the request.

In Mannen's case it had been the patient's own curiosity that had caused it to break the silence.

"You have told me," Lioren said slowly and patiently, "that the attention and questions of the medical staff here are an irritation to you, because they swarm like tiny insects around a behemoth while behaving as if they had the authority of a parent. Have you considered that, in spite of their small size, they feel toward you the same concern and need to help you that is a parent's? The insect analogy is as distasteful to me as it is to the others, if you have told them of it, for we are not mindless insects.

"I much prefer," Lioren went on, "the analogy of the highly intelligent entity with one of lower intelligence of whom it has made a friend, or a pet, if that concept is understood by the Groalterri. Two such entities can often form a strong nonphysical bond with each other and, ridiculous though the idea might seem, should the one of greater intelligence become injured or in distress of some kind, the other will want to give solace and will grieve when it is helpless to do so.

"By comparison with yours," Lioren said, "the intelligence level of those around you is low. But we are not helpless and our purpose here is to relieve many different kinds of distress."

There was no response from the patient, and Lioren wondered if the other was treating his words as the buzzings of an irritating insect. But his pride would not allow him to accept that idea. He reminded himself that while this patient belonged to a superintelligent species, it was a very young member of that species, which should go a long way toward levelling the difference between them; one important characteristic in the young of any species was their curiosity about all things.

"If you do not wish to satisfy my curiosity about you, because of your earlier words being shared with others without your knowledge or consent," Lioren said, "you might be curious about one of the entities who are trying to help you, myself.

"My name is Lioren..."

He was there at Seldal's request because of an age-old and Galaxy-wide truism that in a place of healing there are always entities in worse condition than oneself, and that the one in lesser distress felt sympathy toward its less fortunate fellow and seemed to benefit in the nonclinical area thereby. Plainly the Nallajim Senior was hoping for a similar response from this patient, but Lioren wondered whether an entity so massive in size and intellect, and so tremendously long-lived as this one, was capable of feeling sympathy for the stupid, ephemeral insect hovering above its closed eye.

It took much longer than on the previous telling, because then Mannen had known about the Federation and the Monitor Corps and court-martial as well as the swarm of intelligent insects called the Cromsaggar that Lioren had all but exterminated. Many times his manner lost its clinical objectivity as the words caused him to live again the terrible events on Cromsag, and he had to remind himself several times that his memories were being used as a psychological tool that caused pain to its user, but finally it was over.

Lioren waited, glad of the patient's lack of response that was enabling him to drive away those fearful images and regain control of his mind.

"Lioren," the Groalterri said suddenly, without opening its eye, "I did not know that it was possible for a small entity to bear such a great load of suffering. Only by not looking at you can I continue to believe it, for in my mind I see an old and greatly distressed Parent seeking help. But I cannot give you that help just as you cannot help me because, Lioren, I, too, am guilty."

Its voice had grown so quiet that the translator required full amplification to resolve the word-sounds as it ended, "I am guilty of a great and terrible sin."

CHAPTER 14

More than an hour passed before Lioren returned to the Nurses' Station to find Seldal, its atrophied wings twitching and feathers ruffled in the Nallajim sign of anger, awaiting him.

"Nurse tells me that you ordered the voice recorders switched off," it said before Lioren could speak, "and the earlier conversations with the patient to be erased. You exceeded your authority, Lioren, which is a bad habit of yours that I thought you had given up after the Cromsag business. But you have spoken with the patient at greater length than all of the medical staff combined since its arrival. What did it say to you?"

Lioren was silent for a moment, then he said, "I cannot tell you exactly. Much of the information is personal and I have not yet decided what can and cannot be divulged."

Seldal gave a loud, incredulous cheep. "This patient must have given you information that will help me in its treatment. I cannot order a member of your department to reveal psychosensitive information about another entity, but I can request O'Mara to order you to do so."

"Senior Physician," Lioren said, "whether it was the Chief Psychologist or any other authority my response would have to be the same."

The Hudlar nurse had moved away so as to absent itself and avoid embarrassing its department head by overhearing an argument that entity was losing.

"May I assume that I still have your permission to continue visiting the patient?" Lioren asked quietly. "It is possible that I might be able to obtain information arrived at by observation and deduction and the detection of facts, material of nonpersonal nature about itself or its species which would assist you. But great care is needed if it is not to take offense, because it places great importance on the contents of its mind and the words used to reveal it."

Seldal's feathers were again lying like a bright and unruffled carpet around its body. "You have my permission to continue visiting. And now I presume you have no objection to me talking to my own patient?"

"If you tell it that the speech recorders will remain switched off," Lioren said, "it might talk to you."

As Seldal departed the Hudlar nurse returned to its position on the monitors. Quietly, it said, "With respect, Lioren, the Hudlar organ of hearing is extremely sensitive and cannot be turned off other than by swathing it in a bulky muffling device, the need for which was not foreseen in this ward and so it was not available to me."

"Did you hear everything?" Lioren asked, feeling a sudden anger that the patient's confidence had been breached and that Seldal, from whom he had been keeping the conversation a secret, would shortly be able to hear it all on the hospital grapevine. "Including the crime it is supposed to have committed prior to its arrival here?"

"I was instructed not to hear," the Hudlar said, "so I did not hear, and cannot discuss what I did not hear with anyone other than the entity who forbade me to hear."

"Thank you, Nurse," Lioren said with great feeling. He stared for a moment at the other's identification patch, which bore only the hospital staff and department symbols because Hudlars used their names only among the members of the family or those whom they proposed to mate, and memorized it so that he would know the nurse again. Then he asked, "Do you wish to discuss some aspect of that which you did not hear with me now?"

"With respect," the Hudlar said, "I would prefer to make an observation. You appear to be gaining the patient's confidence with remarkable speed, by speaking freely about yourself and inviting an exchange in kind."

"Go on," Lioren said.

"On my world and, I believe, among the majority of your own population on Tarla," the nurse said, "it would not matter because we believe that our lives begin at birth and end with death, and we do not distinguish between the forms of wrong-doing which seem to be troubling the patient. But among the Groalterri, and in many other cultures throughout the Federation, you would be treading on dangerous philosophical ground."

"I know," Lioren said as he turned to leave. "This is no longer a purely medical problem, and I hope the library computer will give me some of the answers. At least I know what my first question will be."

What is the difference between a crime and a sin?

When he returned to the department, Lioren was told that O'Mara was in the inner office but had left instructions not to be disturbed. Braithwaite and Cha Thrat were about to leave for the day, but the Sommaradvan held back, plainly wanting to question him. Lioren tried to ignore its nonverbal curiosity because he was not sure what, if anything, he could allow himself to say.

"I know that you are seriously troubled in the mind," Cha Thrat said, pointing suddenly at his screen. "Has your distress increased to the level where you are seeking solace in . . . Lioren, this is uncharacteristic and worrying behavior in a personality as well integrated as yours. Why are you requesting all that study material on the Federation's religions?"

Lioren had to pause for a moment to consider his answer, because it was suddenly borne in upon him that, since he had become involved with Seldal and its patients, he had spent much more time thinking about the troubles of Manner and the Groalterri than his own. The realization came as a great surprise to him.

"I am grateful for your concern," he replied carefully, "but my distress has not increased since last we spoke. As you already know, I am investigating Seldal by talking to its patients, and the process has become ethically complicated, so much so that I am uncertain of how much I can tell you. Religion is a factor. But it is a subject about which I am totally ignorant, and I should not want to be embarrassed if I were to be asked questions about it."

"But who would ask questions about religion," Cha Thrat asked, "when it is a subject everyone is supposed to avoid? It causes arguments that nobody wins. Is it the terminal patient, Mannen, who might ask these questions? If it needs help of that kind, I wonder at it asking you rather than a member of its own species. But I understand your reticence."

Allowing another person to arrive at a wrong conclusion was not the same as lying, Lioren told himself.

Cha Thrat made a Sommaradvan gesture the significance of which Lioren did not know, and went on, "Speaking clinically, Lioren, I would say that you have been forgetting to eat as well as sleep. You can call up that stuff on your room console as well as from here. I cannot help you where Earth-human beliefs are concerned, but let us go to the dining hall and I will tell you all about the religions—there are five of them altogether—of Sommaradva. It is a subject about which I can speak with full knowledge if less than complete conviction."

During their meal and continued discussion in Lioren's quarters, Cha Thrat did not press him for information that he was unwilling to give, but he did not have such an easy time at his next visit to Mannen.

"Dammit, Lioren," the ex-Diagnostician said, who seemed no longer to be troubled by breathlessness, "Seldal tells me that you have been talking to the Groalterri, and it to you, for longer than anyone else in the hospital, and that you refuse to tell anyone about it. And now you want me to give you an ethical justification for your silence without telling me the reason why you won't speak.

"What the hell is going on, Lioren?" it ended. "Curiosity is killing me."

"Curiosity," Lioren said calmly, looking at the age-wasted body and face with its youthful eyes, "would only be a contributing factor."

The patient made an untranslatable sound. "Your problem, if I understand it correctly, is that during your second and much lengthier visit to the Groalterri you were given, presumably in exchange for personal data on yourself and information regarding the worlds and peoples of the Federation, a large amount of information about the patient, its people, and its culture. Much of this information is impersonal and clinical and extremely valuable both to the physician in charge of the Groalterri's treatment and to the cultural-contact specialists of the Monitor Corps. You, however, feel that you have sworn yourself to secrecy. But surely you know that neither you nor the patient have the right to conceal such information."

Lioren kept one eye directed toward the biosensors, watching for signs of respiratory distress following that long speech. He did not find any.

"The personal stuff, yes," Mannen went on. "My earlier attempt to get you to shorten my waiting time here was not to become general knowledge, for it affected only myself and had no bearing on the treatment of a patient of a new species or that culture's future relations with the Federation. The clinical or otherwise nonpersonal information you have been able to gather or deduce is pure knowledge that you have no right to keep to yourself. It should be available to everyone just as the operating principles of our scanners or the hyperdrive generators are available to those able to understand and use them without risk, although for a while in the bad old days the hyperdrive was considered to be a top secret, whatever that meant. But knowledge is, well, knowledge. You might just as well try to keep secret a natural law. Have you tried explaining all this to your patient?"

"Yes," Lioren said. "But when I suggested making the nonpersonal sections of our conversation public, and argued that it would not be breaking a confidence because it was clearly impractical to ask every single Groalterri in their population for their permission to reveal this information, it said that it would have to think carefully about its reply.

I'm sure it would like to help us, but there may be a religious constraint, and I would not want to cause an adverse reaction through impatience. If it became angry, it is capable of tearing a hole through the structure and opening the ward to space."

"Yes," Mannen said, showing its teeth. "Children, no matter how large they happen to be, can sometimes throw tantrums. Regarding the religious aspect, there are many Earth-humans who believe that—"

It stopped speaking because suddenly the small room was being invaded, first by Chief Psychologist O'Mara, followed by Senior Physicians Seldal and Prilicla, who flew in and attached itself with spidery, sucker-tipped legs to the ceiling, where its fragile body would be in less danger from unguarded movements by its more physically massive colleagues. O'Mara nodded in acknowledgment of Lioren's presence and bent over the patient. When it spoke its voice had a softness that Lioren had never heard before.

"I hear that you are talking to people again," O'Mara said, "and that you especially want to talk to me, to ask a favor. How do you feel, old friend?"

Mannen showed its teeth and inclined its head in Seldal's direction. "I feel fine, but why not ask the doctor?"

"There has been a minor remission of symptoms," Seldal responded before the question could be asked, "but the clinical picture has not changed substantially. The patient says that it is feeling better, but this must be a self-delusion and, whether it remains here or goes elsewhere in the hospital, it could still terminate at any time."

O'Mara's mention of the patient wanting a favor worried Lioren. He thought that it was the same favor Mannen had asked of him, except that now it would be a more public request for early termination, and he felt both sorrow and shame that it should be so. But the empath, Prilicla, was not reacting as Lioren would have expected to such an emotionally charged situation.

"Friend Mannen's emotional radiation," Prilicla said, the clicks and trillings of its voice like a musical background to the words, "is such that it should not cause concern to a psychologist or anyone else. Friend

O'Mara does not have to be reminded that a thinking entity is composed of a body and a mind, and that a strongly motivated mind can greatly influence the body concerned. In spite of the gloomy clinical picture, friend Mannen is indeed feeling well."

"What did I tell you?" Mannen said. It showed its teeth again to O'Mara. "I know that this is a fitness examination, with Seldal insisting that I am dying, Prilicla equally insistent that I am feeling well, and you trying to adjudicate between them. But for the past few days I have been suffering from nonclinical, terminal boredom in here, and I want out. Naturally, I would not be able to perform surgery or undertake any but the mildest physical exertion. But I am still capable of teaching, of taking some of the load off Cresk-Sar, and the technical people could devise a mobile cocoon for me with protective screens and gravity nullifiers. I would much prefer to terminate while doing something than doing nothing, and I—"

"Old friend," O'Mara said, holding up one digit to indicate the biosensor displays, "will you for God's sake stop for breath!"

"I am not entirely helpless," Mannen said after the briefest of pauses. "I bet that I could arm-wrestle Prilicla."

One of the Cinrusskin's incredibly fragile forelimbs detached itself from the ceiling and reached down so that its slender digits rested for a moment on the patient's forehead. "Friend Mannen," Prilicla said, "you might not win."

Lioren had strong feelings of pleasure and relief that the favor Mannen was asking would reflect neither shame nor dishonor on the ex-Diagnostician's reputation. But there was also a selfish feeling of impending loss, and for the first time since the others had entered the room, Lioren spoke.

"Doctor Mannen," he said, "I would like . . . That is, may I still go on talking to you?"

"Not," O'Mara said, turning to face Lioren, "until you damn well talk to me first."

On the ceiling Prilicla's body had begun to tremble. It detached itself, made a neat half loop, and flew slowly toward the door as it said,

"My empathic faculty tells me that shortly friends O'Mara and Lioren will be engaged in an argument, accompanied as it must surely be by emotional radiation of a kind I would find distressing, so let us leave them alone to settle it, friend Seldal."

"What about me?" Mannen said when the door had closed behind them.

"You, old friend," O'Mara said, "are the subject of this argument. You are supposed to be dying. What exactly did this ... this trainee psychologist, do or say to you to bring about this insane urge to return to work?"

"Wild horses," Mannen said, showing its teeth again, "wouldn't drag it out of me."

Lioren wondered what relevance a nonintelligent species of Earth quadruped had to the conversation, and had decided that the words had a meaning other than that assigned by his translator.

O'Mara swung around to face him and said, "Lioren, I want an immediate verbal and later a more detailed written report of all the attendant circumstances and conversations that took place between this patient and yourself. Begin."

It was not Lioren's intention to be disobedient or insubordinate by refusing to speak, it was simply that he needed more time to separate the things he could say from those which should on no account be revealed. But O'Mara's yellow-pink face was deepening in color, and he was not to be given any time at all.

"Come, come," O'Mara said impatiently. "I knew that you were interviewing Mannen in connection with the Seldal investigation. That was an obvious move on your part even though, if Mannen did not ignore you as he had everyone else, it carried the risk of you revealing what you were doing to the patient—"

"That is what happened, sir," Lioren broke in, knowing that they were on a safe subject and hoping to stay there. "Doctor Mannen and I discussed the Seldal assignment at length, and while the investigation is not yet complete, the indications so far are that the subject is sane—"

"For a Senior Physician," Mannen said.

O'Mara made an angry sound and said, "Forget that investigation for the moment. What concerns me now is that Seldal noticed a marked, nonclinical change in its terminal patient which it ascribed to conversations with my trainee psychologist. Subsequently it asked that you talk to its Groalterri patient, who was stronger but being just as silent as Mannen, with the result that when it did speak you forbade the use of speech recorders."

When the Chief Psychologist went on, his voice was quiet but very clear, in the way that Tarlans described as shouting in whispers, as it went on, "Tell me, right now, what you said to these two patients, and they to you, that brought about the change in the Groalterri's behavior and caused this, this particular act of constructive insanity in a dying man."

One of its hands moved to rest very gently on Mannen's shoulder and even more quietly it said, "I have professional, and personal, reasons for wanting to know."

Once again Lioren searched his mind in silence for the right words until he was ready to speak.

"With respect, Major O'Mara," Lioren said carefully, "some of the words that passed between us contained nonpersonal information that may be revealed, but only if the patients give their agreement to my doing so. Regrettably the rest, which I expect is of primary interest to you as a psychologist, I cannot and will not divulge."

O'Mara's face had again deepened in color while Lioren was speaking, but gradually it lightened again. Then suddenly the Chief Psychologist twitched its shoulders in the peculiarly Earth-human fashion and left the room.

CHAPTER 15

Y ou ask questions," the Groalterri said, "endlessly."
In such a massive creature it was impossible to detect changes of expression, even if the gargantuan features were capable of registering them, and the nonverbal signals he had been able to learn were few. Lioren had the feeling that this was not going to be a productive meeting.

"I also answer questions," Lioren said, "for as long as they are asked."

Around and below him the tightly curled tentacles stirred like great, organic mountain ranges caught in a seismic disturbance, and became still again. Lioren was not unduly worried, because the tantrum of his first visit had not been repeated.

"I have no questions," the patient said. "My curiosity is crushed by a great weight of guilt. Go away."

Lioren withdrew to indicate his willingness to obey, but only by a short distance to show that he still wanted to talk.

"Satisfying my curiosity," he said, "makes me forget my own guilt for a time, as does satisfying the curiosity of others. Perhaps I could help you to forget your guilt, for a while, by answering the questions you do not ask."

The patient did not move or speak, and Lioren, as he had done when previously faced with this form of negative reaction, took it as a reluctant acquiescence and went on talking.

The Groalterri was physiologically unsuited to travel in space, so he talked about one of the other species who were similarly hampered and others for whom star travel should have been impossible but was not. He spoke of the great strata creatures of Drambo, whose vast bodies could grow like a living carpet to cover the area of a subcontinent, who used as eyes the millions of flowers that made of their backs a light-sensitive skin, and who, in spite of the vegetable metabolism that made physical movement so slow, had minds that were quick and sharp and powerful.

He told of the vicious, incredibly violent and mindless Protectors of the Unborn, who neither slept nor ceased fighting from the moment they were born into their incredibly savage environment until they died because of the weakness of age and the inability to protect themselves from their lastborn. But within that organic fighting and killing machine there was an embryo whose telepathic mind was rich and full and gentle, taught as it was by the telepathy of its unborn brothers, and whose ability to think was tragically destroyed after its long gestation by the process of birth.

"Protectors of the Unborn have been brought to this hospital," Lioren went on, "where we are trying to devise ways of birthing their offspring without the consequent mind destruction, and of training these newly born not to attack and kill everyone on sight."

While Lioren had been speaking, the Groalterri remained still and silent. He resumed, but gradually his subject was changing from descriptions of the physiological attributes of the beings who made up the Federation to the philosophical viewpoints which joined or sometimes separated them. He wanted to know what was troubling the patient, so the change was deliberate.

Lioren went on. "An act which is considered to be a great wrong by one species because of an evolutionary imperative or, less often, by a too-narrow philosophical education, can be viewed by another as normal and blameless behavior. Often the judge, who is never physically present but has others to speak for it, is an immaterial entity who is believed to be the all-knowing, all-powerful, and all-merciful Creator of All Things."

Below and around him the tentacles stirred restively, the eye that had been regarding him steadily closed, but there was no other reaction. Lioren knew that he was taking a risk by continuing in this vein, but there was suddenly a need within him to understand the mind of this great and greatly troubled being.

"My knowledge of this subject is incomplete," he continued, "but among the majority of the intelligent species it is said that this omnipotent and immaterial being has manifested itself in physical form. The physiological classifications vary to suit the environments of the planets concerned, but in all cases it manifests itself as a teacher and lawgiver who suffers death at the hands of those who cannot at first accept its teachings. But these teachings, in a short time or long, form the philosophical foundation of mutual respect, understanding, and cooperation between individuals of that species which eventually lead to the formation of a planetary and interstellar civilization.

"There are many beings who hold the belief that it is the same being in every case who, whenever its creation is threatened and its teachings are most needed, manifested or will manifest itself on all worlds. But the common factors in all these beliefs are sympathy, understanding, and forgiveness for past wrongs, whatever form they have taken and no matter whether they be venial or of the utmost gravity. The quality of this forgiveness is demonstrated by the manifestation's death, which is reported in all cases to be shameful and physically distressing. On Earth it is said that termination occurred after being attached with metal spikes to a wooden cross, and the Crepellian octopoids used what they called the Circle of Shame, in which the limbs are staked out at full extension on dry ground until death by dehydration occurs, while on Kelgia—"

"Small Lioren," the Groalterri said, suddenly opening its eye, "do you expect this omnipotent being to forgive your own grievous wrong?"

After the patient's long silence the question took Lioren by surprise.

"I don't... What I mean is, there are others who believe that these teachers and lawgivers arise naturally in any intelligent culture which is in transition between barbarism and the beginnings of true civilization. On some worlds there have been many lawgivers, whose teachings vary in small details, not all of whose adherents believe them to be manifestations of an omnipotent being. All of these teachers advocated showing mercy and forgiveness to wrongdoers, and they usually died at the hands of their own people. Was there an entity of that kind, a great teacher and forgiver, in Groalterri history?"

The eye continued to regard him, but the patient's speaking membrane remained still. Perhaps the question had been offensive in some fashion, for it was plain that the Groalterri was not going to answer it. Sadly, Lioren ended, "I do not believe I can be forgiven because I cannot forgive myself."

This time the response was immediate, and utterly surprising.

"Small Lioren," the Groalterri said, "my question has brought a great hurt to your mind, and for this I am sorry. You have been engaging my mind with stories of the worlds and peoples of your Federation, and of their strangely similar philosophies, and for a time my own great hurt was diminished. You deserve more of me, and shall be given more, than a hurt in return for a kindness.

"The information I shall now give you, and this information only, you may relay to and discuss with others. It concerns the origins and history of the Groalterri and contains nothing that is personal to myself. Any previous or subsequent conversations between us must remain private."

"Of course!" Lioren said, so loudly that in his excitement he overloaded his translator. "I am grateful; we will all be grateful. But—but our gratitude to you is impersonal. Can you at least tell me who and what you are?"

He stopped, wondering if asking the other's name had been a mistake, perhaps his last mistake.

One of the creature's tentacles uncurled suddenly and its bony tip whistled past Lioren's head to strike the metal wall, where it made deafening, intermittent contact for a few seconds before being as quickly withdrawn.

At the center of one of the few-areas of plating left unscarred after its previous tantrum there was a perfect geometrical figure of an eight-pointed star. The lines making it up were straight and of equal depth and thickness, something between a deep, bright scratch and a fine, shallow trench in the metal, and the lines of the figure were accurately joined without gaps or overlapping.

"I am Small Hellishomar the Cutter," it said quietly. "You, Lioren, would call me a surgeon."

CHAPTER 16

Hellishomar concentrated its attack on an area where the skin was thin and the underlying tissues soft, tearing into the flesh with all four blades until the bloody crater was large and deep enough to admit its body and equipment. Then it closed and sealed the flap of the entry wound behind it, switched on the lighting and eye-cover washers, checked the level of the flammables tank, and resumed burrowing.

This Parent was old, old enough to be the parent of Hellishomar's parent's parent, and the gray rot that afflicted the aged was already well established all over and deep within its gargantuan body. As was usual with Parents, it had concealed the early symptoms so as to avoid the days of severe pain and violence that surgery would entail until the visibly growing cancers had left it unable to move, and one of the passing Smalls had reported its condition to the Guild of Cutters.

Hellishomar was old for a Small as well as large for a Cutter, but its extensive knowledge and unrivaled experience more than made up for the damage caused by the size of the entry wounds it was forced to make; and here the deeper tissues were soft so that often he was able to squeeze through a single incision rather than hacking a bloody tunnel into perfectly healthy flesh.

Avoiding the larger blood vessels or heat-sealing those that could not be avoided, and ignoring the severed capillaries which would close naturally, Hellishomar cut rapidly and accurately without waste of time. During deep work the compressed air tanks had to be small, otherwise the entry wound would have been larger, the damage greater, and the progress slower.

Then suddenly it was visible, the first internal evidence of the growth, and precisely in the predicted position.

Lying diagonally across the newly deepened incision there was a thin, yellow tube whose tough walls and oily surface had enabled it to slide away from the blade tentacle. It pulsed faintly as it drew nutrient from the gray, necrotic growth spreading over the Parent's surface tegument to the heart-root, or roots, deep inside the body. Hellishomar changed direction to follow it down.

Within a few moments there was another yellow tube visible on one side of the tunnel, then another and another, all converging towards a single point below him. Hellishomar cut and squeezed through them until the heart-root itself lay exposed like a veined, uneven globe that seemed to glow with its own sickly yellow light. In size it was only a little smaller than Hellishomar's head. Quickly he excised a clear space all around and above it, severing in the process more than twenty of the rootlets and two thicker tubes which were the connections to secondaries. Then, taking up a position which would allow the heat and bloody steam to escape and disperse along the entry wound rather than stewing the Cutter in his own body fluids, Hellishomar attacked the foul thing with his burner turned up to full intensity.

Hellishomar did not stop until the heart-root was converted to ash, and then he gathered the ashes into a small pile and flamed them again. He followed the connector to the secondary, burning it behind him as he went, until he found another heart-root and removed that. When the external Cutters had completed their work, the fine root connections to the surface growths, severed at both ends and starved of nutrient, would wither and shrink so that they could be withdrawn from the Parent's body with the minimum of discomfort.

In spite of the wipers that were laboring to keep the eye-covers clear, there was an increasing and irregular impairment of Hellishomar's vision. His movements were becoming slower, the strokes of his cutting blades less precise, and the quality of his surgery diabolical. He diagnosed the condition as a combination of heat exhaustion and asphyxiation and turned at once to begin cutting a path to the nearest breathing passage.

A sudden increase of resistance to the cutters indicated that he had encountered the tough outer membrane of a breathing passage. Carefully Hellishomar forced through an incision large enough to allow entrance to his head and upper body only so as to minimize bleeding from the wound, then stopped and uncovered his gills.

Water not yet warmed by the Parent's body heat washed past Hellishomar's overheated body, replacing the stale tanked air in his lungs and clearing both vision and mind. His pleasure was short-lived because a few moments later the flood of clear, gill-filtered water diminished to a trickle as the Parent changed to air-breathing mode. Quickly withdrawing the rest of his body from the wound, Hellishomar uncoiled his cutter-tipped tentacles to full extension, making the shallow, angled incisions in the breathing passage wall which would enable it to maintain position above the wound when the storm of inhaled air blew past.

The Parent's nerve network made it aware of everything that occurred in its vast body and the exact position of the events as they took place, and it also knew that wounds healed more readily in air than in water. As he expertly drew together the edges of the exit wound with sutures, Hellishomar wished that just once one of the great creatures would touch its mind, perhaps to thank him for the surgical intervention that would extend its life, or to criticize the Small selfishness which made it want thanks, or merely to acknowledge the fact of its existence.

Parents knew everything, but spoke of their knowledge to none but another Parent.

The wind of inhalation died and there was a moment of dead calm as the Parent prepared to exhale. Hellishomar made a final check on the wound sutures, released its grip on the wall, and dropped onto the soft floor of the breathing passage. There it rolled itself tightly into a ball of its own tentacles, and waited.

Suddenly its body was lifted and hurled along the breathing passage by a hurricane which coughed it onto the surface of the outside world . . .

"There Hellishomar had rested and replaced its consumables," Lioren went on, "because this Parent was old and large and there was still much work to do."

He paused so as to give O'Mara a chance to respond. When he had requested permission to make an immediate verbal report on his return from the Groalterri ward, the Chief Psychologist had expressed surprise in a tone which Lioren now recognized as sarcastic, but thereafter it had listened without interruption or physical movement.

"Continue," O'Mara said.

"I have been told," Lioren went on, "that the history of the Groalterri is composed entirely of memories handed down over the millennia. I have been assured of their accuracy, but archaeological evidence to support them is not available. The culture has, therefore, no presapient history, and in this respect my report must be deductive rather than factual."

"Then by all means," O'Mara said, "deduce."

No early historical records had been kept on the mineral-starved swamp and ocean world of the Groalterri, because the life span of its people was longer and their memories clearer and more trustworthy than any marks placed upon animal skins or layers of woven vegetation that would fade and rot long before the lives of the writers would be ended. Groalter was a large world that orbited its small, hot sun once every two and one-quarter Standard Years, and one of its gigantic intelligent life-forms would have had to be unhealthy or unfortunate indeed not to have witnessed five hundred such rotations.

It was only with the recent advent—recent as the Groalterri measured the passage of time—of Small technology that permanent written records had been kept. These were concerned principally with the discoveries and observations made by the scientific bases that had been established, with great difficulty and loss of Small life, in the heavy-gravity conditions of the polar regions. Groalter's rapid rotation gave low levels of gravity only in a broad band above and below the equator, where the tidal effects of its large satellite kept the vast, inhabited oceans and swamps constantly in motion, and this continuing tidal action had long since eroded away its few equatorial landmasses.

In time—a long time even as the Groalterri measured it—their great, uninhabited moon would spin closer until it and the mother planet collided in mutual destruction.

The Small made such advances in technology as were possible in their impermanent environment. And every day of their young lives they tried to control the animal nature within them so that they might arrive more quickly at the mental maturity of the Parents, who spent their long lives thinking great thoughts while they controlled and conserved the resources of the only world that, because of their great size, they could ever know.

"There are two distinct cultures on Groalter," Lioren continued. "There are the Small, of which our overlarge patient is a member, and the Parents, of whom even their own children know little."

Within their first Groalter year the Small were forced to leave the Parents, to be cared for and educated by slightly more senior children. This seeming act of cruelty was necessary to the mental health and continued survival of the Parents because, during their years of immaturity, the Small were considered to be little more than savage animals whose quality of mentation and behavior made them utterly repellent to the adults.

In spite of being unable to bear their violent and unsettling presence, the Parents loved them dearly and watched over their welfare at a distance.

But the mind of a Small of the Groalterri, when compared with the level of intelligence and social behavior possessed by the average member species of the Federation, was neither savage nor stupid. For many thousands of Earth-standard years, during their long wait between birth and achieving adulthood, they had been solely responsible for the development of Groalterri physical science and technology. During that period they had no communication with their elders, and their physical contacts were incredibly violent and restricted to surgical interventions aimed at prolonging the Parents' lives.

"This behavior," Lioren continued, "is beyond my experience. Apparently the Small hold the Parents in high regard, and they respect and obey and try to help them as much as they are able, but the Parents do not respond in any way other than by passively and at times reluctantly submitting to their surgery.

"The Small use a spoken and written language, and the Parents are said to have great but unspecified mental powers which include wide-band telepathy. They use them to exchange thoughts among themselves, and for the control and conservation of every nonintelligent living creature in Groalter's ocean. For some reason they will not use telepathy to talk to their own young or, for that matter, to the Monitor Corps contact specialists presently in orbit above their planet.

"Such behavior is totally without precedent," Lioren ended helplessly, "and beyond my understanding."

O'Mara showed its teeth. "It is beyond your present understanding. Nevertheless, your report is of great interest to me and of greater value to the contact specialists. Their ignorance of the Groalterri is no longer total, and the Corps will be grateful and pleased with their onetime Surgeon-Captain. I, however, am impressed but not pleased because the report of the lowest-ranking member of my department, Trainee Lioren, is far from complete. You are still trying to hide important information from me."

Clearly the the Chief Psychologist was better at reading Tarlan facial and tonal expressions than Lioren was at reading those of an Earth-human. It was Lioren's turn to remain silent.

"Let me remind you," O'Mara said in a louder voice, "that Hellishomar is a patient and this hospital, which includes Seldal and you and myself, is charged with the responsibility for solving its medical problem. Clearly Seldal suspected that there might be a psychological component to this clinical problem and, having observed the results of your talks with Mannen and knowing that it could not approach me officially because this department's responsibility lies only with the mental health of the staff, it asked you to talk to the patient. This may not be a psychiatric hospital, but Hellishomar is a special case. It is the first Groalterri ever to have spoken with us, or more accurately, with you. I want to help it as much as you do, and I have greater experience than you in tinkering with other-species mentalities. My interest in the case is entirely professional, as is my curiosity regarding any personal information it may have disclosed to you, information which will be used therapeutically and not discussed with anyone else. Do you understand my position?"

"Yes," Lioren said.

"Very well," O'Mara said when it was obvious that Lioren would say nothing more. "If you are too stupid and insubordinate to accede to a superior's request, perhaps you are intelligent enough to take suggestions. Ask the patient how it came by its injuries, if you haven't already done so and are hiding the answer from me. And ask whether it was Hellishomar or someone else who broke the Groalterri silence to request medical assistance. The contact specialists are puzzled by the circumstances of the distress call and wish clarification."

"I did try to ask those questions," Lioren said. "The patient became agitated and gave no answers other than to say that it personally had not requested assistance."

"What did it say?" O'Mara said quickly. "What were its exact words?"

Lioren remained silent.

The Chief Psychologist made a short, untranslatable sound and sat back in its chair. "The Seldal investigation you were given is not in itself important, but the constraints placed on you most certainly were. I knew that you would have to work through Seldal's patients to gather information, and that one of them was Mannen. I hoped that putting the two of you together, the patient suffering from preterminal emotional distress and refusing all contact with friends and colleagues, and a Tarlan whose problems made Mannen's look minor indeed, would cause him to open up to the stage where I might be able to help him. Without further intervention by me, you achieved results that were much better than I could have hoped for, and I am truly grateful. My gratitude and the minor nature of the affair allowed me to ignore your tiresome insubordination, but this is a different matter.

"It was Seldal's idea, not mine, that you should talk to the Groalterri," O'Mara continued, "and I did not learn of it until after the event. Until now I knew nothing of what passed between you, and now I want to know everything. This involves a first-contact situation with a species that is both highly intelligent and until now completely uncommunicative. But you have been able to talk to one of them, and for some reason have achieved more in a few days than the Monitor Corps in as many years. I am impressed and so will be the Corps. But surely you must see that withholding information, any information regardless of its nature, that might help widen contact is stupid and criminal.

"This is not the time for playing ethical games, dammit," O'Mara ended in a quieter voice. "It is much too important for that. Do you agree?"

"With respect—" Lioren began, when a sudden movement of O'Mara's hand silenced him.

"That means no," the Chief Psychologist said angrily. "Forget the verbal niceties. Why don't you agree?"

"Because," Lioren said promptly, "I was not given permission to pass on this kind of information, and I feel that it is important that I continue to do as the patient requests. Hellishomar is becoming more willing to give information about Groalter, at least, for general distribution. If I had not respected its confidence from the beginning, it is likely that we would have been given no information of any kind. Much more data on the Groalterri will be forthcoming, but only if you and the Corps are patient and I remain silent unless specifically directed otherwise by the patient. If I break confidence with Hellishomar, the flow of information will cease."

While he had been speaking, O'Mara's facial pigmentation had grown a dark shade of pink again. In an effort to avert what promised to be a major emotional outburst, Lioren went on. "I apologize for my insubordinate behavior, but the continuing insubordination is being forced on me by the patient rather than any lack of respect. It is grossly unfair to you, sir, because you wish only to help the patient. Even though it is not deserved, I would welcome any help or advice that you would be willing to give."

O'Mara's fixed, unblinking stare was making Lioren uneasy. He had the feeling that the other's eyes were looking directly into his mind and reading every thought in it, which was ridiculous because Earth-human DBDGs were not a telepathic species. Its face had lightened in color but there was no other reaction.

"Earlier," Lioren said, "when I said that the Groalterri behavior was beyond my understanding, you said that it was beyond my present understanding. Were you implying that the situation has a precedent?"

O'Mara's face had returned to its normal coloration. It showed its teeth briefly. "It has many precedents, almost as many as there are member species in the Federation, but you were too close to the situation to see them. I ask you to consider the sequence of events that occurs when an embryo is growing between the time of conception and birth, although for obvious reasons I shall discuss these events as they affect my own species."

The Chief Psychologist clasped its hands loosely together on the desktop and adopted the calm, clinical manner of a lecturer. "Growth changes in the embryo within the womb follow closely the evolutionary development of the species as a whole, although on a more compressed time scale. The unborn begins as a blind, limbless, and primitive water-dweller floating in an amniotic ocean, and ends as a small, physically helpless, and stupid replica of an adult person, but with a mind which will in a relatively short time equal or surpass that of its parents. On Earth the evolutionary path that led to the four-limbed land animal becoming the thinking creature Man was long, and with many unsuccessful side turnings which resulted in creatures that had Man's shape but not his intelligence."

"I understand," Lioren said. "It was the same on Tarla. But what is the significance in this case?"

"On Earth as on Tarla," O'Mara went on, ignoring the question, "there was an interim stage in the development of a fully intelligent, self-aware form of life. On Earth we called the early, less intelligent men Neanderthal and the form that violently replaced it Cro-Magnon. There were small physical variations between the two, but the important difference was unseen. Cro-Magnon man, although still little more than a savage animal, possessed what was called the New Mind, the type of mind which enables civilizations to grow and flourish and cover not one world but many. But should they have tried to teach their forebears beyond their ability to learn or left them alone? On Earth in the past there were many unhappy experiences between so-called civilized men and aboriginals."

At first Lioren did not understand the reason for O'Mara speaking in such oversimplified generalities, but suddenly he saw where the other was leading him.

"If we return to the analogy of prenatal and prehistoric evolution," the Chief Psychologist continued, "and assuming that the gestation period of the Groalterri is proportional to their life span, isn't it possible that they also experienced this preliminary stage of lesser intelligence? But let us also assume that their young experience it, not before but after they are born. This would mean that during the time from birth to prepuberty the Small belong temporarily to a different species from that of their elders, a species considered by the Parents to be cruel and savage and, relatively speaking, of low intelligence and diminished sensitivity. But these young savages are the well-beloved off-spring of these Parents."

O'Mara showed its teeth again. "The highly intelligent and hypersensitive Parents would avoid the Small as much as possible, because it is likely that making telepathic contact with such young and primitive minds would be unpleasant in the extreme. It is also probable that the Parents do not make contact because of the risk of damaging their young minds, and retarding their later philosophical development by trying to instruct them before their immature brains are physiologically ready to accept adult teaching.

"That is the type of behavior we expect of a loving and responsible Parent."

Lioren turned all of his eyes on the aging Earth-human, trying vainly to find the words of respect and admiration that were suited to the occasion. Finally, he said, "Your words are not supposition. I believe them to describe the facts of the situation in every important respect. This information will greatly aid my understanding of Hellishomar's emotional distress. I am truly grateful, sir."

"There is a way that you can show your gratitude," O'Mara said.

Lioren did not reply.

O'Mara shook its head and looked past Lioren at the office door. "Before you leave," it said, "there is information you should have and a question we would like you to ask the patient. Who requested medical assistance for it, and how? The usual communications channels were not used, and telepathy, originating as it does from an organic nondirectional transmitter of very low power, is supposed to be impossible at distances over a few hundred yards. There is also great mental discomfort when a telepath tries to force communication with a nontelepath.

"But the facts," the Chief Psychologist went on, "are that Captain Stillson, the commander of the orbiting contact ship, reported having a strange feeling. He was the only member of the crew to have this feeling, which he likened to a strong hunch that something was wrong on the planetary surface. Until then nobody had even considered making a landing on Groalter without permission from the natives, but Stillson took his ship down to the precise spot where the injured Hellishomar was awaiting retrieval and arranged to transport the patient without delay to Sector General, all because he had a very strong feeling that he should do these things. The captain insists that at no time was there any outside influence and that his mind remained his own."

Lioren was still trying to assimilate this new information, and wondering whether or not it should be given to the patient, when O'Mara spoke again.

"It makes me wonder about the mental capabilities of the adult Groalterri," it said in a voice so quiet that it might have been talking to itself. "If they do not, as now seems evident, communicate with their own young because of the risk of stunting subsequent mental and philosophical development, that must also be the reason they refuse all contact with our supposedly advanced cultures of the Federation."

CHAPTER 17

Lioren's next meeting with Hellishomar was very useful and intensely frustrating. It gave many interesting pieces of information about the life and behavior of the Small, and said that Lioren was free to discuss the material with others, but it seemed to be talking too much about a subject that was not on its mind. The Monitor Corps would be delighted with the details of Groalterri Small society that he was discovering, but Lioren had a strong feeling that the patient was talking to avoid talking about something else. After three hours of listening to information that was becoming repetitious, Lioren lost patience.

During the next pause he said quickly, "Hellishomar, I am pleased and grateful, as will be my colleagues, for this information about your home world. But I would prefer to hear, and I have the feeling that you would prefer to speak, about yourself."

The Groalterri stopped talking.

Lioren forced patience on himself and tried to find the right words of encouragement. Speaking slowly and with many pauses, so as to give Hellishomar every chance to interrupt his questions with an answer, he asked, "Are you concerned about your injuries? There is no need because Seldal assures me that the treatment, although delayed because of the size difference between surgeon and patient, is progressing well and your life is no longer threatened by the infection that has penetrated your body. Are you not a skilled Cutter and highly respected by the Small, who will soon welcome you back to continue the work of extending the lives of Parents? Surely these ailing Parents must also hold you in high regard because of the surgical skills that you can still—"

"I have grown too large to help the Parents," Hellishomar said suddenly, "or to continue as a Cutter. The Small will not want me, either. I am nothing but a failure and an embarrassment to all of them, and I am doubly ashamed because of the great wrong I have done."

Lioren wished that he had more time to think about the implications of this information, and his need to question Hellishomar more closely about it was like a great hunger in his mind. But he was moving into a sensitive area that had been approached before without success. It was likely that too many questions on this subject might seem to Hellishomar like an interrogation, might even imply a judgment and the apportioning of guilt on Lioren's part. His instincts told him that this was a time for further encouragement rather than questions.

"But surely you have grown in surgical experience as well as physical size," Lioren said. "You have said as much yourself. Among many of the peoples of the Federation, an entity who has amassed great knowledge, and who is no longer capable of the physical work involved, makes that knowledge available to the young and less experienced members of its profession. You could become a teacher, Hellishomar. Your knowledge could be passed on to others of the Small who are sure to be grateful to you for it, as would the Parents for the lives you will indirectly have saved. Is this not so?"

Hellishomar's enormous tentacles moved restively, heaving like great, fleshy waves on an organic ocean. "It is not so, Lioren. The Small will pretend that I do not exist, so that my shame will drive me to the loneliest and most inhospitable part of the swamp that I can find, and the Parents . . . The Parents will ignore and never speak with their minds to me. There are precedents, thankfully a very few, in Groalterri history for what will happen to me. I will be an outcast for the whole of my very long life, with only my thoughts and my guilt for company, for that is the punishment I deserve."

The words, thought Lioren with a sudden rush of remembered pain and guilt, were an echo of those he had used so often to himself, and for a moment he could think of nothing but the Cromsaggar. Frantically he tried to return his mind to Hellishomar's sin, which could not possibly be as grievous as that of wiping out a planetary population. Perhaps one of the Small, or even a Parent, had died because of something Hellishomar had or had not done. With Lioren's crime there could be no real comparison.

In an unsteady voice Lioren said, "I cannot know whether or not your punishment is deserved unless you tell me of the crime, or the sin, you have committed. I know nothing of Groalterri philosophy or theology, and I would be pleased to learn of these matters from you if you are allowed to discuss them. But from my recent studies I know that there is one factor common to all the religions practiced throughout the Federation, and that is forgiveness for sins. Are you sure the Parents will not forgive you?"

"The Parents did not touch my mind," Hellishomar replied. "If they did not do so before I left Groalter, they never will."

"Are you sure?" Lioren said again. "Did you know that the Parents touched the mind of the officer commanding the ship orbiting your planet? The touch was gentle and almost without trace, and it was the first and only time that a Groalterri made direct contact with an offworlder, but nevertheless the captain was directed accurately to the place where you were dying."

Without giving Hellishomar time to respond, Lioren continued. "You have already told me that the Parents are philosophically incapable of inflicting physical damage or pain, and that even the most skilled Cutters among the Small are too crude and awkward in their methods to undertake surgery on one of their own kind; only the oldest and largest Parents become sick, the Small never. It is certain that your Small colleagues could never equal the delicacy and precision of the work performed by Seldal. You know this to be so, and you know also that if you had not been taken to this hospital you would be dead.

"That being so," Lioren went on quickly, "is it not possible, indeed is it not a certainty that the Parents responsible for your presence here have already forgiven you? By their willingness to break with Groalterri tradition to ask help from an off-planet species, have they not given proof that they have forgiven you, that they value you and are doing all that they can to help you return to full health?"

While he had been speaking, the patient's great body had remained absolutely motionless, but it was the stillness of extreme muscular tension rather than repose. Lioren hoped that the Hudlar nurse on the tractor beam was alert to the situation and ready to pull him out.

"They spoke to a strange, Small-minded off worlder," Hellishomar said, "but not to me."

Be careful, Lioren told himself warningly, *this might be a very hurt and angry Groalterri.* "I had assumed from what you told me earlier that the Parents did not touch the minds of the Small for any reason. Was I mistaken? What do they say to you?"

Hellishomar's great muscles were still fighting each other, and so evenly matched were they that its body remained motionless. "Are you less intelligent than I assumed, Lioren? Don't you realize that the Small do not remain the Small forever? In preparation for the transition into adulthood of the most senior among us, the Parents touch our minds gently and instruct us in the great laws that guide and bind the long lives of the Parents. We are given the reasons why they seek to live for as long as possible in spite of sickness and physical pain—so that they may be adequately prepared to Go Out. All of these laws are passed on in simplified form to the very young among us by Small teachers who are on the verge of maturity.

"I have waited with patience for the Parents to speak to me," Hellishomar went on, "because I have grown old and large and should rightly have been a young Parent by now. But they do not speak to me. In Groalterri history there are precedents for my situation, a very few of them, fortunately, so I knew that a long, lonely, unhappy and uneventful mental life lay ahead of me. Then in my great despair I committed the most grievous sin of all, and now the Parents will never speak to me."

As the implications of what the other had been saying became clear to Lioren, a great wave of sympathy washed over his mind, and with it the growing excitement of being on the verge of a full understanding of Hellishomar's problem. He was remembering Seldal's description of the patient's clinical condition and Hellishomar's insistence that the Small were impervious to illness. Now he knew the nature of the great sin that Hellishomar had committed, because Lioren had come very close to committing it himself.

He wished that there was some way that he could bring consolation to this gravely troubled being, or relieve the inner distress of knowing that among its own highly intelligent kind it was mentally retarded. That had been the reason Hellishomar had tried to end its own life.

He said gently, "If the Parents touch the minds and speak to the Small who are nearing maturity, and for the first time to an off-worlder ship captain in the hope that your injuries could be successfully treated, then they must have a high regard, perhaps a great affection, for you. The reason they do not speak and tell you so is because you cannot hear them. Am I right, Hellishomar?"

"To my shame," Hellishomar replied, "you are right."

"It is possible," Lioren said, carefully avoiding all mention of Hellishomar's other shame, "that your future life will not be lonely. If embarrassment or other reasons keep the Small from talking to you, and you cannot hear the words of the Parents, there are others who would gladly speak and listen and learn from you. The off-worlders would be pleased to set up a base on the polar hard ground and make it as comfortable as possible for you. If the Parents do not allow this, you could be provided with communications devices which would enable two-way contact to be maintained from orbit. Admittedly, this would not be as satisfactory as full telepathic contact with the Parents, but many questions would be asked and answered by the off-worlders and yourself. Their curiosity about the Groalterri is as great as is yours about the Federation, and will require a long time to satisfy. It is said by many of our foremost thinkers that, to a truly intelligent entity, the satisfaction of curiosity is the greatest and most lasting of pleasures. You would not be lonely, Hellishomar, nor would there be little to occupy your mind."

Around and below Lioren the patient's body was stirring although muscular tension was still evident.

"You would not be exchanging mere words," Lioren went on quickly, "or the verbal questions and answers and descriptions that have passed between us here. When you are well again, large-screen viewing facilities will be made available to you. The visuals will be three-dimensional and in full color. Not only will they show you the physical structure of the galaxy in which we live and the tiny fraction of it that is populated by the Federation, but display to you in as much detail as you desire the science and cultures and philosophies of the many and widely varied intelligent life-forms who are its members. Arrangements could be made that would enable you to question these life-forms and, visually and aurally, to live among many of them. Your life would be long, Hellishomar, but full and interesting so that the absence of Parent mental contact would not be so—"

"*No!*"

Once again the razor-edged, bony tip of a cutting tentacle whistled past Lioren's head to crash against the wall plating. Surprise and fear paralyzed both his body and mind, but only for an instant. Before the metallic reverberations had died away he was talking urgently to the Hudlar in the Nurses' Station, telling it not to pull him out. If Hellishomar had wanted that cutting blade to strike him, he would have been a bloody, dismembered corpse by now. With a great effort he forced himself to speak calmly.

"Have I offended you?" Lioren asked. "I do not understand. If nobody else is willing to speak to you, why do you refuse contact with the Fed—"

"Stop talking about it!" Hellishomar broke in, its voice loud and unmodulated as that of a person who could not hear itself speak. "I am unworthy, and you tempt me to an even greater sin."

Lioren was deeply puzzled by this sudden change in the other's behavior, but decided to give the words and circumstances that had led up to it more serious thought at another time. He hoped that the ban on conversation referred to the one hypersensitive topic, whatever that was. But now he had to apologize without knowing what he was apologizing for.

"If I have given offense," Lioren said, "such was not my intention and I am truly sorry. What is it that I've said that offends you? We can discuss a subject of your choosing. The work of this hospital, for example, or the Monitor Corps's continuing search for inhabited worlds in the unexplored reaches of our galaxy, or scientific disciplines practiced throughout the Federation that are unknown to a water world like Groalter—"

Lioren broke off, his body and tongue alike paralyzed with fear. The razor edge of a cutting blade had swept up to within a fraction of an inch of his forebody and face. Any higher and it would have lopped off two of his eyestalks. Suddenly the flat of the blade pressed hard against his chin, chest, and abdomen, pushing him away. Hellishomar's tentacle continued to uncurl to full extension, and the blade was not withdrawn until Lioren had been deposited back at the entrance to the Nurses' Station.

"Officially I have heard nothing," said the Hudlar nurse on duty, after it had satisfied itself that Lioren was uninjured, "but unofficially I would say that the patient does not want to speak to you."

"The patient needs help . . ." Lioren began.

He fell silent then because his thoughts were rushing far ahead of his words. The recent conversation with Hellishomar, together with the information he had already gathered or deduced about the Groalterri culture, was forming a picture in his mind that grew clearer with every moment that passed. Suddenly he knew what had to be done to and for Hellishomar and the entities who were capable of doing it, but there were serious moral and ethical considerations that worried him. He was sure, or as sure as it was possible to be before the event, that he was right. But he had been right on a previous occasion, right and proud and impatient in his self-confidence, and the population of a world had all but died. He did not want to take on the responsibility for destroying another planetary culture, not alone.

"And so do I," he finished.

CHAPTER 18

He found Senior Physician Prilicla in the dining hall, its four sets of slowly beating, iridescent wings maintaining a stable hover above the tabletop while it ingested a yellow, stringy substance which the menu screen identified as Earth-human spaghetti. The process by which the little empath drew the strands from the platter and used its delicate forward manipulators to weave them into a fine, continuous rope which disappeared slowly into its eating mouth was one of the most fascinating sights that Lioren had ever seen.

As he was about to apologize for interrupting the other's meal, Lioren discovered that the musical trills and clicks of the Cinrusskin's speech came from a different orifice.

"Friend Lioren," Prilicla said. "I can sense that you are not feeling hunger, or even repugnance at my unusual in-flight method of eating, and that your predominant feeling and probable reason for approaching me is curiosity. How may I satisfy it?"

Cinrusskin GLNOs were empaths, emotion-sensitives who were forced to do everything in their power to insure that the emotional radiation of those around them was as pleasant as possible because to do otherwise would have caused them to suffer the identical feelings that they had caused. In their words and deeds Cinrusskins were invariably pleasant and helpful, but Lioren was nonetheless relieved and grateful for the reminder that it was unnecessary to waste time on verbal politeness.

"I am curious about your empathic faculty and in particular its similarities to full telepathy," he said. "My special interest is in the organic structures, the nerve connections, blood supply, and operating mechanism of an organic transmitter-receiver, and the clinical signs and subjective effects on the possessor should the faculty malfunction. If permitted, I would like to interview any telepaths among the hospital staff or patients, or entities like yourself who do not depend solely on aural channels of communication. This is a private project and I am finding great difficulty obtaining information on the subject."

"That is because the information available is sparse," Prilicla said, "and too speculative as yet to be given to the clinical library. But please, friend Lioren, rest your mind. The growing anxiety you are feeling indicates a fear that news of your private project will be passed to others. I assure you that this will not happen without your prior permission ... Ah, already you are feeling better and, naturally, so am I. Now I will tell you what little is known."

The seemingly endless rope of spaghetti disappeared, and the platter had been consigned to the disposal slot when the Cinrusskin made a feather-light landing on the table.

"Flying aids the digestion," it said. "Telepathy and empathy are two vastly different faculties, friend Lioren, although it is sometimes possible for an empath to appear telepathic when words and behavior and knowledge of the background support the emotional radiation. Unlike telepathy, empathy is not a rare faculty. Most intelligent beings possess it to a certain extent, otherwise they could never have progressed to civilization. There are many who believe that the telepathic faculty was present in all species, and that it became dormant or atrophied when the more accurate verbal and visually reproducible language evolved. Full telepathy is rare and telepathic contact between different species is rare indeed. Have you had any previous experience of mind contact?"

"Not that I was aware of," Lioren said.

"If it had happened, friend Lioren," the empath said, "you would have been aware of it."

Full telepathy was normally possible only between members of the same species, Prilicla went on to explain. When a telepath tried to make contact with a nontelepath, the stimulation of a faculty long dormant in the latter had been described as an attempted exchange of signals between two mismatched organic transmitter-receivers. Initially the subjective effects on the nontelepath were far from pleasant.

At present there were three telepathic species in the hospital, all of whom were patients. The Telfi life-forms were physiological classification VTXM, a group-mind species whose small, beetlelike bodies lived by the direct conversion of hard radiation. Although individually the beings were quite stupid, the gestalt entities were highly intelligent. Investigating their ultra-hot metabolism closely was to risk death by radiation poisoning.

Access to the remaining telepathic life-forms was restricted. They were the Gogleskan healer Khone and its recent offspring and two Protectors of the Unborn, all of whom were at Sector General for clinical and psychological investigation by Diagnostician Conway, Chief Psychologist O'Mara, and Prilicla itself.

"Conway has had successful contact as well as surgical experience with both of these life-forms," the empath went on, "although it is still too recent and radical to have found its way into the literature. Your colleague Cha Thrat has also had extended contact with the Gogleskan, Khone, and helped deliver its child. It would save time and effort if you simply talked to these entities, or asked that the relevant clinical notes be made available to you . . . I am sorry, friend Lioren. From the intensity of your emotional radiation it is clear that my suggestion was not helpful."

Prilicla was trembling as though its fragile body and pipestem limbs were being shaken by a great wind that only it could feel. But it was an emotional gale whose origin was Lioren himself, so he strove to control his feelings until the empath's body was again at rest.

"It is I who should apologize for distressing you," Lioren said. "You are correct. I have strong, personal reasons for not involving other members of my department, at least until I know enough to speak without wasting their time. But I would dearly like to read the Diagnostician's clinical notes and visit the patients you mentioned."

"I can feel your curiosity, friend Lioren," Prilicla said, "but not, of course, the reasons for it. My guess is that it has something to do with the Groalterri patient."

It paused and once again its body trembled, but only for a moment. "Your control of your emotional radiation is improving, friend Lioren, and I compliment and thank you for it. But there is no cause for the fear in your mind. I know that you are hiding something from me, but not being a telepath I do not know what it is. I would not relay my suspicions to others in case I caused emotional distress in you that would rebound on myself."

Lioren relaxed, feeling grateful and reassured, and knowing that with this entity he did not have to vocalize his feelings. But the empath was still speaking.

"It is common knowledge," Prilicla said, "that you are the only being within the hospital who has talked freely with Hellishomar. Because my empathic faculty is bound by the inverse square law, it increases in sensitivity with proximity to the radiating mind. I have deliberately avoided approaching the Groalterri because Hellishomar is a deeply distressed and desperately unhappy entity, full of guilt and grief and pain, and it has a mind so powerful that there is nowhere within the hospital that I can escape completely from these terrible and continuing feelings. However, since you began to visit Hellishomar there has been a marked decrease in the intensity of this distressing emotional radiation and for that, friend Lioren, I am truly grateful.

"When Hellishomar's name is mentioned," the empath went on before Lioren could speak, "I detected from you an emotion that is closer to a strong hope than an expectation. It was strongest when telepathy was mentioned. That is why you will be allowed to visit the telepathic patients. Copies of the relevant clinical files will be made available to you for study. If now is a convenient time, we will begin by visiting the Protectors of the Unborn."

The Cinrusskin's six iridescent wings began to beat slowly and it rose gracefully into the air above the table.

"You are radiating an intense feeling of gratitude," Prilicla went on as it flew above Lioren toward the dining-hall entrance, "but it is not strong enough to conceal an underlying anxiety and suspicion. What troubles you, friend Lioren?"

His first impulse was to deny that anything was troubling him, but that would have been like two Kelgians trying to lie to each other—his deepest feelings were as visible to Prilicla as a Kelgian's mobile fur. "I am anxious because these are Conway's patients, and if you are allowing me to visit them without permission you might find yourself in trouble. My suspicions are that Conway has already given its permission and for some reason you are not telling me why."

"Your anxiety is unfounded," Prilicla said, "and your suspicions are accurate. Conway was about to ask you to visit these patients. They are here for close observation and investigation which, to them, is the clinical equivalent of a prison sentence of unknown duration. They are cooperative but not happy and are missing their home planets. We know of two patients, Mannen and Hellishomar, who have benefited from talking to you and, with apologies for any hurt to your feelings, friend Conway thought that visits from you would do no harm even if they did no good.

"I don't know what it is that you say to them," the empath went on, "and according to the grapevine you won't even tell O'Mara precisely how you achieve your results. My own theory is that you use the reversal technique, so that instead of the doctor extending sympathy to the patient the opposite occurs, and proceed from there. I have used this technique myself on occasions. Being fragile and emotionally hypersensitive myself, people are inclined to feel sorry for me and allow me, as Conway describes it, to get away with murder. But for you, friend Lioren, they can really feel sorry because—"

For a moment Prilicla's hovering flight became less than stable as the terrible memories of a depopulated planet came flooding back into his mind. Of course they all felt sorry for him, but no less sorry than he felt for himself. Desperately he fought to push those memories back to the safe place he had made for them, where they could trouble only his sleep, and he must have succeeded because the Cinrusskin was flying straight and level again.

"You have good control, friend Lioren," Prilicla said. "Your close-range emotional radiation is uncomfortable to me but no longer as distressing as it was during and after the court-martial. I am glad for both our sakes. On the way there I will tell you about the first two patients."

The Protector of the Unborn belonged to physiological classification FSOJ, a large, immensely strong life-form with a heavy, slitted carapace from which protruded four thick tentacles, a heavy, serrated tail, and its head. The tentacles terminated in a cluster of sharp, bony projections which made them resemble spiked clubs. The main features of the head were the well-protected, recessed eyes, the large upper and lower mandibles, and teeth which were capable of deforming all but the strongest metal alloys.

They had evolved on a world of shallow seas and steaming jungle swamps where the line of demarcation between animal and vegetable life, so far as physical mobility and aggression were concerned, was unclear. To survive at all, a life-form had to be immensely strong, highly mobile, and unsleeping, and the dominant species on that planet had earned its place by fighting and moving faster and reproducing its kind with a greater potential for survival than any of the others.

The utter savagery of their environment had forced them to evolve a physical form that gave maximum protection to the vital organs. Brain, heart, lungs, and greatly enlarged womb, all were housed deep inside the organic fighting machine that was the Protector's body. Their gestation period was abnormally extended because the embryo had to grow virtually to maturity before parturition, and it was rare for an adult to survive the reproduction of more than three offspring. An aging parent was usually too weak to defend itself against attack by its lastborn.

The principal reason for the Protectors' rise to dominance on their world was that their young were already fully educated in the techniques of survival long before they were born. In the dawn of their evolution the process had begun as a complex set of survival characteristics at the genetic level, but the small physical separation of the brains of the parent and its developing fetus had led to an effect analogous to induction of the electro-chemical activity associated with thought. The result was that the embryos became short-range telepaths receiving everything the parent saw or felt.

And before the fetus was half-grown there was taking form within it another embryo that was also increasingly aware of the violent world outside its self-fertilizing grandparent, until gradually the telepathic range increased until communication became possible between embryos whose parents came close enough to see each other.

To minimize damage to a parent's internal organs, the growing fetus was paralyzed within the womb, and the prebirth deparalysis also caused loss of both sentience and the telepathic faculty. A newborn Protector would not survive for long in its incredibly savage environment if it was hampered by the ability to think.

With nothing to do but receive impressions from the outside world, exchange thoughts with the other Unborn, and try to extend their telepathic range by making contact with various forms of nonsentient life around them, the embryos developed minds of great power and intelligence. But they could not build anything, or engage in any form of technical research, or do anything at all that would influence the activities of their parents and protectors, who had to fight and kill and eat continually to maintain their unsleeping bodies and the unborn within them.

"That was the situation," Prilicla went on, "before friend Conway was successful in delivering an Unborn without loss of sentience. Now there are the original Protector and its offspring, who is itself a young Protector, and the embryos growing within both of them, all but the original parent in telepathic contact. Their ward, which was built to reproduce the FSOJs' home environment, is the next opening on the left. You may find the sight disturbing, friend Lioren, and the noise is certainly horrendous."

The ward was more than half-filled by a hollow, endless cylinder of immensely strong metal latticework. The diameter of the structure was just wide enough to allow continuous, unrestricted movement in one direction to the FSOJ patients it contained, and which curved and twisted back on itself so that the occupants could use all of the available floor area that was not required for access by the medical attendants or environmental support equipment. The cylinder floor reproduced the uneven ground and natural obstacles like the mobile and voracious triproots found on the Protectors' home planet, while the open sections gave the occupants a continuous view of the screens positioned around the outer surface of the cylinder. Onto the screens were projected moving, tri-d pictures of the indigenous plant and animal life which they would normally encounter.

The open lattice structure also helped the medical attendants to bring to bear on the patients the more positive aspects of the life-support system. Positioned between the projected screen images were the mechanisms whose sole purpose was to beat, tear, or jab at the occupants' rapidly moving bodies with any required degree of frequency or force.

Everything possible was being done, Lioren noted, to make the Protectors feel at home.

"Will they be able to hear us?" Lioren shouted above the din. "Or we them?"

"No, friend Lioren," the empath replied. "The screaming and grunting sounds they are making do not carry intelligence, but are solely a means of frightening natural enemies. Until the recent successful birthing the intelligent Unborn remained within the nonsentient Protector and heard only the internal organic sounds of the parent. Speech was impossible and unnecessary for them. The only communication channel open to us is telepathy."

"I am not a telepath," Lioren said.

"Nor are Conway, Thornnastor, and the others who have been contacted by the Unborn," Prilicla said. "The few known species with the telepathic faculty evolved organic transmitter-receivers that are automatically in tune for that particular race, and for this reason contact between members of different telepathic species is not always possible. When mental contact occurs between one of these entities and a nontelepath, it usually means that the faculty in the latter is dormant or atrophied rather than nonexistent. When such contact occurs the experience for the nontelepath can be very uncomfortable, but there are no physical changes in the brain affected nor is there any lasting psychological damage.

"Move closer to the exercise cage, friend Lioren," Prilicla went on. "Can you feel the Protector touching your mind?"

"No," Lioren said.

"I feel your disappointment," the empath said. A faint tremor shook its body and it went on, "But I also feel the young Protector generating the emotional radiation characteristic of intense curiosity and concentrated effort. It is trying very hard to contact you."

"I'm sorry, nothing," Lioren said.

Prilicla spoke briefly into its communicator, then said, "I have stepped up the violence of the attack mechanisms. The patient will suffer no injury, but we have found that the effect of increased activity and apparent danger on the endocrine system aids the process of mentation. Try to make your mind receptive."

"Still nothing," Lioren said, touching the side of his head with one hand, "except for some mild discomfort in the inter-cranial area that is becoming very . . ." The rest was an untranslatable sound which rivaled in volume the noise coming from the Protectors' life-support system.

The sensation was like a deep, raging itch inside his brain combined with a discordant, unheard noise that mounted steadily in intensity. This must be what it is like, Lioren thought helplessly, when a faculty which is dormant is awakened and forced to perform. As in the case of a muscle long unused, there was pain and stiffness and protest against the change in the old, comfortable order of things.

Suddenly the discomfort was gone, the unheard storm of sound in his mind faded to become a deep, still pool of mental silence on which the external din of the ward had no effect. Then out of the stillness there came words that were unspoken from a being who did not have a name but whose mind and unique personality were an identification that could never be mistaken for any other.

"You are feeling seriously disturbed, friend Lioren," Prilicla said. "Has the Protector touched your mind?"

Rather, Lioren answered silently, *it has almost swamped my mind.* "Yes, contact was established and quickly broken. I tried to help it by suggesting ... It asked for another visit at a later time. Can we leave now?"

Prilicla led the way into the corridor without speaking, but Lioren did not need an empathic faculty to be aware of the Cinrusskin's intense curiosity. "I did not realize that so much knowledge could be exchanged in such a short time," he said. "Words convey meaning in a trickle, thoughts in a great tidal wave, and problems explained instantly and in the fullest detail. I will need time alone to think about everything it has told me so that my answers will not be confused and half-formed. It is impossible to lie to a telepath."

"Or an empath," Prilicla said. "Do you wish to delay your visit to the Gogleskan?"

"No," Lioren replied. "My lonely thinking can wait until this evening. Will Khone use telepathy on me?"

Prilicla had a moment of unstable flight for some reason, then recovered. "I certainly hope not."

The empath explained that adult Gogleskans used a form of telepathy which required close physical contact, but, except when their lives were threatened, they did everything possible to avoid such contact. It was not simple xenophobia that ailed them, but a pathological fear of the close approach of any large creature, including nonfamily members of their own species. They possessed a well-developed spoken and written language which had allowed the individual and group cooperation necessary for growth of civilization, but their verbal contacts were rare and conducted over the greatest practicable distance and in the most impersonal terms. It was not surprising that their level of technology had remained low.

The reason for their abnormally fearful behavior was a racial psychosis implanted far back in their prehistoric past. It was a subject which Lioren was strongly advised to approach with caution.

"Otherwise," Prilicla said as it checked its flight above the entrance to the side ward reserved for the Gogleskans, "you risk distressing the patient and endangering the trust that has gradually been built up between Khone and those responsible for its treatment. I am unwilling to subject it to the emotional strain of a visit from two strangers, so I shall leave you now. Healer Khone is a frightened, timid, but intensely curious being. Try to converse impersonally as I have suggested, friend Lioren, and think well before you speak."

A wall of heavy, transparent plastic stretching from floor to ceiling divided the room into equal halves. Hatches for the introduction of food and remote handling devices hung apparently unsupported like empty white picture frames. The treatment half of the ward contained the usual tools of medical investigation modified for use at a distance and three viewscreens. Only two of them were visible to the adult Gogleskan, the third being a repeater for the patient monitor in the main ward's nursing station. Not wishing to risk giving offense by staring at Khone directly, Lioren concentrated his attention on the picture on the repeater screen.

The Gogleskan healer, Lioren saw at once, was classification FOKT. Its erect, ovoid body was covered by a mass of long, brightly colored hair and flexible spikes, some of which were tipped by small, bulbous pads and grouped into digital clusters so as to enable eating utensils, tools, or medical instruments to be grasped and manipulated. He was able to identify the four long, pale tendrils that were used during contact telepathy lying amid the multicolored cranial hair. The head was encircled by a narrow metal band that supported a corrective lens for one of the four, equally spaced and recessed eyes. Around the lower body was a thick skirt of muscle on which the creature rested, and whenever it changed position four stubby legs were extended below the edge of the muscular skirt. It was making untranslatable moaning sounds, which Lioren thought might be wordless music, to its offspring, who was almost hairless but otherwise a scaled-down copy of its parent. The sound seemed to be coming from a number of small, vertical breathing orifices encircling its waist.

Beyond the transparent wall, the metal plating had been covered with a layer of something that resembled dark, unpolished wood, and several pieces of low furniture and shelves of the same material were placed around the inner three walls. Clumps of aromatic vegetation decorated the room, and the lighting reproduced the subdued orange glow of Gogleskan sunlight that had been filtered through overhead branches. Khone's accommodation was as homelike as the hospital's environment technicians could make it, but Khone was too timid to complain about anything except a sudden and close approach of strangers.

A timid entity, Prilicla had described it, who was perpetually fearful and intensely curious.

"Is it permitted," he asked in the prescribed impersonal manner, "for the trainee Lioren to examine the medical notes of the patient and healer, Khone? The purpose is the satisfaction of curiosity, not to conduct a medical examination."

A personal name could be given only once, at the Time of First Meeting, Prilicla had told him, for the purpose of identification and introduction, and never mentioned again except during written communication. Khone's body hair stirred restively and for a moment it stood out straight from the body, making the little entity appear twice its real size and revealing the long, sharply pointed stings that lay twitching close against the curvature of the lower torso. The stings were the Gogleskans' only natural weapon, but the poison they delivered was instantly lethal to the metabolism of any warm-blooded oxygen-breather.

The moaning sound died away. "Relief is felt that clinical examination by another fearsome but well-intentioned monster is not imminent," Khone said. "It is permitted and, since access to the medical notes cannot be forbidden, gratitude is felt for the polite wording of the request. May suggestions be made?"

"They would be welcomed," Lioren said, thinking that the Gogles-kan's forthright manner was not what he had expected. Perhaps the timidity was not evident during verbal exchanges.

"The entities who visit this ward are invariably polite," Khone said, "and frequently politeness retards conversation. If the curiosity of the trainee is specific rather than general, there would be an advantage if the patient rather than the medical notes were consulted."

"Yes, indeed," Lioren said. "Thank you . . . That is, helpfulness has been shown and gratitude is felt. The trainee's primary interest lies in the—"

"It is presumed," the Gogleskan went on, "that the trainee will answer as well as ask questions. The patient is an experienced healer, by Gogleskan standards, and knows that both parent and firstborn are healthy and are protected from physical danger or disease. The firstborn is too young to feel anything other than contentment, but the parent is prey to many different feelings, the strongest of which is boredom. Does the trainee understand?"

"The trainee understands," Lioren replied, gesturing toward the inward-facing display screens, "and will try to relieve the condition. There is interesting visual material available on the worlds and peoples of the Federation—"

"Which shows monstrous creatures inhabiting crowded cities," Khone broke in. "Or packed tightly together in close, nonsexual contact inside air or ground vehicles, or similar terrifying sights. Terror is not the indicated cure for boredom. If knowledge is to be obtained about the visually horrifying peoples and practices of the Federation, it must be slowly and of one person at a time."

Even a Groalterri, Lioren thought, would not live long enough to do that. "As the uninvited guest is it not proper for the trainee to give answers before asking questions of the host?"

"Another unnecessary politeness," Khone replied, "but appreciation is felt nonetheless. What is the trainee's first question?"

This was going to be much easier than he had expected, Lioren thought. "The trainee desires information on Gogleskan telepathy, specifically on the organic mechanisms which enable it to function and the physical causes, including both the clinical and subjective symptomology present if the faculty should malfunction. This information might prove helpful with another patient whose species is also tele—"

"No!" Khone said, so loudly that the young one began making agitated, whistling sounds that did not translate. A large patch of the Gogleskan's body hair rose stiffly outward and, in a manner that Lioren could not see clearly, wove the strands into the shorter growth of its offspring and held it close to the parent's body until the young one became quiet again.

"I'm very sorry," Lioren began, in his self-anger and disappointment forgetting to be impersonal. He rephrased quickly. "Extreme sorrow is felt, and apologies tendered. It was not the intention to cause offense. Would it be better if the offensive trainee withdrew?"

"No," Khone said again, in a quieter voice. "Telepathy and Gogleskan prehistory are most sensitive subjects. They have been discussed in the past with the entities Conway, Prilicla, and O'Mara, all of whom are strange and visually threatening but well-trusted beings. But the trainee is strange and frightening and not known to the patient.

"The telepathic function is instinctive rather than under conscious control. It is triggered by the presence of strangers, or anything else that the Gogleskan subconscious mind considers a threat that, in a species so lacking in physical strength, is practically everything. Can the trainee understand the Gogleskan's problem, and be patient?"

"There is understanding—" Lioren began.

"Then the subject can be discussed," Khone broke in. "But only when enough is known about the trainee for the patient to be able to close its eyes and see the person enclosed in that visually horrendous shape, and so override the instinctive panic reaction that would otherwise occur."

"There is understanding," Lioren said again. "The trainee will be pleased to answer the patient's questions."

The Gogleskan rose a few inches onto its short legs and moved to the side, apparently to have a better view of Lioren's lower body, which had been hidden by one of the display screens, before it spoke.

"The first question is," it said, "what is the trainee training to be?"

"A Healer of the Mind," Lioren replied.

"No surprise is felt," Khone said.

CHAPTER 19

The questions were many and searching, but so polite and imper-sonal was the interrogation that no offense could be taken. By the time it was over, the Gogleskan healer knew almost as much about Lioren as he did himself. Even then it was obvious that Khone wanted to know more.

The young one had been transferred to a tiny bed at the back of the compartment, and Khone had overcome its timidity to the extent of moving forward until its body touched the transparent dividing wall.

"The Tarlan trainee and onetime respected healer," it said, "has an-swered many questions about itself and its past and present life. All of the information is of great interest, although plainly much of it is dis-tressing to the listener as well as the speaker. Sympathy is felt regarding the terrible events on Cromsag and there is sorrow and helplessness that the Gogleskan healer is unable to give relief in this matter.

"At the same time," Khone went on, "there is a feeling that the Tarlan, who has spoken openly and in detail of many things normally kept secret from others, is concealing information. Are there events in the past more terrible than those already revealed, and why does the trainee not speak of them?"

"There is nothing," Lioren said, more loudly than he had intended, "more terrible than Cromsag."

"The Gogleskan is relieved to hear it," Khone said. "Is it that the Tarlan is afraid lest its words be passed on to others and cause embarrassment? It should be informed that a healer on Goglesk does not speak of such matters to others unless given permission to do so. The trainee should not feel concern."

Lioren was silent for a moment, thinking that his utter and impersonal dedication to the healing art and the self-imposed discipline that had ruled his past life had left him neither the time nor the inclination to form emotional ties. It was only after the court-martial, when any thought of career advancement was ridiculous and the continuation of his life was the cruelest of all punishments, that he had become interested in people for reasons other than their clinical condition. In spite of their strange shapes and even stranger thought processes, he had begun to think of some of them as friends.

Perhaps this creature was another.

"A similar rule binds the healers of many worlds," he said, "but gratitude is expressed nonetheless. The reason other information has been concealed is that the beings concerned do not wish it to be revealed."

"There is understanding," Khone said, "and additional curiosity about the trainee. Has the repeated telling reduced the emotional distress caused by the Cromsag Incident?"

Lioren was silent for a moment; then he said, "It is impossible to be objective in this matter. Many other matters occupy the trainee's mind so that the memory returns with less frequency, but it still causes distress. Now the trainee is wondering whether it is the Gogleskan or the Tarlan who is better trained in other-species psychology."

Khone gave a short, whistling sound which did not translate. "The trainee has provided information that will enable a troubled mind to escape for a time from its own troubles because this healer, too, has thoughts which it would prefer not to think. Now the Tarlan visitor no longer seems strange or threatening, even to the dark undermind that feels and reacts but does not think, and there is an unpaid debt. Now the trainee's questions will be answered."

Lioren expressed impersonal thanks and once again sought information on the functioning, and especially the symptoms of malfunctioning, of the Gogleskan telepathic faculty. But to learn about their telepathy was to learn everything about them.

The situation on the primitive world of Goglesk was the direct opposite of that on Groalter. Federation policy had always been that full contact with a technologically backward culture could be dangerous because, when the Monitor Corps ships and contact specialists dropped out of their skies, they could never be certain whether they were giving the natives evidence of a technological goal at which to aim or a destructive inferiority complex. But the Gogleskans, in spite of their backwardness in the physical sciences and the devastating racial psychosis that forced them to remain so, were psychologically stable as individuals, and their planet had not known war for many centuries.

The easiest course would have been for the Corps to withdraw and write the Gogleskan problem off as insoluble. Instead they had compromised by setting up a small base for the purposes of observation, long-range investigation, and limited contact.

Progress for any intelligent species depended on increasing levels of cooperation between individuals and family or tribal groups. On Goglesk, however, any attempt at close cooperation brought a period of drastically reduced intelligence, a mindless urge to destruction, and serious physical injury in its wake, so that the Gogleskans had been forced into becoming a race of individualists who had close physical contact only during the periods when reproduction was possible or while caring for their young.

The situation had been forced on them in presapient times, when they had been the principal food source of every predator infesting Goglesk's oceans. Although physically puny, they had been able to evolve weapons of offense and defense—stings that paralyzed or killed the smaller life-forms, and long, cranial tendrils that gave them the faculty of telepathy by contact. When threatened by large predators they linked bodies and minds together in the numbers required to englobe and neutralize with their combined stings any attacker regardless of its size.

There was fossil evidence that a bitter struggle for survival had been waged between them and a gigantic and particularly ferocious species of ocean predator for millions of years. The presapient Gogleskans had won in the end, but they had paid a terrible price.

In order to englobe and sting to death one of those giant predators, physical and telepathic linkages between hundreds of presapient FOKTs were required. A great many of them had perished, been torn apart and eaten during every such encounter, and the consequent and often repeated death agonies of the victims had been shared telepathically by every member of the group. A natural mechanism had evolved that had fractionally reduced this suffering, diluting the pain of group telepathy by generating a mindless urge to destroy indiscriminately everything within reach that was not an FOKT. But even though the Gogleskans had become intelligent and civilized far beyond the level expected of a primitive fishing and farming culture, the mental wounds inflicted during their prehistory would not heal.

The high-pitched audible signal emitted by Gogleskans in distress that triggered the joining process could not be ignored at either the conscious or unconscious levels. That call to join represented only one thing, the threat of ultimate danger. And even in present times, when the danger was insignificant or imaginary, it made no difference. A joining led inevitably to the mindless destruction of everything in their immediate vicinity—housing, vehicles, crops, farm animals, mechanisms, book and art objects—that they had been able to build or grow as individuals.

That was why the present-day Gogleskans would not allow, except in the circumstances Khone had already mentioned, anyone to touch or come close to them or even address them in anything but the most impersonal terms while they fought helplessly and, until the recent visit of Diagnostician Conway to Goglesk, hopelessly against the condition that evolution had imposed on them.

"It is Conway's intention to break the Gogleskan racial conditioning," Khone went on, "by allowing the parent and offspring to experience gradually increasing exposure to a variety of other life-forms who were intelligent, civilized, and obviously not a threat. It was thought that the young one, in particular, might become so accustomed to the process that its subconscious as well as its conscious mind would be able to control the blind urge that previously caused a panic reaction leading to a joining. Mechanisms have also been devised by the hospital which distort the audible distress signal so that it becomes unrecognizable. The triggering stimulus and subsequent urge to mindless destruction would then be limited to the capabilities of one rather than a large group of persons acting in concert. Another solution which has doubtless already occurred to the trainee would be to excise the tendrils which allow contact telepathy and make it impossible for a joining to occur. But that solution is not possible because the tendrils are needed to give comfort and later to educate the very young, as well as to intensify the pleasures of mating, and the Gogleskans suffer privations enough without becoming voluntary emotional cripples.

"It is Conway's expectation and our hope," Khone concluded, "that this two-pronged attack on the problem will enable the Gogleskans to build with permanence and advance to a level of civilization commensurate with their intelligence."

Normally Lioren found it difficult to detect emotional overtones in translated speech, but this time he felt sure that there was a deep uncertainty within the other's mind that had not been verbalized.

"This trainee may be in error," Lioren said, "but it senses that the Gogleskan healer patient is troubled. Is there dissatisfaction with the treatment it is receiving? Are there doubts regarding the abilities or expectations of Conway—?"

"No!" Khone broke in. "There was one brief and accidental sharing of minds with the Diagnostician when it visited Goglesk. Its abilities and intentions are known and are beyond criticism. But its mind was crowded with other minds full of strange experiences and thoughts so alien that the Gogleskan wanted to call for a joining. Much was learned from the mind of Conway and much more remains incomprehensible, but it was plain that the proportion of the Diagnostician's mind available for the Goglesk project was small. When doubts were first expressed, the Diagnostician listened and its words were confident, reassuring, and dismissive, and it may be that Conway does not fully understand the nonmedical problem. It cannot or will not believe that, out of all the intelligent races that make up the Federation, the Gogleskan species alone is accursed and doomed forever to self-inflicted barbarism by the Authority which Orders All Things."

Lioren was silent for a moment, wondering if he was about to become involved once again in a problem that was philosophical rather than clinical, and unsure of his right or ability as a Tarlan unbeliever to engage in a debate on other-species theology. "If there was a telepathic touching," he said, "then the Diagnostician must have seen and understood what is in the healer's mind, so that the doubts may be groundless. But the trainee is completely ignorant in this matter. If the healer wishes it, the trainee will listen to these doubts and not be dismissive. A fear was mentioned that the situation on Goglesk would never change. Can the reason for this fear be explained more fully?"

"Yes," Khone said in a quieter voice. "It is a fear that one entity cannot change the course of evolution. It was evident from Conway's mind, and from the thoughts and beliefs of those entities who shared that mind when the touching occurred, that the situation on Goglesk is abnormal. On the other worlds of the Federation there is a struggle between the destructive forces of environment and instinctive, animal behavior on one side and the efforts of thinking and cooperating beings on the other. By some entities it is called the continuing battle to impose order upon chaos, and by many the struggle between good and bad, or God against the Evil One. On all of these worlds it is the former, at times with great difficulty, who is gaining ascendancy over the latter. But on Goglesk there is no God; only the prehistoric but still all-powerful Devil rules there . . ."

The Gogleskan's erect, ovoid body was trembling, its hair was raised like clumps of long, many-colored grass, and the four yellow spikes that were its stings were beaded with venom at the tips. For it was seeing again the images that had been indelibly printed into its racial memory, the terrible pictures complete with their telepathically shared death agonies as the gigantic predators had torn its joined forebears into bloody tatters. Lioren suspected that the signal of ultimate distress, the Call for Joining, would have already gone out if Khone had not controlled its instinctive terror with the reminder that the only other Gogleskan capable of linking telepathically with it was its own sleeping offspring.

Gradually Khone's trembling diminished, and when the erect hair and stings were again lying flat against its body, it went on. "There is great fear and even greater despair. The Gogleskan feels that the help of the Earth-human Diagnostician, with good-will and the resources of this great hospital at its disposal, are not enough to alter the destiny of a world. It is a stupid self-delusion on the part of this healer to think otherwise, and a gross act of ingratitude to tell Conway of these feelings. Everywhere in the Federation there is a balance between order and chaos, or good and evil, but it is inconceivable that a Gogleskan and its child could alter the destiny, the habits and thinking and feelings of an entire planetary population."

Lioren made the sign of negation, then realized that the gesture would be meaningless to Khone. "The healer is wrong. There are many precedents on many different worlds where one person was able to do just that. Admittedly, the person concerned was an entity with special qualities, a great teacher or lawgiver or philosopher, and many of its followers believed that it was the manifestation of their God. It is not certain that the healer and its child, with Conway's assistance, will change the course of Gogleskan history, but it is possible."

Khone made a short, wheezing sound which did not translate. "Such wildly inaccurate and extravagant compliments have not been received since the prelude to first mating. Surely the Tarlan is aware that the Gogleskan healer is neither a teacher nor a leader nor a person with any special qualities. That which the trainee suggests is ridiculous!"

"The trainee is aware," Lioren said, "that the healer is the only member of its species to have faced its Devil, to have broken its racial conditioning to the extent of coming to a place like Sector General, a place filled with monstrous but well-intentioned beings the majority of whom are visually more terrifying than the Dark One that haunts the

Gogleskan racial memory. And the trainee disagrees because it is self-evident that the healer possesses special qualities.

"For it has demonstrated beyond doubt," Lioren went on before Khone could react, "that it is possible for one Gogleskan who was continually in fear of the close approach of its own kind to overcome and, with practice and great strength of will, to understand and even befriend many of the creatures out of nightmare who live here. This being so, is it not possible, even probable, that it will be able to find and teach this quality to others of its kind, who will in time spread its teachings throughout their world until gradually the Dark One loses all power over the Gogleskan mind?"

"That is what Conway believes," Khone said. "But is it not also probable that the followers will say that the teacher is damaged in the brain, and be fearful of the great changes that they would have to make in their customs and habits of mind? If it persisted in its attempts to make them think in new and uncomfortable ways, they might drive the teacher from them and inflict serious injury or worse."

"Regrettably," Lioren said, "there are precedents for such behavior, but if the teaching is good it outlives the teacher. And the Gogleskans are a gentle race. This teacher should feel neither fear nor despair."

Khone made no response and Lioren went on. "It is a truism that in any place of healing a patient will invariably find others in a more distressed condition than itself, and derive some small comfort from the discovery. The same holds true among the distressed worlds. The healer is also wrong, therefore, in thinking that Goglesk is uniquely accursed by fate or whichever other agency it feels is responsible.

"There are the Cromsaggar," Lioren went on, maintaining a quiet tone within the sudden clamor of memories the word aroused, "whose curse was that they were constantly ill and constantly at war because fighting each other was the only cure for their disease. And there are the Protectors, who fight and hunt and kill mindlessly for every moment of their adult lives, and who would make the long-extinct Dark Ones of Goglesk seem tame by comparison. Yet within these terrible organic killing machines live, all too briefly, the telepathic Unborn whose minds are gentle and sensitive and in all respects civilized. Diagnostician Thornnastor has solved the Cromsag problem, which was basically one of endocrinology, so that the few surviving natives of that planet will no longer be condemned to unending, reluctant warfare. Diagnostician Conway has made itself responsible for freeing the Protectors of the Unborn from their evolutionary trap, but everyone feels that it is the Gogleskan problem which will be more easily solved—"

"These problems have already been discussed," Khone broke in, its whistling speech increasing in pitch as it spoke. "The solutions, although complex, involve medical or surgical conditions that are susceptible to physical treatment. It is not so on Goglesk. There the problem is not susceptible to physical solution. It is the most important part of the genetic inheritance that enabled the species to survive since presapient times and cannot be destroyed. The evil that drives the race to self-destruction and self-enforced solitude was, is, and always will be. On Goglesk there has never been a God, only the Devil."

"Again," Lioren said, "it is possible that the healer is incorrect. The trainee hesitates lest offense is given through ignorance of Gogleskan religious beliefs that may be held by the—"

"Impatience is felt," Khone said, "but offense will not be taken."

For a moment Lioren tried desperately to remember and organize the information he had recently abstracted from the library computer. "It is widely taught and believed throughout the Federation that where there is evil there is also good, and that there cannot be a devil without God. This God is believed to be the all-knowing, all-powerful but compassionate supreme being and maker of all things, and is also held to be ever-present but invisible. If only the Devil is evident on Goglesk it does not necessarily mean that God is not there because all of the beliefs, regardless of species, are in agreement that the first place to look for God is within one's self.

"The Gogleskans have been struggling against their Devil since they first developed intelligence," Lioren went on. "Sometimes they have lost but more often of late they have made small gains. It could be that there is one Devil and many who unknowingly carry their God within them."

"These are like the words spoken by Conway," Khone said. "But the Diagnostician encourages with advanced medical science and advises more rigorous training in the mental disciplines. Is Goglesk's benefactor unable to believe in God or our Devil or any other form of nonphysical presence?"

"Perhaps," Lioren said. "But regardless of its beliefs the quality of its assistance remains unaltered."

Khone was silent for so long that Lioren wondered if the interview was over. He had a strong feeling that the other wanted to speak, but when they eventually came the words were a complete surprise.

"Additional reassurance might be felt," Khone said, "if the Tarlan spoke of its own beliefs."

"The Tarlan," Lioren said carefully, "knows of many different beliefs held by its own people as well as those on other worlds, but the knowledge is recently acquired, incomplete, and probably inaccurate. It has also discovered in the histories of the subject that such beliefs, if they are strongly held, are matters of faith which are not susceptible to change through logical argument. If the beliefs are very strongly held, the discussion of alternative beliefs can give offense. The Tarlan does not wish to offend, and it does not have the right to influence the beliefs of others in any fashion. For these reasons it would prefer that the Gogleskan takes the lead by describing its own beliefs."

It had been obvious from the beginning that Khone was deeply troubled, even though the precise nature of the problem had been unclear. This was not an area where advice could be given in total ignorance.

"The Tarlan is being evasive," Khone said, "and cautious."

"The Gogleskan," Lioren said, "is correct."

There was a short silence, then Khone said, "Very well. The Gogleskan is frightened, and despairing, and angry about the Devil that lives within the minds of its people and constantly tortures and binds them in chains of near-barbarism. It is preferred that nothing be spoken of the nonmaterial supports its people use to solace and encourage themselves because this Gogleskan, as a healer, doubts the efficacy of nonmaterial medication. It asks again, what kind of God does the Tarlan believe in?

"Is it a great, omniscient, and all-powerful creator," Khone went on before Lioren could reply, "who allows or ignores pain and injustice? Is it a god who heaps undeserved misfortune on a few species while blessing the majority with peace and contentment? Does it have good or even godly reasons for permitting such terrible events as the destruction of the Cromsaggar population, or for the evolutionary trap which imprisons the Protectors of the Unborn and for the dreadful scourge it has inflicted on the Gogleskans? Can there be any sin committed in the past so grievous that it warrants such punishment? Does this God have intelligence and ethical reasons for such apparently stupid and immoral behavior, and will the Tarlan please explain them?"

The Tarlan has no explanations, thought Lioren, because he is an unbeliever like yourself. But he knew instinctively that that was not the answer Khone wanted, because if it was truly an unbeliever it would not be so angry with the God it did not believe in. This was a time for soft answers.

CHAPTER 20

"As has already been stated," Lioren said quietly, "the Tarlan will give information but will not try to influence the beliefs or disbeliefs of others. The religions on the majority of the Federation planets, and the god worshiped by their followers, have much in common. Their god is the omniscient, omnipotent, and omnipresent Creator of All Things, as has already been stated, and is in addition believed to be just, merciful, compassionate, deeply concerned for the well-being of all of the intelligent entities it has created, and forgiving of the wrongs committed by them. It is generally believed that where there is God there is also the Devil, or some evil and less well defined entity or influence which constantly seeks to undo God's work among its thinking creatures by trying to make them behave in the instinctive manner of the animals, which they know they are not. Within every thinking creature there is this constant struggle between good and evil, right and wrong. Sometimes it seems that the Devil, or the tendency to animal behavior that is in all thinking beings, is winning and that God does not care. But even on Goglesk good has begun to make gains, minor though they may be, over evil. Had this not been so the Gogleskan healer would not be here and undergoing instruction in the use of the antijoining sound distorters. Because it is also said that God helps even those who do not believe in its existence—"

"And punishes those who do," Khone broke in. "The questions remain. How does the Tarlan explain a compassionate God who allows such massive cruelty?"

Lioren did not have an answer, so he ignored the question. "It is often said that belief in God is a matter of faith rather than physical proof, that it does not depend on the level of intelligence possessed by the believer and that when the quality of mentation is weak the faith is stronger and more certain. The implication is that only the relatively stupid believe in the metaphysical or the supernatural or a life after physical death, while the more intelligent entities know better and believe only in themselves, the physical reality they experience around them and their ability to change it for the better.

"The complexities of this external reality, from the galaxies that stretch out to infinity and the equally complex microuniverses of which it is made, are given scientific explanations which are little more than intelligent guesses that are subject to continual modification. Most unconvincing of all are the explanations for the presence of creatures who have evolved in the area between the macro- and microcosm, creatures who think and know, and know that they know, and who try to understand the whole of which they are but the tiniest part while striving to change it for the better. To the enlightened few among these thinkers it is considered right to behave well toward each other and cooperate individually and as peoples and other-planet species so that peace, contentment, and scientific and philosophical achievement is attained for the greatest number of beings. Any person or group or system of thinking which retards this process is considered wrong. But to the majority of these thinkers good and evil are abstractions, and God and the Devil but the superstitions of less intelligent minds."

Lioren paused, trying to find the right words of certainty and reassurance about a subject of which he felt very uncertain. "For the first time in its history, the Galactic Federation has been contacted by a superintelligent, philosophically advanced, but technologically backward race called the Groalterri. The contact was indirect because this species believes that direct mental contact would result in irreversible philosophical damage to those races which hitherto considered themselves to be highly intelligent. One of their young sustained injuries which they were unable to treat, and they requested the hospital to accept it as a patient and gave reassurances that the young one was not yet intelligent enough for contact with it to be psychologically damaging. During conversations with it the Tarlan discovered, among other things, that it and the hyperintelligent adult members of its race are not unbelievers."

Tufts of stiff, bristling fur were standing out from Khone's body, but the Gogleskan did not speak.

"The Tarlan feels no certainty about this," Lioren said, "and wishes only to make an observation. It may be that all intelligent species pass through a stage when they think that they know the answers to everything, only to progress further to a truer realization of the depth of their ignorance. If the most highly intelligent and philosophically advanced species yet discovered believes in God and an afterlife then—"

"Enough!" Khone broke in sharply. "The existence of God is not the question. The question, which the Tarlan is trying to avoid by providing other and more interesting material for debate, remains the same. Why does this all-powerful, just, and compassionate God act so cruelly and unjustly where some of its creatures are concerned? To the Gogleskan the answer is important. Great distress and uncertainty is felt."

But what exactly do you believe or disbelieve, Lioren wondered helplessly, *so that I can try to relieve your distress?* Because he did not believe in prayer he wished desperately for inspiration, but all that he could find to talk about were the recently learned beliefs of others.

"The Tarlan does not know or understand the purposes and behavior of God," he said, "It is the creator of all things and must therefore possess a mind infinitely superior and more complex than that possessed by any of its creations. But certain facts are generally accepted about this being which may assist in understanding behavior that, as the healer has noted, is very often at variance with what is believed to be its intentions.

"For example: It is believed to be the omniscient creator of all things," Lioren continued, "who has the deep concern of a parent for the welfare of each and every one of its creations, although the more general belief is that this love is reserved principally for its thinking creations. Yet all too often it appears to behave as an angry, irrational, or uncaring parent than a loving one. It is also widely believed that the creator works its purpose within all of its thinking creatures, whether or not they believe in its existence.

"Another belief held by most species is that God created them in its own image and that they will one day live forever in happiness with their creator in an afterlife which has as many names as there are inhabited planets. This belief is particularly troublesome to many thinkers for the reason that the variety of physiological classifications among intelligent life-forms encountered within the known Galaxy makes this a logical and physical impossibility—"

"The Tarlan is restating the question," Khone said suddenly, "not providing an answer."

Lioren ignored the interruption. "But there are others who have come to share a different belief and think that they know a different god. These beings are not as intelligent as the Groalterri, whose thoughts on this subject are and will probably always remain unknown to us. They were unhappy with the idea that such a complex but perfectly ordered structure as the universe around them is without purpose and came into being by accident. It troubled them that there were probably more stars in their sky than individual grains of sand on the beaches surrounding Goglesk's island continent. It troubled them that the more they discovered about the subatomic unreality that is the foundation of the real world, the more hints there were of a vast and complex macrostructure at the limits of resolution of their most sensitive telescopes. It also troubled them that intelligent, self-aware creatures had come into being with a growing curiosity and need to explain the universe they inhabit. They refused to believe that such a vast, complex, and well-ordered structure could occur by accident, which meant that it had to have had a creator. But they were a part of that creation, the only part composed of self-aware entities, creatures who knew and were aware that they knew, so they believed all intelligent life to be the most important part of the creation so far as the creator was concerned.

"This was not a new idea," Lioren continued, "because many others believed in a God who had made them and loves them and watches over them, and who would take them to itself in the fullness of time. But they were troubled by the uncharacteristic actions of this loving god, so they modified their idea of God's purpose so that its behavior might be more easily explained.

"They believe that God created all things including themselves," Lioren said slowly, "but that the work of creation is not yet complete."

Khone had become so still and silent that Lioren could not hear its normally loud respiration. He went on. "The work is not complete, they say, because it began with the creation of a universe that is still young and may never die. Exactly how it began is unknown, but at present it contains many species who have evolved to high intelligence who are spreading in peace among the stars. But the rise from animal to thinking being, the process of continuing creation, or evolution if one is an unbeliever, is not a pleasant process. It is long and slow and often many necessary cruelties and injustices occur among those who are part of it.

"They also believe," Lioren continued, "that the present differences in physiology and enviromental requirements are unimportant since evolution, or creation, is leading toward increased sentience and a reduced dependence on specialized appendages. The result, in the greatly distant future, will be that thinking creatures will have evolved beyond their present need for the physical bodies that house their minds. They will become immortal and join together to achieve goals that cannot be envisaged by the near-animals of the present. They will become Godlike and a true image, as they were and are promised, of the being who created them. It is held that the spirits or souls of the mentally and philosophically immature entities who have and will inhabit this universe for many eons to come will also share in this future immortality and be one with their God, because it is believed to be a philosophical absurdity that the creator of all things would discard the most important, if presently incomplete, parts of its own creation."

Lioren paused to await Khone's reaction; then another thought occurred to him. "The Groalterri possess very high intelligence and they are believers, but will not talk about their beliefs or anything else with those of lower intelligence levels lest they damage immature minds. It may be that every intelligent species must find its own way to God, and the Groalterri are further along the path than the rest of us."

There was another long silence; then Khone asked very quietly, "Is this, then, the God in which the Tarlan believes?"

From the other's tone Lioren knew that his answer should be "Yes," because he felt sure now that the Gogleskan was a doubter who desperately wanted its doubts dispelled, and that he should take advantage of the situation by quickly reassuring the patient if he wished to obtain the telepathy information he wanted. But an unbeliever telling a lie in the hope of making a doubter believe was dishonorable and dishonest. It was his duty to give what reassurance he could, but he would not lie.

Lioren thought for a long moment, and when he replied he was surprised to discover that he meant every word.

"No," he said, "but there is uncertainty."

"Yes," Khone said, "there is always uncertainty."

CHAPTER 21

Lioren's answer had satisfied the Gogleskan, or perhaps had satisfactorily reinforced its doubts, because Khone did not ask any more questions about God.

Instead, it said, "Earlier the Tarlan expressed curiosity regarding the organic structures associated with the Gogleskan telepathic faculty and reasons why a loss or a diminution of function takes place. As is already known by the Tarlan, the solitary nature of the Gogleskan life-form precluded the development of sophisticated surgical techniques, and only a very few healers could force themselves to investigate internally a Gogleskan cadaver. The information available is sparse and regret is felt for any disappointment caused. But a debt is owed and it is now encumbent upon the Gogleskan to answer rather than ask questions."

"There is gratitude," Lioren said.

Khone's fur twitched, rose and stood out in long, uneven tufts all over its body—a clear indication of the mental effort required to discuss personal matters. But the reaction, Lioren discovered quickly, was also intended as a demonstration.

"Contact telepathy is used only on two occasions," Khone said, "in response to a tribal Call for Joining when a real but more often an imaginary danger threatens, or for the purpose of reproduction. As has already been explained, the emotional trigger of the signal is highly sensitive. A minor injury, a sudden surprise or change in normal conditions, or an unexpected meeting with a stranger can cause it to operate unintentionally, whereupon a group forms by intertwining the body fur and telepathic tendrils. This fear-maddened group entity reacts to the real or imagined threat by destroying everything that is not a Gogleskan in the immediate vicinity as well as causing self-inflicted injuries to individual members. At such times the mental state makes it impossible to be objective or qualitative about the functioning or malfunctioning of the telepathic faculty, since the ability to make clinical observations, or even to think coherently, is submerged in the panic reaction.

"Doubtless the Tarlan will know from experience that a similar but much more pleasant emotional upheaval occurs between partners during the process of sexual conjugation. But here the Gogleskan telepathic linkage insures that the sensations of both are shared, and doubled. Small variations or diminution of sensation, if present, would be difficult to detect or remember afterward."

"The Tarlan is without experience in this area," Lioren said. "Healers on Tarla expecting advancement to high positions in the profession are required to forgo such emotional distractions."

"There is deep sympathy," Khone said. It paused for a moment, then went on, "But an attempt will be made to describe in detail the physical preliminaries and telepathically reinforced emotional responses associated with the Gogleskan sex act—"

It broke off because another person had entered the room. It was a DBDG female wearing the insignia of a Charge Nurse and pushing a food-dispenser float before it.

"Apologies are tendered for this interruption," the nurse said, "which has been delayed for as long as possible in the expectation that this discussion would soon be concluded. But the patient's principal meal is long overdue and harsh words will be directed toward the medical entity charged with its care should a convalescent patient be allowed to starve to death. If hunger is also felt by the visitor and it wishes to remain with the patient, food can be provided that is metabolically acceptable, although perhaps not entirely palatable, to the Tarlan lifeform."

"Kindness is shown," Lioren said, realizing for the first time how long Khone and himself had been talking and how hungry he was, "and gratitude is felt."

"Then please defer further discussion until the food has been served," the Charge Nurse said, making the soft, barking sound that its species called laughter, "and spare my maidenly, Earth-human blushes."

As soon as the Charge Nurse left them, Khone reminded him that it had more than one mouth and was therefore capable of eating and answering questions at the same time. By then Lioren had reconsidered and decided that the Gogleskan's information, interesting though it might be in itself, would not enlarge his knowledge of possible dysfunction in the organic transmitter-receiver mechanism of Groalterri telepathy. Apologetically and impersonally, he told the other that the information was no longer required.

"Great relief is felt," Khone said, "and offense is not taken. But a debt remains. Are there other questions whose answers might be helpful?"

Lioren stared at Khone for a long time, contrasting the tiny, upright, ovoid body of an adult Gogleskan with that of Small Hellishomar the Cutter, who completely filled a ward large enough to accommodate an ambulance ship, and tried to frame another polite refusal. But suddenly he felt so angry and disappointed and helpless that it required a great effort to make the proper, impersonal words come.

"There are no more questions," he said.

"There should always be more questions," Khone said. The spikes of fur drooped and the body slumped onto its apron of muscle so that Lioren could almost feel its disappointment. "Is it that the ignorant Gogleskan lacks the intelligence to answer them, and now the Tarlan wishes to leave without further waste of time?"

"No," Lioren said firmly. "Do not confuse intelligence with education. The Tarlan requires specialist information that the Gogleskan has had no chance to learn, so it is not intelligence that is lacking. To the contrary. Has the healer more questions?"

"No," Khone said promptly. "The healer has an observation to make, but hesitates lest it give offense."

"Offense will not be taken," Lioren said.

Khone rose to its full height again. "The Tarlan has demonstrated, as have many entities before it, that a suffering shared is a suffering diminished, but in this case it appears that the sharing is not equal. The Cromsag Incident, which makes the problem with the Dark Devil of Goglesk seem insignificant by comparison, has been described in detail, but its full effect upon the entity responsible for it has not. Much has been said about the beliefs and Gods, or perhaps the one God, of others, but nothing about its own God. Perhaps the God of Tarla is special, or different, and does not possess the qualities of understanding and justice with compassion where the most important parts of its creation are concerned. Does it expect its creatures to do no wrong at all, even by accident? The excuse given for the Tarlan's silence, that it does not wish to influence unfairly the beliefs of another with its more extensive knowledge, is laudable. But the excuse is weak indeed, for even an ignorant Gogleskan knows that a belief, even one that is often weakened by self-doubt, is not susceptible to change by logical argument. And yet the Tarlan speaks freely about the beliefs of others while remaining silent about its own.

"It is assumed," Khone went on before Lioren could reply, "that the Tarlan is deeply troubled by guilt over the Cromsaggar deaths, a guilt that is increased because the punishment it considers due for this monstrous crime has been unjustly withheld. Perhaps it seeks both punishment and forgiveness and believes that both are being withheld."

It was obvious that Khone was trying to find a way of helping him, but so far its lengthy observation had been neither offensive nor helpful, for the good reason that Lioren was beyond help.

"If the Creator of All Things is unforgiving," Khone went on, "or if the Tarlan does not believe in the existence of this Creator, there can be no forgiveness there. Or if that small part of God, or if there is disbelief and a nonreligious word is preferred, the good that struggles constantly with the evil in all intelligent creatures, then the Tarlan will not be able to forgive itself. The Cromsag Incident cannot be wholly forgotten or its psychological scars entirely healed, but the wrong must be forgiven if the Tarlan's distress is to be relieved.

"It is the Gogleskan's advice and strong recommendation," Khone ended, "that the Tarlan should seek forgiveness from others."

Not only was Khone's observation lengthy and inoffensive, it was a complete waste of time. Lioren had difficulty controlling his impatience as he said, "From other, less morally demanding Gods? From whom, specifically?"

"Is it not obvious?" Khone said in a tone no less impatient than his own. "From the beings who have been so grievously wronged—from the surviving Cromsaggar."

For a moment Lioren was so deeply shocked and insulted by the suggestion that he could not speak. He had to remind himself that an insult required knowledge of the target to give it force, and this one was based on complete ignorance.

"Impossible," he said. "Tarlans do not apologize. It is utterly demeaning, the act of a misbehaving young child trying to reduce or turn away the displeasure of a parent. The small wrongs of children can be forgiven by the wronged, but Tarlans, adult Tarlans, fully accept the responsibility and the punishment for any crime they have committed, and would never shame themselves or the person they have wronged with an apology. Besides, the patients in the Cromsaggar ward are cured and under observation rather than treatment. They would probably become demented with hate and terminate my life on sight."

"Was not that the fate which the Tarlan desired?" Khone asked. "Has there been a change of mind?"

"No," Lioren replied. "Accidental termination would resolve all problems. But to, to *apologize* is unthinkable!"

Khone was silent for a moment; then it said, "The Gogleskan is expected to break its evolutionary conditioning and to think and behave in new ways. Perhaps in its ignorance it considers that the effort needed to best the Dark Devil in its mind is small compared with that required to apologize to another thinking entity for a well-intentioned mistake."

You are trying to compare subjective devils, Lioren thought. Suddenly his mind was filled with the sight and sound and touch of Cromsaggar warring or mating or dying amid the filthy ruins of a culture they themselves had destroyed. He saw them lying helpless in the aseptic beds of the medical stations and in tumbled, lifeless heaps after the orgy of self-destruction that had come about as the result of his premature cure. Remembrance of the sight and strength and close touch of them came rushing into his mind like a bursting wave of sensation that included the feeling of a wardful of them tearing him apart as they tried to exact vengeance for the death of their race. He felt a strange satisfaction and peace in the knowledge that his life would soon be over and his terrible guilt discharged. And then came the images of probability, of the nurses on duty, heavy-gravity Tralthans or Hudlars, restraining them and rescuing him before lethal damage could be inflicted; and he imagined the long, lonely convalescence with nothing to occupy his mind but the dreadful, inescapable memories of what he had done to the Cromsaggar.

Khone's suggestion was ridiculous. It was not the behavior expected of an honorable Tarlan of a society in which few indeed lacked honor. To admit to a mistake that was already obvious to all was unnecessary. To apologize for that mistake in the hope of reducing the punishment due was shameful and cowardly and the mark of a morally damaged mind. And to lay bare the inner thoughts and emotions before others was unthinkable. It was not the Tarlan way.

Neither, as Khone had just reminded him, was it the Gogleskan way to fight the Dark Devil in their minds; or to make physical contact other than for the purposes of reproduction or comforting the young, or to address another entity who was not a mate, parent, or offspring in anything but the briefest and most impersonal terms, but Khone was trying to do all those things.

Khone was changing its ways, gradually, as were the Protectors of the Unborn. The changes both species had to make were extraordinarily difficult for them and called for a mighty and continuing effort of will, but they were not in themselves cowardly and morally reprehensible acts, as was the one that Khone had suggested that Lioren commit. And suddenly he was thinking about Hellishomar, whose condition was the reason for his present investigation into other-species telepathy as well as the cause of his present mental turmoil.

The young Groalterri, too, was struggling with itself. Against all its natural instincts, its training as a Cutter and the teachings of its near-immortal Parents, it had changed and forced itself to do something reprehensible indeed.

Hellishomar had tried to kill itself.

"I need help," Lioren said.

"The need for help," Khone said, "is an admission of personal in-adequacy. In an entity with pride and authority it might be considered the first step toward an apology. Regrettably, I am unable to give it. Do you know where or from whom this help is available?"

"I know who to ask," Lioren replied, then stopped as the realization came to him that during the last exchange Khone and he had omitted the Gogleskan impersonal manner of address, and that they had spoken to each other as would close members of a family. He did not know what this signified and did not want to risk asking for clarification be-cause Khone had misunderstood him.

From the other's words it was clear that Khone had assumed that the help he wanted was with his own Cromsaggar problem, whereas the truth was that he badly needed specialist assistance with Hellishomar's case. Initially the person he must ask for it was O'Mara, then Conway, Thornnastor, Seldal, and whoever else was qualified to give it. He ad-mitted to himself that he was not qualified, and that interviewing tele-pathic life-forms in an attempt to solve the problem by himself had been a sop to his vanity as well as being an inexcusable waste of time.

Asking help from others, which would of necessity reveal the lack of knowledge and ability within himself, was not the Tarlan way. But he had been receiving help from many entities in the hospital, often without asking for it, and he did not expect that repeating the shameful process would cause any severe emotional trauma.

As he was leaving Khone's ward a few minutes later, Lioren wondered if his own habits of thought were beginning to change.

Very slightly, of course.

CHAPTER 22

Senior Physician Seldal was present because Hellishomar had been its responsibility from the beginning and it had more clinical experience with the patient than any of the others, although that situation was expected to change very soon. The Tralthan Diagnostician-in-Charge of Pathology, Thornnastor, and the equally eminent Earth-human Conway, who had been recently appointed Diagnostician-in-Charge of Surgery, were there to discover why Chief Psychologist O'Mara, who was the only entity with sufficient authority to call such a high-level meeting at short notice, had thought it necessary to bring them together to discuss a patient who was supposedly well on the way to a full recovery.

It reminded Lioren of his recent court-martial, and even though the arguments would be clinical rather than legal, he thought that when it came the cross-examination would be much less polite. Seldal spoke first.

Indicating the big clinical viewscreen, it said, "As you can see, the Groalterri patient presented with a very large number, close on three hundred, punctured wounds that were equally divided over the dorsal and lateral areas and in the anterior region between the tentacles, where the tegument is thin and affords minimum natural protection. The punctures were apparently caused by a fast-flying and burrowing insect species which laid eggs and introduced infection to the wound sites. The

Nallajim operational procedure was judged to be best suited to the treatment of the condition, and I was assigned. Because of the patient's unusually large body mass, progress has been slow, but the prognosis is good except for an unfortunate lack of—"

"Doctor Seldal," Thornnastor broke in, its voice sounding like an impatient, modulated foghorn. "Surely you asked the patient how its wounds were sustained?"

"The patient did not give this information," Seldal said, the rapid, background twittering of its natural voice reflecting its irritation at the interruption. "I had been about to say that it rarely spoke to me, and never about itself or its condition."

"The distribution of the punctures," Diagnostician Conway said, speaking for the first time, "is too localized to suggest a random attack by an insect swarm. To my mind, the angles of penetration and the concentration on one clearly defined area indicates a common point of origin, as in an explosion, although I suppose it is possible that Hellishomar disturbed a hive and the insects attacked the parts of its body that were closest to them. From what little we know of the Groalterri species, they have refused to speak to everyone, so the reticence of the patient may be irritating but not unusual. In the past we have all treated our share of uncooperative patients."

"Hellishomar was cooperative during treatment," Seldal said, "and when it spoke it did so with politeness and respect, but without saying anything about itself. I suspected that the clinical picture might have psychological implications, and I asked Surgeon-Captain Lioren to speak to the patient in the hope that—"

"Surely this is a matter for the Chief Psychologist," Thornnastor said impatiently. "What are a couple of busy Diagnosticians doing here?"

"I," O'Mara said in a quiet voice, "was not consulted."

Thornnastor's four eyes and Conway's two stared at O'Mara for a moment; then all six were directed at Lioren. It was probably fortunate that he could not read Tralthan or Earth-human expressions.

"In the hope," Seldal went on, "that Lioren would have a similar degree of success in making a reticent patient talk as it had achieved with another of my patients, the former-Diagnostician Mannen. At the time I was not sure whether the matter was important enough to ask for the help of the Chief Psychologist. Now Lioren believes that it is, and, after consultation with the Surgeon-Captain, I am in total agreement."

Seldal settled back into its perch, and Lioren placed two of his medial limbs on the table and tried to order his thoughts.

Thornnastor's six elephantine feet thumped restively against the floor in a manner which could have indicated impatience or curiosity. Conway made an untranslatable sound and said, "Surgeon-Captain, for the nonmedical improvement you have brought about in Doctor Mannen, who was my tutor and is my friend, I am most grateful. But how can we help you with what appears to be a psychiatric problem?"

"Before I begin," Lioren said, "I would prefer that you do not use my former title. You know that I am forbidden and have forsworn the practice of medicine, and the reason for it. However, I cannot change the way my mind works, and my past training leads me to the conclusion that Hellishomar's problem is not entirely psychiatric. But first I must discuss briefly the patient's evolutionary and philosophical background."

Thornnastor's feet remained at rest and there were no other interruptions while Lioren described the strangely divided cultures of the telepathic Parents and the more technologically oriented Small, and how strongly the latter were affected by the teachings of the former and by the uncertainties of approaching maturity. He told them how O'Mara had explained that the division was due to an uncompleted stage of their evolution, that the Small were subintelligent by Groalterri standards until they reached maturity, although the concern of the Parents for their Small was very strong. The intelligent macrospecies inhabiting Groalter were so physically massive and extremely long-lived that their numbers had to be strictly controlled if their planet and their race was not to become extinct. Orbital observations had shown that the total Groalterri population of both Parents and Small numbered less than three thousand, so that the birthing of a Small was an extremely rare event and the parental regard for the newborn proportionately large.

Lioren was careful to speak in the most general terms, and he was particularly careful to give only information that Hellishomar had given him permission to pass on, or material that he had been able to deduce for himself.

"Doubtless you will discover for yourselves that the information I am about to give you regarding the patient is incomplete," Lioren went on. "This is a deliberate omission on my part, and I have told the Chief Psychologist O'Mara why he and yourselves must be kept in partial ignorance—"

"You told O'Mara that," Conway broke in, showing its teeth, "and you are still alive?"

"Because Hellishomar is the first and only source of data on the Groalterri culture," Lioren continued, deciding that it was not a serious question. "This information is of great value to the Federation and the hospital, but I have been told that a small proportion of it is not for general distribution. Were I to break confidence with the patient there is a risk, virtually a certainty, that the source of this valuable knowledge would dry up. My observations of the patient's behavior and clinical condition, however, are as complete and accurate as I can make them."

Lioren paused briefly so as to select words that would combine maximum information with complete confidentiality. "Patient Hellishomar came here at the unconscious direction, or suggestion or whatever means was used on the captain of the orbiting vessel, of the Parents because they hoped that it could be treated. They themselves are physically and temperamentally incapable of inflicting pain or injury on another intelligent life-form, and the treatment was not available on Groalter because the surgical procedures of the Small, while precise enough, are too crude for the fine work of removing large numbers of deeply embedded insects. Senior Physician Seldal has been performing this work as only it can, but with the minimum of verbal contact with the patient. I had nothing but verbal contact with Hellishomar and had many opportunities to observe its behavior while we were speaking.

These observations led me to the conclusion, a conclusion with which Seldal and O'Mara now agree, that the infected insect punctures were not the only reason for Hellishomar being sent here."

They were all watching him and so still were they that the whole office with its living contents might have been a holograph.

"From our conversations together," Lioren went on, "it has become obvious that Hellishomar has grown much too old and large to live and practice as a Cutter among the Small, and that by now it should be undergoing the psychological as well as the physical changes that precede full maturity. But the Parents have not touched minds with it, as is customary at this time, or if they have tried to do so it has not been aware of it because the patient is telepathically deaf, and the possibility exists that Hellishomar is mentally retarded."

There was a short silence that was broken by Thornnastor. "Judging by the evidence you have given us so far, Surgeon-Captain, I would say it is a strong probability."

"Please do not use my former title," Lioren said.

The Earth-human, Conway, made a dismissive gesture with one hand. "You still retain the manner of a Surgeon-Captain if not the rank, so the mistake is excusable. But if you are convinced that Hellishomar is mentally defective, that is not the concern of Pathology or Surgery, so what are Thornnastor and myself doing here?"

"I am not fully convinced," Lioren replied, "that the condition is due to a congenital defect. Rather, I favor the theory that there might be a structural abnormality which has temporarily affected the proper development of the patient's telepathic faculty without, however, impairing the other brain functions. This theory is based on behavioral observations by myself as well as those reported by Seldal, and on conversations with the patient which I will not repeat in detail."

O'Mara made an untranslatable sound but did not speak. Lioren ignored the interruption and went on. "Hellishomar is a Cutter, the Groalterri equivalent of a surgeon, and, although the gross differences in its body mass and ours mean that its work seems crude by our standards, it has displayed to me and to the ward's vision recorders a high degree of muscular coordination and precision of control. There was no evidence of the uncoordinated movements or the mental confusion normally expected of a damaged or otherwise abnormal brain. Even though it is only an immature member of a species whose adult minds are immeasurably more advanced than our own, in conversation it displays a mind that is flexible, lucid in its thinking, and well able to debate the finer points of philosophy, theology, and ethics that have arisen between us. This is not, I submit, the physical behavior or the quality of thinking expected of a congenitally defective brain. I believe that the deficiency lies only with the telepathic faculty and that there is a high probability that the abnormality causing it is localized and may be operable."

The Chief Psychologist's office became a still picture once again. "Go on," Conway said.

"For the first time," Lioren resumed, "the Groalterri have contacted the Federation so that we at Sector General might cure one of their ailing Small. Perhaps they are hoping that Hellishomar's cure will be complete. We should do our best not to disappoint them."

"We should do our best," Conway said, "not to kill the patient. Do you realize what you are asking?"

Thornnastor answered the question before Lioren could reply. "It will require the investigation of a living and conscious brain about which we know nothing, because there are no Small cadavers available for prior investigation. We will be looking for structural abnormalities when we do not even know what is normal. Microbiopsies and sensor implants will not give data of the precision required for a cerebral procedure. Our deep scanners cannot be used because the level of radiation needed to penetrate a cranial structure of that size would almost certainly interfere with the locomotor muscle networks, and we cannot risk a patient of Hellishomar's mass making involuntary muscle movements during an op. To a greater or lesser degree, depending on the findings of the nonsurgical investigation, we will be trusting to luck and instinct. Has the patient been informed of the risks?"

"Not yet," Lioren replied. "As the result of a recent conversation with the patient there was an emotional upset of some kind. Hellishomar broke off verbal contact and physically evicted me from the ward, but I am hoping to resume communication soon. I will inform it of the situation and try to obtain its permission and cooperation during the operation."

"Thankfully," Conway said, showing its teeth again, "that is your problem." It turned toward O'Mara. "Chief Psychologist, in matters pertaining to Patient Hellishomar and until further notice I want Trainee Lioren placed under my authority. I shall take overall surgical responsibility for this one, and move it to the top of my operating schedule. Thornnastor, Seldal, and Lioren will assist. And now, if there is nothing further to detain us—"

"With respect, Diagnostician Conway," Lioren said urgently, "I am forbidden to practice—"

"So you have said," Conway broke in as it rose to its feet. "You will not be required to cut, simply to observe and advise and give nonsurgical support to the patient. You are the only one among us who may have sufficient knowledge of the patient's mind and thought processes— and it is Hellishomar's mind that we will be tinkering with—to keep it from ending up a worse mental cripple than you say it already is.

"You *will* assist."

Lioren was still trying to think of a reply when the office had emptied except for O'Mara and himself. The Chief Psychologist had risen to its feet, which was a clear nonverbal signal that Lioren should also leave. He remained where he was.

Hesitantly, he said, "If I had sought personal interviews with Diagnosticians Conway and Thornnastor individually, the result would have been the same, but much time would have been wasted because they are busy entities and appointments with them are difficult to obtain for a trainee. I am grateful for your help in expediting this matter, especially as you and they could not be given full information about the patient. You remained silent so as not to embarrass me by calling attention to my deliberate omission.

"But it is a new and more serious problem," Lioren went on, "which was my prime reason for asking for your help. Again I may only discuss it in general terms—"

The Chief Psychologist seemed to be in respiratory distress for a moment, but it recovered quickly and held up one hand for silence.

"Lioren," O'Mara asked in a very quiet voice, "do you think we are all mentally defective?"

CHAPTER 23

Lioren knew that an answer was not expected because the questioner was about to provide its own.

"Thornnastor and Conway and Seldal are not stupid," O'Mara continued. "My latest records show that their three minds are currently in possession of a total of seventeen Educator tapes, and the donor entities who made those recordings were not stupid, and I, making due allowance for the subjective nature of the assessment, would place my own level of intelligence as well above average."

Lioren was about to agree, but O'Mara gestured for silence.

"Seldal's description of the clinical picture," the Chief Psychologist went on, "together with the knowledge you have already obtained regarding the Groalterri society as a whole, and your new information that the patient is by its race's standards a mental defective, indicates a very high probability that Hellishomar's injuries were the result of a failed suicide attempt. Thornnastor, Conway, Seldal, and myself know this, but we would certainly not embarrass the patient or risk worsening its emotional distress by telling it that we knew or by making the knowledge public. If the circumstances are as you describe, the patient had every reason to destroy itself.

"But now," O'Mara said, raising its voice slightly as if to emphasize the point, "we have to give it an even stronger reason to live whether or not the cranial surgery is successful. You and, if the situation was normal and you were not such a pig-headed, self-righteous trainee, I as your superior should be trying to discover such a reason. You are the sole channel of communication to the patient, and it is better that no other person, myself included, tries to usurp that position. But must I remind you that I am the Chief Psychologist of this weird and wonderful establishment, that I have much experience in prying into the minds of its even weirder staff, and that it is my right and your duty to keep me fully informed so that you can make full use of my experience while talking to this Groalterri. I shall be disappointed and seriously irritated with you if you pretend that the patient did not attempt suicide.

"And now," he ended, "what exactly is this new and more serious problem with Hellishomar?"

For a moment Lioren sat in the quiet desperation of hope, afraid to answer the question in case there was no hope—or worse, that he would have to find the answer for himself. The Chief Psychologist's face had grown pink with irritation at the delay when he spoke.

"The problem," Lioren said, "is with me. I have to make a difficult decision."

O'Mara sat back into its chair, features no longer discolored. "Go on. Is it difficult for you because it may involve breaking the patient's confidence?"

"No!" Lioren said sharply. "I told you this is my problem. Maybe I should not ask your advice and risk making it yours."

The Chief Psychologist showed no sign of irritation at Lioren's insubordinate tone as it said, "And maybe I should not allow you any further contact with Hellishomar, once we have its permission for the operation. Placing together two beings who are so guilt-ridden that both would like nothing better than to end their own lives is a greater risk, to my mind, because the chances are even that the results could be beneficial or disastrous. So far you have managed to avoid a disaster. Please begin by telling me why you think that it is not my problem, and allow me to assess the risks."

"But that would require a long explanation of the problem itself,"

Lioren protested. "I would also have to include background information, much of which is speculative and probably inaccurate."

O'Mara raised one hand from the desk and allowed it to fall again. "Take your time," it said.

Lioren began by describing again the strange, age-segregated Groalterri culture, but he did not take much time because in the beginning he was repeating information that was already known, and O'Mara was not an Earth-human noted for its patience. He said that by virtue of their great size and unguessable abilities, the Parents controlled their population nondestructively and maintained their planet, its nonintelligent animal and vegetable and mineral resources in optimum condition, because they were an extremely long-lived species and this was the only world that they would ever have. On Groalter all life was of value and intelligent life was precious indeed. The control mechanisms, the laws that were to govern every day of a Groalterri's incredibly long life, were taught by the Parents to the pre-adults, who passed them on to the younger Small down to the age when they first began to think and speak. These laws, which governed all future behavior on Groalter, were not physically enforced because the evidence pointed to this being a philosophically advanced and nonviolent race. The Small were taught, verbally when they were very young and telepathically as they approached adulthood, so thoroughly that the process more closely resembled deep conditioning. The guilt felt by a lawbreaker, and the punishment that it inflicted on itself, was of a degree of severity possible only to the recipient of the strictest and most comprehensive form of religious indoctrination.

"Which is a theory supported by the fact," Lioren continued, "that Hellishomar has made several references to committing not a serious crime or an offense but a grievous sin. To the Groalterri the most grievous of all sins is the deliberate and premature destruction of a life. It matters not whether the sin is of commission or omission, or if the life concerned was close to its beginning or near its end. And if the Small and their Parents are deeply religious, that faced me with other questions.

"What kind of god would a life-form that is well-nigh immortal believe in? And what is their hope or expectation of an afterlife?"

"My own hope," O'Mara said, lowering the lines of fur above its eyes, "is that you will eventually get to the point. This could become an interesting religious debate if I could allow myself the time for it, but so far I do not see a problem where you are concerned."

"But there is a problem," Lioren said, "and their religious beliefs are very much involved. And so, to my shame, am I."

"Explain," O'Mara said, "and try to take less time about it."

"In all of the religions that I have recently been studying, I found that their adherents have many beliefs in common. Apart from a few who are fractionally more long- or short-lived than us, all enjoy what we consider to be an average life span..."

In precivilized times, when many religions were originating and beginning to shape the thinking of their adherents toward a respect for the person and property of others that formed the basis of civilized behavior, the hopes and needs of these people were simple. Apart from a few individuals who had seized power, the lives of these beings were unhappy, filled with unremitting toil, plagued by hunger and disease, or under the constant threat of violent and premature death, and their life expectancy was far below the present average.

It was natural that they should hope and dream and finally believe in teachings which gave the promise of another life, a Heaven, in which they would not toil or hunger or feel pain or suffer separation from their friends, and where they would live forever.

"In contrast," Lioren went on, "the Groalterri already possess virtual immortality, so their lives are already long enough for a further physical extension not to be high on their list of priorities. Because of their vast size and lack of mobility, they telepathically control or otherwise cause their food supply to come to them, so they do not have to toil. They are too large to suffer injury, and disease and pain are unknown among them until they are approaching termination, when they call on the Small Cutters to help them further extend their lives before what Hellishomar calls the Escape or the Time of Going Out.

"At first, I assumed this to be the case of a long-lived entity wanting to live even longer in spite of the increasing pain suffered during the terminal decades, but this would be the type of behavior expected of small-minded, selfish entities, which the Parents were not. It came to me that their terminal years, which the Small are sworn to extend for as long as possible, are needed so that they would have the maximum time possible in which to prepare their minds and make themselves worthy of what they expect to find in the afterlife.

"To the tremendous minds and gigantic bodies of the Groalterri," Lioren said, "it may be that Heaven is the place and condition where they can seek and ultimately discover the secrets of all creation, and while doing so, the condition they most desire is mobility. They need it so that they can escape from the great, organic prisons that are their bodies, and from their planet, and Go Out. Perhaps they long to travel freely through a universe that is infinitely large and provides their great minds with an intellectual challenge that is also infinite."

O'Mara raised one hand from the desk, but the interruption seemed to be polite rather than impatient. It said, "An ingenious theory, Lioren, and, I think, very close to the truth. But I still do not see where you have a problem."

"The problem," Lioren said, "lies in the intention of the Parents in sending Hellishomar to us, and my subsequent behavior toward the patient. Did they influence us into bringing it to Sector General in the hope that we might effect a complete cure for their Small Cutter, as would any parents deeply concerned for the welfare of one of their young? Or do they believe that we might not be able to treat the infected wounds that were then threatening its life, much less recognize the patient as a mental defective? Are they hoping that the treatment it receives here, and the people it meets during that treatment, will give a mind that is incapable of further intellectual and spiritual progression an experience that it will find strange and stimulating and enjoyable before it passes into the substandard Heaven or Limbo that is reserved for the few mentally flawed Groalterri?

"Hellishomar is telepathically deaf and dumb," Lioren continued, "so the Parents cannot tell it what their intentions are, or that they have forgiven it for the sin it tried to commit, or that they feel compassion for its distress and are simply doing their best to relieve the suffering of a mental cripple by giving it the memories of what, to a living Groalterri, is a unique experience of leaving its planet. But I believe that the patient is more intelligent, and much stricter in its religious self-discipline, than the Parents realize.

"Hellishomar is trying to refuse their gift.

"When it was brought here," he went on quickly, "Hellishomar offered no resistance and obeyed only the simple requests of Seldal and the nurses during initial examination and treatment. It would not ask or answer questions about itself, and for long periods it kept its eyes closed. Only when I told the patient about myself and it discovered that I, too, had committed a grievous sin and was still suffering from guilt and distress over it, did Hellishomar begin to talk freely about itself. Even then it made me promise not to pass on certain personal information, and it showed great agitation when I tried to talk about the member species and planets of the Federation. When I offered to show supporting visual material it became very agitated and distressed.

"I insist," Lioren said, "or rather I suggest most strongly that its contacts with other species be kept to a minimum, and that information on all subjects other than its forthcoming treatment be withheld, if necessary by switching off the translator and covering its eyes if life-forms new to its present experience are operating—"

"Why?" O'Mara asked sharply.

"Because Hellishomar is a sinner," Lioren replied, "and believes itself unworthy of being given even this tiny glimpse of Heaven. To the highly intelligent and questing minds trapped within the physically massive Groalterri body, Going Out, escaping at death from the imprisonment of their planet, is Heaven. Sector General and all the varied life-forms it contains is a part of that much deserved afterlife."

O'Mara showed its teeth. "This place has been called many things, but never Heaven. I can see that Hellishomar faces a theological problem which we must try to help it resolve, but I still cannot see that you have a problem. What exactly is troubling you?"

"Uncertainty, and fear," Lioren replied. "I don't know what the Parents' intentions were when they touched the mind of the orbiting ship's captain. That touching must have revealed much about the Federation, but they seem to have ignored the religious implications because they caused Hellishomar to be brought here. Perhaps their adult theology is more sophisticated and liberal than the form they have to teach to the less able minds of the Small, or they simply did not realize what they were doing. Maybe, as I have already said, they believed that Hellishomar was about to die of its self-inflicted injuries and they wanted to give it this small experience of Heaven because they were unsure of the fate of a mental cripple in their afterlife and they are a compassionate race. Or perhaps they are expecting us to cure the patient of all its defects and return Hellishomar to take its place among the Parents. But what will happen if we cure only its physical injuries?

"It is the answer to that question which frightens me," Lioren ended, "and that is the problem that so terrifies me that I am afraid to solve it without help."

"Terrifies you, how?" O'Mara asked, in the quiet, absentminded manner of a questioner who is already working out the answer for itself.

"There are precedents on many worlds," Lioren replied, "for prophets and teachers coming out of the wilderness to spread beliefs which attack the old order. On Groalter there is no violence, and no way of silencing a religious heretic who is deaf to the words of its elders. The mental cripple, Hellishomar, might be so filled with its new knowledge that it could not subject itself to the voluntary seclusion expected of it. Instead it might bring to the immature minds of the younger Small the knowledge that Heaven contains great machines for traveling between the stars, as well as other technological wonders, and that it is peopled with a great variety of short-lived creatures who are in many cases less intelligent and certainly less moral in their behavior than the Groalterri. As a result the Small might try using their limited technology and plan-

etary resources to build machines so that a few of them could Go Out
before reaching Parenthood, much less waiting until the end of their
lives, and the many who could not go would cause disaffection and
destabilization among the Small. Worse, they might take Hellishomar's
teachings with them into adulthood, and the delicate physical and philosophical balance that has maintained the Groalterri planet and culture
for many thousands of years would be destroyed.

"I have already destroyed the Cromsaggar," Lioren ended miserably,
"and I fear that I am bringing about an even greater philosophical destruction in the minds of the most advanced culture to be discovered
since the Federation came into being."

O'Mara placed its hands together and looked down at them for a
moment before it spoke. There was a heavy emphasis on the first word
as it said, "We do indeed have a problem, Lioren. The simple answer
would be to lose the patient, allow Hellishomar to terminate here, for
the greater good of its people, naturally. But that is a solution which we
would find ethically unsound, a relic of our presapient past. Our rejection of it would have the agreement of the entire hospital staff, the
Monitor Corps, the Federation, and the Groalterri Parents. We must
therefore do the best that we possibly can do for the patient, in the
hope that the Parents also knew what they were doing when they sent
it to us. Agreed?"

Without waiting for a reply, the Chief Psychologist went on. "The
suggestion that you should be the only contact with the patient is a valid
one. Hellishomar will be isolated from all other visual and verbal contact
during surgery, and I shall certainly not contact it. At least, not directly.

"You have been doing very well," O'Mara continued. "But you lack
my professional experience or, as Cha Thrat insists on describing it, my
knowledge of the subtler spells. You do not know everything, Lioren,
even though you often act as if you do. For example, there are several
well-tried methods of reestablishing communication and friendly relations with an other-species patient who has broken off contact for emotional reasons—"

O'Mara stopped and, with its eyes still directed toward Lioren, one hand moved to the desk communicator. "Braithwaite, reschedule today's appointments for this evening or tomorrow. Be diplomatic; Edanelt, Cresk-Sar, and Nestrommli are Seniors, after all. For the next three hours I am not here.

"And now, Lioren," it went on, "you will listen and I shall talk . . ."

CHAPTER 24

T he modifications to the ward structure necessary for the performance of this operation will be completed within the hour," Diagnostician Conway said, loudly enough to be heard above the din of shouting voices and the metallic clangor of massive equipment being moved into position and given its final operational checks, "and the surgical team is already standing by. But any cranial investigation involving a newly discovered intelligent species, especially of a macro life-form like yourself, must of necessity be exploratory and with a high element of risk. For anatomical and clinical reasons, the sheer body mass combined with our present ignorance regarding the metabolism involved makes any estimate of the quantity of medication required sheer guesswork, so that the procedure will have to be carried out without benefit of anesthetic.

"Such a procedure is completely contrary to normal practice," Conway went on, in a voice which was less than steady, "so that it is the psychological rather than the clinical preparations which Chief Psychologist O'Mara and I must satisfy ourselves are complete."

Hellishomar did not speak. It was probable, thought Lioren, that the Groalterri knew nothing of the tiresome Earth-human habit of asking questions in the form of statements.

Conway looked quickly at the large openings that had been cut in the deck, walls, and ceiling all around them, and at the heavily braced structural supports for the tractor- and pressor-beam installations projecting from them before going on. "It is imperative that you do not move during the procedure, and you have told us several times that you will remain still. But, with respect, that is too much to expect from a fully-conscious patient when the degree of pain being inflicted is unknown, and there is a risk of our instruments stimulating the locomotor network and causing involuntary body movements. Total restraint and immobility will therefore be imposed by use of wide-focus tractor and pressor beams even though we may not, as you have assured us, require them."

Hellishomar remained silent for a moment; then it said, "Surgery under anesthesia is not practiced by Groalterri Cutters, so I would not consider your procedure abnormal or the discomfort associated with the entry wound of major importance. As well, you will remember that Seldal, Lioren, and yourself have assured me that, in the majority of life-forms of your clinical experience, deep cranial surgery can be undertaken without discomfort since the protection afforded by the thickness of the cranium obviates the necessity for pain sensors within the brain itself."

"That is true," Conway said. "But the Groalterri life-form is like no other in the hospital's experience, so it is not a certainty."

"Another and more important reason for the absence of anesthesia," the Diagnostician continued before Hellishomar could reply, "is that we will be forced to call on you from time to time for a report on the subjective effects of our surgery while the operation is in progress. The high intensity of scanner radiation required to penetrate and chart the cranial contents, although harmless in itself, would almost certainly affect the local nerve networks and cause—"

"All this has been explained to me," Hellishomar said suddenly, "by Lioren."

"And it is being explained again by me," Conway said, "because I am performing the operation and must be absolutely sure that the patient is fully aware of the risks. Are you?"

"I am," Hellishomar said.

"Very well," Conway said. "Is there anything else you would like to know about the procedure? Or anything that you would like to do or say, up to and including changing your mind and canceling the operation entirely? This can still be done without any loss of self-respect. In fact I, personally, would consider it to be an intelligent decision."

"I have two requests," Hellishomar said promptly. "Shortly I will be experiencing the first cranial surgery to be performed on a member of my species. As a Cutter as well as the patient I am deeply interested in the procedure and would appreciate a translated description of, and the reasons for, your actions while the operation is in progress. During the operation I might need to talk with the entity Lioren on another channel, but privately. If this conversation becomes necessary, no other entity in the hospital is to overhear our words. That is my second and more important requirement."

Both the Diagnostician and the Chief Psychologist turned to look at Lioren. He had already warned them that Hellishomar would make such a request and that it would not accept a negative answer.

Reassuringly, Conway said, "My intention is to talk through the procedure and record it in sound and vision for staff-training purposes, so there is no reason why you should not overhear the original. We can also arrange for a second communications channel, but you will not be able to operate it yourself because your manipulatory appendages are too massive for the control mechanism. I suggest that both channels be controlled by Lioren, and any private words you have for Lioren be prefixed by its name so that all others can be switched out of the conversation. Would that be satisfactory?"

Hellishomar did not reply.

"We understand that privacy at such times is of great importance to you," O'Mara said suddenly, staring at one of the patient's enormous, closed eyes. "As Chief Psychologist of this establishment I possess the authority of a Parent. I can assure you; Hellishomar, that your second communication channel will be private and secure."

The Chief Psychologist's curiosity regarding the words that had and would pass between Hellishomar and Lioren was personal, professional, and intense. But if there was disappointment in O'Mara's voice, it was lost in translation.

"Then I would like you to proceed with minimum delay," Hellishomar said, "lest I take Diagnostician Conway's good advice and change my mind."

"Doctor Prilicla?" Conway said quietly.

"Friend Hellishomar's emotional radiation fully supports its decision to proceed," the empath said, joining the conversation for the first time. "The feeling of impatience is natural in the circumstances, and the expression of self-doubt may be considered as an oblique verbal pleasantry rather than indecision. The patient is ready."

A great wave of relief, so intense that he could see Prilicla shaking with it as well, burst over Lioren's mind. But the empath's trembling was slow and regular, like the movements of a stately dance, and indicated the presence of emotional radiation that was pleasant rather than painful. Even with O'Mara advising him at every stage, it had taken five days and nearly as many nights of argument, closely reasoned at times but at others purely emotional, to obtain Hellishomar's agreement to the operation. It was only now that he knew they had succeeded.

"Very well," Conway said. "If the team is ready we will go in. Doctor Seldal, I'd be obliged if you would open."

The instruments required for the macroprocedure, the drills and cutters and suction tubes so massive that some of them had to be individually manned, hung in position all around them. The preparations, Lioren had thought, more closely resembled those for a mining operation than a surgical procedure. But the Diagnostician's words were another example of an oblique verbal pleasantry, because the operating team was ready and waiting, and Seldal had already been thoroughly briefed on its part at every stage of the operation.

Politeness was a lubricant, Lioren thought, that reduced friction but wasted time.

Even though Hellishomar was a member of a macrospecies with a head that was large in proportion to its enormous body, the sheer size of the operative field came as a shock to Lioren. The area of the flap of tegument that was excised and drawn back to reveal the underlying bone structure was larger than any of the decorative rugs scattered around his living quarters.

"Doctor Seldal is controlling the subdermal bleeding by clamping off the incised capilliaries," Conway was saying, "which in this patient more closely resemble major blood vessels, while I drill vertically through the cranium to the upper surface of the meningeal layer. The drill is tipped with a vision sensor linked to the main monitor, which will show us when it reaches the surface of the membrane . . . We're there.

"The drill has been withdrawn and replaced by a high-speed saw of identical length," the Diagnostician continued a few minutes later. "This is being used to extend the original bore-hole laterally until a circular opening has been made in the cranium of sufficient diameter so that, when the resulting plug of osseous material is removed, the surgeons will be able to enter the wound and work freely. That's it. The plug is being removed now and will be kept under moderate refrigeration pending its replacement. How is the patient?"

"Friend Hellishomar's emotional radiation," Prilicla said quickly, "suggests feelings of mild discomfort, or more severe discomfort that is under firm control. Feelings of uncertainty and anxiety normal to the situation are also present."

"A reply from me," Hellishomar said, opening the eye nearest to the display screen, "seems unnecessary."

"For the moment, yes," Conway said. "But later I will need the kind of help which only you will be able to give. Try not to worry, Hellishomar, you are doing fine. Seldal, climb aboard."

Lioren wished suddenly that he could find something reassuring to say to the patient, because he, having convinced O'Mara and Conway and finally Hellishomar itself of the necessity for the operation, bore the responsibility for what was to happen here. But he could not excuse breaking into the operating team's conversation without invitation, and the private communication channel was closed to him until or unless

Hellishomar spoke his name, so he remained silent and watchful.

Looking like a pink-flecked, shaven log of a large tree, the bony plug was lifted clear while Seldal, its three spindly legs strapped together so as to minimize bodily projections, was being lifted into Conway's backpack so that only its long, flexible neck, head, and beak were uncovered. A similar pack containing the instruments and inflatable equipment that both surgeons would use was strapped tightly to Conway's chest and abdomen. The Diagnostician's legs were not strapped together, but the sharp contours of its feet were encased in thick padding, and a white, frictionless overgarment was drawn over the limbs and fastened at the shoulders so that only the arms and head were uncovered. A transparent helmet that was free of external projections and large enough to accommodate the necessary lighting and communications equipment was added. Seldal, whose upper body was naturally streamlined, kept its head and beak pressed firmly against the back of Conway's helmet. The Nallajim wore only eye protection and an attachment for the thin air line running into the corner of its mouth.

"Zero gravity in the operative field," Conway said. "Ready, Seldal? We will now enter the wound."

A tractor beam seized their weightless bodies in its immaterial grasp, deftly upended them, and lowered them heads first into the narrow opening. The thick cable loom comprising their air supply, suction and specimen extraction hoses, and the emergency rescue line unreeled like a multicolored tail behind them. Conway's helmet lighting showed the smooth, gray walls of the organic well they had created moving past them, and an enlarged and enhanced image was reproduced on the external display.

"We are at the base of the entry well," Conway said, "level with the internal surface of the cranium, and have encountered what is probably the equivalent of the protective meningeal sheath. The membrane responds to firm hand pressure, in a way which suggests the presence of underlying fluid, and what appears to be the outer surface of the brain itself lies just beyond. A precise estimate of the distance is difficult because either the membrane or the fluid, or perhaps both, are not completely transparent. A small test incision is being made through the membrane. That's strange."

A moment later the Diagnostician went on, "The incision has been extended and opened, but there is still no apparent loss of fluid. Oh, so that's it . . ."

Conway's voice sounded pleased and excited as it went on to explain that, unlike in other species of its experience, the cere-brospinal fluid, which helped protect the brain structure from shocks by acting as a lubricant between the inner cranium and brain, was not in the Groalterri species a fluid. It was instead a transparent, semisolid lubricant with the consistency of a thin jelly. When a small piece of the jelly was cut away for closer examination and then replaced, it immediately rejoined the main body without any trace of the earlier incision. This was fortunate since it enabled them to go through the meninges without having to worry about controlling fluid losses, and they could move laterally with minimal resistance and loss of time between the brain surface and the meningeal layer to the first objective, a deep fissure between two convolutions in the area suspected of housing the Groalterri telepathic faculty.

"Before we proceed," Conway said, "is the patient aware of any unusual physical sensations or psychological effects?"

"No," Hellishomar said.

For a few moments the main screen gave glimpses of Conway's hands and Seldal's beak, brightly lit by the helmet lamp, as they pushed themselves carefully through the clear jelly between the smooth inner meninges and the massively wrinkled outer surface of the cortex and into the narrow crevice.

"As closely as we can estimate," Conway went on, "this fissure extends about twenty yards on each side of our entry point and the average depth is three yards. On the upper brain surface the division between adjoining convolutions is clearly evident, but with depth the walls begin to press together. The pressure is not sufficient to be life-threatening, and the effort required to push the surfaces apart is minimal and does not reduce our mobility, but it would seriously hamper any surgical procedure that may become necessary and quickly cause disabling levels of fatigue. Soon we will have to deploy the rings."

Hellishomar had not spoken directly to Lioren, even on the open channel, so that he had no way of knowing what was going through the patient's mind. But Prilicla's gauzy wings were beating slowly, and the stability of its hovering flight made it plain that there was no source of unpleasant emotional radiation in the area.

"Ease your mind, friend Lioren," the empath said quietly. "At this time your anxiety is greater than friend Hellishomar's."

Greatly reassured, Lioren returned his attention on the main screen.

"This is the lobe where the highest concentration of trace metals occurs," Conway said. "It has been chosen because similar traces have been associated with the telepathic function of the few other species known to possess the faculty, and although the operating mechanism remains unclear, the higher concentration of metal indicates the presence of an organic transmitter-receiver. It is the possible impairment of the patient's higher brain functions, including the telepathic faculty, that we are trying to investigate and correct.

"Regrettably our charting of this area is imprecise," it continued. "This is because the volume and density of the cranial contents would make it necessary to use very high power levels on our deep scanners, which would cause interference with neural activity.

"For this reason the portable, low-powered scanner will be used briefly and only in an emergency.

"The patient's earlier cooperation in making voluntary muscle movements at our direction and submitting to external touch, pressure, and temperature stimuli has enabled us, by observing the local increases in neural activity, to identify those areas and eliminate them from the investigation. This information was obtained by sensor only, a detection system which produces no troublesome radiation, but which lacks the precision of the scanner."

Lioren could not believe that there was anyone in the hospital, either presently on the staff or future trainees, who did not know the difference between a scanner and a sensor, and assumed that the explanation was for the patient's benefit.

"It was expected," Conway went on, "that the brain of a macro life-form would be more open and coarse-structured to correspond with its large body mass. As we can now see, the blood supply network is on the expected large scale, but the neural structure appears to be as highly condensed and finely structured as that of a being of smaller mass. I cannot . . . it is completely beyond my ability to estimate the level of mentation possible to a brain of this size and complexity."

Lioren stared at the enlarged image of Conway's hands as they stretched slowly forward, pushed palms outward to each side, and then moved back out of sight, as if the Diagnostician was swimming endlessly through a fleshy ocean. For a moment he tried to put himself in Hellishomar's place, but the thought of a white, slippery, two-headed insect crawling about in his brain was so repulsive that he had to control a sudden feeling of nausea.

Conway's voice became uneven and its respiration more audible as it went on. "While we cannot be completely certain of what is or is not normal in this situation, it seems that the investigation so far has uncovered no evidence of structural abnormality or dysfunction. Our progress is being gradually impeded by increasing pressure from the fissure walls. At first this was ascribed to increasing fatigue in my arm muscles, but Seldal, who has no arms to tire, notes a similar increase in pressure against the outer surface of its carrying pouch. It is not thought to be a psychosomatic effect caused by claustrophobia.

"Mobility and the field of view are seriously reduced," it added. "We are deploying the rings."

Lioren watched as Conway struggled to pull the first ring over their heads and, with the help of Seldal's incredibly flexible neck and beak, position it at waist level before breaking the compressed-air seal and inflating it around them. Two more rings were inflated at knee and shoulder level and joined into a hollow, rigid cylinder by longitudinal spacers. When the initial triple-ring deployment was complete, they added another ring and spacers to extend the structure forward. By deflating and withdrawing the rearmost ring and attaching it in front, and varying the lengths of the spacers, they were able to move the hollow cylinder and travel within it in any required direction. The open structure provided all-around visibility and ready access to perform surgery.

They were no longer swimmers in a near-solid ocean, Lioren thought, but miners boring through a tunnel that they carried with them.

"We are encountering increasing resistance and pressure from one wall of the fissure," Conway said. "The tissues on that side appear to be both stretched and compressed. You can see there, and over there, where the blood supply has been interrupted. Some of the vessels are distended where the blood has pooled and others deflated and all but empty. This does not appear to be a naturally occurring condition, and the absence of necrosis in the area suggests that the circulation is seriously impeded but so far not completely blocked. The structural adaptation that has taken place also suggests that the condition has been present for a long time.

"Scanning is needed to find its cause and source," Conway went on. "I will use the hand scanner briefly, at minimum penetration, now. How does the patient feel?"

"Fascinated," Hellishomar said.

The Earth-human barked softly. "No emotional or cerebral effects are reported by the patient. I will try again with a little more penetration."

For a few seconds Conway's scanner image appeared on the main screen, then dissolved. The recording was projected onto an adjacent screen and frozen for study.

"The scanner shows the presence of another membrane at a depth of approximately seven inches," the Diagnostician continued. "It is no more than half an inch thick, and has a dense, fibrous structure and a degree of convex curvature which, if continued uniformly, would enclose a spherical body of approximately ten feet in diameter. The underlying tissue structure is still unclear but shows a marked difference o that encountered so far. It may be that this is the site of the lobe esponsible for the telepathic faculty. But there are other possibilities which can only be eliminated by surgical investigation and tissue anal-rsis. Doctor Seldal will make the incision and obtain tissue samples while control the bleeding."

The main screen was filled with a picture of Conway's hands, look-ng enormous and distorted because of the proximity of the helmet's vision pickup, as they fitted a cutter to the Nallajim Senior's beak. Then an index finger moved forward to outline the position and extent of the required incision.

There was a sudden blur of motion as the back of Seldal's head and neck briefly obscured the operative field.

"You can see that the initial incision has not uncovered the membrane," Conway went on, "but the underlying pressure has forced apart the edges of the wound to a degree that, if we don't relieve the situation by extending the incision at once, there is a serious risk of it tearing open at each end. Seldal, would you go a little deeper and extend . . Oh, *damn!*"

It was as Conway had foreseen. The incision had torn apart at each end and weightless globules of blood were drifting out of it and totally obscuring the operative field. Seldal had discarded the cutter because its beak came into view gripping the suction unit, which it moved expertly along and inside the wound so that Conway could find and seal off the bleeders. Within a very few minutes the wound, now with torn, uneven edges and fully three times its original length, was clear and gaping open to reveal at its base a long, narrow ellipse of utter blackness.

"We have uncovered a strong, flexible, and light-absorbent membrane," the Diagnostician resumed, "and two tissue samples have been taken. One is being sent out to you through the suction unit for more detailed study, but my analyzer reading indicates an organic ma-terial that is totally foreign to the surrounding tissues. Its cell structure is more characteristic of a vegetable than an—What the blazes is hap-pening? We can feel the patient moving. It *must* remain absolutely still! We are not supposed to be in an area where accidental stimulation of the motor muscles is possible. Hellishomar, what is wrong?"

The Diagnostician's words were lost in the bedlam of the outer ward, where the tractor and pressor units were emitting audible and visible signals of overload as their operators struggled to keep Hellishomar's heaving body motionless. The Groalterri's enormous head was jerking from side to side against its immaterial restraints, and the ends of the incision were tearing and bleeding again. Prilicla's body was being shaken by an emotional gale, and everyone seemed to be shouting questions, instruction, or warnings at each other.

But it was Hellishomar who succeeded in making itself heard above the din, suddenly and with one word.

"Lioren!"

CHAPTER 25

I am here," Lioren said, switching quickly to the secure channel, but the sounds that the patient was making did not translate.

"Hellishomar, please stop moving," Lioren said urgently. "You could seriously injure, perhaps kill yourself. And others. What is troubling you? Please tell me. Is there pain?"

"No," Hellishomar said.

Telling the patient that it might kill itself would be a waste of time, Lioren thought, because the Groalterri's presence in the hospital was due to it trying to do just that. But the reminder that it was endangering others must have penetrated the frenzy in its mind, because the violence of its struggles was gradually diminishing.

"Please," Lioren asked again. "What is troubling you?"

The reply came slowly at first, as if each and every word had to break through a great, individual wall of fear, shame and self-loathing; then suddenly the words rushed out in a near-incoherent flood that swept away all such barriers. As he listened to Hellishomar pouring out everything that was in its mind, Lioren's confusion changed slowly to anger and then to sadness. This was utterly ridiculous, he told himself. Had he been an Earth-human he might have been barking with laughter by now at this display of ignorance from a member of a species that was the most highly intelligent of any race known to the Federation.

But if Lioren had learned anything since joining O'Mara's department it was that emotional distress was the most subjective of all phenomena, and the most difficult to relieve.

But this was an entity trained in the Groalterri concepts of healing. It was a young and perhaps mentally retarded Cutter whose experience was restricted to peripheral surgery performed on aged members of its own race, and it was viewing an intercranial procedure, on itself, for the first time. In those circumstances ignorance was excusable, he told himself, provided it remained a temporary condition.

"Listen," Lioren said quickly into the first, brief pause in the tirade. "Please listen carefully to what I am saying, ease your mind, and above all, be still. The blackness inside your head is *not* the physical manifestation of your guilt, nor did it grow because of evil thoughts or any sin committed by you. It is likely that it is a bad and a dangerous thing, but it is not your spirit or soul or any part of—"

"It is," Hellishomar broke in. "It is the place where I am. The thinking, feeling, and grievously sinning me who tried to destroy myself lives in that place, and it has a blackness that is beyond hope."

"No," Lioren said firmly. "Every intelligent entity I know of believes that its personality, its soul lives in the brain, usually a short distance behind the visual receptors. They believe this because, even when there has been gross trauma and physical dismemberment, it remains intact. Sometimes there is physical damage or disease that causes the personality to change. But this change does not come about because of an act of will, so the entity concerned cannot be held responsible for subsequent behavior."

Hellishomar remained silent and its body movements had reduced to the point where the overload lights were no longer showing on the tractor-beam installations.

Lioren went on quickly. "It is possible that the inability of your brain to mature to the stage where direct mind-to-mind contact can be achieved with the Parents is due to a genetic defect. But it is also possible that the crimes you blame yourself for committing were the result of a disease or injury to the brain, and the reason for these wrongful thoughts and actions may now have been found. You must know that the black mass that Conway and Seldal have uncovered is not your personality, because you have told me yourself that the soul is immaterial, that when the Parents die and their bodies decay and return their substance to the world, their souls leave Groalterri to begin their never-ending exploration of the universe—"

"While my own soul," Hellishomar said, beginning to struggle against the restraints again, "sinks like a stone into the mud of the ocean floor, to fester in darkness forever."

Lioren felt that he would lose what little control he had gained over the situation if he did not speak quickly, and move the argument from metaphysics to medicine. Focusing one of his eyes on the side screen where the results of Conway's analysis were being displayed, he went on. "It may well rot at the bottom of your ocean if that is where you want it placed, but more likely it will end in a waste-disposal furnace at Sector General. I do not know what it is exactly, but it is not your soul or, for that matter, any other part of you. It is completely foreign material, a vegetable form of life, an invader of some kind. I ask you to be calm and to think, to think as a Groalterri Cutter and healer, and to remember if there was anything in your past experience that resembles this black growth. Please think carefully."

For several moments Hellishomar was silent and absolutely still. The ward was quiet again and he could hear the voice of Conway saying that it was about to resume the operation.

"Please wait, Doctors," Lioren said, switching briefly to the public channel. "I may have important clinical data for you." On the main screen one of the Diagnostician's hands waved acknowledgment, and he returned to the private channel.

"Hellishomar," Lioren said again, "please try to recall anything resembling this black growth, whether the memory is from recent experience, the less certain recollections of infancy, or even the hearsay experiences of others. Can you remember having contact with such a growth, or having suffered an injury, not necessarily to the cranium, which would have allowed it to enter the bloodstream?"

"No," Hellishomar said.

Lioren thought for a moment. "If you do not remember, is it possible that you contracted the disease as a very small infant, before you were capable of forming memories? Can you recall any later reference to something like this happening to you by an older Small charged with your care? This person may not have considered it important at the time, or mentioned it until you were grown and—"

"No, Lioren," Hellishomar broke in. "You are trying to make me believe that this foul thing in my brain is not the result of wrong thinking, and what you are doing is a great kindness. But I have already told you, it is only the very aged Parents who are afflicted with diseases, the Small never. We are strong and healthy and immune. The invisible attackers you have told me about are ignored, and those large enough to be visible are treated as a nuisance and simply brushed away."

Lioren had been hoping that he would discover something useful to Conway and Seldal by questioning the patient, but he was making no progress at all. He was about to signal them to proceed when another thought occurred to him.

"These pests that you brush away," he said. "Please tell me all that you can remember about them."

Hellishomar's replies sounded polite but very impatient, as if it had guessed that the other's only intention was to keep its mind on other things and the answers were unimportant. But gradually its answers became very important indeed and Lioren's questions more precise. Slowly his earlier feeling of hopelessness was changing to one of excitement and mounting anxiety.

"From all that you have told me," Lioren said urgently, "I am convinced that the pest you call a skinsticker is the original cause of your trouble, but I do not want to waste time giving my reasons to you and then again to the operating team. A final question. Will you give me permission to speak of this to the others? Not all that has passed between us, and nothing about your thoughts and fears, only the details of the description and behavior of the skinstickers."

Subjectively it seemed that a very long time elapsed without any response from Hellishomar. Lioren could hear Conway, Seldal, and the support staff in the ward talking together, their words muffled by his earpads but their impatience plain. He tried again.

"Hellishomar," Lioren said, "if my theory is correct, your life may be at risk, and the cerebral damage will certainly render you incapable of future coherent thought. Please, your answer is needed quickly."

"The Cutters inside my skull are also at risk," Hellishomar said. "Tell them."

Without taking time to reply Lioren switched to the public channel and began to speak.

Although he could not be absolutely certain because of the small amount of information that the patient had been able to give him, Lioren said that he felt sure the original cause of the black intercranial growth was due to infestation by a species of parasitic vegetable vermin known to the Groalterri as a skinsticker, which was considered to be a periodic nuisance rather than a threat to life. Nothing was known about the life cycle or reproduction mechanism of the skinsticker because they could be easily removed, brushed away with the manipulatory tentacles or by rubbing the affected area of tegument against a tree, and a life-form with the enormous physical mass and limited dexterity of the Groalterri had neither the desire nor the ability to investigate the habits of a near-microscopic form of plant life.

Skinstickers were black, spherical, and covered with a vegetable adhesive which enabled them to attach themselves to the host's body and extend their single feeder root while they were still too small to be seen. They required only an organic food source and the presence of light and air to grow very quickly to the size when they became a nuisance and were removed. They could be destroyed by crushing between hard surfaces or by burning, and after removal the root, which had a high liquid content, withered quickly and fell out of the wound it had made.

Lioren went on, "My theory is that this case was the result of infestation by a single skinsticker which gained entry via a small abrasion which the patient no longer remembers or through the puncture wound left by the root of an earlier and unsuccessful skinsticker, and was carried through the circulatory system until it lodged in the cranium. Once there it had a virtually limitless food supply but not, apart from the tiny amount of oxygen it was able to absorb from the local blood supply, the light and air its metabolism required for optimum growth. The growth rate was inhibited but it has had a great many years, a young Groalterri's very long lifetime, in which to grow to its present size."

Except for the slow and near-silent beating of Prilicla's wings, the ward might have been a still picture as Lioren finished speaking. It was Conway who reacted first.

"An ingenious theory, Lioren," the Diagnostician said, "and while obtaining this information and discussing it between you, you have succeeded in pacifying our patient. That was well done. But whether or not your theory is correct, and I believe that it is, our procedure must continue as originally planned."

Imperceptibly Conway's manner changed from one of person-to-person conversation to that of lecturer-student instruction as it went on. "This foreign tissue, tentatively identified as a massively overgrown Groalter skinsticker, will be excised in very small pieces whose size will be dictated by the maximum orifice setting of our suction unit. Many hours of patient, careful work will be required to accomplish this, particularly in the later stages if there are adhesions to healthy brain tissue, and rest periods or relays of surgeons may be necessary. However, since the patient has shown no impairment or deterioration in mentation since its arrival here, and the growth has been present for a very long time, its removal may be considered necessary but non-urgent. We will be able to take all the time we need to insure that—"

"No," Lioren said harshly.

"No?" Conway sounded too surprised to be angry, but Lioren knew that the anger would not be long in coming. "Why not, dammit?"

"With respect," Lioren said, "the screen shows that your original incision is widening and extending in length. Let me remind you that the skinsticker grows rapidly in the presence of light and air and, after a great many years in the airless dark, light and air are again present."

For a few moments Conway directed angry and self-abusive words at itself, then suddenly the main screen turned black as it switched off its helmet lighting and said, "This will slow the rate of growth a little. I need time to think . . ."

"You need more surgical assistance," Thornnastor said. "I will—"

"No!" Seldal broke in. "Another set of enormous, awkward feet in here is what we don't need! There isn't enough space as it is to—"

"My feet aren't that big—" Conway began.

"Not yours," said Seldal. "I'm sorry, for a moment I was thinking of—"

"Doctors!" Thornnastor said, speaking suddenly with the voice and authority of the hospital's senior Diagnostician. "This is not the time for arguments about the relative sizes of your ambulatory appendages. Please desist. I was about to say that the Nidian Senior, Lesk-Murog, is available and anxious to assist. Its surgical experience is as large as its feet are small. Conway, what are your instructions?"

The main screen brightened again as Conway switched on its helmet light. "We need a much wider suction unit, a flexible pipe of six inches' diameter or as large as Lesk-Murog can handle, linked to one of the air circulation pumps, so that large pieces of the growth can be excised and withdrawn quickly. We cannot work without light, but we should be able to reduce the air that has leaked from the edges of our breathing masks by withdrawing it with the operative debris and replacing it with an inert gas pumped through the existing suction line. The inert should inhibit the skinsticker's rate of growth as effectively as a complete absence of air, but that is a hope rather than an expectation."

"I understand, Doctor," Thornnastor said. "Maintenance technicians, you know what is required. Lesk-Murog, prepare yourself. Quickly, everyone."

A subjective eternity passed before the equipment was set up and the diminutive Lesk-Murog, looking like a plastic-encased, long-tailed rodent with one end of the new suction pipeline attached to its backpack, disappeared headfirst into the entry wound. Conway and Seldal had already cut through the skinsticker's outer membrane and were excising small pieces and feeding them into the original suction unit, although it was obvious that the black growth was increasing in size in spite of their efforts because the incision continued to widen and tear in both directions. But with the Nidian Senior's arrival the situation changed at once.

"This is much better," said Conway. "We are beginning to make progress now and are excising deeply into the growth. As soon as we have hollowed it out sufficiently, Seldal and Lesk-Murog will go inside and pass the excised material out to me for disposal. Don't cut such large pieces, doctors, please. If this suction unit blocks we'll be in real trouble. And watch where you're swinging that blade, Lesk-Murog, I have no wish to become an amputee. How is the patient?"

"It is radiating anxiety, friend Conway," Prilicla said, "with secondary but still strong feelings of excitement. Neither are at levels to cause distress."

Since a further reply was unnecessary, Hellishomar and Lioren did not speak.

The main screen showed glimpses of rapidly moving Earth-human and Nidian hands and a furiously pecking Nallajim beak plying instruments that glittered brightly against the light-absorbent blackness of the growth. While describing the procedure Conway broke off to say that they were feeling more like miners digging for fossil fuel than surgeons engaged on a brain operation. The Diagnostician's words were complaining but its voice sounded pleased because the environment of inert gas was seriously inhibiting further growth and the work was going well.

"The cavity has been enlarged sufficiently so that all three of us are now able to work inside and attack the growth independently," Conway said. "Doctors Seldal and Lesk-Murog are able to stand upright while I am forced to kneel. It is becoming very warm in here. We would be obliged if the inert gas you are pumping was reduced in temperature so as to avoid the risk of heat prostration. The inner surface of the growth's enclosing membrane has been exposed over several large areas and it is beginning to sag under the weight of the surrounding brain structure. Please increase the internal gas pressure immediately to keep it from collapsing all over us. How is the patient?"

"No change, friend Conway," Prilicla said.

For a time the operation proceeded in silence. It was clear what the surgeons were doing and there was nothing new for Conway to describe, until suddenly he said, "We have discovered the location of the feeder root and are evacuating its liquid content. The root has shrunk to less than half its original circumference and is being withdrawn with negligible resistance. It is very long but appears to be complete. Seldal is making a deep probe to insure that none of it has been left behind. No other roots have been discovered, nor anything resembling connective pathways to a secondary growth.

"The inner surface of the membrane is now totally exposed," the Diagnostician went on. "We are excising it in narrow strips that can be accommodated by the suction unit. Of necessity the work at this stage is slow and carefully performed because we are detaching the membrane from the underlying brain structures and must avoid inflicting further damage. It is most important that the patient remain completely immobile."

Hellishomar spoke for the first time in nearly three hours. It said, "I will not move."

"Thank you," Conway said.

More time passed, slowly for the operating team and interminably for the watchers, until finally all activity on the main screen ceased and the Diagnostician spoke again.

"The last of the skinsticker material has been withdrawn," Conway said. "You can see that the interfacing brain structures displaced by the growth have been seriously compressed, but we have found no evidence of necrosis due to impairment of the local circulation, which is, in fact, being slowly restored. It is unsafe to make categorical statements regarding the clinical condition of a hitherto unknown life-form or a prognosis based on incomplete data, but my opinion is that minimum cerebral damage has been done and, provided the effects were not due to heredity factors, the condition should rectify itself when the pressure which is artificially maintaining this working cavity is gradually reduced to zero. There is nothing more that we can do here.

"You leave first, Lesk-Murog," Conway ended briskly. "Seldal, hop back into the pouch. We will withdraw and close up."

Lioren watched the main screen as they slowly retraced their path, and worried. The operation had been successfully accomplished and the great mass of foreign matter within the Groalterri's brain had been removed, but had it been the only cause of Hellishomar's trouble? The Groalterri had carried that foul thing in its brain for most of its life, and it could never have become a highly respected Cutter had there been any impairment of muscular coordination. Was it not more likely, as Conway had suggested, that the missing telepathic function and all the mental distress which had stemmed from it was due to an untreatable genetic defect and incurable? He looked around for Prilicla, intending to ask it how the patient was feeling, then remembered that the emotion-sensitive had been forced to leave. As a species Cinrusskins lacked stamina and required frequent rest periods.

He should ask the question of Hellishomar himself, Lioren thought, instead of waiting for the patient to signal its private distress by calling his name. But suddenly he was too afraid of what the answer might be. Conway and Seldal had replaced the massive osseous plug and sutured the flap of cranial tegument and were removing their operating garments, and still Lioren could not drive himself to ask the question.

"Thank you, Seldal, Lesk-Murog, everyone," Conway said, looking all around to include the OR and technical support staff. "You all did very well. And especially you, Lioren, by making the patient remain immobile when it was most necessary, by discovering the growth characteristics of that skinsticker, and by warning us in time about the effects of air and light. That was very well done. Personally I think your talents are wasted in Psychology."

"I don't," O'Mara said. Then, as if ashamed of the compliment it had paid, the Chief Psychologist went on, "The trainee is insubordinate, secretive, and has an infuriating tendency to . . ."

Lioren.

They were all listening to O'Mara and seemed not to have heard. Lioren's hand moved instinctively to his communicator to switch to the private channel, wondering desperately what possible words of comfort he could find for this vast being who must again have lost all hope. Then, with his finger on the key, he stopped as a great and joyful realization came to him.

His name had been called but it had not been spoken.

CHAPTER 26

O nce again it was a private conversation, but this time without the deep cranial itching that had preceeded his telepathic contact with the Protector of the Unborn. The answers were given before the questions could be uttered, the other's reassurance negated his concern as soon as it was felt, and the nerve and muscle connections between Lioren's brain and tongue became redundant. It was as if a system for exchanging messages chiseled laboriously on slabs of rock had been replaced by the spoken word, except that the process was much faster than that.

Hellishomar the Cutter, formerly the flawed, the mentally deficient, the telepathically deaf and no longer the Small, was cured.

Gratitude washed over him in a bright, warm flood that only Lioren could see and feel, and with it came knowledge, incomplete and simplified so as to avoid damage to his relatively primitive mentality, that must be his alone. The people who had contributed to the unique and wondrous cure of a mentally disabled Groalterri should not be repaid with knowledge that would cripple their own young minds. Hellishomar had touched the minds of every thinking being within the hospital and the occupants of vessels orbiting beyond it, and knew this to be so.

The entities who had contributed to the success of the operation would be thanked individually and verbally. They would be told that

Hellishomar felt very well, that a significant change for the better had already taken place in the quality of its mentation, and that it was anxious to return to Groalter, where its recuperation would be aided by the greater freedom of physical movement that was not possible in Sector General.

All this was true, but it was not all of the truth. They were not to be told that Hellishomar needed to leave the hospital quickly because the temptation to remain and explore the minds and behavior and philosophies of the thousands of entities who came to work, to visit, or to be cared for in this great hospital was well-nigh irrestistible. For Lioren had been right when he had told O'Mara that to the gross and planet-bound Groalterri the universe beyond the atmosphere was the hereafter that they would need all eternity to explore, and Sector General was a particularly intriguing microcosm of the Heaven that awaited them.

Lioren's concern over the possible effects on the other Groalterri culture of Hellishomar's off-planet experiences had been justified at the time. But now Hellishomar was not returning as one of the Small destined to remain a telepathic mute and crippled by a permanently occluded mind for the remainder of its life. Instead it was returning with all of its faculties restored, as a near-adult who would speak of this wondrous thing only to the Parents. It did not know how they would react to the knowledge he bore, but they were old and very wise and it was probable that the proof that Heaven was as wonderful and mind-stretching as they believed, and even that a small part of it was peopled by short-lived creatures whose minds were primitive and their ethics advanced, would strengthen their belief and cause them to strive even harder for the perfection of mind and spirit that was needed before the Going Out.

A great debt was owed to the Monitor Corps and to the hospital staff who had made Hellishomar whole again, and to the single Tarlan entity who had talked and argued and worked with its mind to obtain the patient's agreement to the operation. An even greater debt was owed by the other Groalterri, but neither debt would be paid. The Federation would not be allowed full contact with the Groalterri for the reasons already given, and neither would Lioren be given the answers to the two questions uppermost in his mind.

During all his contacts with patients Lioren had never allowed himself to influence their nonmaterial beliefs, no matter, in the light of his own greater knowledge and experience, how strange or ridiculous they had seemed to him. He had refused to tamper with their beliefs even though he himself did not believe that he believed in anything. In the circumstances Lioren's behavior had been ethically flawless and Hellishomar could do no less. It would not give its Tarlan friend the benefit of the advanced Groalterri philosophical and theological thinking by telling him what he should believe. And an answer to the second question was unnecessary because Lioren was about to make the decision for himself and do something that was completely foreign to his nature.

Lioren was becoming confused by this highly compressed method of communication, and by answers that come before the questions are fully formed.

It shames me to remind you of the debt you owe, Lioren thought, *and to ask that a small part of it be repaid. When you touch my mind I sense a vastness of knowledge, a great area of brightness that you are hiding from me. If you instructed me I would believe. Why will you not tell me from your greater knowledge what is the truth about God?*

By your own efforts, Hellishomar replied, *you have acquired great knowledge. You have used it to ease the inner hurts of many entities, including my former, retarded self, but you are not yet ready to believe. The question has already been answered.*

Then I repeat the second question, Lioren went on. *Is there any hope of me finding ease or a release from the constant memory and guilt of Cromsag? The decision I have struggled with for so long involves behavior shameful to a Tarlan of my former standing, but no matter. It may also result in my death. I ask only if the decision I have made is the right one.*

Does the memory of Cromsag trouble you continually, Hellishomar thought, *to the extent that you would seek your own death as a release from it?*

No, said Lioren, surprised by the intensity of his feelings. *But that is because so many other matters have recently occupied my mind. I would not welcome death, especially if it came about by accident or as a result of a stupid decision on my part.*

Yet you believe that the decision includes the serious risk of major injury or death, Hellishomar returned, *and I find no indication that you are going to change your mind. I will not tell you whether your decision is right or wrong or stupid, or of the probable results, but shall only remind you that no event in this state of existence occurs by accident.*

This much I will do for you, Hellishomar went on. *Your coming action will not be hampered in any way. Since your decision has now been made, I suggest that you avoid prolonging your distress and uncertainty further and leave without delay.*

There was a moment of mental dislocation as Lioren's mind returned to a working environment in which conversations were conducted by laggard speech and meanings were clouded. It seemed that O'Mara had just finished listing its trainee's shortcomings. Conway was showing its teeth and reminding the Chief Psychologist that it had expressed serious displeasure with everyone in Sector General, and especially those who had risen to become Diagnosticians, and it seemed that every being in the ward was watching Lioren expectantly and trying to move closer.

"The patient is well," Lioren said. "It feels no sensory discomfort and reports a significant and continuing improvement in the quality of its mentation. It wishes to use the public channel to thank everyone here individually."

They were all too excited and pleased to notice him leave. Lioren plotted the fastest route to the Cromsaggar ward and tried to push all second thoughts out of his mind.

He had already checked the duty rosters and knew that there were only two nursing staff on the ward. This was normal practice when patients were fully convalescent and under observation rather than treatment or awaiting discharge, but it was not normal to post an armed Monitor at the ward entrance.

The guard was an Earth-human DBDG, with only two arms and

legs and less than half of Lioren's body mass, and its weapon was a disabler. It could scramble his voluntary muscle system or cause full paralysis, depending on the power setting, but it would not kill him.

"Lioren, Psychology, Department," he said briskly. "I am here to interview the patients."

"And I am here to stop you," the guard said. "Major O'Mara said that you might try to get among the Cromsaggar patients and that you should be forbidden entry for your own safety. Please leave at once, sir."

The guard was showing the consideration and respect due Lioren's former rank as a Surgeon-Captain, but feelings of kindliness and sympathy, however strong, would not cause it to ignore its orders. Surely O'Mara knew enough Tarlan psychology to know that he would not try to escape just punishment by deliberately ending his own life. Perhaps the Chief Psychologist had thought that even this Tarlan could change his mind and his inflexible code of behavior and force himself to commit an act formerly considered dishonorable and had simply taken precautions.

This obstruction, Lioren thought helplessly, had not been foreseen. Or had it?

"I'm glad you understand my position," the guard said suddenly. "Good-bye, sir."

A few seconds later it stamped its feet and, as if to relieve boredom or stiffening leg muscles, began pacing slowly along the corridor. If Lioren had not stepped aside quickly, the guard would have walked straight into him.

Thank you, Hellishomar, Lioren thought, and entered the ward.

It was a long, high-ceilinged room containing forty beds in two opposing rows and with the nurses' station rising like a glass-walled island from the center of the floor. Environmental technicians had reproduced the dusty yellow light of Cromsag's sun and softened the structural projections with native vegetation and wall hangings that looked real. The patients were standing or sitting in small groups around four of the beds, talking together quietly while another group was watching a display screen on which a Corps contact specialist was explaining the

Federation's long-term plans for reconstructing Cromsag's technology and rehabilitating the Cromsaggar. One of the Orligian duty nurses was using the communicator and the other's furry head was swiveling slowly from side to side as it scanned the length of the ward. It was plain that they did not see him and, as with the guard outside, their minds had been touched to render them selectively blind.

Whether or not his decision was the correct one, Hellishomar had promised that he could make it without interruption.

Trying to show neither haste nor hesitation, Lioren walked down the ward in a gathering silence. He looked briefly at the seated or recumbent patients he passed, and they stared back at him. He had never learned to read Cromsaggar facial expressions and had no idea of what they were thinking. When he reached the largest group of patients he stopped.

"I am Lioren," he said.

It was obvious that they already knew who and what he was. The patients who had been sitting or lying on the nearby beds rose quickly to their feet and gathered around him, and those further along the ward hurried to join the others until he was completely encircled by still and silent Cromsaggar.

A sharp, clear memory of his first meeting with one of them rose in Lioren's mind. It had been a female attacking him in defense of an imagined threat to infants sleeping in another part of its dwelling, and even though its body had displayed the discoloration and muscle wastage of disease and malnutrition, it had come close to inflicting serious injury on him. Now he was surrounded by more than thirty Cromsaggar whose bodies and limbs were well-muscled and healthy. He knew well the damage that those horny, long-nailed feet and hard medial hands could inflict because he had seen them fighting each other not quite to the death.

On Cromsag they had fought with ferocity but total control, with the intention of inflicting maximum damage short of killing, and with the sole purpose of stirring their near-atrophied endocrine systems into sufficient activity to enable them to procreate and survive as a species.

But Lioren was not another Cromsaggar and would-be mate; he was the creature responsible for countless thousands of their deaths and of all but destroying their race. They might not want to control the hatred they must feel for him, or the urge to tear his body apart limb from limb.

He wondered whether the distant Hellishomar was still influencing the minds of the guard and the two nurses, for normally they could not have helped seeing the crowd closing in around him and would have attempted a rescue. He wished that the Groalterri would not be so thorough in its mind control because suddenly he did not want his life to end in this or any other fashion, and then he realized that his thoughts were clear to Hellishomar and he felt an even greater shame.

That which he was about to do and say was shameful enough without adding to it the dishonor of personal cowardice. Slowly he looked at each one of the faces surrounding him and spoke.

"I am Lioren," he said. "You know that I am the being responsible for causing the deaths of many thousands of your people. This was a crime too great for expiation and it is only fair that the punishment should lie in your hands. But before this punishment is carried out, I wish to say that I am truly sorry for what I have done, and humbly ask your forgiveness."

The feeling of shame at what he had just done was not as intense as he had expected, Lioren thought as he waited for the onslaught. In fact he felt relieved and very good.

CHAPTER 27

The Monitor guard insists that he did not see you enter the ward," the Chief Psychologist said in a quiet but very angry voice, "and the nurses did not know you were there until the Cromsaggar were suddenly standing around and shouting at you. When the guard went in to investigate you told him that he should not be concerned, that they were having a religious argument which he was welcome to join, although he says that he had heard quieter riots. Tarlans are not noted either for their sarcasm or their sense of humor, so I must assume you spoke the truth. What happened in that ward, dammit? Or have you imposed another oath of secrecy on yourself?"

"No, sir," Lioren replied quietly. "The conversations were public and confidentiality was neither asked for nor implied. When you sent for me I was preparing a detailed report for you on the whole—"

"Summarize it," O'Mara said sharply.

"Yes, sir," Lioren said, and tried to find a balance between accuracy and brevity as he went on. "When I identified myself, apologized, and asked forgiveness for the great wrong I had committed against them—"

"You *apologized*?" O'Mara broke in. "That—that was unexpected."

"So was the behavior of the Cromsaggar," Lioren said. "Considering my crime, I expected a violent reaction from them, but instead they—"

"Did you hope that they would kill you?" O'Mara broke in again. "Was that the reason for your visit?"

"It was not!" Lioren said sharply. "I went there to apologize. That is a shameful enough act for any Tarlan to perform because it is considered to be a cowardly and dishonorable attempt to diminish personal guilt and avoid just punishment. But it is not as shameful as escaping that punishment by deliberately ending one's life. There are degrees of shame, and from my recent contacts with patients I have discovered that there are feelings of shame that may be misplaced or unnecessary."

"Go on," O'Mara said.

"As yet I do not fully understand the psychological mechanism involved," Lioren replied, "but I have discovered that in certain circumstances a personal apology, while shameful to the entity making it, can sometimes do more to ease the hurt of a victim than the simple knowledge that the offender is receiving just punishment. It seems that vengeance, even judicial vengeance, does not fully satisfy the victim and that a sincere expression of regret for the wrong committed can ease the pain or loss more than the mere knowledge that justice is being done. When the apology is followed by forgiveness on the part of the wronged entity, there are much more beneficial and lasting effects for both victim and perpetrator.

"When I identified myself in the Cromsaggar ward," Lioren went on, "there was a strong probability that lethal violence would ensue. It was no longer my wish to die, because the work of this department is very interesting and there may be more that I can do here, but I felt strongly that I should try to ease the hurt of the Cromsaggar with an apology, and did so. I did not expect what happened then."

In a very quiet voice O'Mara asked, "You are still insisting that you, a Wearer of the Blue Cloak of Tarla with all that that implies, apologized?"

The question had already been answered so Lioren continued. "I had forgotten that the Cromsaggar are a civilized race forced by disease to wage war. They fought with great ferocity because they had to try their hardest to engender the fear of imminent death in each other if their formerly impaired sex-involved endocrine systems were to be stimulated to the point where they would become briefly capable of conceiving children. But while fighting they learned to exercise strict mental and emotional control, and refuse to surrender to anger or hatred, because they loved and respected the opponents they were trying so hard to damage almost to the point of death. They had to fight to insure the continual survival of their species, but the wounds they inflicted and sustained were personal to themselves. They could not have continued to fight and respect and love each other if they had not also learned to apologize for and forgive each other for the terrible hurts they were inflicting.

"On Cromsag the ability to forgive is what enabled their society to survive for so long."

Suddenly Lioren was seeing and hearing again the Cromsaggar patients who had crowded around him, and for a moment he could not speak because his emotions were being involved in a way that any self-respecting Tarlan would have considered to be a shameful weakness. But he knew that this was another one of the minor shames that he was learning to accept. He went on. "They treated me as another Cromsaggar, a friend who had done a very great wrong and inflicted much suffering in an attempt to save their race and, unlike themselves, I had succeeded.

"They—they forgave me and were grateful.

"But they were also fearful about the return to Cromsag," he continued quickly. "They understood and were grateful for the rehabilitation program the Monitor Corps had planned for them and said that they would cooperate in every way. It is a psychological problem involving a disbelief in their own ability to exist without severe and continuous stress, coupled with a belief that fate, or a nonmaterial presence whose precise nature was the subject of much argument, might not intend them to live lives of contentment in the material world. Basically it was a religious matter. I told them about the racial memory of the Gogleskans, the Dark Devil which tries to drive them to self-destruction, and how Khone is besting it. And about the problems of the Protectors of the Unborn, and gave what other reassurance I could. My report will cover everything that transpired in detail. I do not foresee the Corps psychologists having serious trouble with the problem. An ensuing religious debate, which the Cromsaggar engage in with great enthusiasm, was interrupted by the arrival of the guard."

O'Mara leaned back into its chair and said, "Apart from taking that insane risk you have done well, but then fortune often favors the stupid. In a very short time you have also become something of an authority on other-species religious beliefs mostly, I have been told, by studying the available material during off-duty periods. This is a very sensitive area which the department normally prefers to leave untouched, but so far you have had no problems with it. So much so that you may now consider yourself to be a full member of the department staff rather than a trainee. This will in no sense improve my behavior toward you because you have become the second most insubordinate and selectively reticent person I have ever known. Why will you not tell me what went on between you and ex-Diagnostician Mannen?"

Lioren decided to treat it as a rhetorical question because he had refused to answer it the first time it had been asked. Instead he asked, "Are there any other assignments for me, sir?"

The Chief Psychologist exhaled with an unusually loud hissing sound, then said, "Yes. Senior Physician Edanelt would like you to talk to one of its post-op patients, Cresk-Sar has a trainee Dwerlan with a nonspecified ethical problem, and the Cromsaggar patients would like you to visit them as soon and as often as you find convenient. Khone says that it is willing to try my suggestion that the transparent wall dividing its compartment be reduced gradually in height and eventually replaced by a white line painted on the floor, and it wants to see you again, as well. There is also the original Seldal assignment, which you seem to have forgotten."

"No, sir, I have completed it," Lioren said, and went on quickly. "From the information given by yourself and my subsequent conversations with and about Senior Physician Seldal it was clear that a marked change in personality and behavior had taken place, although not for he worse. At first the change was apparent in the reduced number of couplings with female Nallajims on the staff, and in its behavior toward colleagues and subordinates. Normally members of that species are physically and emotionally hyperactive, impatient, impolite, inconsiderate, and subject to the rapid changes of mood that make them very unpopular as surgeons-in-charge. Not so Seldal. Its OR and ward staff would do anything it asks and will not allow a word of criticism about their Senior either as a surgeon or a person, and I agree with them. The reason for the change, I am certain, is that one of the Educator-tape personalities Seldal is carrying has assumed partial control or is exerting a considerable amount of influence on the Senior's mind.

"I did not realize that a Tralthan donor was responsible," Lioren continued, "until the incident during the Hellishomar operation when the growth was threatening to get out of control and Conway needed help. Seldal had a moment of extreme stress and indecision during which it must have forgotten who it was. The remark about not wanting another set of big feet in the operative field was intended for Thornnastor, who had offered help, and referred to its six overly large Tralthan feet rather than Conway's, because at that moment the Tralthan tape persona was in the forefront of its mind.

"This is an unusual and perhaps unique situation," Lioren went on, "because observational evidence supports my theory that the partial control of Seldal's mind was relinquished willingly. I would say that the Tralthan donor, rather than being kept under tight control by the host mind, has been befriended by Seldal. The feeling may be even stronger than that. There is professional respect, admiration of a personality that possesses the Tralthan attributes of inner calm and self-assurance that is so unlike Seldal's own, and it is probable that a strong emotional bond has formed between the Senior Physician and this immaterial Tralthan that is indistinguishable from nonphysical love. As a result we have a Nallajim Senior who has willingly assumed the personality traits of a Tralthan and is a better physician and a more content person because of it. That being so I would recommend that nothing whatever be done about the case."

"Agreed," O'Mara said quietly, and for a moment it stared at him in a way which made Lioren wonder again if the Chief Psychologist possessed a telepathic faculty. "There is more?"

"I do not wish to embarrass and perhaps anger a superior by asking this as a question," Lioren said carefully, "but I have formed a suspicion that you, having knowledge of the donor tapes in the Senior Physician's mind, suspected or were already aware of the situation and the Seldal assignment was a fitness test for myself. Its secondary, or perhaps its primary, purpose was to try to make me go out and meet people so that my mind would not be concerned solely with thoughts of my own terrible guilt. I have not nor will I ever be able to forget the Cromsag Incident. But your plan worked and for that I am truly grateful to you, and especially for making me realize that there were people other than myself who were troubled, entities like Khone, Hellishomar, and Mannen who—"

"Mannen is a friend," O'Mara broke in. "His clinical condition has not changed, he could terminate at any moment, and yet he is going around in that antigravity harness like a . . . Dammit, it's a bloody miracle! I would like to know what you said to each other. Anything you tell me will not go into his psych file and I will not speak of it to anyone else, but I want to know. Termination comes to everyone and some of us, unfortunately, may be given too much time to think about it. I will not break this confidence. After all, he is an old friend."

The question was being asked again, but his momentary feeling of irritation was quickly replaced by one of sympathy as he realized that the Chief Psychologist was troubled, however briefly, by the thought of termination and the deterioration of the body and mind which preceded it. His answer must be the same as before, but this time Lioren believed that he could make it more encouraging.

"The ex-Diagnostician is no longer troubled in its mind," he said gently. "If you were to ask your questions of Mannen, as an old friend, I feel sure that it will tell you everything you want to know. But I cannot."

The Chief Psychologist looked down at his desk as if ashamed of its momentary display of weakness, then up again.

"Very well," it said briskly. "If you won't talk you won't talk. Meanwhile the department will have to contend with another soft-spoken, insubordinate Carmody. No disciplinary action will be taken over your Cromsaggar ward visit. Close the door on your way out. Quietly."

Lioren returned to his desk feeling relieved but very confused, and decided that he must try to relieve the confusion; otherwise the quality of his report would suffer. But search as he would, the information he wanted remained hidden, and he was beginning to strike his keyboard as if it were a mortal enemy.

Across the office Braithwaite cleared its breathing passages with a noise which Lioren now knew denoted sympathy. "You have a problem?"

"I'm not sure," Lioren replied. "O'Mara said that it would take no disciplinary action, but it called me . . . Who or what is a Carmody, and where will I find the information?"

Braithwaite swung round to face him and said, "You won't find it there. Lieutenant Carmody's file was withdrawn after his accident. He was before my time but I know a little about him. He came here from the Corps base on Orligia at his own request and managed to survive in the department for twelve years even though he and O'Mara were always arguing. When an incoming ship whose pilot was badly injured lost control and crashed through our outer hull, he accompanied the rescue team and tried to give reassurance to what he thought was a surviving crewmember. It turned out to be a very large, fear-maddened and nonintelligent ship's pet, which attacked him. He was very old and frail and gentle, and did not survive his injuries.

"During his time here Lieutenant Carmody became very well liked and highly respected by all of the staff and long-term patients," Braithwaite concluded, "and his position was not filled, until now."

Feeling even more confused, Lioren said, "The relevance of what you say eludes me. I am neither old nor frail nor particularly gentle, I have been stripped of all Monitor Corps rank, and my arguments with

O'Mara are concerned only with the retention of patient confidences—"

"I know," said Braithwaite, showing its teeth. "Your predecessor called it the Seal of Confession. And the rank doesn't matter. Carmody never used his, and most of the people here did not even use his name. They just called him Padre."

Breinigsville, PA USA
19 November 2010
249691BV00001B/67/A